HOW
NOT
TO
DIE
ALONE

HOW
NOT
TO
DIE
ALONE

Richard Roper

G. P. PUTNAM'S SONS
New York

PUTNAM
— EST. 1838 —

G. P. PUTNAM'S SONS
Publishers Since 1838
An imprint of Penguin Random House LLC
penguinrandomhouse.com

Library of Congress Cataloging-in-Publication Data

Names: Roper, Richard, author.
Title: How not to die alone / Richard Roper.
Description: New York: G. P. Putnam's Sons, 2019.
Identifiers: LCCN 2018049551 | ISBN 9780525539889 (hardcover) |
ISBN 9780525539902 (epub)
Classification: LCC PR6118.O643 H69 2019 | DDC 823 / .92—dc23
LC record available at https://lccn.loc.gov/2018049551
p.   cm.

Printed in the United States of America
1   3   5   7   9   10   8   6   4   2

Book design by Laura K. Corless

This is a work of fiction. Names, characters, places, and incidents either are the product of the author's imagination or are used fictitiously, and any resemblance to actual persons, living or dead, businesses, companies, events, or locales is entirely coincidental.

For Mum and Dad

Public Health (Control of Disease) Act 1984, section 46:
(1) It shall be the duty of a local authority to cause to be buried or cremated the body of any person who has died or been found dead in their area, in any case where it appears to the authority that no suitable arrangements for the disposal of the body have been or are being made otherwise than by the authority.

HOW
NOT
TO
DIE
ALONE

– CHAPTER 1 –

Andrew looked at the coffin and tried to remember who was inside it. It was a man—he was sure of that. But, horrifyingly, the name escaped him. He thought he'd narrowed it down to either John or James, but Jake had just made a late bid for consideration. It was inevitable, he supposed, that this had happened. He'd been to so many of these funerals it was bound to at some point, but that didn't stop him from feeling an angry stab of self-loathing.

If he could just remember the name before the vicar said it, that would be something. There was no order of service, but maybe he could check his work phone. Would that be cheating? Probably. Besides, it would have been a tricky enough maneuver to get away with in a church full of mourners, but it was nearly impossible when the only other person there apart from him was the vicar. Ordinarily, the funeral director would have been there as well, but he had e-mailed earlier to say he was too ill to make it.

Unnervingly, the vicar, who was only a few feet away from Andrew, had barely broken eye contact since he'd started the service.

Andrew hadn't dealt with him before. He was boyish and spoke with a nervous tremor that was amplified unforgivingly by the echoey church. Andrew couldn't tell if this was down to nerves. He tried out a reassuring smile, but it didn't seem to help. Would a thumbs-up be inappropriate? He decided against it.

He looked over at the coffin again. Maybe he *was* a Jake, though the man had been seventy-eight when he died, and you didn't really get many septuagenarian Jakes. At least not yet. It was going to be strange in fifty years' time when all the nursing homes would be full of Jakes and Waynes, Tinkerbells and Appletisers, with faded tribal tattoos that roughly translated as *"Roadworks for next fifty yards"* faded on their lower backs.

Jesus, concentrate, he admonished himself. The whole point of his being there was to bear respectful witness to the poor soul departing on their final journey, to provide some company in lieu of any family or friends. Dignity—that was his watchword.

Unfortunately, dignity was something that had been in short supply for the John or James or Jake. According to the coroner's report, he had died on the toilet while reading a book about buzzards. To add insult to injury, Andrew later discovered firsthand that it wasn't even a very *good* book about buzzards. Admittedly he was no expert, but he wasn't sure the author—who even from the few passages Andrew had read came across as remarkably grumpy—should have dedicated a whole page to badmouthing kestrels. The deceased had folded the corner of this particular page down as a crude placeholder, so perhaps he'd been in agreement. As Andrew had peeled off his latex gloves he'd made a mental note to insult a kestrel—or indeed any member of the falcon family—the next time he saw one, as a tribute of sorts.

Other than a few more bird books, the house was devoid of anything that gave clues to the man's personality. There were no records or films to be found, nor pictures on the walls or photographs on the windowsills. The only idiosyncrasy was the bafflingly large number of Fruit 'n Fibre boxes in the kitchen cupboards. So aside from the fact that he was a keen ornithologist with a top-notch digestive system, it was impossible to guess what sort of person John or James or Jake had been.

Andrew had been as diligent as ever with the property inspection. He'd searched the house (a curious mock-Tudor bungalow that sat defiantly as an incongruous interlude on the terraced street) until he was sure he'd not missed something that suggested the man had any family he was still in touch with. He'd knocked on the neighbors' doors but they'd been either indifferent to or unaware of the man's existence, or the fact it was over.

The vicar segued unsurely into a bit of Jesus-y material, and Andrew knew from experience that the service was coming to a close. He *had* to remember this person's name, as a point of principle. He really tried his best, even when there was no one else there, to be a model mourner—to be as respectful as if there were hundreds of devastated family members in attendance. He'd even started removing his watch before entering the church because it felt like the deceased's final journey should be exempt from the indifference of a ticking second hand.

The vicar was definitely on the home stretch now. Andrew was just going to have to make a decision.

John, he decided. He was definitely John.

"And while we believe that John—"

Yes!

"—struggled to some extent in his final years, and sadly departed the world without family or friends by his side, we can take comfort that, with God waiting with open arms, full of love and kindness, this journey shall be the last he makes alone."

Andrew tended not to stick around after the funerals. On the few occasions he had, he'd ended up having to make awkward conversation with funeral directors or last-minute rubberneckers. It was remarkable how many of the latter you would get, hanging around outside, farting out inane platitudes. Andrew was well practiced at slipping away so as to avoid such encounters, but today he'd briefly been distracted by a sign on the church noticeboard advertising the troublingly jaunty "Midsummer Madness Fete!" when he felt someone tapping him on the shoulder with the insistence of an impatient woodpecker. It was the vicar. He looked even younger close up, with his baby-blue eyes and blond curtains parted neatly in the middle, as if his mum might have done it for him.

"Hey, it's Andrew, isn't it? You're from the council, right?"

"That's right," Andrew said.

"No luck finding any family then?"

Andrew shook his head.

"Shame, that. Real shame."

The vicar seemed agitated, as if he were holding on to a secret that he desperately wanted to impart.

"Can I ask you something?" he said.

"Yes," Andrew said, quickly deciding on an excuse for why he couldn't attend "Midsummer Madness!"

"How did you find that?" the vicar said.

"Do you mean . . . the funeral?" Andrew said, pulling at a bit of loose thread on his coat.

"Yeah. Well, more specifically my part in it all. Because, full disclosure, it was my first. I was quite relieved to be starting with this one, to be honest, because there wasn't anybody here so it sort of felt like a bit of a practice run. Hopefully now I'm fully prepared for when there's a proper one with a church full of friends and family, not just a

4

guy from the council. No offense," he added, putting a hand on Andrew's arm. Andrew did his best not to recoil. He hated it when people did that. He wished he had some sort of squidlike defense that meant he could shoot ink into their eyes.

"So yeah," the vicar said. "How'd you think I did?"

What do you want me to say? Andrew thought. *Well, you didn't knock the coffin over or accidentally call the deceased "Mr. Hitler," so ten out of ten I'd say.*

"You did very well," he said.

"Ah, great, thanks, mate," the vicar said, looking at him with renewed intensity. "I really appreciate that."

He held out his hand. Andrew shook it and went to let go, but the vicar carried on.

"Anyway, I better be off," Andrew said.

"Yes, yes of course," said the vicar, finally letting go.

Andrew started off down the path, breathing a sigh of relief at escaping without further interrogation.

"See you soon I hope," the vicar called after him.

– CHAPTER 2 –

The funerals had been given various prefixes over the years—"public health," "contract," "welfare," "Section 46"—but none of the attempted rebrands would ever replace the original. When Andrew had come across the expression "pauper's funeral" he'd found it quite evocative; romantic, even, in a Dickensian sort of way. It made him think of someone a hundred and fifty years ago in a remote village—all mud and clucking chickens—succumbing to a spectacular case of syphilis, dying at the fine old age of twenty-seven and being bundled merrily into a pit to regenerate the land. In practice, what he experienced was depressingly clinical. The funerals were now a legal obligation for councils across the UK, designed for those who'd slipped through the cracks—their death perhaps only noticed because of the smell of their body decomposing, or an unpaid bill. (It had been on several occasions now where Andrew had found that the deceased had enough money in a bank account for direct debits to cover utility bills for months after their death, meaning the house was kept warm enough to speed up their body's decomposition. After the fifth harrowing instance of this, he'd considered mentioning it in the "Any other comments" section on his annual job satisfaction survey. In the end he went with asking if they could have another kettle in the shared kitchen.)

Another phrase he had become well acquainted with was "The Nine O'Clock Trot." His boss, Cameron, had explained its origin to him while violently piercing the film on a microwavable biryani. "If you die alone"—stab, stab, stab—"you're most likely buried alone too"—stab, stab, stab—"so the church can get the funeral out of the way at nine o'clock, safe in the knowledge that every train could be canceled"—stab—"every motorway gridlocked"—stab—"and it wouldn't make a difference." A final stab. "Because nobody's on their way."

In the previous year Andrew had arranged twenty-five of these funerals (his highest annual total yet). He'd attended all of them, too, though he wasn't technically required to do so. It was, he told himself, a small but meaningful gesture for someone to be there who wasn't legally obligated. But increasingly he found himself watching the simple, unvarnished coffins being lowered into the ground in a specially designated yet unmarked plot, knowing they would be uncovered three or four more times as other coffins were fitted in like a macabre game of Tetris, and think that his presence counted for nothing.

———

As Andrew sat on the bus to the office, he inspected his tie and shoes, both of which had seen better days. There was a persistent stain on his tie, origin unknown, that wouldn't budge. His shoes were well polished but starting to look worn. Too many nicks from churchyard gravel, too many times the leather had strained where he'd curled his toes at a vicar's verbal stumble. He really should replace both, come payday.

Now that the funeral was over, he took a moment to mentally file away John (surname Sturrock, he discovered, having turned on his phone). As ever, he tried to resist the temptation to obsess over how John had ended up in such a desperate position. Was there really no niece or godson he was on Christmas-card terms with? Or an old school friend who called, even just on his birthday? But it was a slippery slope. He had to stay as objective as possible, for his own sake, if only to be mentally strong enough to deal with the next poor person who ended up like this. The bus stopped at a red light. By the time it went green Andrew had made himself say a final good-bye.

He arrived at the office and returned Cameron's enthusiastic wave with a more muted acknowledgment of his own. As he slumped into his well-weathered seat, which had molded itself to his form over the years, he let out a now sadly familiar grunt. He'd thought having only just turned forty-two he'd have a few more years before he began accompanying minor physical tasks by making odd noises, but it seemed to be the universe's gentle way of telling him that he was now officially heading toward middle age. He only imagined before too long he'd wake up and immediately begin his day bemoaning how easy school exams were these days and bulk-buying cream chinos.

He waited for his computer to boot up and watched out of the corner of his eye as his colleague Keith demolished a hunk of chocolate cake and methodically sucked smears of icing from his stubby little fingers.

"Good one, was it?" Keith said, not taking his eyes off his screen, which Andrew knew was most likely showing a gallery of actresses who'd had the temerity to age, or something small and furry on a skateboard.

"It was okay," Andrew said.

"Any rubberneckers?" came a voice from behind him.

Andrew flinched. He hadn't seen Meredith take her seat.

"No," he said, not bothering to turn around. "Just me and the vicar. It was his very first funeral, apparently."

"Bloody hell, what a way to pop your cherry," Meredith said.

"Better that than a room full of weepers, to be fair," Keith said, with one final suck of his little finger. "You'd be shitting piss, wouldn't you?"

The office phone rang and the three of them sat there not answering it. Andrew was about to bite but Keith's frustration got the better of him first.

"Hello, Death Administration. Yep. Sure. Yep. Right."

Andrew reached for his earphones and pulled up his Ella Fitzgerald playlist (he had only very recently discovered Spotify, much to Keith's delight, who'd spent a month afterward calling Andrew "Granddad"). He felt like starting with a classic—something reassuring. He decided on "Summertime." But he was only three bars in before he looked up to see Keith standing in front of him, belly flab poking through a gap between shirt buttons.

"Helloooo. Anybody there?"

Andrew removed his earphones.

"That was the coroner. We've got a fresh one. Well, not a fresh body obviously—they reckon he'd been dead a good few weeks. No obvious next of kin and the neighbors never spoke to him. Body's been moved so they want a property inspection a-sap."

"Right."

Keith picked at a scab on his elbow. "Tomorrow all right for you?"

Andrew checked his diary.

"I can do first thing."

"Blimey, you're keen," Keith said, waddling back to his desk. *And you're a slice of ham that's been left out in the sun*, Andrew thought. He went to put his earphones back in, but at that moment Cameron emerged from his office and clapped his hands together to get their attention.

"Team meeting, chaps," he announced. "And yes, yes, don't you worry—the current Mrs. Cameron has provided cake, as per. Shall we hit the break-out space?"

The three of them responded with the enthusiasm a chicken

might if it were asked to wear a prosciutto bikini and run into a fox's den. The "break-out space" consisted of a knee-high table flanked by two sofas that smelled unaccountably of sulfur. Cameron had floated the idea of adding beanbags, but this had been ignored, as were his suggestions of desk-swap Tuesdays, a negativity jar ("It's a swear jar but for negativity!") and a team park run. ("I'm busy," Keith had yawned. "But I haven't told you which day it's on," Cameron said, his smile faltering like a flame in a draft.) Undeterred by their complete lack of enthusiasm, Cameron's most recent suggestion had been a suggestion box. This, too, had been ignored.

They gathered on the sofas and Cameron doled out cake and tea and tried to engage them with some banal small talk. Keith and Meredith had wedged themselves into the smaller of the two sofas. Meredith was laughing at something Keith had just whispered to her. Just as parents are able to recognize variants in the cries of their newborns, so Andrew had begun to understand what Meredith's differing laughs denoted. In this particular instance, the high-pitched giggle indicated that someone was being cruelly mocked. Given that they kept very obviously sneaking glances in his direction, it seemed it was probably him.

"Rightio, lady and gents," Cameron said. "First things first, don't forget we've got a new starter tomorrow. Peggy Green. I know we've struggled since Dan and Bethany left, so it's super-cool to have a new pair of hands."

"As long as she doesn't get 'stressed' like Bethany," Meredith said.

"Or turn out to be a knob like Dan," Keith muttered.

"*Anyway*," Cameron said, "what I actually wanted to talk to you about today is my weekly . . . honk! Honk!"—he honked an imaginary horn— ". . . fun idea! Remember, guys, this is something you can all get involved with. Doesn't matter how crazy your idea is. The only rule is that it has to be fun."

Andrew shuddered.

"So," Cameron continued. "My fun idea this week is, drumroll please . . . that every month we have a get-together at one of our houses and we do dinner. A sort of *Come Dine with Me* vibe but without any judgment. We'll have a bit of food, I daresay a bit of vino, and it'll give us a chance to do some real bonding away from the office, get to know each other a bit better, meet the family and all that. I'm mega-happy to kick things off. Whaddya say?"

Andrew hadn't heard anything past "meet the family."

"Is there not something else we can do?" he said, trying to keep his voice steady.

"Oh," Cameron said, instantly deflated. "I thought that was actually one of my better ideas."

"No, no, it is!" Andrew said, overcompensating now. "It's just . . . couldn't we just go to a restaurant instead?"

"Toooo expensive," Keith said, spraying cake crumbs everywhere.

"Well, what about something else? I don't know—Laser Quest or something. Is that still a thing?"

"I'm vetoing Laser Quest on the grounds I'm not a twelve-year-old boy," Meredith said. "I like the dinner party idea. I'm actually a bit of a secret Nigella in the kitchen." She turned to Keith. "I bet you'd go crazy for my lamb shank." Andrew felt bile stir in his stomach.

"Go on, Andrew," Cameron said, confidence renewed by Meredith's giving his idea her blessing. He attempted a matey arm punch that caused Andrew to spill tea down his leg. "It'll be a laugh! There's no pressure to cook up anything fancy. And I'd love to meet Diane and the kids, of course. So, whaddya say? You up for this, buddy?"

Andrew's mind was racing. Surely there was something else he could suggest as an alternative? Life drawing. Badger baiting. *Anything.* The others were just looking at him now. He had to say something.

"Bloody hell, Andrew. You look like you've seen a ghost," Meredith said. "Your cooking can't be that bad. Besides, I'm sure Diane's a fabulous chef, among all her other talents, so she can help you out."

"Hmmm," Andrew murmured, tapping his fingertips together.

"She's a lawyer, right?" Keith said. Andrew nodded. Maybe there'd be some catastrophic world event in the next few days, a lovely old nuclear war to make them all forget about this stupid idea.

"You've got that beautiful old town house Dulwich way, haven't you?" Meredith said, practically leering. "Five-bed, isn't it?"

"Four," Andrew said. He hated it when she and Keith got like this. A tag team of mockery.

"Still," Meredith said. "A lovely big four-bed, smart kids by all accounts, and Diane, your talented, breadwinning wife. What a dark old horse you are."

Later, as Andrew prepared to leave the office, having been too distracted to do any meaningful work, Cameron appeared by his desk and dropped down onto his haunches. It felt like the sort of move he'd been taught in a course.

"Listen," he said quietly. "I know you didn't seem to fancy the dinner party idea, but just say you'll have a think about it, okay, mate?"

Andrew needlessly shuffled some papers on his desk. "Oh, I mean . . . I don't want to spoil things, it's just . . . okay, I'll think about it. But if we don't do that I'm sure we can think of another, you know, fun idea."

"That's the spirit," Cameron said, straightening up and addressing them all. "That goes for all of us, I hope. Come on, team—let's get our bond on sooner rather than. Yeah?"

———

Andrew had recently splashed out on some noise-canceling earphones for his commute, so while he could see the man sitting opposite's ugly sneeze and the toddler in the vestibule screaming at the utter injustice of being made to wear not one but two shoes, it simply appeared as a silent film incongruously soundtracked by Ella Fitzgerald's soothing voice. It wasn't long, however, before the conversation in the office started to repeat itself in his head, vying with Ella for his attention.

"Diane, your talented, breadwinning wife . . . smart kids . . . Beautiful old town house." Keith's smirk. Meredith's leer. The conversation dogged him all the way to the station and continued as he went to buy food for that night's dinner. That's when he found himself standing in the corner shop by multi-bags of novelty potato chips named after celebrities and trying not to scream. After ten minutes of picking up and putting down the same four ready meals, feeling incapable of choosing one, he left empty-handed, walking out into the rain and heading home, his stomach rumbling.

He stood outside his front door, shivering. Eventually, when the cold became too much to bear, he brought out his keys. There was usually one day a week like this, when he'd pause outside, key in the lock, holding his breath.

Maybe this time.

Maybe this time it *would* be the lovely old town house behind that door: Diane starting to prepare dinner. The smell of garlic and red wine. The sound of Steph and David squabbling or asking questions about their homework, then the excitable cheers when he opened the door because Dad's home, Dad's home!

When he entered the hallway the smell of damp hit him even harder than usual. And there were the familiar scuff marks on the corridor walls and the intermittent, milky yellow of the faulty strip light. He trudged up the stairs, his wet shoes squeaking with each step, and slid the second key around on his key ring. He reached up to right the wonky number 2 on the door and went inside, met, as he had been for the last twenty years, by nothing but silence.

– CHAPTER 3 –

Five Years Previously

Andrew was late. This might not have been so much of a disaster if on the CV he'd submitted ahead of that morning's job interview he hadn't claimed to be "extremely punctual." Not just punctual: *extremely* punctual. Was that even a thing? *Were* there extremities of punctuality? How might one even go about measuring such a thing?

It was his own stupid fault, too. He'd been crossing the road when a strange honking noise distracted him and he looked up. A goose was arrowing overhead, its white underside lit up orange by the morning sun, its shrill cries and erratic movement making it seem like a damaged fighter plane struggling back to base. It was just as the bird steadied itself and continued on its course that Andrew slipped on some ice. There was a brief moment where his arms windmilled and his feet gripped at nothing, like a cartoon character who'd just run off a cliff, before he hit the ground with an ugly thud.

"You okay?"

Andrew wheezed wordlessly in reply at the woman who had just helped him to his feet. He felt like someone had just taken a sledgehammer to his lower back. But it wasn't this that stopped him from finding the words to thank the woman. There was something about the way she was looking at him—a half smile on her face, how she brushed her hair behind her ears—that was so startlingly familiar it left him breathless. The woman's eyes seemed to be searching his face, as if she too had been hit with an intense feeling of recognition and pain. It was only after she'd said, "Well, bye then," and walked off that Andrew realized she'd actually been waiting for him to thank her. He wondered if he should hurry after her to try to make amends. But just then a familiar tune began to play in his head. *Blue moon, you saw me standing alone.* It took all his concentration to shake it away, squeezing his eyes shut and massaging his temples. By the time he looked again the woman was gone.

He dusted himself down, suddenly aware that people had seen him fall and were enjoying their dose of schadenfreude. He avoided eye contact and carried on, head down, hands thrust into his pockets. Gradually his embarrassment gave way to something else. It was in the aftermath of mishaps like this where he would feel it stir at his core and start to spread out, thick and cold, making it feel like he was walking through quicksand. There was nobody for him to share the story with. No one to help him laugh his way through it. Loneliness, however, was ever vigilant, always there to slow-clap his every stumble.

Though somewhat shaken up after his slip, he was fine apart from a small graze on his hand. (Now that he was nearing forty he was all too aware there was a small but visible spot on the horizon where such a standard slip would become "having a little fall." He secretly welcomed the idea of a sympathetic stranger laying their coat over him as they waited for an ambulance, supporting his head and squeezing his hand.) But while he hadn't suffered any damage, unfortunately the same couldn't be said for his white shirt, which was now splattered with dirty brown water. He briefly considered trying to make something out of this and the graze to impress his interviewer. "What, this? Oh, on my way here I was briefly diverted by diving in front of a bus/bullet/tiger to save a toddler/puppy/dignitary. Anyway, did I mention I'm a self-starter and I work well on my own *and* as part of a team?" He decided on the more sensible option and dashed into the nearest Debenhams for a new shirt. The detour left him sweaty and out of breath, which was how he announced himself to the receptionist at the cathedral of concrete that was the council offices.

He took a seat as instructed and sucked in some deep, steadying breaths. He needed this job. Badly. He'd been working in various admin roles for the council of a nearby borough since his early twenties, finally finding a position that had stuck, and which he had been in for eight years before unceremoniously being made redundant. Andrew's boss, Jill (a kind, rosy-cheeked Lancastrian with a "hug first, ask questions later" approach to life), had felt so terrible at having to let him go that she'd apparently called every council office in London asking about vacancies. The interview today was the only one that had come out of Jill's calls, and her e-mail to him describing the job was frustratingly vague. From what Andrew could tell it was similar to what he'd been doing before, largely admin based, though it involved something to do with inspecting properties. More importantly, it paid exactly the same as his last job and he could start the following month. Ten years ago there had been a chance he might have considered a fresh start. Traveling, maybe, or a bold new career move. But these days just having to leave the house left him with an unspecific feeling of anxiety, so hiking to Machu Picchu or retraining as a lion tamer wasn't exactly on the cards.

He tore at a loose flap of skin on his finger with his teeth, jiggling his knee, struggling to relax. When Cameron Yates finally appeared Andrew felt certain he'd met him before. He was about to ask if that was actually the case—perhaps he'd be able to use it to curry favor—but then he realized that he only recognized Cameron because he was a dead ringer for a young Wallace from *Wallace and Gromit*. He had bulbous eyes that were too close together and large front teeth that jutted down unevenly like stalactites. The only real differences were his tufty black hair and home counties accent.

They exchanged some awkward small talk in the coffin-sized lift, and all the while Andrew couldn't tear his eyes away from the stalactites. *Stop looking at the fucking teeth*, he told himself, while staring directly at the fucking teeth.

They waited for someone to bring them two blue thimbles of lukewarm water before finally the interview began in earnest. Cameron started by rattling through the job description, barely pausing for breath as he outlined how, if Andrew were to get the role, he'd be dealing with all deaths covered under the Public Health Act. "So that's liaising with funeral directors to organize the services, writing death notices in the local paper, registering deaths, tracing family members, recovering funeral costs through the deceased's estates. There's an awful lot of the old paperwork malarkey, as you can imagine!"

Andrew made sure to nod along, trying to take it all in, inwardly cursing Jill for neglecting to mention the whole "death" thing. Then, before he knew it, the spotlight was on him. Disconcertingly, Cameron seemed as nervous as he was, switching from simple, friendly questions to meandering, confusing ones, a harsher edge to his voice—as if he were playing good cop/bad cop by himself. When Andrew was afforded a second to respond to Cameron's nonsense, he found himself stumbling over his words. When he did manage to string a sentence together his enthusiasm sounded like desperation, his attempts at humor just seeming to confuse Cameron, who on more than one occasion looked past Andrew's shoulder, distracted by someone walking past in the corridor. Eventually it got to a point where he felt so despondent he considered giving up on the spot and just walking out. In among his depression at how things were going he was still distracted by Cameron's teeth. For one thing, he'd started to question whether it was stalactites or *stalagmites*. Wasn't there a thing about pulling down tights that helped you remember? It was at that moment that he realized Cameron had just asked him something—he had no idea what—and was now waiting for an answer. Panicked, he sat forward. "Ermmm," he said, in a tone he hoped conveyed that he was appreciative of such a thoughtful question and thus needed to give it due consideration. But this was clearly a mistake, judging from Cameron's growing frown. Andrew realized the question must have been a simple one.

"Yes," he blurted out, deciding to keep the answer short. Relief flooded him as Cameron's trampled Wallace smile reappeared.

"Wonderful. And how many?" he said.

This was trickier, though Andrew sensed a lightheartedness in Cameron's tone so this time plumped for a general, breezy response.

"Well, I suppose I sort of lose track sometimes," he said, trying a rueful smile. Cameron reacted with a false-sounding laugh, as though he couldn't quite tell if Andrew was joking. Andrew decided to fire back, hoping for more information.

"Do you mind me asking you the same question?" he said.

"Of course. I've just got the one myself," Cameron said enthusiastically. He reached into his pocket and started rummaging. The thought briefly crossed Andrew's mind that the man interviewing him for a job was about to pull out a lone testicle, as if he asked this question of every man he met, hoping desperately for a solo-ball owner. Instead, Cameron produced his wallet. It was only when he brought out a picture from within of a child trussed up in winter gear with skis on that Andrew understood what the question had been. He quickly replayed the conversation from Cameron's perspective.

"Do you have kids?"

"Ermmm . . . Yes."

"Wonderful. And how many?"

"Well, I suppose I sort of lose track sometimes."

Christ, had he just given the impression to a potential new boss that he was some sort of prolific Lothario who'd spent his life shagging around town and leaving a succession of women pregnant and homes broken?

He was still just looking at the photo of Cameron's child. *Say something!*

"Lovely," he said. "Lovely . . . boy."

Oh good, now you sound like the Child Catcher. That'll go down well. You start on Monday, Mr. Pedophile!

He grasped his plastic water beaker, long since empty, and felt it crack in his hand. This was a fucking disaster. How could he have blown things already? He could tell from Cameron's expression that he was past the point of no return. Quite what he'd say if Andrew just admitted to accidentally lying about having children he wasn't sure, but it seemed unlikely that it would suddenly turn things around. He decided his best option now was just to get through the rest of the interview while saving as much face as possible—like continuing to do mirror, signal, maneuver on a driving test having just run over a lollipop lady.

As he let go of the plastic beaker he noticed the graze on his palm and thought about the girl who'd helped him that morning. The wavy brown hair, that inscrutable smile. He could feel the blood starting to throb in his ears. What would it be like—to have a moment where he could just pretend. To play out a little fantasy all for himself. Where was the harm? Where, really, was the harm in spending the briefest moment imagining that everything had actually worked out fine and not fallen to pieces?

He cleared his throat.

Was he going to do this?

"How old is he?" he asked, handing the photo back to Cameron.

"He's just turned seven," Cameron said. "And yours?"

Was he actually going to do this?

19

"Well . . . Steph's eight and David's four," he said.

Apparently, he was.

"Ah, wonderful. It was when my boy Chris turned six that I really started to get the sense of what sort of person he was going to be," Cameron said. "Though Clara, my wife, always reckoned she could tell all that before he'd even left the womb."

Andrew smiled. "My wife Diane said exactly the same," he said.

And, just like that, he had a family.

They talked about their wives and children for a while longer, but all too soon Cameron brought the interview back around to the job, and Andrew felt the fantasy slipping away like water through his fingers. Before too long their time was up. Disconcertingly, instead of trucking out the usual line of whether Andrew had any questions for *him*, Cameron instead asked whether he had "any last words," as if he were about to be taken away and hanged. He managed to dredge up some vague waffle about what an interesting role it seemed and how much he'd relish the chance to work in Cameron's dynamic-sounding team.

"We'll be in touch," Cameron said, spoken with the sincerity of a politician pretending to like an indie band during a radio interview. Andrew forced a smile and remembered to make eye contact as he shook Cameron's hand, which was cold and wet, as if he'd been fondling a trout. "Thanks for the opportunity," Andrew said.

―――――――――

He found a café and used the free Wi-Fi to search for jobs, but he was too distracted to look properly. When he'd thanked Cameron "for the opportunity" it had nothing to do with the job, it was because he'd been given the chance to indulge, however briefly, in the fantasy of having a family. How strangely thrilling and scary it had been to feel so normal. He tried to forget about it, forcing himself to concentrate.

If he wasn't going to get another council job he'd need to expand his search, but it felt like an impossibly daunting task. There was nothing he could find that he seemed qualified for. Half the job descriptions themselves were baffling enough. He stared hopelessly at the large muffin he'd bought but not eaten, picking at it instead until it looked like a molehill. Maybe he'd make other animal burrows out of food and enter the Turner Prize competition.

He sat in the café for the rest of the afternoon, watching important businesspeople having their important business meetings and tourists thumbing excitedly through guidebooks. He stayed there long after all had left, pressing himself up against the radiator and trying to remain invisible to the young Italian waiter stacking chairs and sweeping up. Eventually he asked Andrew if he wouldn't mind leaving, the apologetic smile disappearing from his face as he spotted the muffin molehill crumbs that had spilled onto the table.

Andrew's phone rang just as he stepped outside. An unknown number.

"Andrew?" the person on the end of the line said. "Can you hear me?"

"Yes," Andrew said, though he barely could with the combination of a blustery wind and an ambulance driving past, siren screaming.

"Andrew, it's Cameron Yates. I just wanted to give you a call to say that it was really good to meet you earlier today. You really seemed to get the can-do culture I'm trying to build here. So, to cut a long story short, I'm very pleased to say I'd love you to come on board."

"I'm sorry?" Andrew said, jamming a finger in his free ear.

"We're offering you the job!" Cameron said. "There'll be the usual formalities, of course, but can't see any problems there, mate."

Andrew stood there, buffeted by the wind.

"Andrew? Did you catch that?"

"Gosh. Yes, I did. Wow. That's great. I'm . . . I'm delighted."

And he was. So delighted in fact that he beamed at the waiter through the window. The waiter rewarded him with a slightly be-mused smile.

"Andrew, listen, I'm just heading off to a seminar, so I'll ask some-one to ping you an e-mail with all the deets. I'm sure there'll be a few bits and pieces to chat through, but don't sweat any of that now. You get home and give Diane and the kids the good news."

– CHAPTER 4 –

It was hard for Andrew to believe that it was only five years since he'd been standing in that windswept street, trying to take in what Cameron had just said. It felt like a lifetime ago.

He stirred listlessly at the baked beans currently spluttering in the travel saucepan on the stovetop, before depositing them on a crust of whole wheat he'd cut with his one still-sharp knife, its plastic handle warped and burned. He looked intently at the square of cracked tiles behind the cooker, pretending it was a camera. "So what I've done there is to combine the beans and the bread, and now I'll just add a blob of ketchup (I use Captain Tomato but any brand is fine) to make it a tasty trio. You can't freeze any of the leftovers, but luckily you'll have wolfed it all down in about nine seconds and you'll be too busy hating yourself to worry about that."

He could hear his neighbor humming downstairs. She was relatively new, the previous tenants having moved out a few months ago. They were a young couple—early twenties, both startlingly attractive; all cheekbones and toned arms. The sort of aesthetically pleasing appearance that meant they'd never had to apologize for anything in their lives. Andrew would force himself to make eye contact with them and summon up a breezy greeting when they crossed paths in the hallway, but they never really bothered to reply. He was only aware that someone new had moved in when he heard the distinctive humming. He hadn't seen his new neighbor, but, oddly, he *had* smelled her. Or at least he'd smelled her perfume, which was so strong that it lingered permanently in the hallway. He tried to picture her, but when he tried to see her face it was just a smooth, featureless oval.

Just then, his phone lit up on the countertop. He saw his sister's name and his heart sank. He checked the date in the corner of his screen: March 31. He should have known. He pictured Sally checking her calendar, seeing a red ring around the thirty-first and swearing under her breath, knowing it was time for their quarterly call.

He took a fortifying gulp of water and picked up.

"Hello," he said.

"Hey," Sally said.

A pause.

"Well. How are you, little bro?" Sally said. "Everything cool?"

Christ, why did she still have to speak as though they were teen-agers?

"Oh, you know, the usual. You?"

"Can't complain, dude, I guess. Me and Carl are doing a yoga retreat this weekend, help him learn the teaching side of it and all that jazz."

Carl. Sally's husband. Usually to be found guzzling protein shakes and voluntarily lifting heavy objects up and down.

"That sounds . . . nice," Andrew said. Then, after the sort of short silence that clearly denotes it's time to move on to the most pressing matter: "And how's it going with your tests and everything?"

Sally sighed.

"Had a bunch more last month. Results all came back inconclusive, which means they still know sweet FA, basically. Still, I feel much better. And they think that it's probably not a heart thing, so I'm not likely to do a Dad and kick the bucket without warning. They just keep telling me the usual BS, you know how it is. Exercise more, drink less, blah blah blah."

"Well, good that they're not unduly concerned," Andrew said, thinking that if Sally shouldn't talk like a teenager he probably shouldn't talk like a repressed Oxford don. He'd have thought that after all these years it wouldn't feel like they were strangers. It was still that simple checklist of topics: Work. Health. Family (well, Carl, the only person who came close to a shared family member). Except, this time, Sally decided to throw in a curveball.

"So, I was thinking . . . maybe we should meet up sometime soon. It's been, like, five years now after all."

Seven, Andrew thought. *And the last time was at Uncle Dave's funeral in a crematorium opposite a KFC in Banbury. And you were high.* Then again, he conceded, he hadn't exactly been inundating Sally with invitations to meet up since.

"That . . . that would be good," he said. "As long as you can spare the time, of course. Maybe we could meet halfway or something."

"Yeah, it's cool, bro. Though we've moved, remember? We're in Newquay now—Carl's business, and everything? So halfway is somewhere else these days. But I'm going to be in London seeing a friend in May. We could hang then, maybe?"

"Yes. Okay. Just let me know when you're coming up."

Andrew scanned the room and chewed his lip. In the twenty years since he'd moved into the flat barely a thing had changed. Consequently, his living space was looking not so much tired as absolutely knackered. There was the dark stain where the wall met the ceiling in the area that masqueraded as a kitchen; then there were the battered gray sofa, threadbare carpet and yellowy-brown wallpaper that was meant to suggest autumn but in fact suggested digestive biscuits. As the color of the wallpaper had faded, so had the chances of Andrew's actually doing anything about it. And his shame at the state of the place was only matched by the terror he felt at the thought of changing it or, worse, living anywhere else. There was at least one benefit to being on his own and never having anyone around—nobody could judge him for how he lived.

He decided to change the subject, recalling something Sally had told him the last time they'd spoken.

"How are things going with your . . . person?"

He heard a lighter sparking and then the faint sound of Sally exhaling smoke.

"My person?"

"The person you were going to see. To talk about things."

"You mean my therapist?"

"Yes."

"Ditched her when we moved. To be honest, dude, I was glad of the excuse. She kept trying to hypnotize me and it didn't work. I told her I was immune but she wouldn't listen. But I've found someone new in Newquay. She's more of a spiritual healer, I guess? I bumped into her while she was putting up an advert next to Carl's yoga class flyer. What are the chances?"

Well . . . , Andrew thought.

"So, listen, man," Sally said. "There was something else I wanted to talk to you about."

"Right," Andrew said, instantly suspicious. First arranging to meet, now this. Oh god, what if she was going to try to make him spend time with Carl?

"So—and I normally wouldn't do this as I know that . . . well, it's not something we'd normally talk about. But, anyway, you know my old pal Sparky?"

"No."

"You do, bud. He's the one with the bong shop in Brighton Lanes?"

Obviously.

"Okay . . ."

"He's got this friend. Julia. She lives in London. Crystal Palace way, actually, so not too far from you. She's thirty-five. And about two years ago she went through a pretty shitty-sounding divorce."

Andrew held the phone away from his ear. *If this is going where I think it's going . . .*

"But she's come out of the other side of it now, and from what Sparky tells me she's looking to, you know, get back in the saddle. So, I was just thinking, that, like, maybe you might—"

"No," Andrew said. "Absolutely not. Forget it."

"But, Andrew, she's super nice from what I can tell—pretty too, from the pics I've seen—and I reckon you'd like her a lot."

"That's irrelevant," Andrew said. "Because I don't want . . . that. It's not for me, now."

"'It's not for me.' Jesus, man, it's love we're talking about, here, not pineapple on pizzas. You can't just dismiss it."

"Why not? Why can't I? It's not hurting anyone, is it, if I do? If anything it's guaranteeing that nobody gets hurt."

"But that's no way to live your life, dude. You're forty-two, still totally in your prime. You gotta think about putting yourself out there, otherwise you're, like, actively denying yourself potential happiness. I know it's hard, but you have to look to the future."

Andrew could feel his heart start to beat that little bit faster. He had a horrible feeling that his sister was building up the courage to ask him about something they'd never ever discussed, not for want of trying on Sally's part. It was not so much the elephant in the room as the brontosaurus in the closet. He decided to nip things in the bud.

"I'm very grateful for your concern, but there's no need for it. Honestly. I'm fine as I am."

"I get that, but, seriously, one day we're gonna have to talk about . . . you know . . . stuff."

"No, we don't," Andrew said, annoyed that his voice had come out as a whisper. Showing any sort of emotion was going to come across like an invitation to Sally to keep up this line of questioning, as if he secretly did want to talk about "stuff," which he definitely, absolutely, didn't.

"But, bro, we have to at some point, it's not healthy!"

"Yes, well neither is smoking weed your whole life, so I'm not sure you're in any position to judge, are you?"

Andrew winced. He heard Sally exhale smoke.

"I'm sorry. That wasn't called for."

"All I'm saying," Sally said, and there was a deliberateness to her tone now, "is that I think it would be good for you to talk things through."

"And all *I'm* saying," Andrew said, "is that I really don't feel like that's something I want to do. My love life, or lack thereof, isn't something I feel comfortable getting into. And when it comes to 'stuff,' there's really nothing to say."

A pause.

"Well, okay, man. It's up to you I guess. I mean, Carl keeps telling me to stop bothering you about it, but it's hard not to, you know? You're my brother, bro!"

Andrew felt a familiar pang of self-loathing. Not for the first time, his sister had reached out and he'd basically told her to take a running jump. He wanted to apologize properly, to tell her that of course it meant a lot to him that she cared, but the words stuck in his throat.

"Listen," Sally said. "I think we're nearly ready to sit down to eat. So, I guess . . . speak to you later?"

"Yeah," Andrew said, screwing his eyes shut in frustration. "Definitely. And thanks, you know, for the call and everything."

"Sure. No problem, bro. Look after yourself."

"Yes. I will. Absolutely. And you too."

As Andrew made his way the short distance from the kitchenette to his computer he nearly walked straight into the Flying Scotsman, which chugged on unconcerned. Of all his locomotives, the Scotsman seemed to carry itself with the most cheerful insouciance (compared to the Railroad BR InterCity, for example, which always seemed petulant at being made to travel at all). It was also the very first engine, and the very first part of his model train collection as a whole, that he'd owned. He'd received it as a gift when he was a teenager, and he was instantly infatuated. Perhaps it was the unexpected source of the present rather than the thing itself, but over time he began to appreciate just how perfect it was. It took him years before he could afford to buy another engine. And then another. And then a fourth. And then track and sidings and platforms and buffers and signal boxes, until eventually all of the floor space in his flat was taken up with a complicated system of interweaving tracks and various accompanying scenery: tunnels made to look like they were cut into mountains, cows grazing by streams, entire wheat fields, allotments with rows of tiny cabbages being tended to by men wearing floppy hats. Before too long he had enough scenery to actively mirror the real seasons. It was always a thrill when he felt the change in the air. Once, during a funeral attended exclusively by the deceased's drinking pals, the vicar had made reference to the clocks going back as part of a clunky metaphor in his eulogy, and it was all Andrew could do not to punch the air with joy at the prospect of a whole weekend of replacing the currently verdant landscape with something much more autumnal.

It was addictive, building these worlds. Expensive, too. Andrew's meager savings had long since been spent on his collection, and other than rent, his pay packet now went almost exclusively to upgrading and maintenance. He no longer worried about all the hours, or sometimes whole days, he spent browsing the Internet for ways to improve his setup. He couldn't remember the point at which he'd discovered and then signed up to the ModelTrainNuts forum, but he'd been on it every day since. The majority of people who posted there made his interest seem positively amateurish, and Andrew thoroughly admired every single one of them. Anyone—anyone at all—who thought to log on to a message board at 2:38 a.m. and post the message: PLEASE HELP A NEWBIE: Stanier 2–6–4T Chassis CRACKED. HELP?? was nearly as much of a hero to him as the *thirty-three* people who replied within minutes offering tips, solutions and general words of encouragement. In truth, he understood about 10 percent of all that was talked about in the more technical conversations, but he always read them post by post, feeling genuine joy when queries, sometimes having lain dormant for months, were resolved. He would occasionally post on the main forum with general messages of goodwill, but the game changer was after he began regularly chatting to three other users and was invited—via private message no less!—to join an exclusive subforum. This little haven was run by BamBam67, one of the longest-serving members of the site, who had recently been granted moderator rights. The two others invited into the fold were TinkerAl, by all accounts a young and passionate enthusiast, and the more experienced BroadGaugeJim, who'd once posted a photo of an aqueduct he'd built over a running stream that was so beautiful Andrew had needed to have a lie-down.

The subforum had been set up by BamBam67 to show off his new moderator privileges (and Bam *did* like to show off, often accompanying his posts with photos of his train setup that seemed to be more about letting them see the size of his very beautiful home). They discovered early on that they all lived in London, except for BroadGauge (the enthusiastic, avuncular member of the group), who had been "keeping it real in Leatherhead" for over thirty years, but the idea of their meeting up in real life had never been raised. This suited

Andrew (who went by Tracker) just fine. Partly because it meant there were times when he could modify his online persona to mask his real-life inadequacies (this, he had realized early on, was the entire point of the Internet), but also because these were the only (and therefore best) friends he had, and to meet them in real life and find out they were arseholes would be a real shame.

There was a marked difference between what happened on the main forum and the subforum. A delicate ecosystem existed in the former. Conversation had to be strictly on topic, and any user who flouted the rules was duly punished, sometimes severely. The most infamous example of this had been when TunnelBotherer6 had persistently posted about baseboards in a gears topic and had been branded a "waste of space" by the moderator. Chillingly, TB6 never posted again. But in the subforum, away from prying main-board moderator eyes, a slow shift occurred. Before long, it became a place where personal issues were discussed. It felt terrifying at first. It was like they were the Resistance poring over maps under a single light-bulb in a dusty cellar as enemy soldiers drank in the bar above. It had been BroadGaugeJim who'd been the first one to bring up an explicitly non-train issue.

Listen, chaps, **he'd written,** I wouldn't normally want to bother you with something like this, but to be perfectly honest I'm not quite sure who else to ask. Basically, my daughter Emily got caught "cyberbullying" someone at school. Mean messages. Photoshopped pics. Nasty stuff, from what I've seen. She tells me she wasn't the ringleader and feels really bad (and I believe her), but I still feel like I need to make sure she understands she can't be part of anything like that ever again, even if it means losing her mates. Just wondered if any of you might have any advice for a useless duffer like me!! No worries if not!!!!!

Andrew's scrambled eggs went cold as he waited to see what happened. It was TinkerAl who responded first, and the advice he gave was simple, sensible, yet obviously heartfelt. So much so that Andrew felt momentarily overwhelmed. He tried writing his own response, but he couldn't really think of anything better than what TinkerAl had said. Instead, he just backed up Tinker's suggestion with a couple of lines, and resolved (perhaps a little selfishly) to be the helpful one next time.

———

Andrew logged on, heard the reassuring sound of the Scotsman rushing past behind him, and waited in eager anticipation of the little breeze that followed in its wake. He adjusted his monitor. He'd bought the computer as a thirty-second birthday present for himself. At the time it had seemed like a sleek and powerful machine, but now, a decade later, it was impossibly bulky and slow compared to the latest models. Nevertheless, Andrew felt an affection for the clunky old beast that meant he'd cling on to it for as long as it still spluttered into life.

Hi, all, **he wrote.** Anybody on for the night shift?

As he waited for the reply he knew would come within a maximum of ten minutes, he maneuvered carefully across the rail tracks to his record player and thumbed through his LPs. He kept them in a wonky pile rather than in neat rows on a shelf—that diminished the fun of it. In this more ramshackle style of ordering he could still occasionally surprise himself. There were some other artists and albums in there—Miles Davis, Dave Brubeck, Dizzy Gillespie—but Ella vastly outnumbered all of them.

He slid *The Best Is Yet to Come* out of its sleeve but changed his mind and put it back. When he altered his railway landscapes that was because of the changing seasons, but there wasn't as straightforward a logic when choosing which of Ella's records to listen to. With her, it was just a case of what felt right in the moment. There was only one exception—her version of "Blue Moon." He hadn't been able to play that particular song for twenty years, though that didn't stop the tune from filtering into his head on occasion. As soon as he recognized the first notes, pain would grow at his temples, his vision would fog, and then came the sound of piercing feedback and shouting, mixing with the music, and the uncanny sensation of hands gripping his shoulders. And then, just like that, it was gone, and he'd be looking at a confused pharmacist or realizing he'd missed his bus stop. On one occasion a few years before, he'd walked into a record shop in Soho and realized that the song was playing on the shop's speakers. He'd left so hastily he'd ended up in a tense encounter with the shopkeeper and a passing off-duty police officer. More recently, he'd been channel-hopping and found himself watching a football match. Minutes later he was desperately searching for the remote to turn it off, because apparently "Blue Moon" was what the Manchester City fans sang. To hear the actual song was bad enough, but fifty thousand people bellowing it out of sync was on another level. He tried to tell himself that it was simply one of those unusual afflictions people suffer and just have to tolerate, like being allergic to sunlight, or having night terrors, but the thought lingered that at some point, probably, he would have to talk to someone about it.

He ran his fingers down the uneven record pile. Tonight it was *Hello Love* that caught his eye. He carefully dropped the needle and went back to his computer. BamBam67 had been first to reply.

Evening, all. Night shift for me too. House to myself thankfully. Seen they're repeating that BBC thing from last year tonight? James May sitting in his shed rebuilding a Graham Farish 372–311 N Gauge steam loco. Apparently they did it all in one take. Anyway, don't bother with it. It's awful.

Andrew smiled and refreshed. There was TinkerAl right on cue:

HAHA! Knew it wouldn't be your c.o.t.! I loved it I'm afraid!

Refresh. Here was BroadGaugeJim:

Evening shift for me too, squires. I watched the May thing first
time around. Once he'd argued in favor of cork underlay over
ballasted I'm afraid I couldn't really take the rest of it seriously.

Andrew rolled his head around on his shoulders and sank down
low in his chair. Now that the four of them had posted, now that Ella
was crooning and a train was rattling around the room, defeating the
silence, he could relax.

This was when everything came together.

This was everything.

– CHAPTER 5 –

As Andrew's packed lunches went, this was another textbook effort, even if he said so himself. "Ham *and* cheese," he boasted to the camera. "Blob of pickle goes central, then we'll just spread it out to each corner. I like to imagine it's a traitor's body parts being sent to the four corners of England, but come up with whatever metaphor you want. Hang on, is this a bit of iceberg lettuce? You bet it is. So who's coming with? A packet of salt and vinegar from the multi-bag? Tick. And how about a satsuma from the Big Red Net? Ditto. Though do be careful to check it's not one of those sneaky ones who's pretending to be fine despite the fact its bottom's gone moldy. I always picture a vainglorious young soldier protesting he wants to go on patrol despite a shattered fibula, but again, do choose your own metaphor."

He was about to launch into an explanation of his Tupperware system when he faltered, staring ahead as if the autocue had broken, the wholly unwelcome reminder of Keith and Meredith's tag-team interrogation coming into his mind.

Sitting on the train to work (wedged into the armrest by a man whose legs were spread so far apart Andrew could only assume he was performing some sort of interpretive dance about what a *great guy* he was), he found himself thinking back to his very first day in the office. After his momentary excitement at getting the job, he'd spent the following days desperately panicking about how he was going to set things straight with Cameron about the small matter of his made-up family. He reasoned his best chance would be to get on with Cameron very, very quickly—to go against all instincts and actively befriend him. A few illicit chats in the corridor slagging other people off, a pint of lager after work on a Friday—that's what people did, wasn't it?—then he'd confess, say it had been a moment of madness between you and me, mate, and they'd chalk the whole thing up to one of those white lies everyone told in interviews.

Unfortunately, it wasn't to be. As is dictated by UK law, Andrew had said a brief hello to his new colleagues before immediately locking himself out of his e-mails and sitting in silence for an hour because he was too embarrassed to ask for help.

That's when he saw Cameron appear. This was Andrew's first big chance to get on friendly terms. He was just planning a witty opening gambit about his current admin crisis when Cameron, having interrupted to wish him a happy first day and rambled on and on about "KPIs" without giving him a chance to speak, concluded by asking in a voice clearly loud enough that everyone else could hear, "How's the family? Steph and David okay?"

So thrown was he that Cameron had blown the whole thing this early, he responded to the question of how his children were by saying, "They seem fine, thanks."

It would have been an appropriate response to an optician asking how his new lenses were, but not so much when referring to the well-being of his flesh and blood. Flustered, he gabbled on about them seeming to have lots of homework at the moment.

"Well," Cameron said when Andrew had finished rambling. "Easter hols, soon. You and Diane off anywhere nice?"

"Um . . . France," Andrew said.

"Oh, top banana," Cameron said. "Whereabouts?"

Andrew considered this.

"South," he said. "South France."

And that was that.

In those early days, when conversation turned to family he was forced to think on his feet. He learned quickly that he could pretend to be distracted by something on his computer, or ask for a question to be repeated as if he hadn't quite caught it, to buy him time, but he knew he needed a more long-term strategy. In his second week, there were a few days when nothing came up, and he wondered if he might be out of the woods. Looking back, he'd been incredibly naive. This was *family*. This was what normal people talked about. The situation wasn't helped by the fact that Meredith seemed to exist on a diet of nosiness and gossip, constantly pressing Andrew for more specific information. A case in point had been when she, Keith and a nervous graduate called Bethany were talking about weddings.

"Oh it was so excruciating," Meredith said, gloating about a friend's nuptials that weekend. "They were standing there up at the altar and they just couldn't fit the ring on his big fat finger."

"My dad thinks it's a bit namby-pamby for men to wear a wedding ring," Bethany said in her quivering voice that made her sound like she was perpetually being driven over a cattle grid.

"You seeeee?" Keith said, spreading his arms wide to make his point and revealing the sweat patches under his arms. "That's what I've always said."

"Oh, I don't know," Meredith said. "If my Graham didn't wear one I know he'd have all sorts of slappers crawling all over him."

She strained her neck to try to see over Andrew's screen.

"Do you wear one, Andrew?"

Stupidly, he actually checked his finger before saying no.

"Is that for any particular reason, or . . . ?"

Shit.

"No, no," he said. "I just . . . didn't think I'd like how it felt."

Nobody questioned this, but he could still feel his neck starting to burn with embarrassment. He realized then that it wasn't good enough just knowing the simple facts, having the general overview. He was going to have to accentuate the broad brushstrokes with finer ones. And so, later that evening, with Ella on in the background, he opened up a blank spreadsheet and began to fill in his family's story. He started by establishing as many "factual" things as possible: middle names, ages, hair colors, heights. Then, over the following weeks, he began to add subtler details—remembering snippets of strangers' conversations from which he'd take some minor detail, or asking himself how someone else's news might have been dealt with by his own family. Before too long you could have asked him almost anything and he'd have had a response prepared. To look at the spreadsheet at random you might have found that David enjoyed touch rugby but had recently sprained his ankle. He was shy and preferred playing on his own rather than with friends. He'd begged for months for a pair of trainers that had heels that lit up when you walked, until Andrew had finally relented.

Steph had terrible colic when she was a baby, but apart from the odd case of conjunctivitis now and then they rarely had to see a doctor with her these days. She asked scarily intelligent questions in public, which often left them embarrassingly stumped. She had once played a shepherd at the nativity to mixed reviews from her costars, though of course they'd never been prouder.

It was the "they" part—him and Diane—that he found more difficult. It had felt okay when he'd allowed himself to fantasize during the interview, but this was another level altogether. Nevertheless, the details were all there: Diane had recently been made partner in the law firm (her field was human rights), and though she worked long hours she'd now stopped checking the dreaded BlackBerry on weekends. Their wedding anniversary was September 4, but they also had a mini-celebration on November 15—the anniversary of their first kiss (standing outside in the snow after an impromptu party in a friend's halls of residence room). Their first proper date had been to see *Pulp Fiction* at the cinema. They went to her parents' for Christmas and tended to holiday with the kids in France in the summer and Center Parcs in the autumn half term. They'd gone to Rome for their tenth wedding anniversary. When they could get a babysitter they'd go to the theater—but nothing too avant-garde, because they'd decided their time and money were too precious to fritter away on something without at least one of the leads having been in a Sunday night costume drama. Diane played tennis every Sunday morning with her friend Sue and was on the PTA at Steph's school. She used to wear bright orange-rimmed glasses before taking the plunge with laser surgery. She had a little scar above her eyebrow from where a boy at school called James Bond had thrown a crabapple at her.

All of this had been such a full-on job that Andrew had barely found time to think about how his actual new role was going. He'd already been to two funerals and made difficult phone calls to several relatives (one of which involved having to explain to a man that if he wanted the council to pay for his uncle's funeral then he'd have to return the laptop he'd taken from the house so that they could sell it to pay for the service). He'd even come along with Keith to his first property inspection and seen the room where a woman had taken her final breath. But all that felt like a walk in the park compared to keeping his deceit undiscovered. He was constantly on edge, waiting for the moment he got himself tangled up in knots or completely contradicted himself. But then a month passed, and another, and slowly he started to relax. All his hard work was paying off.

The moment that nearly changed everything came on a Friday at lunchtime, Andrew having spent a fruitless morning searching for next-of-kin clues in a shoebox full of papers recovered from a property search. He was absentmindedly watching some shop-bought macaroni and cheese rotate in the microwave and engaging in some idle chitchat with Cameron when the subject of allergies came up.

"That's the hard part," Cameron was saying. "You have to be totally prepared. It just means you're on edge rather a lot. Especially when it comes to nuts. With Chris we just have to be extra vigilant, you know?"

"Mmm," Andrew said, distractedly peeling back the plastic film and jabbing the pasta around with his fork. "Steph's allergic to bee stings, so I know what you mean."

It was only when he got back to his desk and was halfway through his lunch that he considered this little exchange. He hadn't needed to mentally refer to his spreadsheet or desperately improvise something; instead he had quite calmly volunteered this information about Steph without even thinking about it, as if it had come from his subconscious. The fact that the detail had appeared so easily left him deeply unsettled. It may have helped his cause overall, another little piece of information to put meat on the bones, but it was the first time he'd really lost sight of why he was having to make things up in the first place. Allowing the fantasy to take over like that felt scary. So much so, in fact, that when he got home that evening, rather than updating his spreadsheet he spent the time looking for another job.

A week later, he had just come out of the church, having attended the funeral of a seventy-five-year-old former driving instructor who'd drowned in the bath, when he turned on his phone to find a voicemail from an HR person asking him to interview for one of the jobs he'd applied for. Ordinarily this would have thrown him into a panic, but he always felt curiously numb after the funerals, so when he heard the message he felt calm enough to call back immediately to arrange the interview. This was his chance to escape and finally stop the lies.

Another week later, he was climbing the stairs at the council office and feeling horribly out of breath, trying to convince himself that this was because he was suffering from a disease—possibly fatal—and nothing to do with the fact he hadn't exercised for two decades, when his phone rang again. A few seconds later, he was wheezing that yes he'd be very happy to come in for a second interview. He spent the rest of the afternoon sitting at his desk and imagining how it would feel to tell Cameron he was handing in his notice already.

"You and the family up to anything nice this weekend, Andrew?" Bethany asked.

"Barbecue on Saturday if the weather's nice," Andrew said. "Steph's decided she's vegetarian, so not quite sure what's going to be on the menu for her."

"Oh, I am too! It's fine—just do some halloumi cheese and some Linda McCartney sausages. She'll love it."

They were still discussing weekend plans some minutes later when Andrew got an e-mail from Adrian, the recruitment person who'd called him, asking him to confirm what dates he was free for the second interview. Andrew excused himself and escaped to a toilet cubicle. He didn't want to admit to himself quite how warm and comforted he felt after little moments like this with Bethany and the others when discussing family stuff. The thought returned to him again: Where was the harm in what he was doing? He wasn't upsetting anyone. People had *actual* families that they did *actual* diabolical things to, harming loved ones in all sorts of awful ways, and what he was doing wasn't comparable to that in any way.

By the time he'd gotten back to his desk he'd made up his mind. He would make peace with what he was doing. He wasn't going to turn back now.

Hi Adrian,

I'm really glad for the opportunity to have met with Jackie, but after a bit of soul-searching I've decided to keep on in my current role. Thank you for your time.

From then on, things started to get easier. He could happily join in with family chat feeling guilt-free, and, for the first time in a very long while, he felt happy more often than he felt lonely.

– CHAPTER 6 –

Andrew emerged from the station and—soddiest of sod's laws—found himself walking just behind Cameron. He hung back and pretended to check his phone. To his surprise, he actually had a new text. To his disappointment, it was from Cameron. He read it and swore under his breath. He wanted to like Cameron, he really did, because he knew that his heart was in the right place. But it was hard to warm to a person who a) commuted on one of those mini-scooters that had suddenly been deemed acceptable for people above the age of five, and b) was unwittingly trying to ruin his life, having waited barely twelve hours before texting him to ask whether he'd had a chance to reconsider the dinner party plan.

The idea of losing his family didn't bear thinking about. Yes, there was still the occasional tricky moment in conversation that sent him briefly off balance, but it was worth it. Diane, Steph and David *were* his family now. They were his happiness and his strength and the thing that kept him going. Didn't that make them just as real as everyone else's family?

He made a cup of tea, hung his coat on its usual peg and turned to see there was a woman sitting in his seat.

He couldn't see her face because it was obscured behind his computer, but he could see her legs, clad in dark green tights, under his desk. She was dangling one of her black pumps on her toes. Something about the way she was flicking it back and forth reminded Andrew of a cat toying with a mouse. He stood there, mug in hand, not quite knowing what to do. The woman was swiveling in his chair and tapping a pen—one of *his* pens—on her teeth.

"Hello," he said, realizing that even for him this was a record, to feel his cheeks reddening as the woman smiled and offered him a cheery hello in response.

"Sorry, but you're, um, sitting in . . . that's sort of technically my seat."

"Oh god, I'm so sorry," the woman said, jumping to her feet.

"It's okay," Andrew said, adding, rather needlessly, another "sorry" himself.

The woman had dark, rusty red hair that was piled high on top of her head with what looked like a pencil poking through it, as if to pull it out would make her hair cascade down like some sort of Kerplunk Rapunzel. Andrew guessed she was a few years younger than him, late thirties perhaps.

"What a great first impression to make," she said, getting to her feet. Then, seeing Andrew's confusion, "I'm Peggy—it's my first day."

Just then Cameron appeared and bounded over like a quiz-show presenter on a now-defunct digital channel.

"Excellent, excellent—you two've met!"

"And I've already stolen his chair," Peggy said.

"Ha, *stolen his chair*," Cameron laughed. "So anyway. Pegs—do you mind if I call you Pegs?"

"Um . . . No?"

"Well, Pegs, Peggy—the Pegster!—you're going to be shadowing Andrew for a while just to get you up to speed. I'm afraid you're rather in at the deep end this morning as I believe Andrew has a property inspection. But, well, no time like the present to get stuck in, I suppose."

He proffered a violent double thumbs-up and Andrew watched Peggy recoil involuntarily, as if Cameron had just pulled out a knife. "Righto," Cameron said, oblivious to this, "I shall leave you in Andrew's capable hands."

———

Andrew had forgotten they had a new person starting, and he felt uneasy at the prospect of being shadowed. Entering a dead person's house was still strange and unsettling, and the last thing he wanted was someone else to worry about. He had his own methods, his own way of doing things. He didn't really want to have to keep stopping to explain everything along the way. At the start, Keith had been the one to show Andrew the ropes. He had seemed to take it relatively seriously at first, but before long he started to just sit in the corner and play games on his phone, pausing only to make crude jokes at the deceased's expense. Andrew might have welcomed a bit of gallows humor, though it wasn't really his style, but Keith didn't seem to possess a shred of empathy. Eventually, Andrew had approached him in the office kitchen and suggested he carry out inspections on his own. Keith had mumbled his agreement, barely seeming to notice what Andrew had said (though this may have been due in part to him struggling to extract his finger from the can of energy drink it was stuck in).

From then on, Keith stayed with Meredith in the office, registering deaths and arranging funerals. Andrew much preferred doing the inspections alone. The only problem with being unaccompanied was that news traveled fast when someone died, and suddenly a person who'd expired in complete solitude now had posthumous well-wishers and dear, *dear* friends who arrived during his inspections—caps in hand, beady eyes darting about the place—to pay their respects, and, just on the off chance, check if that watch the deceased had promised them in the event of their death, or fiver they owed them, happened to be on the premises. It was always the worst part, having to shoo these people away, the threat of violence hanging in the room long after they'd gone. So at least with the newbie alongside him he'd have a bit of backup.

"I meant to say," Peggy said. "Before we left, Cameron cornered me and told me to try and persuade you that us all having 'dinner party bonding sessions' together was a good idea. He said be subtle about it, but, well, that's not really my area of expertise . . ."

"Ah," Andrew said. "Well, thanks for letting me know. I think I'll just ignore that for now." He hoped that was *that* nipped in the bud.

"Righto," Peggy said. "Probably for the best as far as I'm concerned.

"Cooking isn't my bag, really. I managed to get to the age of thirty-eight without realizing I've been pronouncing 'bruschetta' wrong all my life. Turns out it's not 'brusheta,' according to my neighbor. Then again he does wear a pink sweater tied around his shoulders like he lives on a yacht, so I'm reluctant to take any of his advice."

"Right," Andrew said, slightly distracted, having realized they were running low on supplies ahead of the property inspection.

"I suppose it's a team-building thing, is it?" Peggy said. "To be fair I'd prefer that than clay pigeon shooting or whatever it is these middle managers get up to."

"Something like that," Andrew said, pulling his rucksack around and searching it to see if he was missing anything.

"And so we're, um, actually going to see a house now where a bloke's just died?"

"Yes, that's right." Shit, they *did* need supplies. They'd have to make a detour. He looked around in time to see Peggy puffing out her cheeks and then realized how unwelcoming he was being. He felt a familiar wave of self-loathing, but the words to rectify the situation wouldn't come, so they walked on in silence until they got to the supermarket.

"We just need to make a quick stop-off here," Andrew said.

"Midmorning snack?" Peggy asked.

"Afraid not. Well, not for me. But feel free to get something for yourself. I mean, not that you need my permission. Obviously."

"No, no, I'm fine. I'm actually on a diet anyway. It's the one where you eat an entire wheel of brie and then have a bit of a cry. You know the one?"

Andrew remembered to smile this time.

"I'll just be a minute," he said, shuffling off. When he returned with everything he needed he found Peggy standing in an aisle by the books and DVDs.

"Just look at this lass," she said, showing him a book whose cover displayed a woman smiling to the camera, apparently halfway through preparing a salad. "No one should look that delighted while holding an avocado." She put the book back on the shelf and looked at the air freshener and aftershave in Andrew's basket.

"I've got a horrible feeling I don't know what I'm letting myself in for," she said.

"I'll explain a bit more when we get there," Andrew said. He made his way to the tills, watching Peggy as she strolled toward the exit. She had a curious way of walking, her arms flat against her sides but her fists gently clenched and pointing out sideways, so that it looked like she had two treble clefs attached to her sides. As Andrew punched his pin into the card reader the tune of Ella and Louis Armstrong's version of "Would You Like to Take a Walk?" drifted into his head.

———

They were standing at a crossroads, Andrew checking they were going the right way on his phone. Peggy filled the silence with a story about a particularly moving TV episode she'd watched the night before. ("Admittedly I can't remember the name of the show, or the lead character, or when or where it's set—but if you can track it down it's brillo.") Satisfied they were going in the right direction, Andrew was about to lead the way when there was a sudden crash behind him. He spun around to see where the noise had come from and saw a builder leaning over some scaffolding, about to toss an armful of rubble down into a dumpster.

"Everything okay?" Peggy said. But Andrew was rooted to the spot, unable to take his eyes off the builder as he hurled another lot of bricks down with an even harsher clang. He began to clap dust off his hands but saw Andrew looking at him and stopped.

"Problem, mate?" he said, leaning over the scaffolding. Andrew swallowed hard. He could feel pain beginning to grow at his temples, the sound of harsh feedback slowly filtering into his head. Underneath the static came the faint strains of "Blue Moon." With great effort, he managed to get his legs moving, and, to his relief, by the time he'd crossed the road and walked further on both the pain and noise had subsided. He looked around sheepishly for Peggy, wondering how he was going to explain this, but she was still standing by the dumpster, talking to the builder. From the expressions on their faces, it looked as if Peggy was patiently trying to teach an incredibly stupid dog how to do a trick. Abruptly, Peggy walked off.

"You all right?" she said when she'd caught up with him.

Andrew cleared his throat. "Yes, fine," he said. "Thought I might have a migraine coming on, but thankfully not." He nodded back at the builder. "What were you talking to him about?"

"Oh," Peggy said, still seeming distracted with concern for him, "he made some unsolicited comments about my appearance so I took the time to explain that I sensed a deep, unquenchable sadness in his eyes. Are you sure you're okay, though?"

"Yes, fine," Andrew said, realizing too late that his arms were rigid at his sides, like a toy soldier's.

They set off again, and even though he braced himself, the distant crash of rubble still made him jump.

The deceased's flat was part of the Acorn Gardens estate. The name was written in white on a green sign featuring the names of the various blocks on the estate: Huckleberry House, Lavender House, Rose Petal House. Underneath that someone had spray-painted "Fuck cops," and underneath that a sketch of a cock and balls.

"Blimey," Peggy said.

"It's okay. I've actually been here before, I think. Nobody bothered me that time so I'm sure we'll be fine," Andrew said, in part trying to reassure himself.

"Oh no, I'm sure it will be. I just meant that." Peggy nodded at the sketch. "Impressive detail."

"Ah, right. Yes."

As they walked through the estate Andrew noticed people closing their windows and parents calling their kids inside, as if it were a Western and he was an outlaw hell-bent on chaos. He just hoped his attempted friendly smile conveyed the fact it was a coverall and some Febreze in his bag, rather than a shotgun.

The flat was on the first floor of Huckleberry House. Andrew paused at the bottom of the concrete steps and turned to face Peggy.

"How much detail has Cameron gone into with you about what happens at the property inspections?" he said.

"Not a huge amount," Peggy said. "It would be great if you could fill me in a bit more. Because I'll level with you, Andrew, I'm ever-so-slightly completely bloody terrified." She laughed nervously. Andrew dropped his gaze. Part of him wanted to laugh along to reassure her, but at the same time he was aware that if there were any neighbors or friends of the deceased watching it wouldn't look very professional. He squatted and reached into his bag.

"Here you go," he said, handing Peggy a pair of surgical gloves and mask. "So, the deceased's name is Eric White. He was sixty-two. The coroner referred the death to us because from what they can tell from the initial search by police there's no obvious sign of a next of kin. So we've got two goals today: firstly to piece together as much as we can about Eric and find out if there really isn't a next of kin, and secondly to try and work out if he's got enough money to pay for the funeral."

"Wow, okay," Peggy said. "And what's the going rate for a funeral these days?"

"It depends," Andrew said. "Average cost is about four thousand. But if the deceased hasn't got any sort of estate, and no relatives or anyone else willing to pay for it, then the council are legally obliged to bury them. Without frills—no headstone, flowers, private plot and the like—that's about a grand."

"Jeez," Peggy said, snapping a glove on. "Does that happen a lot—the council doing that?"

"Increasingly," Andrew said. "In the last five years or so there's been about a twelve percent increase in public health funerals. More and more people are passing away on their own, so we're always busy."

Peggy shivered.

"Sorry, I know it's a bit bleak," Andrew said.

"No, it's that expression—'pass away.' I know it's meant to soften the blow, but it just seems so, I dunno, flimsy."

"I agree, actually," Andrew said. "I don't usually say it myself. But sometimes people prefer it described that way."

Peggy cracked her knuckles. "Ah, you're all right, Andrew. I'm quite hard to shock. Ha—cut to me in five minutes' time legging it out of here." From the couple of wafts Andrew had already smelled coming through the door, he wouldn't be at all surprised if that was what happened. What was the protocol then? Would he have to chase after her?

"So what else did the coroner have to say about this poor chap?" Peggy asked.

"Well, the neighbors realized they hadn't seen him for a while and called the police, who forced entry and found his body. He was in the living room and he'd been there for a while so was in a fairly bad state of decomposition."

Peggy reached up and twiddled one of her earrings.

"Does that mean it might be a bit . . ." She tapped her nose.

"Afraid so," Andrew said. "It will have had time to air out a bit, but you can't . . . it's hard to explain, but . . . it's a very specific sort of smell."

Peggy was starting to look a little pale.

"But that's where this comes in," Andrew said quickly, holding up the aftershave, sounding unintentionally like he was in an advert. He shook the bottle and sprayed it liberally inside his mask, then did the same for Peggy, who strapped her mask over her nose and mouth.

"I'm not entirely sure this is what Paco Rabanne had in mind," came her muffled voice. This time Andrew smiled for real, and though Peggy's mouth was obscured he could tell from her eyes that she was smiling back.

"I've tried all sorts of different things over the years—but it's only ever the expensive stuff that seems to work."

He took the keys from an envelope in his bag.

"I'll go and have a quick look first, if that's okay?"

"Be my guest," Peggy said.

With the key in the lock, this was usually the point where Andrew took a moment to remind himself why he was there: that he was to treat the place with as much respect as possible, no matter how bad the conditions. He was by no means a spiritual person, but he tried to make sure he carried out his work as if the deceased were watching on. On this occasion, not wanting to make Peggy any more uncomfortable than she already was, he only went through this little ritual—putting his phone on silent, too—after he'd stepped inside and shut the door gently behind him.

When Peggy had asked him about the smell, he was glad he'd managed to censor himself. Truthfully, what she was about to experience would change her forever. Because, as Andrew had discovered, once you've smelled death it never leaves you. Once, not long after his first-ever house inspection, he'd been walking through an underpass and had caught the same smell of decomposition as he'd experienced at the house. Glancing to one side, he saw among the leaves and rubbish on the floor a small stretch of police tape. It still made him shudder whenever he thought about it, to feel so highly tuned to death.

It was hard to tell from the little hallway what condition the flat was going to be in. In Andrew's experience, the places fell into two categories: either they were immaculately clean—no dust, no cobwebs, not a thing out of place—or they were overpoweringly squalid. It was the former that Andrew found the most upsetting by far, because to him it never felt as simple as the deceased's just being house-proud. Instead, it seemed more likely that they knew that when they died they were going to be found by a stranger and couldn't bear the thought of leaving a mess. It was like a more extreme version of people who spent the morning feverishly tidying in preparation for the cleaner. Of course there was a certain dignity to it, but it made

Andrew's heart break to think that, for some people, the moments immediately following their death were more of a pressing concern than whatever time they had left to live. Chaos, on the other hand—clutter and filth and decay—never felt quite as upsetting. Maybe the deceased had just been unable to look after themselves properly in their last days, but Andrew liked to think that they were actually giving the finger to convention. Nobody had bothered to hang around to look after them, so why should they carry on giving a shit? You can't go gently into the good night when you're laughing uproariously imagining some mug from the council slipping on some shit on the bathroom floor.

The fact that he was forced to shoulder open the door to the little living room suggested this was going to be the latter of the two scenarios, and, sure enough, the smell hit him with an overwhelming intensity, greedily seeking out his nostrils. He usually refrained if possible from spraying air freshener, but to really be able to spend time there he would have to. He fired off a generous burst in each corner, picking his way through the mess, and reserved the most prolonged spray for the center of the room. He would have opened the grimy window but the key was presumably lost somewhere in all the clutter. The floor was covered by an ocean of blue corner-shop bags stuffed with empty crisp packets and cans of soft drinks. In one corner, a mound of clothes. In another, newspapers and mail, mostly unopened. In the middle of the room there was a green camping chair, a can of cherry Coke in each cup holder, opposite a television that was propped up on an uneven pile of telephone directories, so that it sloped to one side. Andrew wondered if Eric had suffered from a crick in his neck from having to angle his head at the listing screen. On the floor in front of the chair was an upturned microwave meal, yellow rice spilled all around it. That was probably where it happened. That chair. Andrew was about to make a start on the pile of mail when he remembered Peggy.

"How is it?" she said when he stepped outside.

"It's pretty messy, and the smell isn't . . . ideal. You can always wait outside if you'd prefer."

"No," Peggy said, clenching and unclenching her hands at her sides. "If I don't do it the first time then I never will."

She followed him into the living room, and apart from the fact she was holding her mask to her face so firmly her knuckles were faintly white, she didn't seem too distressed. They surveyed the living room together.

"Wow," Peggy eventually mumbled through her mask. "There's something so, I dunno, *static* about all this. It's like the place died with him."

Andrew had never really thought about it that way. But there *was* something eerily still about it all. They reflected in silence for a moment. If Andrew had known any profound quotes about death this would have been the perfect time for one. It was then that an ice-cream van went past outside, cheerily blasting out "Popeye the Sailor Man."

———————

Under Andrew's instruction, they began to sort through all the paper.

"So what am I actually looking for?" Peggy said.

"Photos, letters, Christmas or birthday cards—anything that might indicate a family member, their phone number or a return address. Oh, and any bank statements so we can get a sense of his finances."

"And a will, presumably?"

"Yes, that too. That usually depends on whether he's got a next of kin. The vast majority of people without one won't have a will."

"Makes sense, I guess. Here's hoping you had a bit of cash, Eric old boy."

They worked methodically, Peggy following Andrew's lead by

clearing a space as best as possible on the floor and creating separate piles for documents depending on whether they contained any useful information or not. There were utility bills and a TV license reminder, along with a catalog from the official Fulham Football Club shop, scores of takeaway menus, a warranty for a kettle and an appeal from the Shelter charity.

"I think I've got something," Peggy said after twenty minutes of fruitless searching. It was a Christmas card, featuring some laughing monkeys in Christmas hats with the caption: "Chimply Having a Wonderful Christmastime!" Inside, in handwriting so small it was as if the person were *trying* to remain anonymous, it read:

To Uncle Eric,
Happy Christmas
Love from Karen

"He's got a niece then," Peggy said.

"Looks like it. Any other cards there?"

Peggy dug about and did her best not to flinch when a horribly dozy fly was disturbed and flew past her face.

"Here's another one. A birthday card. Let's see now. Yep, it's from Karen again. Hang on, there's something else written here: '*If you ever want to give me a call, here's my new number.*'"

"There we go," Andrew said. Ordinarily he would have called the number there and then, but he felt self-conscious with Peggy beside him so he decided to wait until they were back at the office.

"Is that it, then?" Peggy said, making subtle movements toward the door.

"We still need to see about his financial situation," Andrew said. "We know he had a small amount in a current account, but there might be something else here."

"Cash?" Peggy said, looking around at all the mess.

"You'd be surprised," Andrew said. "The bedroom's usually a good place to start."

Peggy watched from the doorway as Andrew headed for the single bed and dropped to his knees. The light coming from the window was catching the dust in the air. Every time he shifted on the floor another bloom of it billowed up, disturbing the rest. He tried not to grimace. This was the part that he found hardest, because it felt even more invasive to be poking around in someone's bedroom.

He made sure to tuck his sleeves into his protective gloves before reaching under the mattress at one end, slowly sweeping his hand along.

"Say he does have ten grand stashed away somewhere," Peggy said. "But he *hasn't* got a next of kin. Where would the money go?"

"Well," Andrew said, readjusting his position, "any cash or assets he has first of all go to paying for the funeral. What's left over is kept in the safe at the office. If nothing comes to light about someone who's clearly entitled to the money—extended family and so on—then it goes to the Crown Estate."

"What, so old Betty Windsor gets her hands on it?" Peggy said.

"Um, sort of," Andrew said, sneezing as some dust went up his nose. He found nothing on the first sweep, but after bracing himself and reaching in further he touched something soft and lumpy. It was a sock—Fulham FC branded—and inside was a bundle of notes, mostly twenties, held in place by an elastic band. For no discernible reason the elastic band had been almost entirely colored in with blue pen. Whether it denoted something vitally important or was just an act of idle doodling, Andrew wasn't sure. It was this kind of detail that stayed with him long afterward: odd little elements of a forgotten life, the reasons for their existence unknowable, leaving him with a subtle feeling of unresolved tension, like seeing a question written down without a question mark.

From the amount of notes there he knew it was going to be enough for Eric to cover the cost of his funeral. It would be up to his niece how much she wanted to help out too.

"So, is that it?" Peggy said. Andrew could tell she was now really rather keen to be outside and breathe fresh air again. He remembered that feeling from his own first time—that first gulp of polluted London air was like being reborn.

"Yep, that's us done."

He gave the place one final check in case they'd missed anything. They were just preparing to leave when they heard movement by the front door.

The man in the hallway clearly hadn't been expecting anyone to be there, judging from the surprise on his face and the fact he immediately took two steps back toward the door when he saw them. He was squat and noticeably perspiring—a bowling ball of a beer belly threatening to escape from under his polo shirt. Andrew braced himself for confrontation. God, how he despised encounters with these cynical, desperate opportunists.

"You police?" the man said, eyeing their protective gloves.

"No," Andrew said, making himself look the man in the eye. "We're from the council."

The fact the man visibly relaxed at this point—even taking a step forward—was enough for Andrew to know why he was there.

"You knew the deceased?" he asked, trying to stand tall in the small hope the man might mistake him for a retired bare-knuckle boxer rather than someone who got vaguely out of breath watching snooker.

"Yeah, that's right. Eric."

A pause.

"Real shame about, you know, him passing on and that."

"Are you a friend or relative?" Peggy said.

The man looked her up and down and scratched his chin, as if appraising a secondhand car.

"Friend. We were tight. Really tight. We went way back."

As the man went to smooth what remained of his greasy hair against his head, Andrew noticed his trembling hand.

"How long we talking?" Peggy said.

Andrew was glad Peggy was taking the lead. The way she spoke, the steeliness of her voice, sounded much more authoritative.

"Oh, blimey, there's a question. A long old time," the man said. "You lose track of these things, don't you?"

Apparently confident that Peggy and Andrew weren't anything to worry about, he was now distracted by trying to look past them into the living room. He took another step forward.

"We were just about to lock up," Andrew said, showing the key in his hand. The man eyed it with barely concealed magpie-like intent.

"Right, yeah," the man said. "I was just here to pay my respects and whathaveyou. As I say we were good mates. I don't know if you found a will or anything . . ."

Here we go, Andrew thought.

". . . but he'd actually said if he *were* to pass away, you know, suddenly and that, he'd want me to have a couple of his things."

Andrew was about to explain, as calmly as he could, that anything that made up Eric's estate needed to remain untouched until everything was clarified, but Peggy got in ahead of him.

"What was it Mr. Thompson was going to leave you?" she said.

The man shifted his feet and cleared his throat. "Well, there was his telly, and truth be told he did owe me a little bit of cash too." He flashed a yellow smile. "To make up for all the drinks I'd bought him over the years, you know."

"Funny that," Peggy said. "His name was Eric White. Not Eric Thompson."

The man's smile vanished.

"What? Yeah, I know. White. What . . ." He looked at Andrew and spoke to him out of the side of his mouth, as if Peggy wouldn't be able to hear him. "Why'd she do that, try and trick me, when a man's just died?"

"I think you probably know why," Andrew said quietly.

The man was suddenly consumed by a hacking cough.

"Bollocks, you've no idea," he spluttered. "No idea," he said again, yanking the front door open.

Andrew and Peggy waited awhile before they went outside. The man had clumped down the steps and was now halfway across the estate, his hands in his jacket pockets. He turned briefly, backpedaling as he looked up and gave the finger. Andrew took off his mask and gloves and Peggy did the same before wiping a sheen of sweat from her forehead.

"So what did you think of your first property inspection, then?" Andrew said, watching the man disappear around the corner with a final middle finger salute.

"I think," Peggy said, "that I need a stiff bloody drink."

– CHAPTER 7 –

Andrew had assumed Peggy was joking even as she marched them into the first pub they came to around the corner from the estate. But then the next thing he knew she'd ordered a pint of Guinness and asked what he was having. He checked his watch. It had only just turned one o'clock.

"Oh, really? Well, I shouldn't . . . I'm not . . . um . . . okay then. A lager, I suppose, please."

"Pint?" the barman asked.

"A half," Andrew said. He suddenly felt like a teenager again. He used to practically hide behind Sally as she'd confidently order them beers in their local. He'd have to hold the pint glass with both hands, like a toddler drinking milk from a bottle.

Peggy was drumming her fingers on the bar impatiently as the barman waited for her half-full Guinness to settle. She looked ready to jump over and drink straight from the tap.

Aside from a couple of regulars who looked so gnarled and settled in, it was as if the structural integrity of the building depended on their presence, they were the only ones there. Andrew was still hanging his coat on the back of a chair when Peggy clinked her glass against his on the table and drank three hearty gulps.

"Christ, that's better," she said. "Don't worry, I'm not an alkie," she added quickly. "This is my first drink in about a month. That was just pretty intense for a first morning's work. Usually it's just seeing where the toilets are and forgetting the name of everyone you're introduced to. Still, better to properly go for it. It's like getting into cold water, isn't it? And I've got enough holiday memories of slowly inching my way into the sea, like I could somehow trick my body into not realizing what was happening, to know you've just got to get it over with."

Andrew took a tentative sip of beer. He couldn't actually remember the last time he'd had an alcoholic drink, but he was fairly certain it hadn't been lunchtime on a Wednesday.

"How often do chancers like that guy turn up and try and scam money?" Peggy said.

"It's quite common," Andrew said. "The stories are usually very similar, though sometimes you get a person with something better prepared, more believable."

Peggy wiped some foam off her lip. "I'm not sure what's worse. Maybe the people who concoct a proper story are the real shits, not that dopey idiot back there."

"I think you're right," Andrew said. "At least with Eric we've got what looks like a next of kin. That usually settles things—stops the chancers trying to get something when there's family on the scene."

One of the locals at the bar began an impressive sneezing fit, entirely ignored by the others dotted around him. He eventually recovered enough to inspect whatever he'd hacked up into a handkerchief with a mixture of surprise and pride before ramming it back up his sleeve.

"Is it usually blokes who, you know, end up like this?" Peggy said, eyeing the sneezer as if he might be their next case.

"Nearly always, yes. I've only had one woman"—Andrew went red before he could stop himself—"you know, a dead one." *Oh god!* "I mean . . ."

Peggy was trying very hard not to smile. "It's okay, I know what you mean. You've only ever done one house inspection where the deceased was female," she said, very deliberately.

"That's right," Andrew said. "It was my first inspection, actually."

The pub door opened and an elderly couple came in, regulars too, it would seem, judging from the way the barman acknowledged them with a nod and began pouring a pint and a half of bitter without needing to be asked.

"What was that like, then, your first?" Peggy asked.

The memory of that day was still very clear in Andrew's mind. The woman's name was Grace, and she'd been ninety when she'd died. Her house had been so immaculate it was as if she might have expired as a result of a particularly vigorous clean. Andrew recalled the intense relief he'd felt when he and Keith had entered the house. Maybe it would always be like this: little old ladies who'd had a good innings and passed away in their sleep; savings in a Mrs. Tiggy-Winkle money jar; *Brideshead Revisited* on VHS; a kindly next-door neighbor doing the weekly shop and replacing lightbulbs.

That was before he found the note under Grace's pillow.

In the event of my death: make sure that evil bitch next door gets nothing. She'll be after my wedding ring—mark my words!

He realized Peggy was looking at him expectantly.

"It was largely fine," he said, deciding that dropping another grim tale into the mix might not be helpful.

They sipped their drinks and Andrew realized he should really ask Peggy some questions about herself. But his mind was blank. That was the problem when you spent your entire adult life treating small talk like it was Kryptonite. Luckily, Peggy had that rare quality of making a silence seem comfortable. After a while, she broke it. "So is there nobody at the funerals if we've not found a next of kin?"

"Well," Andrew said, "and this isn't strictly part of the job, but if it doesn't look like anyone's going to turn up—no neighbors or ex-colleagues or anything—then I go myself."

"That's very good of you. Going above and beyond, like that."

"Oh no. Not really," Andrew said quickly, squirming with embarrassment. "It's quite common in this job, I think. I'm sure I'm not the only one."

"Must be tough, though," Peggy said. "Are they usually okay—as much as they can be—the funerals? Nothing really distressing's happened?"

"Not so much distressing," Andrew said. "But there are unusual moments."

"Like what?" Peggy said, leaning forward slightly.

Andrew immediately pictured the chair man.

"A man once turned up with a blue armchair," he said. "I'd not been able to find any friends or family, so I wasn't expecting anyone there. It turned out this man—Phillip—had been on holiday when his friend died. He was the one person who was allowed into the guy's house. The deceased was obsessed with this chair getting somehow damaged, though the color had already begun to fade. Phillip wasn't sure why he was so attached to it, but he had a feeling his friend's late wife used to sit there. Phillip eventually persuaded the man to let him take it away and get the color restored, but by the time he'd come to collect it from the repair place after his holiday the man had died. Phillip saw the notice I'd put in the local paper that morning and headed straight to the funeral. He even brought the chair into the church so it was next to us during the service."

"Wow," Peggy said, sitting back. "That's heartbreaking."

"It is, yes," Andrew said. "But—" He stopped abruptly.

"What?" Peggy said.

Andrew cleared his throat.

"Well, it actually made me determined to keep going to the funerals."

"How come?"

"Oh, well, I'm not exactly sure," Andrew said. "It just felt like I sort of . . . had to."

The truth was that it had made him see that everyone who died alone had their own version of that chair. Some drama or other, no matter how mundane the rest of their existence was. And the idea that they'd not have someone there to be with them at the end, to acknowledge that they'd been a person in the world who'd suffered and loved and all the rest of it—he just couldn't bear the thought of it.

Andrew realized he'd been spinning his glass on the table. He stopped and the liquid swirled for a moment before falling into a gentle rotation. When he looked up at Peggy, she seemed to be studying him, as if recalibrating something.

"Well, what a first morning on the job this has been," she said.

Andrew took a big gulp of beer, enjoying the fact that tipping liquid into his face meant the onus on him to talk briefly disappeared.

"Anyway," Peggy said, seeming to sense Andrew's discomfort, "we should talk about something more cheery. Like, who am I going to hate working with in the office?"

Andrew relaxed slightly. This felt like safer territory. He weighed the question up. If he were being professional about it he'd toe the party line and say that while of course it could be a challenging environment to work in, which meant there was the occasional personality clash, everyone always pulled together in the end. But then again he had just had half a pint of lager at one p.m. on a Wednesday, so sod it.

"Keith."

"Keith?"

"Keith."

"I think I remember him from my interview. He sat in with Cameron. He kept putting his finger in various parts of his body and eating whatever came out when he thought I wasn't looking."

Andrew winced. "Yeah, that's sort of the tip of the iceberg when it comes to his personal hygiene."

Still feeling somewhat reckless, Andrew found himself divulging his theory that there was something going on between Keith and Meredith. Peggy shuddered.

"Sadly, Keith reminds me a bit of this boy I had a dalliance with in my teenage years. He smelled like unwashed PE kit and had long, greasy hair, but I was besotted. And I wish I could say that was because he was incredibly charming and kind, but he was a complete idiot. He *was*, however, the lead guitarist in a local band, a band I subsequently joined to play maracas in." Andrew was instantly transported back to his teenage local and watching the first—and last—performance by Sally and (then boyfriend) Spike's band, Driftwood, where they nervously murdered Joni Mitchell covers in front of an audience of Andrew and twenty empty chairs. Sally had seemed unusually vulnerable that night, Andrew recalled, feeling a rush of affection for his sister.

"What was your band called?" he said to Peggy.

She looked at him with an unmistakably mischievous glint in her eye. "Get another round in and I'll tell you."

———

It turns out that if you haven't had a drink for a long time, two halves of 4 percent lager on an empty stomach will actually have quite a strong effect. Andrew didn't feel drunk as such, just fuzzy and warm and aware that he would happily punch a puffin if it meant he'd get some crisps.

As promised, Peggy revealed the name of the band she'd been in (Magic Merv's Death Banana), and they'd moved on to talking about their previous jobs. Peggy had also been axed from her position in a different part of the council and been shunted across. "I was 'business support officer for the Access, Inclusion and Participation Team,'" she said, "which was as fun as it sounds."

Andrew had been trying to place her accent. He thought it was probably Geordie. Was it rude to ask that question? He rubbed at his eyes. God, this *was* a bit ridiculous. They should really have gone straight back to the office. Not that he had any desire at all to do so. But two beers, though. Two! At lunchtime! What was he going to do next—throw a television out of a window? Ride a motorbike into a swimming pool?

Just then the quiet was broken as a group of women bustled in, all talking loudly over each other. Their boisterousness was entirely at odds with the subdued atmosphere, but they didn't seem at all embarrassed, as Andrew would have been, to be causing any sort of disruption. He got the sense that this was a regular fixture, a midweek tradition, perhaps: the way they all headed for a particular table without deliberation. *Why is it that we find traditions comforting?* he thought, stifling a belch. He looked at Peggy and was suddenly struck by the promise of asking her this incredibly profound question. Inevitably, it didn't sound quite so clever when he said it out loud.

"Hmm," Peggy said, not looking fazed, to Andrew's relief. "I suppose it's probably just because it's a moment in time where you know exactly what's about to happen, so there are no nasty surprises waiting for you. I dunno, maybe that's a bit of a pessimistic way of looking at it."

"No, I know what you mean," Andrew said. He pictured Sally looking at the calendar, realizing it was time for their quarterly call. Maybe there was some solace, some comfort, in the regularity of their interaction. "I suppose it's about having a balance," he said. "You need to keep making new traditions, otherwise you start to resent the old ones."

Peggy lifted her glass. "I feel like I need to toast that. To new traditions."

Andrew looked dumbly at her for a minute before quickly grabbing his glass and knocking it clumsily into hers with an ugly clink.

There was a collective cooing from the women in the corner. Peggy looked past Andrew's shoulder at them. After a moment she leaned forward and looked at him conspiratorially. "Be subtle," she said, "but don't you just love looking at everyone's reactions when someone's talking about getting engaged?"

Andrew swiveled around.

"Whoa, whoa, whoa—I said subtle!"

"Sorry."

This time, he half turned in his chair and pretended to be inspecting a framed caricature of a drunken cricketer on the wall. He glanced as casually as possible at the group before turning back. "Was there something specific I was supposed to notice?" he said.

"Look at their smiles. It's all in the eyes."

Andrew was lost.

"Most of them are genuinely happy for her, but there are at least a couple of them who don't think this is a good idea," Peggy said. She went to take a gulp of beer, then decided what she had to say was more important. "Me and my friend Agatha, right, for ages we had this game that whenever we found out someone we knew was getting married and we didn't really approve we'd guess what their first post-proposal argument would be about."

"That's . . . that's a bit . . ."

"Mean? Awful? You betcha. I very much learned my lesson after I got engaged to my fella, Steve. When I saw Agatha I jokingly made her guess what our first fight had been. Unfortunately it backfired in a pretty major way."

"How so?"

"She guessed that it was because Steve had told me he was already having cold feet about the whole thing."

"And what was it about really?"

"It was over a badly washed-up spatula."

"Oh."

"Yep. Turns out she'd never really approved of him at all. But we made up in the end, thankfully. All it took was five years of stubborn silence before bumping into each other, both hammered, in a kebab shop and putting the world to rights. She even bought me a spatula for mine and Steve's tenth wedding anniversary. Funnily enough, that was the first thing I reached for to chuck at his head the other night when he came back from a two-day bender having 'just popped out for a quick drink.' God, life's weird sometimes." Peggy let out a hollow laugh and Andrew joined in, unsurely. Peggy took a long gulp of Guinness and landed her glass with a thud. "I mean," Peggy said, "go out, get wasted, we've all been there, right?"

Thankfully, Andrew judged this to be rhetorical and kept quiet.

"But just don't *lie* about it, you know?"

"Absolutely," Andrew said. "That's the last thing you should do."

Peggy sighed. "Sorry, this is stupidly unprofessional of me, banging on about my marital problems."

"Not at all, it's fine," Andrew said. He suddenly realized what he'd just opened the door to. He could sense the question coming a mile away.

"You married, yourself?"

"Mm-hmm."

"So I can't now *not* ask you: what was your first post-proposal argument?"

Andrew thought for a moment. What would it have been? He had the feeling it should be something equally as trivial as Peggy's.

"Whose turn it was to take the trash out, I think," he said.

"A classic. If only all the arguments were about domestic chores, eh? Anyway . . . just nipping to the loo."

For one dreadful second Andrew nearly stood up, too, out of politeness. *Calm down, Mr. Knightley*, he thought, watching Peggy disappear around a corner in search of the toilets. He looked around, accidentally catching the eye of a man sitting at the bar, who gave him the slightest of nods. *Here we are*, the look seemed to say. *On our own. As usual.*

Well, not me this time, Andrew thought, feeling a prickle of defiance. When Peggy returned he looked at the man, feeling rather smug.

There was a shriek of laughter from the other table. However insincere her friends were being, the bride-to-be was very obviously glowing with happiness.

"Bloody hell," Peggy said. "Last time I smiled like that it was after I'd found a twenty-pound note in my dressing gown. I screamed so loud the dog farted."

Andrew laughed. And perhaps it was just the beer on an empty stomach, or the fact he hadn't had to go straight back to the office to face another afternoon of Keith and the others, but he was feeling really rather happy and relaxed all of a sudden. He made a mental note to try to remember how it felt not to have his shoulders tensed so much that they were practically touching his ears.

"Sorry again for dragging you to the pub," Peggy said.

"No, no, it's fine. I'm actually having a good time," Andrew said, wishing he hadn't sounded quite so surprised. If Peggy found this an odd thing to say, then thankfully her face didn't show it.

"By the way, how are you at pub quizzes?" she said, half distracted by a man on a mobility scooter edging his way through the door, shepherded by the barman.

"Pub quizzes? I'm . . . I don't really know," Andrew said. "Normal, I suppose?"

"A few of us get babysitters and do the one at the Rising Sun on the South Bank. We come last every time and Steve usually ends up getting into a fight with the quizmaster, but it's always a laugh. You should come."

Before he could stop himself, Andrew said, "I'd love to."

"Champion," Peggy yawned, rolling her head around her shoulders. "I hate to be the one to say this, but it's nearly two—I suppose we better get back?"

Andrew looked at his watch, hoping that there had been some sort of glitch in time so that they had another few hours. Sadly, it wasn't to be.

Even when they were approaching the office and climbing the rain-slick steps outside, which seemed especially keen to have him slip on them today, Andrew found he couldn't stop grinning. What an unexpectedly pleasant end to the morning that had been.

"Hang on a sec," Peggy said as they came out of the lift. "Remind me: Keith, Cameron . . . Melinda?"

"Meredith," Andrew said. "The one I've decided has a thing for Keith."

"Oh yeah. How could I forget? A late summer wedding, maybe?"

"Hmm, spring, I think," Andrew said, and in the moment it felt somehow perfectly natural for him to perform a semitheatrical bow as he held the door, gesturing for Peggy to go through first.

Cameron, Keith, and Meredith were sitting on one of the sofas in the break-out space and all got up straightaway when Andrew and Peggy walked in. Cameron's face was ashen.

Oh shit, Andrew thought. *We've been rumbled. They know about the pub.* Maybe Peggy was just a stooge, hired as a one-off to investigate improper practices. The pub trip was all just a fucking ruse and it served him right for daring to hope to pretend he could be happy. But a quick glance at Peggy and he saw she was as nonplussed as he was.

"Andrew," Cameron said, "we've been trying to get in touch. Has someone managed to call you?"

Andrew pulled his phone out of his pocket. He'd forgotten to turn it off silent after leaving Eric White's flat.

"Is everything okay?" he said.

Keith and Meredith shared an uneasy glance.

"Someone called earlier, with some news," Cameron said.

"Right?"

"It's about your sister."

– CHAPTER 8 –

Andrew had been three and Sally eight when their father had died of a heart attack. Rather than this bringing the two siblings together, Andrew's early memories of his sister tended to feature her slamming doors in his face, screaming at him to leave her alone, and their occasionally vicious scraps when he was brave enough to stand up to her. He sometimes wondered if their dad had been around how their relationship might have differed. Would they have bonded more, or would their dad have had to be constantly intervening to stop them from fighting, getting angry himself at their relentless squabbling, or perhaps using a gentler approach—telling them in a soft voice how they were upsetting Mum. For her part, their mother was never on hand to stop their squabbling. "She's taken to her bed," was the confusing expression Andrew had once overheard a neighbor say, unaware that he was lying in the border by the garden fence, recovering from Sally's latest pummeling. At the time he couldn't comprehend that his mum was crippled with grief. Nobody explained this to him. All he knew was that if she'd opened her bedroom blinds it was going to be a good day—and on good days he got sausage and mash for dinner. Occasionally she'd let him climb into bed with her. She'd lie facing away from him, her knees pulled up to her chest. She would hum songs and Andrew would rest the tip of his nose on her back, feeling the vibration of her voice.

By the time Sally was thirteen she was already a good six inches taller than the biggest boy at school. Her shoulders grew broad, her legs meaty. There was a large part of her that seemed to embrace being different, stalking the corridors, actively seeking out people to intimidate. Looking back, Andrew realized this was obviously a defense mechanism, a way for Sally to strike preemptively against any bullies, while also providing an outlet for her grief. He might have been more understanding if he hadn't been her punching bag of choice on quite so many occasions.

When some of the boys came back after summer holidays having had growth spurts, the bravest of them were confident enough to tease Sally, provoking her until she went for them, pursuing them across the playing fields, a manic glint in her eye, windmilling her arms at whoever she managed to corner.

One day shortly after Andrew had turned eleven, he had waited until Sally had gone downstairs before creeping into her bedroom and just standing there, smelling his sister's smell, wanting desperately to perform some sort of spell that would change her and make her care about him. He had his eyes closed, tears pooling behind his eyelids, when he heard Sally hurrying up the stairs. Maybe the spell had worked; maybe Sally had felt the urgent call to find him and tell him everything was going to be fine. It only took Andrew a split second to realize that Sally advancing toward him was going to end with a punch in the gut, not an arm around the shoulder. He received a gruff apology later that day, though he couldn't be sure if it was guilt that made Sally do it, or a rare instance of their mother stepping in. In any case, Andrew was only afforded a few days' respite before another scrap.

But then out of nowhere came along Sam "Spike" Morris, and everything changed. Spike had only joined the school when he was sixteen, but he had a quiet confidence about him that meant he soon made friends. He was tall, with shoulder-length black hair, and, much to the jealousy of his bumfluff-sporting male peers, possessed a full-on folk singer's beard. Almost immediately, the word went around that Spike had somehow incurred Sally's wrath, and that he was in for a windmilling if he crossed her again.

Andrew saw the telltale signs that a fight was happening somewhere as the other kids—as if by some innate instinct, like animals heading for higher ground before a tsunami—all began hurrying toward the portable buildings. He got there in time to see Spike and his sister squaring up, circling each other warily. Spike, Andrew noticed, was wearing a badge with the peace symbol on it.

"Sally," Spike said in an unexpectedly soft voice, "I don't know why you've got this beef with me, but I'm not going to fight you, yeah? Like I said, I'm a pacifist." Sally had tackled him to the ground before the "ist" was out of his mouth. It was at this point that Andrew got caught up in the melee of kids around him and was knocked to the ground, so for a few moments all he could hear was the approving roars as the fight continued out of sight. But then the roars suddenly gave way to jeers and wolf whistles. When Andrew finally managed to get to his feet and see what was happening he was met by the sight of Sally and Spike locked in a passionate embrace, sharing an almost violent kiss. They broke apart briefly and Spike grinned. Sally returned the smile, then swiftly gave him a vicious knee to the balls. She marched away, hands raised in victory, but when she looked back at Spike writhing on the ground, Andrew was sure he saw concern tempering her triumph. As it turned out, Sally clearly felt something deeper than just concern for Spike Morris's welfare, and against all odds, the two of them became an item. If Andrew was surprised at this, nothing could have prepared him for the effect it seemed to have on Sally. The change was instant. It was as if Spike had tinkered with a pressure valve somewhere and all her fury had been released. At school they were inseparable, loping around with hands clamped together, their long hair swaying softly in the breeze, handing out spliffs to the other kids they towered over, like benevolent giants who'd wandered down from the mountains. Sally's voice began to change, eventually morphing into a slow, monotonous drawl. At home, she started not only talking to Andrew but inviting him to hang out with her and Spike in the evenings. She never acknowledged her previous reign of terror, but letting him spend time with them, watching films and listening to records, seemed to be her way of trying to make up for it.

At first, Andrew—like most of the other kids at school—thought this was some sort of psychotic playing-the-long-game tactic; Sally was only sneaking him into pubs and inviting him to watch Hammer horrors on ropey VHS to make the inevitable beatings afterward unexpected and even more brutal. But no. Spike, it seemed, had softened her with love. That and the weed. There was the odd flash of anger, usually directed at their mother, whose torpor Sally took for laziness. But she would always apologize afterward, and of her own volition.

Most surprisingly of all, shortly after Andrew turned thirteen, Sally went out of her way to source him a girlfriend. He'd been minding his own business, reading *The Lord of the Rings* in his usual spot by the fight-zone portable building, when Sally appeared at the other side of the playground along with two other girls Andrew had never seen before, one Sally's age, one closer to his. Sally strode over to him, leaving the other girls behind.

"Hey, Gandalf," she said, pulling Andrew to his feet.

"Hello . . . Sally."

"See that girl over there? Cathie Adams?"

Ah yes, he did recognize her now. She was in the year below.

"Yes."

"She fancies you."

"What?"

"As in, she wants to go out with you. Do you want to go out with her?"

"I don't really know. Maybe?"

Sally sighed. "Of course you do. So now you need to go and talk to her sister, Mary. She wants to see if she approves. Don't worry, I'm doing the same with Cathie." And with that she signaled to Mary with a thumbs-up and pushed Andrew roughly in the back. He stumbled forward, just as Mary shoved Cathie in his direction. They crossed in the middle of the playground and exchanged nervous smiles, like captured spies being exchanged across an exclusion zone.

Mary swiftly interrogated him, at one point leaning close and taking a tentative sniff. Seemingly satisfied, she turned him by his shoulders and shoved him back the way he'd come. A similar process had occurred with Sally and Cathie, it would seem, and the end result was that the next few weeks seemed exclusively to involve his holding Cathie's hand in mute acceptance as she paraded them around school at break times, her head held high in the face of jeers and wolf whistles. Andrew was beginning to wonder what the point of all this was when one evening, following a school play and two and a half bottles of Woodpecker cider, Cathie pinned him against a wall and kissed him, before he promptly vomited on the floor. It was the best evening of his entire life.

But such are the cruel twists of fate that only two days later Sally sat him down to deliver him the terrible news, as passed on to her by Mary, that Cathie had decided to end things. Before Andrew had time to process this, Sally was hugging him ferociously, explaining that everything happened for a reason and that time was a great healer. Andrew had no idea how he felt about Cathie Adams's decision, but as he rested his head on Sally's shoulder, enjoying the pain that came from her fierce embrace, he thought whatever had happened was probably worth it.

The following Saturday, when Andrew came back upstairs after having been dispatched to make popcorn, he looked through a gap in the door and saw Sally and Spike kneeling, foreheads resting together, whispering softly. Sally opened her eyes and kissed Spike delicately on his forehead. Andrew had no idea his sister was capable of anything so tender. He could have kissed Spike Morris himself for performing this miracle. After everything, he'd finally gotten a big sister. Unbeknownst to him, that evening would be the last time he'd see her for years.

He had no idea how Sally and Spike had managed to sneak out of their separate homes and get to the airport, never mind how they'd afforded the flights to San Francisco (it later transpired that when Spike turned eighteen he was entitled to a large sum of money that had been left to him by his grandparents). Andrew found a note in his sock drawer from Sally explaining that they'd "gone to the States for a while. Don't want to cause drama, little bro," she added, "so please can you explain everything to dear old Mother, but not until tomorrow?"

Andrew did as he was told. His mum reacted to the news from her bed with a sort of affected panic, saying, "Oh dear. Dearie, dearie me. Really, that's unbelievable. I can't believe it."

There followed a surreal meeting with Spike's parents, who arrived outside the house in a VW camper van and a haze of marijuana. Andrew's mum spent the morning fretting exclusively about which sort of snacks she should put out and Andrew, terrified that she'd now gone entirely mad, scratched so hard at the spots on his cheeks that he bled.

He spied on the conversation by lying on the landing and peering down through the banister. Spike's father, Rick, and mother, Shona, were a jumble of long brown hair and potbellies. Hippies, it turned out, didn't age well.

"The thing is, Cassandra," Rick said, "we kind of feel that as they're two consenting adults we can't stop them from following their hearts. Besides, we went on our own trip at that age and it didn't do us any harm."

The way Shona was clinging to Rick as if they were on a roller coaster made Andrew ever-so-slightly doubt this statement. Rick was American, and the way he pronounced the word "adults," with the emphasis on the second syllable, seemed so impossibly exotic to Andrew he wondered whether he might just up sticks and get on a plane across the pond, too. But then he remembered their mother. Sally might not have had a conscience, apparently, but he still did.

At first, there was no word from Sally. But after a month a postcard arrived, postmarked New Orleans, with a picture of a jazz trombonist in smoky sepia.

"The Big Easy! Hope you're cool, dude."

Andrew chucked it on his bedroom floor, furious. But the next day he couldn't resist the temptation to study it again, and then he found himself sticking it to the wall by his pillow. It would be joined later by Oklahoma City, Santa Fe, the Grand Canyon, Las Vegas, and Hollywood. Andrew used up what little pocket money he had on a US map, tracking his sister's movements with a marker pen and trying to guess where she'd post from next.

By now his mother would oscillate wildly from angry rants about why Sally thought she could just go swanning off like that, to tearful laments about Andrew's now being her only child—cupping his face in her hands and making him promise several times that he'd never leave her.

It was with grim irony, then, that five years later Andrew found himself sitting at what his mother now referred to, with no sense of how upsetting this was to him, as her deathbed. The cancer was aggressive, and the doctor gave her weeks. Andrew was supposed to be going to university—Bristol Polytechnic—to study philosophy that

September, but he deferred to look after her. He hadn't told her he'd gotten a place at university. It was just easier this way. The problem was that he'd not been able to get in touch with Sally to tell her their mother was dying. The postcards had dried up, the last one coming the previous year from Toronto with the message "Hey, bud, freezin' here. Hugs from us both!" But more recently there had been a phone call. Andrew had answered with a mouthful of fish fingers and nearly choked when the echoey sound of Sally's voice came through the receiver. The line was terrible, and they barely managed a conversation, but Andrew did manage to hear her telling him she'd call again on August 20, when they'd be in New York.

When the day came he sat waiting by the phone, half willing the call to come, half hoping it never would. When it finally did he had to wait for it to ring several times before he could face picking up.

"Heyyyy, man! It's Sally. How's the line? Hear me okay?"

"Yeah. So listen, Mum's ill. As in, really ill."

"What's that? Ill? Like, how bad?"

"As in, not-getting-better ill. You need to get on a plane now or it might be too late. The doctors think it might be less than a month."

"Holy shit. Fuck. Are you serious?"

"Of course I'm serious. Please come home as soon as you can."

"Jesus, bro. That's . . . that's nuts."

Sally's return was as clandestine as her exit. Andrew was coming down for breakfast as usual when he heard the kitchen tap running. His mum hadn't been out of bed for weeks, let alone made it downstairs, but he felt a flash of hope: maybe the doctors had gotten it wrong. But it was Sally, standing at the sink, a ponytail seemingly featuring every color of the rainbow stretching all the way down to her lower back. She was wearing what looked like a dressing gown.

"Brother, fuck!" she said, pulling Andrew into a bear hug. She smelled of something musty and floral. "How the hell are you?"

"I'm okay," Andrew said.

"Jesus, you've grown about twenty feet."

"Yeah."

"How's school?"

"Yeah, fine."

"You do good in your exams?"

"Yeah."

"What about girls? You got a new chick yet? Nah, too busy playing the field I bet. Hey, you like my sweater? It's a Baja. I could get you one if you want."

No, what I want is for you to come and talk to our dying mother.

"Where's Spike?" Andrew said.

"He's stayed out in the States. Gonna go back to him when it's all, you know . . . over."

"Right," Andrew said. So that answered that. "Do you want to go up and see Mum?"

"Um, yep, okay. As long as she's up and everything. Don't wanna disturb her."

"She doesn't really get up anymore," Andrew said, heading toward the stairs. He thought for a moment that Sally wasn't going to follow, but then he saw she was just kicking off her shoes.

"Force of habit," she said with a sheepish smile.

Andrew knocked on the door once, twice. Nothing. He and Sally looked at each other.

It was almost as if she'd planned to die before the three of them were together, just to make things extra painful.

"Classic Mum," Sally said later in the pub, though she pronounced it "Mom" and Andrew was very tempted to pour his pint over her head, suddenly no longer in awe of the accent.

Their mother's funeral was attended by two great-aunts and a handful of reluctant ex-colleagues. It was impossible for Andrew to sleep that night. He was sitting on his bed, reading yet failing to follow Nietzsche on suffering, when he heard the front door click shut. He was suddenly aware of the squawking starlings in the nest on the porch who'd mistaken the security light for dawn. He peered through his curtains and saw his sister, laden down with a backpack, walking away, and wondered if this time she was going for good.

As it turned out, it was only three weeks later—Andrew having spent the majority of that time lying on the sofa wrapped in the duvet from his mum's bed, watching daytime TV—when he came downstairs and found Sally once more standing by the sink. She'd come back for him. Finally, something had gotten through that thick skull. When Sally turned around Andrew saw her eyes were puffy and red, and this time it was he who crossed the room and hugged her. Sally said something, but her voice was muffled against his shoulder.

"What's that?" Andrew said.

"He left me," Sally said, sniffing violently.

"Who did?"

"Spike, of course! There was just a note in the apartment. He's gone off with some fucking girl, I know it. Everything's ruined."

Andrew shook Sally off and took a step back.

"What?" Sally said, wiping her nose on her sleeve. Then a second time, louder, when Andrew said nothing. There it was again, that old anger flashing in her eyes. But this time Andrew wasn't afraid. He was too furious.

"What do you think?" he spat. And then Sally was advancing on him and pushing him back against the fridge, an arm against his throat.

"What, are you fucking glad or something? Pleased that he's left me?"

"I couldn't care less about him," Andrew gasped. "What about Mum?" He struggled to pull Sally's arm away from his throat.

"What about her?" Sally said through gritted teeth. "She's dead, isn't she? Dead as a doornail. How can you be that upset? That woman didn't have a maternal bone in her body. When Dad died it was all over for her. She just fell apart. Would she really have done that if we mattered to her?"

"She was ill! And given what a mess you are about getting dumped I don't think you're one to judge about someone falling apart."

Sally's face flashed with renewed anger, and she managed to free her arm to hit him. Andrew staggered backward, his hands over his eye. He braced himself for another impact, but when it came it was Sally taking him gently in her arms, saying "I'm sorry" over and over. Eventually they both slid down to the floor, where they sat, not speaking, but calm. After a while Sally opened the freezer and passed Andrew some frozen peas, and the simplicity of the act, the kindness of it in spite of her being the reason for his pain, was enough to cause tears to leak from his uninjured eye.

The next few weeks followed the same pattern. Andrew would return from his job working in the pharmacy on the high street and cook pasta with tomato sauce, or sausage and mash, and Sally would get high and watch cartoons. As Andrew watched her suck up spaghetti strands, sauce dribbling off her chin, he wondered just what sort of a person she would turn out to be. The fiery bully and the hippie were still living Jekyll and Hyde–like inside her. How long, too, before she left again? He didn't have long to wait, it turned out, but this time he caught her sneaking out.

"Please just tell me you're not going to try and find Spike?" he said, shivering in the doorway against the dawn chill. Sally smiled sadly and shook her head.

"Nah. My pal Beansie got me a job. Or at least he thinks so. Up near Manchester."

"Right."

"I just need to get myself back on track. Time for me to grow up. I just can't do that here. It's too fucking grim. First Dad, now Mum.

I was . . . I was going to come and see you. Say good-bye and every-thing. But I didn't want to wake you up."

"Uh-huh," Andrew said. He looked away, scratching at the back of his neck. When he looked back he saw that Sally had just done the same. A mirror image of awkwardness. This, at least, made them both smile. "Well. Let me know where you end up," Andrew said.

"Yeah," Sally said. "Deffo." She went to close the door but stopped and turned. "You know, I'm really proud of you, man."

It sounded like something Sally had rehearsed. Maybe she'd hoped to wake him after all. He couldn't work out how that made him feel.

"I'll call as soon as I get settled, I promise," she said.

She didn't, of course. The call only came months later, by which time Andrew had gotten his place sorted at Bristol Poly, and already it felt like an unbridgeable gap had opened between them.

They did spend a Christmas together, though, where Andrew slept on the sofa in the little flat Sally shared with Beansie (real name Tristan), the three of them drinking Beansie's home-brewed beer that was so strong, at one point Andrew was convinced he'd briefly gone blind. Sally was seeing someone called Carl, a lean, languid man who was obsessed with working out and the subsequent refueling. Every time Andrew turned around he was eating something: a whole bag of bananas or great slabs of chicken—sitting there in his workout clothes, licking grease from his fingers like an Adidas-clad Henry the Eighth before he'd let himself go. Eventually Sally moved in with Carl and that's when Andrew stopped seeing her altogether. The system of reg-ular phone calls came into play not through any spoken agreement; it was just how things began to work. Every three months, for the past twenty years. It was always Sally that called. Sometimes, back in the early days, they'd talk about their mother. Enough time had passed for them to see some of her eccentricities through rose-tinted glasses. But as the years went by, their reminiscing became forced, a desperate attempt to keep alive a connection that seemed to diminish every time they spoke. These days, the conversations had always felt like a real effort, and sometimes Andrew had wondered why Sally still bothered to call him. But then there were moments—often in the silences, when there was only the sound of their breathing—when Andrew had still felt an undeniable bond.

– CHAPTER 9 –

Andrew left the office in a daze, shaking off offers from Cameron and Peggy to accompany him home. He needed fresh air, to be on his own. It took all his strength to pick up the phone and call Carl. But Sally's husband—Sally's widower—wasn't the one to answer. Instead, it was someone who introduced herself as "Rachel, Carl's best friend"—a strange way for a grown adult to describe herself, especially given the circumstances.

"It's Andrew. Sally's brother," he said.

"Of course. Andrew. How *are* you?" And then before Andrew could actually answer: "Carl says there's no room for you at the house, unfortunately. So you'll have to stay at the B & B down the road. It's very near the church . . . for the funeral and everything."

"Oh. Right. Has that all been arranged already?" Andrew said.

There was a pause.

"You know our Carl. He's very organized. I'm sure he won't want to worry you with all of the little details."

Later, as the Newquay-bound train pulled away from London and copses replaced concrete, it wasn't grief or even sadness that he felt. It was guilt. Guilt that he hadn't cried yet. Guilt that he was dreading the funeral, that he'd actually considered the possibility of not going.

When the conductor appeared, Andrew couldn't find his ticket. When he finally found it in his inside jacket pocket he apologized so profusely for wasting the conductor's time that the man felt compelled to put his hand on Andrew's shoulder and tell him not to worry.

———

He spent a week in a damp B & B, listening to angry seagulls keening outside, fighting the urge to leave and get straight back on a train to London. When the morning of the funeral arrived, he ate a breakfast of stale cereal alone in the B & B "restaurant," the proprietor watching on throughout, standing in the corner with his arms folded, like a death row prison guard observing him eating his final meal.

Walking into the crematorium, the coffin resting on his shoulder, he was aware that he had no idea who the men were on the other side (it had seemed impolite to ask).

Carl—who had entered his fifties in disgustingly healthy and stylish fashion, all salt-and-pepper hair and wristwatch the value of a small market town—spent the service with his head raised stoically, tears spilling metronomically down his cheeks. Andrew stood awkwardly next to him, fists clenched at his sides. At the moment the coffin went through the curtains Carl let out a low, mournful howl, unburdened by the self-consciousness that consumed Andrew.

———

Afterward, at the wake, surrounded by people he had never seen, let alone met, before, he felt more alone than he had in years. They were in Carl's house, in the room dedicated to his burgeoning yoga business, Cynergy. The room had been temporarily cleared of mats and exercise balls so there was space for trestle tables struggling to support the regulation wake spread. Andrew looked at the homemade sandwiches, pale and precisely cut, and was reminded of a rare occasion he'd seen his mother laughing, having recalled the Victoria Wood line about a typical British reaction to the news that someone had died: "Seventy-two baps, Connie. You slice, I'll spread," she'd said in a perfect imitation, tweaking Andrew's ear and dispatching him to put the kettle on.

As he chewed on a damp sausage roll, he suddenly got the sense that he was being watched. Sure enough, Carl was looking at him from across the room. He had changed out of his suit into a loose white shirt and beige linen trousers, and was now barefoot. Andrew couldn't help but notice he'd kept his expensive watch on. Andrew realized Carl was about to make his way over, so he quickly put down his paper plate and was up the stairs as fast as he could go and into the thankfully unoccupied bathroom. As he washed his hands his eye was drawn to a shaving brush on an ornate white dish on the windowsill. He picked it up and ran his finger across the top of the bristles, specks of powder flicking off into the air. He brought it to his nose and smelled the familiar rich, creamy scent. This had belonged to his father. His mother had kept it in the bathroom. He couldn't remember talking to Sally about it. She must have formed an especially sentimental attachment to want to keep hold of it.

Just then someone tapped on the door, and Andrew quickly slipped the brush into his trouser pocket.

"Just a minute," he said. He paused and forced an apologetic smile onto his face. When he emerged, Carl was standing outside with his arms crossed, biceps straining against his shirt. Up close, Andrew could see that Carl's eyes were raw from crying. He caught the scent of Carl's aftershave. It was rich and overpowering.

"Sorry," Andrew said.

"No problem," Carl said, though he didn't move to let Andrew pass.

"I was thinking I might head off soon," Andrew said. "It's a long journey back," he added, more defensively than he'd intended.

"Of course you were," Carl said.

Andrew chose to ignore this comment. "See you then," he said instead, stepping around Carl and heading for the stairs.

"After all," Carl said, "this must be much easier for you now that Sally's gone."

Andrew stopped at the top of the stairs and turned. Carl was looking at him, unblinking.

"What," Carl said, "you don't agree? Come on, Andrew, it wasn't as if you were ever really there for her, no matter how much that obviously hurt her."

That's not true, Andrew wanted to say. *She was the one who abandoned me.*

"Things were complicated."

"*Oh*, I've heard all about it, believe me," Carl said. "In fact, there wasn't really a week that went by when Sally didn't talk about it—going over it all again and again and again, trying to work out how to get through to you, how to make you care, or at least stop hating her."

"Hating her? I didn't hate her—that's ridiculous."

"Oh is it?" Renewed anger flashed in Carl's eyes and he moved toward Andrew, who dropped down a couple of stairs. "So you didn't hold such a grudge about her apparently 'abandoning' you for America that you basically refused to ever see her again?"

"Well no, that's not—"

"And even when she spent weeks on end—months, actually—trying to reach out and help you sort your life out, you were so pathetically fucking stubborn that you wouldn't let her in, even though you knew how much it was hurting her." Carl pressed his fist to his mouth and cleared his throat.

Oh god, please don't cry, Andrew thought.

"Carl, it . . . it was com—"

"Don't you *dare* fucking say it was complicated again," Carl said. "Because it's actually very simple. Sally was never really happy, Andrew. Not really. Because of you."

Andrew dropped down another step and nearly stumbled. He swiveled and used the momentum to keep on going. He needed to be as far away as possible from this. *He's got no idea what he's talking about,* Andrew thought as he slammed the front door behind him. But the doubt that had begun to nag at him as he left only intensified during the train journey home. Was there some truth to what Carl had said? Had Sally really been so cut up about their relationship that it had somehow contributed to her decline? It was a thought too painful to even consider.

———

With all the lights off, the brightness of the screen was harsh on Andrew's eyes. TinkerAl's forum avatar (a dancing, laughing tomato), usually a cheering sight, seemed malevolent tonight.

Andrew made himself look at the words he had typed and untyped so many times he'd lost count.

I buried my sister today

The cursor flashed back at him expectantly. He moved the mouse until it was over the "post" button, but took his hand away, reaching for his plastic tumbler of foamy beer instead. He'd been drinking in an attempt to re-create the comforting sense of warmth he'd felt in the pub with Peggy, before Cameron's awkwardly delivered bombshell, but it had just left him with a dull, repetitive throbbing behind his eyes. He sat up straight and felt the bristles of the shaving brush in his pocket poking into his leg. It was three a.m. Carl's words were still swimming in his head—the confrontation still horribly vivid. What he'd have given now for loved ones around him. Gentle words. Mugs of tea. A moment when a family was more than the sum of its parts.

He looked again at the screen. If he were to refresh, there would be tens, maybe hundreds of messages now shared between BamBam, TinkerAl, and Jim. Something about spotting some limited-edition rolling stock or a platform footbridge for sale. They were the closest he had to friends, but he couldn't bring himself to confide in them about this yet. It was just too hard.

He moved his finger to the delete key.

I buried my sister today
I buried my
I buried
I

CHAPTER 10

Despite Cameron insisting he could take off as much time as he needed, Andrew went back to work two days after the funeral. He'd barely slept, but it had been bad enough spending one day sitting around with nothing to distract him—he'd much rather have dealt with dead people he'd never met. He braced himself for the onslaught of sympathy. The head tilting. The sad-eyed smiles. People not even being able to *imagine* how hard it was for him. He'd have to nod and say thanks, and all the while he'd be hating them for saying such things and hating himself because he didn't deserve their sympathy. It was to his considerable confusion, then, that Peggy had spent the majority of the first hour that morning talking to him about moorhens.

"Very underrated birds, if you ask me. I saw a one-legged one once at Slimbridge Wetland Centre. It was in quite a small pond and it just seemed to be swimming in circles around the perimeter in a sort of sad victory lap. My daughter Maisie wanted me to rescue it so she could 'invent it a new leg.' Ambitious, eh?"

"Mmm," Andrew said, batting a fly out of his face. Bearing in mind this was only Peggy's second property inspection, she seemed to have acclimatized remarkably well, especially given that Jim Mitchell's house was in an even worse state than Eric White's.

Jim had died in bed, on his own, at the age of sixty. The flat's kitchen, bedroom, and living room were all in one, with a separate shower room choked with mildew, its floor boasting an impressive range of stains whose origins Andrew tried not to think about.

"This is the sort of room my estate agent would describe as a 'compact, chic washroom,'" Peggy said, sweeping a moldy curtain aside. "What the hell," she yelped, stepping back. Andrew rushed over. The whole bathroom window was covered in little red bugs, like blood spatter from a gunshot wound. It was only when one of them flapped its little wings that Andrew realized they were ladybugs. They were the most colorful thing in the entire flat. Andrew decided that they'd leave the window open in the hope it would encourage an exodus.

They were dressed in the full protective suits this time. Peggy had specifically requested this outside so that she could pretend to be a lab assistant in a James Bond film, having watched *You Only Live Twice* the previous evening. "My Steve used to have a bit of Pierce Brosnan about him when we were first going out. That was before he discovered pork pies and procrastination." She sized Andrew up. "I reckon you might pass for—who's the baddie in *GoldenEye*?"

"Sean Bean?" Andrew said, moving over to the kitchenette.

"Yeah, that's the one. Reckon you've got a touch of the Sean about you."

As Andrew caught sight of his reflection in the filthy oven door—the receding hairline, patchy stubble, bags under his eyes—he suspected that Sean Bean might have been doing a lot of things at that moment in time, but he almost certainly wasn't scrambling around on the kitchen floor of a South London bedsit with a Mr. Chicken! takeaway menu stuck to his knee.

After twenty minutes of searching they went outside to take a breather. Andrew was so tired he felt almost weightless. A police helicopter went past overhead and they both craned their necks to watch it as it banked and flew back in the direction it had come from.

"Phew, they weren't after me then," Peggy said.

"Mmm," Andrew murmured.

"You know, I've never had to talk to the police before. I feel like I'm missing out, somehow, you know? I just want to report a minor misdemeanor, or be called on to make a statement—that's the dream. Have you ever had to do anything like that?"

Andrew had zoned out.

"Sorry, what?"

"Ever had any encounters with the old bill? The rozzers. The . . . peelers, is that one right?"

Andrew was transported back to the record shop in Soho. The sudden awareness that the song playing over the speakers was "Blue Moon." The blood draining from his face. Rushing to the exit and wrenching the door open. The strangled cry of the shop owner. "Fuck! Stop him, he's nicked something!" Running straight into the man outside and bouncing off him onto the floor, lying winded. The man looming over him. "I'm an off-duty police officer." The furious face of the shop owner coming into view. Being hauled to his feet. Arms held. "What have you taken?" The owner's breath smelling of nicotine gum.

"Nothing, *nothing*," he'd said. "Honestly, you can search me."

"Why the hell'd you run then?"

What could he have said? That hearing that song crippled him with pain? That even as he lay winded on the pavement, the fading bars lodged in his head made him want to curl into the fetal position?

"Bloody hell," Peggy laughed, "you look like you've seen a ghost!"

"Sorry," Andrew said, but his voice cracked and only half the word came out.

"Don't tell me—you got done for pinching chocolate from Woolworths?"

Andrew's eyelid was twitching uncontrollably. He was desperately trying to stop the tune from coming into his head.

"Or some naughty parking ticket action?"

Blue Moon, you saw me standing alone.

"Oh, dear—it was littering, wasn't it?"

She nudged him on the arm and Andrew felt the voice coming up from somewhere deep inside him, sharp and unstoppable. "Leave it, okay?" he snapped.

Peggy's face fell as she realized he wasn't joking.

Andrew felt a miserable wave of shame hit him. "I'm sorry," he said. "I didn't mean to snap like that. It's just been a strange couple of weeks."

They stood in silence for a long time, both of them clearly too embarrassed to speak first. Andrew could practically hear Peggy attempting to regroup, the cogs whirring as she decided to change the subject. This time he was going to be ready and attentive.

"My daughter's invented this game, right?"

"A game?"

"Yeah. And I'm not sure if I should be worried about her or not, but it's called the Apocalypse Game."

"Right," Andrew said.

"So, the scenario is this: a massive bomb has gone off and everyone's been wiped off the face of the earth. It appears that you are the only person in the country to have survived. What do you do?"

"Not sure I understand," Andrew said.

"Well, where do you go? What do you do? Do you find a car and go blasting up the M1 trying to look for people? Or do you just head straight to your local and drink the bar dry? How long before you try and make your way across the channel, or go to America, even? If nobody's there could you break into the White House?"

"And that's the game . . . ?" Andrew said.

"Pretty much," Peggy said. Then, after a pause: "I tell you what I'd do to kick us off. I'd go to Silverstone and do a lap of the track in the Fiesta. Then, I'd either hit golf balls off the top of the Houses of Parliament or cook myself a fry-up in the Savoy. At some point I'd probably go across to Europe and see what's what—though I slightly worry I'd end up having to be part of some sort of 'resistance,' smuggling people across the border and that sort of thing. And I'm not sure I'm a good enough person to get involved in that if there's nobody left at home to see my Facebook status about it."

"Understandable," Andrew said. He tried to concentrate but his mind was blank.

"I don't quite know what I'd do," he said. "I'm sorry."

"Ah well. It's not for everyone," Peggy said. "By the way, if you fancy heading off early I'm sure I can crack on by myself."

"No, I'm all right," Andrew said. "Quicker with two of us anyway."

"Right you are. Oh, I nearly forgot to say, I brought a flask of coffee today. Let me know if you want a mug. And I *attempted* brownies too."

"I'm fine, thanks," Andrew said.

"Well, let me know if you change your mind," Peggy said, heading back into the house. Andrew followed her, a waft of fetid air hitting him before he'd even crossed the threshold. Luckily, before long, Peggy found something.

"It's one of those Christmas 'round robin' things," she said, her voice strained because of having to breathe through her mouth. She passed what she'd found to Andrew. The paper felt brittle, as if it had been crumpled up and straightened out countless times. In among the pages detailing uneventful holidays and unremarkable school sports days there was a photo of the family, their faces looking pixelated from where the paper had been scrunched up.

"I wonder how many times he nearly threw this out but couldn't quite bring himself to," Peggy said. "Hang on, look, there's a phone number there on the back."

"Well spotted. Right, I'll give them a call," Andrew said, reaching for his phone and turning it on.

"Are you sure you're all right to?" Peggy asked, her tone deliberately casual.

"I'm fine, but thank you," he said. He dialed the number and waited for it to connect. "I'm sorry again, about snapping," he said.

"Don't be silly," Peggy said. "I'm just going to head outside for a second."

"Sure," Andrew said. "See you in a minute."

Someone picked up on the first ring.

"Sorry, Brian, lost you there," the person on the line said. "So like I said, this is just something we'll chalk up to experience."

"Sorry," Andrew said, "this is actually—"

"No, no, Brian, time for apologies is over. Let's clean-slate this one, okay?"

"I'm not—"

"'I'm not,' 'I'm not'—Brian, you're better than this, yeah? I'm putting the phone down now. I'll see you in the office tomorrow. I don't want to hear any more about it, okay? Right, good. See you later."

The line went dead. Andrew sighed. This was going to be a tricky one. He hit redial and walked over to the living room window. At first he thought Peggy was doing some sort of exercise—she was squatting down and rocking on her heels slightly, as if she were about to bounce up into a star jump. But then he saw her face. She'd gone very pale. There were tears pooling in her eyes and she was taking in deep lungfuls of air. It was then that Andrew realized that of course she hadn't acclimatized at all to being inside a house in this state. And then there were the coffee and the brownies and the games and the talking—all designed to cheer him up, without even a hint of patronizing him or doing the sad head tilt. All that time she'd been feeling awful but pretending not to, and he hadn't even realized. Peggy's kindness, her selflessness, was so overwhelming that Andrew felt a lump forming in his throat.

The man who'd answered the phone was letting it ring out this time—presumably letting poor Brian stew in his own juice. Andrew watched Peggy stand up and take one final breath before going toward the front door. He hung up the phone and cleared his throat, trying to get rid of the lump.

"Not good?" Peggy said, eyeing the phone in his hand.

"He thought I was someone who he worked with calling him back and he wouldn't let me speak."

"Oh."

"And he used the term 'clean slate' as a verb."

"What a cock."

"My thoughts exactly. I'll try him again later, I think."

They stood still for a moment, looking around at the mess. Andrew scratched at the back of his head.

"I, um, just wanted to say thank you," he said, "for, being here and chatting and the brownies and everything. I really do appreciate it."

Some color returned to Peggy's cheeks, and she smiled.

"No bother, pal," she said. "So, back to the office?"

"You should go back," Andrew said, not wanting Peggy to be there a second longer than she needed to. He pulled a roll of trash bags out of his rucksack.

"Is there not more to do then?" Peggy said, looking at the trash bags.

"No, it's just . . . When it's as bad as this I like to clear up the worst of the rubbish. Just doesn't seem right to leave the place like this. Like I said, you can go back."

Andrew wasn't quite sure what the look Peggy was giving him meant, but he felt like he might have said something embarrassing.

"I think I'd rather stay," Peggy said, arm outstretched. "Chuck us a bag."

As they cleared up, Andrew willed his imagination into action until, eventually, he had something.

"I'd go to Edinburgh, by the way," he said.

"Edinburgh?" Peggy said, looking confused.

"During the apocalypse. I'd see if I could drive a train up there. Then try and break into the castle. Or climb Arthur's seat."

"Aha, not a bad shout at all," Peggy said, tapping her chin contemplatively. "I have to say, though, I still think I win with my Savoy fry-up or Parliament golf plan. Just saying."

"I didn't realize there was a winner," Andrew said, folding up a pizza box that had chunks of greasy mozzarella stuck to it.

"I'm afraid there has to be. And given that I lose to my kids every single time, do you mind if I have this one, you know, to regain a bit of pride?"

"Fair enough," Andrew said. "I'd shake your hand to congratulate you, but there seems to be quite a lot of moldy cheese on mine."

There was a moment where Peggy looked at his hand in horror, where Andrew thought he might have said something far too weird, but then Peggy let out a huge belly laugh and said, "Jesus, what *is* this job?" and Andrew felt awake for the first time that day.

———

They'd worked their way through the majority of the rubbish when Peggy said, "I wanted to say I'm sorry, you know, about your sister. I just didn't know when was the right time."

"That's okay," Andrew said. "I'm . . . It's . . . I don't know, really . . ." He trailed off, caught halfway between saying how he felt and saying what he thought he was supposed to say.

"I lost my dad nine years ago," Peggy said.

Andrew felt like someone had stuck him on pause. "I'm sorry," he managed to say, after what felt like an age.

"Thanks, pet," Peggy said. "It's a while ago now, I know, but . . . I still remember afterward, there were days—especially at work—where all I wanted was to hide away, but there were others when it was all I wanted to talk about. And that's when I noticed people avoiding me, deliberately not catching my eye. Of course I realize now they were just embarrassed about not knowing what to say to me, but at the time it felt like I had something to be ashamed about, that I'd done something wrong and was inconveniencing everybody somehow. What made it harder was that my feelings were all over the place." Peggy gave Andrew a look as if wondering whether she should continue.

"How do you mean?" he said.

Peggy chewed her lip. "Let's just say kindness wasn't exactly in my dad's DNA. The abiding memory of my childhood is sitting in the living room and holding my breath when I heard his footsteps on the drive. I could tell from how the sound varied what mood he was going to be in. He never hurt us, or anything, but he got in these moods where nothing me or my sister or my mam did was good enough, and he left us in doubt as to exactly how we'd let him down. Then one day he just up and left. Ran off with some lass from work, so my sister later found out. Mam never accepted that, though. That was the hardest part. She talked about him like he'd been God's gift, as if he were a war hero who'd drifted out to sea on a raft never to be heard of again, despite the fact he was shacked up with this woman four streets away."

"That must have been hard," Andrew said.

Peggy shrugged. "It's complicated. I still loved him, even though I barely saw him after he left. People think loss is the same for everyone, but it's different in every case, you know?"

Andrew tied a trash bag closed. "That's true," he said. "I think when you've not been through that sort of loss you just imagine you'll feel it in one big wave of sadness, that you're immediately devastated and then it just goes away over time." He looked up quickly at Peggy, worried that he was sounding callous, but her expression was neutral. Andrew continued. "With my sister, I sort of . . . well, it's complicated, like you said about your dad. And the idea of people looking at me all sympathetic—I just can't deal with that."

"Yep, I hear you," Peggy said, joining him to pick up the remaining rubbish with a litter picker. "I mean, their hearts are in the right place, but if you've not been through it, then it's impossible to understand. It's like we're in 'the club' or something."

"The club," Andrew murmured. He felt a burst of adrenaline pass through him. Peggy looked at him and smiled. And Andrew, remembering his failed attempts at properly saying cheers in the pub, suddenly found himself raising his litter picker in the air, an empty bag of Doritos in its pincers, and saying, "To the club!" Peggy looked at him in surprise, and Andrew's hand wavered, but then she reached her own picker aloft. "The club!" she said.

After a slightly awkward pause they lowered their pickers and carried on with their tidying.

"Now then, Andrew," Peggy said after a while. "Back to more important matters."

Andrew raised his eyebrows. "Is this going to be about the apocalypse, by any chance?"

———

An hour later they were nearly done, Andrew having had a surprisingly enjoyable time clearing away rubbish and playing end-of-the-world-themed games, when Peggy said, "If you want a slightly more structured mental test, it's that pub quiz I mentioned tonight if you fancy it."

Maybe, actually, Andrew *did* fancy it. It would be something else to take his mind off things after all, and this way he could make it up to Peggy properly for snapping at her, if not with his atrocious general knowledge then with pints of Guinness.

"Yes, why not," he said, trying to sound like this was the sort of thing he was always doing.

"Top stuff," Peggy said, and the smile she gave him was so warm and genuine that he actually had to look away. "And bring Diane! I want to meet her."

Oh yes. That.

———

Maybe Diane would magically appear in the bathroom mirror and find him a better shirt than this orange monstrosity. He'd panic-bought it after work on the way home, suddenly very aware that the last time he'd specifically bought clothes for a night out people were still worried about the Millennium Bug. He had no real idea what was fashionable these days. Occasionally he thought about replacing some of his particularly old stuff, but then he'd see someone young and apparently trendy wearing a shirt that looked exactly like one he'd hung on to since the early nineties, so what was the point? It was just lucky that his stubbornness and loathing of clothes shopping were neatly complemented by the cyclical nature of fashion.

He moved his face closer to the mirror. Maybe he should buy some cream or other to sort out those dark circles under his eyes. But then again, he did feel an odd sort of attachment to them, perhaps because they were the closest thing to a distinguishing feature he had. Everything else about him was just so . . . normal. Part of him longed to have "a thing"—like those men who decide to compensate for being five foot five by spending hours in the gym, ending up incredibly muscly yet still having to walk a bit faster than their friends to keep up.

Or maybe he'd choose a dominating nose, or jutting-out ears—the sort of feature that, if possessed by a celebrity, would lead to their being described as "unconventionally attractive" by the press. "Ordinary"-looking women were saddled with "Plain Jane." There didn't seem to be an equivalent for men. Maybe, Andrew thought, he would take on that mantle. "Standard Andrew"? "Standy Andy"? The benchmark for men with light brown hair and unremarkably straight teeth. It would be one way to leave a legacy.

He stepped back and smoothed out a crease on his shirtsleeve. "You know what you look like? A wilted carrot with a face drawn on it." He puffed out his cheeks. What in god's name had he been thinking to agree to this?

The Sentinel 4wDH was speeding around at a pleasing pace, hypnotic on the figure-eight track he'd set up. He'd deliberately chosen Ella's "But Not for Me"—smooth and languid and beautiful—to try to calm him down, but it wasn't helping much. This was why he didn't socialize, because just the thought of it was making his stomach cramp up. The temptation to stay in and carry on his conversations on the forum was very much in danger of winning out. But in the end he forced himself to leave the house. Diane, he had decided, was having to pull a late one at work, but he'd managed to get a babysitter last minute.

He Googled the pub before he left and was concerned that it might be dangerously close to "cool," judging by the ominous photos of chalkboards by the door with their aggressive slogans promising—with 50 percent accuracy—"beer and good times," but when he got there he was relieved to see it looked fairly normal, from the outside at least. Nevertheless, he did three walk-bys, pretending to be on his phone so if Peggy or her friends saw him from the inside he could pretend he'd just been finishing a call before he came in. The timing of his arrival was crucial. If he got there too early he'd be forced into making conversation. Too late and he'd feel like an interloper. Ideally he'd join them in time to say a quick hello *just* before the quiz began—then the focus would be on the questions and nobody would feel like they had to make an effort to include him in conversation.

The next time he passed by he glanced through the window and spotted a group of people in the far corner. It was them. Peggy was sitting next to a man in a leather jacket who had long brown hair and a goatee. Steve, presumably. He seemed to be in the middle of an anecdote, his gestures getting more expansive as he built to what was obviously the punch line. He banged the table as the others laughed. Andrew saw a few people standing at the bar looking around to see the reason for the noise. Peggy, he noticed, was only half joining in with the laughter.

He braced his hand against the door, but then he froze.

This wasn't him. This wasn't what he did. What if he literally didn't know one correct answer in this quiz, or was forced to take sides in a heated debate? What if they were on course to win and then he ruined it for everyone? And even then, it wasn't as if the quiz was continuous—there'd be gaps where people could question him about his life. He knew how to deal with people at work when it came to talking about his family. He could predict what things they'd ask him and knew when to duck out of conversations when he felt uncomfortable about where they were going. But this was uncharted territory, and he'd be trapped.

A car pulled up behind him and he heard someone get out and offer a familiar "Have a good night"—a farewell that could mean only one thing. He turned and saw the cab's yellow light, a welcoming beacon promising sanctuary. He rushed over and rattled off his address to the driver, yanking the door open and throwing himself inside. He sank down low into the seat, his heart racing as if he were in a getaway car leaving a bank robbery. A quarter of an hour later he was outside his building, his evening over, twenty pounds down and he hadn't even bought a drink.

Inside his building's hallway, in among the junk mail delivered that morning there was an envelope addressed to him in pen. He quickly stuffed it into his pocket and hurried up the stairs. Inside his flat, his urgency to get music on and a train moving around the track felt even greater than usual.

He pushed the needle down roughly on the record player and turned the volume up, then knelt down and tugged at the rail track, pulling the middle of the eight apart and pushing it out to create one loop instead of two. He set the train running and sat in the newly created circle, his knees folded to his chest. Here, he was calm. Here, he was in control. Trumpets howled and cymbals crashed, and the train fizzed around the track, encircling him, guarding him, keeping him safe.

After a while he remembered the envelope in his pocket. He took it out and opened it, pulling out the message inside. As he did so he was hit by a waft of rich aftershave.

Your disappearing act meant you weren't around long enough to hear Sally's will being read this morning. You little bastard. Did you know? Because I certainly didn't. Twenty-five grand in her savings— you'd have thought she'd have mentioned that to me, wouldn't you? After all, we were trying to grow the business—that was the dream. So you can imagine it came as something of a shock to find out about it, and that she had decided to leave the money not to me, but to you.

Maybe now you'll begin to realize just how sick with guilt she was, all because you never forgave her, no matter how hard she tried to help you. You were like a brick tied around her ankles, weighing her down. Well, I hope you're happy now, Andrew. It was all worth it, wasn't it?

———

Andrew read Carl's letter through several times, but it still didn't make sense. Surely Sally giving him money was some sort of administrative mistake? Ticking a wrong box? Because the alternative explanation, that it was a last-gasp attempt to make things right, to rid herself of guilt that she had lived with and that he could, and should, have absolved her of, was too desperately sad for him to contemplate.

– CHAPTER 11 –

For the next three months, each time he returned home it was with trepidation at the prospect of another envelope addressed to him in Carl's spidery scrawl.

The letters arrived erratically. Some weeks there would be two or three—tearstained and inkblotted—then there would be four weeks without one at all. But Carl's anger never wavered—if anything he furiously doubled down on how Andrew had conned Sally out of her money. *You are pathetic and cowardly and worthless, and you don't deserve Sally's forgiveness* was how he'd ended his latest note. Andrew wondered if Carl would be surprised to know that he was broadly in agreement with this assessment.

Each time he opened the door to find a letter he would trudge upstairs and sit on the side of his bed, turning the envelope around in his hands. He told himself to stop opening them, but he was trapped in an unforgiving cycle: the more he read, the guiltier he felt, and the guiltier he felt, the more he thought he deserved Carl's anger. This was especially true when Carl once more accused Andrew of contributing to Sally's ill health by never reaching out to her, because the more he thought about it, the more he started to convince himself that this was true.

———————

It was long enough now after Sally's death for some sense of normality to have returned in the way that people were treating him. Cameron had gone through a phase of putting a hand on his shoulder when he spoke to him, looking at him with his sad, bulbous eyes and knitted eyebrows and doing the head tilt, but thankfully that had now stopped. More of a relief still was the fact that Keith, who had briefly restrained himself, was now back to being a complete arsehole.

After several aborted attempts, he'd finally built up the courage to tell the subforum about Sally.

Hi, chaps. Sorry I've been a bit quiet of late. Had some sad news. I lost my sister. I'm still feeling a bit numb about it all, to be honest. As soon as he'd hit "post" he wondered if he'd done the wrong thing, but they'd all responded with sympathetic, well-judged messages and, in a move of touching solidarity, had changed their avatars from dancing tomatoes and cheerful fat controllers to match Andrew's plain, sky-blue square.

But while things were largely back to normal, there was something that had been brought sharply into focus, something that Andrew was finding hard to ignore. He had always justified continuing to lie about having a family on the grounds that it was harmless. But, subconsciously, the fact that Sally was still around (no matter how strained their relationship) had meant that the fantasy he'd created just existed alongside his real life, and he knew deep down that he had something tangible to fall back on in his sister. But now, with her gone, he was feeling increasingly uncomfortable about Diane, Steph and David. As a result, when family came up in conversation with

Cameron, Keith and Meredith, he no longer felt the little thrill he used to when inventing some mundane detail about how things were at school or what his weekend plans were. But it was worse—much worse—when it came to Peggy. The day after he'd bailed on the pub quiz, he'd been racked with guilt and apologized far more earnestly than was necessary, much to Peggy's amusement and confusion. After a few more weeks in her company Andrew realized she wasn't the sort of person to sweat the small stuff like that. She had continued to shadow him, so they had spent almost all their time at work together: attending more property inspections, as well as the office grind of registering deaths and compiling details of unclaimed estates to send on to the treasury.

And then there had been the funeral.

Andrew had mentioned in passing to Peggy that he was going to attend the service of Ian Bailey, having not been able to track down any friends or family. He wasn't expecting Peggy to ask if she could come.

"You don't have to," he said. "It's not compulsory—or technically part of the job, in fact."

"I know, but I'd like to," Peggy said. "I'm just following your lead, really. If the point is to help see the person off with some company, then me doubling the numbers is a good thing to do, right?"

Andrew had to concede that this was a good point.

"Not to sound patronizing," he said, "but it's maybe worth taking a bit of time to prepare yourself for it. As I've said, they can be pretty bleak affairs."

"Don't worry," Peggy said. "I was thinking I could do a bit of karaoke to cheer things along. 'Africa' by Toto, something like that?"

Andrew looked at her blankly. He saw her face falter. God, why couldn't he just respond normally to things? He forced himself to try to rectify the situation.

"I'm not sure that'd be appropriate," he said. Then, before Peggy could respond sincerely, "I think 'The Final Countdown' might be more fitting."

Peggy chuckled while Andrew went back to his screen, torn between self-reproach at trivializing the funeral and relief and pride at managing to successfully devise and deliver a real-life joke to a real-life human being.

That Thursday they stood in church, waiting for Ian Bailey to arrive.

"It's nice—well, not *nice*, but, you know, a good thing, there being two of us today." Andrew winced slightly at how clumsily this had come out.

"Three of us actually," Peggy said, pointing up at the rafters, as a sparrow flitted over from one beam to another. They were quiet for a moment, watching the bird, which then briefly disappeared out of sight.

"Have you ever imagined your own funeral?" Peggy asked.

Andrew kept his eyes on the rafters. "I can't say I have; you?"

Peggy nodded. "Oh yeah. Loads. When I was about fourteen I got really obsessed and planned the whole thing, right down to the readings and the music. I seem to remember everyone was going to be dressed in white, so it was different from normal, and Madonna was going to do "Like a Prayer" a cappella. Is that weird? I mean, the planning of it, not the Madonna part—I *know* that's weird."

Andrew saw the sparrow flit to another beam. "I don't know," he said. "I suppose it makes sense. We're all going to have one, so why not think about how you want it to go?"

"Most people don't want to think about it, do they? Understandably, of course. But then for some of us, it's always at the back of our minds. I think that's the only real explanation why some people do such stupid, impulsive things."

"Like what?" Andrew said, giving in to neck ache and lowering his head.

"Like people who embezzle money from their business even though they're *obviously* going to get found out. Or . . . that woman who was on the news for getting caught pushing a cat into a wheelie bin. It's like, in that moment, they're sticking a middle finger up to death. *You're coming for me, I know you are—but watch this!* It's like a pure burst of living, isn't it?"

Andrew frowned. "You're saying pushing a cat into a bin is a pure burst of living?"

Peggy had to cover her mouth to stop herself from laughing, and for one dreadful moment Andrew thought they were both about to get the giggles, like naughty schoolchildren. Then a memory came to him, quite out of the blue, of he and Sally convulsing with laughter in a fish and chip shop as they exchanged fire with chips across the table, while their mother was distracted by a conversation with a friend at the counter.

Try as he might, as the service proceeded he found it impossible not to think about Sally. Surely there had been more moments like that? Had her leaving for America been such an all-consuming betrayal that it had biased his memory? After all, he thought, suddenly feeling faint, there had been one particular memory that he'd spent the last twenty years trying to let go, where Sally had done her utmost to help him, and he hadn't let her. He pictured himself in his flat, rooted to the spot, hearing the phone ringing on and on and on, unable to answer. When he'd finally picked up, he heard her voice, pleading with him to talk to her, to let her help. He'd let the phone slip from his hand. He told himself he'd answer the next day when she called, and then the day after that, and every day for the next month after, but he never did.

Andrew's mouth had gone very, very dry. He was only vaguely aware of the vicar's soft address. At Sally's funeral, he had been numb, horribly self-conscious next to Carl. But now, all he could think of was why he hadn't answered the phone.

His breathing had become shallow. The vicar had just finished delivering part of the service and nodded to the back, whereupon an organ clunked into life. As the first chord filled the church, Peggy leaned over to Andrew. "Are you okay?" she whispered.

"Yes, I'm fine," he said. But as he stood there, the music getting louder, his head bowed, the church floor swam in front of his eyes, and he had to grasp onto the pew in front with both hands to stop himself from falling. His breaths were coming in shuddering bursts, and as the music echoed around the church, and he realized he was finally beginning to mourn his sister, he was vaguely aware of Peggy's hand gently rubbing his back.

By the time the service was over he had managed to compose himself. As he and Peggy walked out of the churchyard he felt it necessary to explain.

"Back there," he said, "I was a bit . . . upset . . . because I was thinking about my sister. Not the person—Ian. Not that I *wasn't* thinking about him, but . . ."

"It's okay, I get it," Peggy said.

They walked on in silence for a while. Andrew began to feel the tightness leaving his throat and the tension draining from his shoulders. He realized Peggy was waiting for him to be the one to speak first, but he couldn't think of anything to say. Instead, he found himself softly humming Ella's "Something to Live For." He'd been listening to it the previous evening—the version from *Ella at Duke's Place*. He'd always had an odd relationship with the song. He loved it for the most part, but there was a particular moment that always seemed to leave him with a gnawing pain in his gut.

"There's a piece of music," he said, "which is one of my favorites. But there's this moment, right at the end, that's jarring, and loud, and sort of shocking, even though I'm expecting it. So when I'm listening to the song, as much as I'm enjoying it, it's always sort of spoiled by the fact I know this horrible ending is coming. But there's nothing I can do about it, is there? So, in a way, it's like what you were saying earlier, about people who are comfortable with the fact they're going to die: if I could just accept the ending's coming, then I could concentrate on enjoying the rest of the song so much more."

Andrew glanced at Peggy, who seemed to be trying to suppress a smile.

"I cannot believe that you had that pearl of wisdom up your sleeve," she said, "when you let me wang on about someone pushing a cat into a bin."

———————

Peggy began to attend all the funerals with him after that. Without really thinking about it, Andrew realized that he now felt relaxed around her, glad to have her company. It was an odd sensation to feel so normal discussing everything from the meaning of life to whether the vicar was wearing a wig. He was even starting to hold his own when it came to playing along with the games she and her kids had invented. His proudest moment had been coming up with one of his own, devising a challenge where you had to argue in favor of arbitrary opponents: the color red versus Tim Henman, for example. On occasion, at home in the evenings, he found his mind wandering, thinking about what Peggy might be up to at that moment.

Schedules permitting, they would have lunch in the pub every Friday, where they would review the week, marking property inspections from one to ten on the "harrowing scale," reminding each other of the latest personal hygiene disaster from Keith or snarky comment from Meredith. It was as he was on the way to one of these lunches, enjoying the sun on his back after days of gray skies, when Andrew had a sudden realization and stopped dead in the street, causing a man behind him to take evasive action. Could it really be true? He supposed it must be. No, there were no two ways about it: he was dangerously close to making a friend. The thought actually made him laugh out loud. How on earth had this happened? It was as if he'd managed to do it behind his own back. He carried on toward the pub with a new swagger, so much so that he overtook the man whose path he'd just accidentally blocked. As soon as he sat down, though, unable to stop grinning like an idiot, Peggy raised her eyebrows and jokingly speculated that he'd just popped over to Diane's office "for a quickie or something."

And therein lay the problem: the closer they got, the worse it was when he had to lie. It felt like a ticking time bomb—like it was only a matter of time before Peggy found out the truth and he'd lose the first friend he'd made in years. One way or another, he knew that something had to give. As it turned out, he didn't have to wait long.

———————

The day had begun with a particularly grueling house inspection, not helped by the fierce July heat. Terry Hill had slipped in the bath and lain there dead for seven months. Nobody had missed him. It was only when his overseas landlord finally stopped receiving rent that his body was found. The TV had still been on. A knife, fork, plate and water glass sat gathering dust on the kitchen table. Andrew had opened the microwave to find something festering inside and accidentally inhaled a great waft of rancid air, coughing and retching as he ran from the room. He was still feeling like he might be sick when Peggy, who valiantly dealt with the microwave horror while he recovered, turned to him and said, "We've not talked about tonight, have we?"

"What's tonight?" Andrew said.

"So, the week you were off work, before the funeral, Cameron started on again about his stupid *Come Dine with Me* family dinner party thing. Every day it'd be an e-mail or he'd mention it out of nowhere in a meeting."

"Jesus," Andrew said. "Why is he so *obsessed* with this idea?"

"Well, I think there are probably two explanations."

"Go on . . ."

"Okay, one: it's something he's been taught to do in a course. It's a box-ticking exercise to show he's getting the team to bond, and he'll be flavor of the month with the bosses."

"Hmm. And two?"

"He hasn't got any friends."

"Oh," Andrew said. The bluntness of it caught him off guard, but thinking about it, Cameron's general behavior did seem to make more sense if that was the case.

"That would explain a lot," he said.

"I know," Peggy said. "So anyway, he made us get a date in the diary—we delayed it as far down the line as possible, obviously. He didn't want to ask you about it when you were away, but I ended up saying I'd ask you, largely just to get him off my back for five minutes. I just haven't found the right moment to tell you. But as far as Cameron's concerned, you're coming."

Andrew started to protest but Peggy interrupted. "Look, look, I *know* it's a massive pain in the arse, but I for one cannot bear him going on and on about it all the time with his sad face all crumpled in disappointment when we put it off. He's going to host it tonight, the others and I are going. His missus will be there but it's optional if we want to bring partners."

Well that's one thing at least, Andrew thought.

"I think you should come," Peggy said. "It might be fine—okay, it'll definitely be awful, but . . . well, what I'm really saying is, *please* just come so we can get shitfaced together and ignore the others." She put her hand on Andrew's arm, smiling hopefully.

Andrew could think of many things he'd rather be doing that evening—most of them involving his testicles, some jam and some aggrieved hornets—but he suddenly felt a rather strong urge not to disappoint Peggy.

———————

That evening he arrived at Cameron's carrying a bottle of corner shop merlot and feeling firmly out of his comfort zone.

Who even likes dinner parties, anyway? he thought. Dutifully doling out compliments just because someone's managed to shovel some stuff into a pot and heated it to a point where it won't kill anyone. And then there was all the competitive conversation about books and films: *"Oh you simply* must *see it. It's a Portuguese art-house epic about triplets who befriend a crow."* What a lot of nonsense. (Andrew did take the occasional bit of enjoyment from hating things he'd never actually experienced.)

Keith and Meredith had been particularly abhorrent that afternoon, with Cameron in particularly irritating form. Quite why the man thought their all spending an increased amount of time together in an enclosed space was going to help, Andrew had no idea. It was like trying to force the negative ends of magnets together.

He was looking forward to spending time with Peggy, of course, although she'd seemed unusually subdued when she'd left the office, something that was possibly connected to the phone call he'd overheard her having on the back stairs, during which she had employed the word "wanker" several times. Delivered in her Geordie twang, it sounded like music to him.

He rang Cameron's doorbell and hoped to god that Peggy was already there. Ideally they could just sit next to each other, ignoring the others and arguing whether tiramisu was better than Michael Flatley, Lord of the Dance.

The door was answered by what appeared to be a very short Victorian dandy, wearing a velvet jacket complete with waistcoat and bow tie. It took Andrew a moment to register that this was, in fact, a child.

"Do come in. I'll take your coat?" the child said, holding Andrew's jacket between thumb and forefinger as if he'd been handed a sack of dog turds. Andrew followed him into the hall as Cameron appeared, aggressively brandishing nibbles at him. "Andrew! You've met Chris, I see?"

"It's Christopher," the boy said, turning from the coat hook, smiling frustratedly. Andrew had already gotten the impression that Christopher held his father to very high standards that Cameron rarely met.

"Clara?" Cameron called.

"What now?" someone hissed back.

"Darling, our first guest's arriiiiived!"

"Oh, just a second!" This voice bore almost no resemblance to the first. Clara appeared in an apron, smiling to reveal several thousand pristine white teeth. She had closely cropped auburn hair and was so pretty that Andrew felt flustered even before they exchanged an awkward handshake, which became a hug and then a kiss on each cheek, a three-for-the-price-of-one greeting, Clara pulling him toward her as if leading him in a ballroom dance. Cameron handed Andrew a bowl of cashew nuts and asked Clara how the starters were coming along. "Well," she said, through ever-so-slightly gritted teeth, "if someone hadn't turned the stove all the way off we would have been bang on time."

"Oh dear—guilty!" Cameron said, clapping his hand to the top of his head and grimacing theatrically. Andrew looked at Christopher and the boy rolled his eyes as if to say, *Tip of the iceberg.*

Meredith and Keith arrived together—not by coincidence, Andrew guessed, his suspicions confirmed by the fact that they were both clearly quite tipsy. Keith ruffled Christopher's neatly parted hair and the boy left the room with a murderous look in his eyes, returning—to Andrew's disappointment—brandishing a comb and not a revolver.

By the time Peggy arrived they had already sat down for the starters. "Sorry I'm late," she said, hurling her coat onto an empty chair. "Got stuck on a bus. The traffic was an utter bastard." She glanced at Christopher. "Oh, sorry, is that a child? Didn't mean to swear."

Cameron laughed uncertainly. "I'm sure you've heard worse from us, haven't you, Chriss-o?" Christopher muttered something darkly into his soup.

Conversation was stop-start, in the way that magnified every slurp of food and clink of cutlery. They all agreed that the soup was delicious, although Meredith did add a caveat that it was a "bold choice" to have added quite so much cumin. Keith smirked at this, apparently enjoying the backhanded compliment, and Andrew was suddenly, horribly aware that there was some knee touching going on under the table. He wanted to bring this to Peggy's attention, if only to share the burden of horror, but she seemed distracted, pushing soup slowly around her bowl like a disillusioned painter mixing colors in their palette. Andrew felt a strong urge to get her away from the others and ask if she was okay, but it was hard when you had Cameron to contend with. He had clearly anticipated lulls in conversation and was beginning to bring up topics that were as disparate as they were fruitless, the latest being their taste in music.

"Peggy? What tickles your fancy in that regard?" he asked.

Peggy yawned. "Oh, you know, acid house, dubstep, Namibian harpsichord stuff. All the classics." Meredith hiccupped and dropped her spoon on the floor, disappearing to retrieve it and nearly sliding off her chair in the process. Andrew raised his eyebrows at Peggy. He had never really understood the point in getting hammered at social events like this. Surely you were just more likely to say something stupid and then spend the rest of the evening regretting it? Then you'd need another drink just to get over that.

("That," Peggy would later say to him, "is drinking in a nutshell.")

Once they'd finished the main course Clara asked with exaggerated winsomeness if Cameron could give her a hand in the kitchen.

"You're sure I won't just be in the way?" Cameron asked with a little chuckle.

"No, no. Just don't go near the stove," Clara said.

Cameron headed after her with a *You got me there!* gesture and shut the door after him. A symphony of slammed cupboard doors occurred shortly afterward. "There may be trouble ahead," Peggy sang quietly.

Meredith and Keith, again by total coincidence, decided that they needed the toilet at exactly the same time. Andrew and Peggy listened to the sounds of excited footsteps on the stairs.

"Those two are definitely shagging then," Peggy said. "Sorry for swearing again, Christopher," she added. Andrew had entirely forgotten the boy was still there.

"Not at all," Christopher said. "I better go and see what's happening in the kitchen."

Peggy waited till the door was closed, then leaned over to Andrew.

"At least the poor sod's got his mother's looks. Anyway, bollocks to this, I'm off."

"Oh, are you . . . Do you think you should just . . . wait?"

"Absolutely not," Peggy said, swinging her coat on and making for the door. "I've had a rubbish enough day as it is without having to endure another second of this. You coming or what?"

Andrew hesitated, but Peggy wasn't going to hang around for an answer. He swore under his breath and dashed to the kitchen, opening the door to find Clara in full flow.

"You *know* Wednesday is book club night, yet as usual you didn't give any bloody consideration to what I might— Andrew! Is everything okay?"

Cameron spun around.

"Andrew! Andy-boy. What's up?"

"Peggy's not feeling very well so I thought I better make sure she gets home okay."

"Oh, are you sure? There's ice cream!" Cameron said, eyes wide in desperation. Luckily, Clara stepped in and, with a bit too much intensity for Andrew's liking, said, "There'll always be ice cream, Cameron. It's chivalry that's in short supply."

"Look, I better go . . . ," Andrew said, hearing the argument renewed in earnest as soon as he'd closed the front door.

―――――

He had to jog to catch up with Peggy. When he arrived at her side he was too out of breath to say anything, and Peggy only offered a quick "All right?" before falling quiet. They walked on without speaking, Andrew's breathing finally leveling out, until gradually their steps became in sync. It was a comfortable silence, but it felt charged in a way that Andrew couldn't put his finger on. As they waited to cross the road at some traffic lights, Peggy pointed out a pool of dried blood on the pavement.

"I've walked past a similar patch on my road every day this week and it's barely faded," she said. "Why is it that blood takes ages to wash away?"

"I think it's because it carries all the proteins and iron and everything," Andrew said. "And it's so thick because it coagulates. Hard to get rid of, blood."

Peggy snorted. "'Hard to get rid of, blood.' Now, that's the most serial killer–y thing I've heard in a while."

"Ah. God, I hadn't . . . I just meant that—"

Peggy laughed and nudged him with her elbow. "I'm only messing." She puffed out her cheeks. "God, I shouldn't have come out tonight. I really wasn't in the mood for it. Think anyone noticed?"

"I'm sure they didn't," Andrew said, trying not to picture Cameron's forlorn face. "Is everything all right?"

"Oh I'm fine, really. I'm just having a bit of a hard time of it. With Steve, actually."

Andrew wasn't quite sure how to respond, but Peggy didn't need a prompt.

"You remember I told you about my friend Agatha, the one who clearly didn't approve of him?"

Andrew nodded. "The spatula. The one that you, well . . ."

"Chucked at his head? Yes, well. That's not the only thing I've felt like throwing at him recently. It's just so bloody hard, sometimes. I remember when Agatha told me her doubts about him when he first proposed, I just couldn't even consider what she was saying. I was so fiercely proud of what I had, I thought she was just jealous. Sure we used to row a bit, but we'd make up. Better that than those couples who never raise their voices but keep each other awake grinding their teeth."

"And what seems to be the problem?" Andrew said, wincing at how he'd managed to somehow sound like a 1950s doctor talking disapprovingly to his patient about their libido.

"So there's the drinking," Peggy replied. "I know things are on the verge of going tits-up when he starts singing, and last night it was 'Yes Sir, I Can Boogie.' Next thing he's getting all boisterous and asking complete strangers to dance, buying shots for everyone in the pub. Then he finally has too much and starts getting confrontational with people for no reason. But it's the *lying* about the drinking that I really can't stand. It's just relentless. Last night I went home before him as he was having 'one for the road.' He gets back steaming at two a.m. Usually I can handle him by giving him a quick bollock-wallop, but last night he was determined to go and say good night to the girls, but it was so late it was practically morning, and I didn't want him to go and wake them up, so then it became 'Oh, you're not letting me see my own kids.' He ended up sleeping on the landing under a *Finding Nemo* duvet in some sort of protest. I left him there snoring this morning. My youngest, Suze, came out and saw him lying there. She just looked at me, shook her head and said, 'Pathetic.' *Pathetic!* I didn't know whether to laugh or cry."

An ambulance flashed past, lights on but no siren, ghosting through a gap in the traffic.

"You got an apology this morning, presumably?" Andrew said, not entirely sure why he'd decided to play devil's advocate.

"Not exactly. I tried to talk to him, but he gets this scrunched-up face when he's hungover and it's hard to take him seriously. Honestly, it goes all mad and blotchy. Like he's a clumsy beekeeper. We'd have had it out this evening if I hadn't had this nonsense to go to. The only reason I stayed as long as I did was because you were there. I mean, that lot are just the absolute worst, aren't they?"

"They really are," Andrew said, wondering whether Peggy had seen just how wide he'd smiled about him apparently being the only reason she'd stayed.

"I wonder if Meredith and Keith are still up in that bathroom," Peggy said with a shudder. "Oof, it really doesn't bear thinking about."

"It really, really doesn't," Andrew said.

"And yet now I can't stop picturing them sweating away."

"Oh god, *sweating*?!"

Peggy sniggered and linked her arm into his.

"Sorry, there was no need for that, was there?"

"There absolutely wasn't, no," Andrew said. He cleared his throat.

"I have to say, it's felt like a lifetime, having to deal with those idiots by myself, so it's nice . . . it's been really good to have, you know, a friend, to share the burden with."

"Even when I make you think of them *at it*?" Peggy said.

"Okay, maybe not then." Andrew wasn't exactly sure why his heart was beating almost uncomfortably hard. Or, for that matter, why he'd allowed them to walk past at least three stops from which he could have caught a bus home.

Peggy groaned. "I've just realized Steve's going to have written me an apology song on his stupid guitar. I actually can't stand the thought of it."

"Hmm, well, we can always head back to Cameron's for pudding," Andrew said. Peggy elbowed him again.

They were both quiet for a moment, lost in their own thoughts. A siren sounded in the distance. Perhaps it was the same ambulance that had gone past with just its lights on, Andrew thought. Had the paramedics been on the radio, waiting to hear if they were needed after all?

"Are your lot still going to be up when you get in?" Peggy said.

Andrew winced. *Not this. Not now.*

"Diane, maybe," he said. "The kids should be asleep by now."

They were approaching the station Andrew guessed Peggy was getting her train from.

"Is it bad," he said, fighting the voice in his head warning him that this wasn't a good idea, "that sometimes I just sort of wish I could escape from it all?"

"From what?" Peggy said.

"You know, the family . . . and everything."

Peggy laughed and Andrew immediately backtracked. "God, sorry, that's ridiculous, I didn't mean to—"

"No, are you kidding?" Peggy said. "I dream of that on a regular basis. The bliss of it all. The time you could actually spend doing things you wanted to do. I think you'd be mad *not* to fantasize about that. I spend half my life daydreaming about what I'd be doing with myself if I wasn't stuck where I was . . . and then that's usually when one of the kids ruins it by drawing something beautiful for me or being inquisitive or loyal or kind, and I feel like my heart's going to explode with how much I love them, and then it's all over. Nightmare, eh?"

"Nightmare," Andrew said.

They hugged good-bye outside the station. Andrew stayed for a while after Peggy had gone, watching people coming through the ticket barriers, blank face after blank face. He thought of the property inspection that morning and Terry Hill with his knife, fork, plate and water glass. And that's when the thought hit him so hard it practically winded him: living this lie would be the death of him.

He thought about how he'd felt in the brief moment Peggy had hugged him. This wasn't physical contact through formality—an introductory handshake. Nor was it the unavoidable touch of the barber or dentist, or a stranger on a packed train. It had been a genuine gesture of warmth, and for that second and a half he was reminded about how it felt to let someone in. He had resigned himself to the fate of Terry Hill and all those others, but maybe, just maybe, there was another way.

– CHAPTER 12 –

When it came to model trains, one of the most satisfyingly simple things Andrew had learned was that the more you ran a locomotive, the better it performed. With repeated use, an engine starts to glide around the track, seeming to grow in efficiency with every circuit. When it came to making connections with people, however, he was less of a smoothly running locomotive and more a rail replacement bus rusting in a rest stop.

After he'd left Peggy at the station he'd practically floated home, suddenly buoyed by possibility. He'd half considered turning on his heel and running after her to improvise some sort of grand gesture— perhaps spelling out "I am terrified of dying alone and I think it's probably weird when adults make friends this late in life but shall we do it anyway?" in discarded Coke cans at the side of the tracks. In the end he managed to contain himself and jogged halfway home, buying four cans of lukewarm Polish lager from the corner shop, drinking them in quick succession and waking up hungover and afraid. He forced himself out of bed and fried some bacon while listening to

"The Nearness of You"—Ella and Louis Armstrong from 1956—five times in a row. Each time the vocals kicked in he could feel the sensation of Peggy's arm interlinked with his again. If he closed his eyes tightly enough he could see the smile she'd given him as they parted from their hug. He looked at his watch and decided he had just enough time for one more spin of the record, but as he went to move the needle back, the miserable sound of "Blue Moon" suddenly came into his head, as clear as if it were coming through the record player. *No no no. Not now. Stay in the moment for once.* He scrabbled to put "The Nearness of You" on again and bent down by the speaker, his ear so close that it hurt, his eyes screwed shut. After a moment there was a piercing shriek and he opened his eyes to see the room was hazy with smoke, the alarm triggered by the now-cremated bacon.

———————

It was still too early to go to work, so he sat at his computer with two cups of tea in an attempt to alleviate his hangover—taking sips from alternate mugs—and pondered on how he might go about cementing a proper friendship with Peggy, something that elevated things above simply spending time together at work. Just the idea of suggesting they go for coffee, or to the cinema or whatever, left him firmly out of his comfort zone, and *god* how he loved that zone. It was a world where Pickled Onion Monster Munch was seen as the height of culinary experimentation, where ice-breaker games were punishable by death.

He thought about what he and Peggy had bonded over so far. Well, there were the chats about the meaning of life and loss, and the idea of "the club." But it wasn't as if he could go steaming in there and suggest they get matching litter picker tattoos via a quick trip to the aquarium, was it? At the heart of that conversation, though, had been the fact that Peggy had been trying to comfort him. She'd used the Apocalypse Game as a fun distraction—that had been a gesture of real kindness. And now it was Peggy who was clearly in a bad way because of Steve. If he was able to comfort her as she had him, then that would surely be the basis of a real connection. So what could he do to try to cheer *her* up?

What he really needed was advice, and there was only one place he could go to for that. A few clicks of the mouse and he was on the forum. The only issue was that he felt too embarrassed to just come straight out with it and ask for help. He'd have to improvise, see where that got him first. Morning, chaps, he wrote. I'm after some advice. I happened to meet someone recently who's having a bad time with a seller. They'd been promised a China Clay 5 Plank Wagon Triple Pack but the seller lied and ended up going with another bidder at the last minute. They're very upset, so any help on how to cheer them up would be greatly appreciated!

TinkerAl replied within seconds: Hmmm. Well it's the Beckenham & West Wickham Vintage Toy Train Show next weekend. Could take them to that?

BamBam67: Why would they POSSIBLY have wanted a China Clay 5 Plank Wagon Triple Pack when for the same money they could probably have got a Dapol B304 Westminster?

Hmmm. Andrew drummed his fingers on his knees. If he was actually going to get any useful advice he'd have to take the plunge properly. He wrote and rewrote a message several times, eventually hitting "post":

Okay, truth be told, the person I was talking about is having a bad time of it at the moment, but she's not actually into trains (for her sins!). I'm just a bit rusty when it comes to this sort of thing. Any advice on fun activities and the like would be really helpful.

BroadGaugeJim: Aha! I'd been curious about whether there was a Mrs. Tracker on the scene!

Tracker: No, no, it's nothing like that.

TinkerAl: Ah. Sounds like Tracker isn't that keen to expand on the specifics, Jim. But we're here for you, mate, if you do want to!

Andrew felt a pang of something between embarrassment and affection.

Thanks, TA. In all honesty, part of my being so rubbish at all this, hence why I'm asking for advice, is because I'm not exactly a people person. But it just feels a bit different with her. In a good way. It's been a very long time since I had someone in my life like this, and it's been really nice. But there's still a nagging doubt that I should just leave things as they are.

BamBam67: I can understand that.

TinkerAl: Yeah, me too.

BroadGaugeJim: Ditto. I'm not the biggest people person myself. Sometimes it's just easier to go it alone in life. No dramas that way.

Andrew went to the kitchen and put the kettle on (just a single tea, this time), thinking about what BroadGauge had said. He knew that he was comforted by how much control he had with this simple little life of his. It was consistent and unspectacular and he had absolutely no desire to jeopardize that. But there were moments—when he saw groups of friends sitting in neat, symmetrical rows on pub benches, or couples holding hands in the street, and he felt a wave of embarrassment that he, a forty-two-year-old man, hadn't exchanged so much as a cup of tea with an acquaintance or a flirtatious smile with someone on a train in years—that he scared himself with how intense the feeling of longing was. Because maybe, actually, he did want to find people to be close to, to make friends and perhaps even find someone to spend the rest of his life with. He'd gotten adept at sweeping that feeling away as quickly as he could, telling himself that it would only lead to unhappiness. But what if he let it grow—nourished it, in fact? Maybe that was the only way forward. The past was the past and maybe this time, once and for all, he could stop it from dictating his life.

He sipped his tea and replied to BroadGauge.

I don't know, BG, I thought maybe I was too stuck in my ways, but maybe not! Anyway, perhaps we should get back to train chat, eh? I appreciate the help, though. Opening up like this isn't really my forte. Feels a bit unnatural, like going for a poo with your coat on. (He decided on balance to delete this last line before posting.)

TinkerAl: Well, let us know how you get on, mate!

BroadGaugeJim: Absolutely!

BamBam67: Indeed!

———

Despite his newfound determination to get out of his comfort zone, to be part of Peggy's world and vice versa, Andrew was all too aware that honesty was something of a given when it came to friendship, and as far as Peggy knew he was a happily married father of two, living in relative luxury. He briefly considered the idea of Diane running away to Australia with a surfing instructor, taking the kids with her. But even then, say he managed to convince Peggy it was all just too painful ever to talk about; ten years down the line he still wouldn't be able to show her a picture of the kids, let alone explain why he hadn't been out to visit them. His only option was to hope they could get to a point where he could tell her the truth and pray that, somehow, against all odds, she'd accept it.

But his attempts to try to properly cement their friendship got off to a tricky start. Andrew had spent a frustrating Tuesday afternoon working his way through the contacts on an old Nokia phone he'd recovered from a property search, none of his calls being answered. As he plucked up the courage to call a contact saved as "Big Bazza," he decided to craft what he hoped was a funny e-mail to Peggy. He crowbarred in some in-jokes and generally tried to come across as charming and irreverent, signing off by suggesting they should run away to the pub "right bloody now!!"

Andrew had never before experienced regret quite as potent as he did immediately after hitting "send." He was wondering whether he had time to locate a hammer and smash up the building's power supply, or his own face, when Peggy's response arrived.

"Ha, yeah."

Oh.

A second message arrived. Here it was—the moment where she saw quite how brilliant and hilarious he was.

"By the way, I finally tracked down the will executor of that bloke who died on Fenham Road. Do you think 'I want nothing to do with that bastard' counts as a 'formal revocation of duty'?"

This was going to be harder than he thought. He knew he was being impatient, but what if Peggy decided she'd suddenly had enough for some reason and quit the job and moved away? What made things worse was that as each day passed he was increasingly aware of how much she was starting to mean to him, and the more he realized this the more ridiculous his behavior became. How the hell was he supposed to seem like someone Peggy wanted to spend time with when he sat there worrying himself into a state of panic that he was looking at her left eye more than her right and, for reasons that were hopelessly unclear, talking to her for a very long time about soup?

What he really should just do was casually inquire if Peggy wanted to meet outside of work. If she didn't want to, then that was fine. He'd get the message that it was just a work friendship situation and that would be that. So the only thing for it was to be very calm and confident and ask her very directly if, perhaps, and fine if not, of course, she wanted to do something one evening, or at the weekend. On balance, he realized the Beckenham & West Wickham Vintage Toy Train Show was probably an ambitious opening gambit, but a drink, say, or dinner, that was what he should go for. And, just so there could be no backing out, he decided to set himself a deadline—Thursday that week seemed as good as any—where he had to ask her by the time they left work. He just hoped she could deal with him being weird until he'd worked up the courage.

There was, he admitted, a very, *very* slight chance that he was overthinking things.

———

Inevitably, by the time Thursday afternoon arrived he still hadn't asked her. In retrospect he might have decided that delaying things by a day or so was preferable to making his move as they sorted through rubbish in a dead man's home, but at the time it really felt like it was now or never.

Derek Albrighton had lived to the age of eighty-four before his heart stopped beating. His flat was right on the borough's boundary edge—one street across and he would've been dealt with by another team. The coroner had sounded unusually grumpy when she'd called Andrew and asked him to investigate.

"No obvious next of kin. Neighbors called the police after they'd not seen him for a couple of days. The attending officers were about as useful as a mudguard on a tortoise, as per. Would be great to get this one sorted as soon as poss, Andrew. I'm on holiday soon and I've got paperwork up to my ears."

Derek's flat was one of those places you felt could never get warm no matter how much you heated it. It was tidy, on the whole, apart from the dull white powder that was spread out on the kitchen lino-leum, with footprints in it, as if it were pavement covered in a thin layer of snow.

"It's flour," Peggy said. "Either that or rat poison. Did I mention I'm a crap cook? Ah, but what have we here?" She reached for a large biscuit tin that was sitting on top of the microwave. She cooed as she removed the lid, beckoning Andrew over to show him the still-pristine Victoria sponge that was inside.

"Shame he didn't get to eat it after all the effort he clearly went to," Andrew said.

"A tragedy," Peggy said, reverently replacing the lid, as if it were a time capsule they were about to bury. Andrew decided to try out a lean against the kitchen counter, one leg crossed behind the other, an eyebrow raised in what he hoped suggested an irreverent take on early-years Roger Moore Bond.

"So, you a big fan of . . . cake, then?" he said. Unfortunately, or, perhaps not, Peggy was busying herself with some paperwork she'd found and was only half paying attention.

"Yeah, course, who isn't?" she said. "I wouldn't trust anyone who says they aren't a fan of cake, to be honest. It's like those people who say they don't like Christmas. Get over yourself, of course you do. What else don't you like? Wine and sex and bloody . . . ten-pin bowling."

Andrew winced. This wasn't going well. For one thing, he *hated* ten-pin bowling.

"Nothing here, no phonebook or anything either," Peggy said, shuffling the bits of paper newsreader-style. "Bedroom?"

"Bedroom. Sure thing . . . *you*," Andrew said. He tapped out a little rhythm on the countertop to show how devil-may-care he was—how music ran through his soul—pausing only very briefly to deal with the massive coughing fit he was suffering as a result of his jaunty drumming's disturbing yet more flour. Peggy was looking at him with a mixture of suspicion and confusion, like a cat that's seen itself in the mirror.

The bedroom was dominated by a surprisingly plush double bed, with purple satin sheets and brass headboard—incongruous next to the tattered blinds, worn carpet and cheap chest of drawers at the foot of the bed. On top sat an ancient-looking TV and VHS machine. Andrew and Peggy knelt at either side of the bed and began checking under the mattress.

"I was thinking," Andrew said, emboldened slightly by the fact Peggy couldn't see him, "you know that pub we went to after your first property inspection?"

"Uh-huh," Peggy said.

"That was nice, wasn't it?"

"Not sure I'd say nice, but there was beer there and that always feels like a plus in a pub."

"Ha . . . yeahhh."

Not there then.

"I didn't see what the food was like," he said. "Do you . . . have a favorite sort of cuisine, for, you know, when you're out?"

Cuisine?

"Hang on," Peggy said. "I've got something."

Andrew edged around to the foot of the bed.

"Oh," Peggy said. "It's just a receipt. For some socks."

Andrew was starting to feel desperate. He was really going to have to say something now before he bottled it. "So I was just, you know . . . wondering-if-you-fancied-going-for-dinner-or-something-after-work-sometime-soon." As he went for another casual lean his elbow pushed a button on the television, which began to turn itself on with a series of clunks and whines, sounds that seemed to entirely encapsulate the 1980s. Moments later, the room was filled with the unmistakable sounds of sex. Andrew spun around to see a middle-aged woman on the screen in nothing but a pair of high heels being taken from behind by a man naked apart from a white baseball cap.

"Oh my god," Peggy said.

"Oh my god," the man in the baseball cap answered.

"You like that, don't ya, ya dirty sod?" the woman grunted, rhetorically, it would seem. As Andrew backed away to fully take in the horror, he trod on something. It was a video case—the cover of which featured a shot of the couple on-screen in midflow. Red block capitals announced the film's title: *IT'S QUIM UP NORTH!*

Andrew slowly rotated the case so that Peggy could see. She had already been crying silently with laughter, but this, apparently, was the final straw, and she let out a loud, gleeful cackle. After a moment Andrew began edging toward the TV as if he were going back to a lit firework, weight on his back foot, one hand covering his face, jabbing randomly at the buttons until he hit "pause" and a grotesque tableau shuddered on the screen.

In the end they managed to compose themselves enough to finish the rest of their search with the requisite solemnity. It was Andrew who found a tattered documents folder in a drawer that had a phone number for a "Cousin Jean" written on the flap.

"Well I for one am not calling Cousin Jean," Peggy said.

"It does seem a bit strange after . . . that," Andrew said.

Peggy shook her head, bewildered. "I was going to suggest we should get a coin and toss for it, but that seems a horribly inappropriate thing to say now."

Andrew snorted. "I can't quite work out what to think about Derek Albrighton."

"Well it's clear to me that the bloke had life absolutely figured out," Peggy said.

Andrew raised his eyebrows.

"Oh come on," Peggy said. "If I get to eighty-four and my day consists of baking a cake and celebrating that achievement with a wank, then I'll be pretty bloody happy."

———

"You two look pleased with yourselves," Keith said when they arrived back at the office.

"Thick as thieves," Meredith said, clacking a pen between her top and bottom teeth.

"Bit like you two at Cameron's the other night," Peggy said calmly, which shut them up. She hung her coat on the back of her chair and winked at Andrew. He grinned back goofily. Peggy might not have had time to answer his question about dinner—randy Derek Albrighton had put paid to that—but it had been such a fun walk back to the office that he couldn't feel too despondent. Cameron chose that moment to amble out of his office and, in an uncharacteristically solemn voice, ask them to join him in the break-out area. Ever since the disastrous dinner party he'd carried himself with the air of a well-meaning schoolteacher who'd let his students bring in a game on the last day of term, only for them to spray Silly String all over the place and write rude words on their desks. The five of them sat in a semicircle and Cameron steepled his fingers against his chin.

"I've been mulling over whether to actually say anything, guys, but I've decided I'd like to talk to you all about what happened last week at my house. Before I speak, would any of you like to say anything?" The water cooler hummed. A strip light overhead flickered. Outside, a vehicle announced that it was reversing.

"Okay," Cameron said. "Well, what I wanted to say to you was that—and, believe me, I hate to say this—I was really rather disappointed"—his voice cracked, and he had to stop and gather himself—"*disappointed* with you all. What with two of you running off early and two of you disappearing upstairs. What should have been a nice evening for all of us to bond ended up having the opposite outcome. I mean, talk about low-hanging fruit, guys." He waited for this to sink in. Andrew hadn't realized he'd taken it this badly. "However," Cameron continued. "I very much believe in second chances, so let's give this another go and see how we get on, okay, team? Meredith has kindly volunteered to host the next evening. Andrew, you can be next."

Andrew instantly pictured the stain on his kitchen wall, the battered old sofa and the distinct lack of a family there, and bit down hard on his cheeks.

Cameron kept them for further blather about budgets and targets, then decided to regale them with a spectacularly dull anecdote about he and Clara losing each other in the supermarket, before finally they were all allowed to go back to their desks. Not long after, Peggy sent Andrew an e-mail. "I don't know about you, but all I was thinking about during that was whether they ever made *It's Quim Up North 2*."

"Would you need to have seen the first one to understand the sequel?" Andrew replied.

A minute later he received two messages at once. The first was from Peggy: "Ha! Quite possibly. Oh, and I forgot to say: Yes to dinner. Where are we going?"

The second was a text from an unknown number: *How many letters am I going to have to send you before you grow some balls and reply? Or are you too busy thinking about what you'll spend Sally's money on?*

– CHAPTER 13 –

It took Andrew six attempts to dial Carl's number without hanging up before it connected. He hadn't thought about what he was going to say. He just knew he had to stop this.

"Hello, Cynergy?" A hollow sense of friendliness in the voice.

"It's Andrew."

A pause.

"Oh. You finally decided to call then."

"These letters. Please—please just stop sending them," Andrew said.

"The truth hurts, doesn't it." A statement, not a question.

"What do you want me to say?" Andrew said.

"How about an apology. It was *you* that made her ill. You did this." Carl's voice was shaking already. "Can't you see that? She spent the last twenty years trying to make things right, and you never let her. You were too stubborn to forgive her, and her heart was a fucking wreck because of you."

"That's not true," Andrew said, unsure of the words even as he said them.

"You're pathetic, you know that? God, I just keep imagining what Sally would be thinking now—how much she'd regret what she'd done. I bet she'd—"

"Okay, okay—you can have the money. I never asked for it in the first place. As soon as I get it I'll transfer it over, but you have to promise to just . . . leave me alone."

He heard Carl sniff and clear his throat. "I'm glad you've come to your senses. I will 'leave you alone,' as you put it. But I'll be in touch again when I know you've got the money, you can be sure of that." Then the line went dead.

Andrew made some beans on toast and logged on to the subforum, eager to forget about his conversation with Carl.

I'm after a bit of restaurant advice, chaps, **he wrote.** Somewhere nice but not TOO expensive. Think LNER 0-6-0T "585" J50 Class rather than LNER 0-6-0 "5444" J15. Within minutes the subforum had come up trumps with several suggestions. Eventually, he settled on an Italian restaurant that was trendy enough not to put pound signs on the menu but not so fancy that the meals were described in a Tuscan mountain dialect.

The next morning they were at a property inspection and Andrew reminded Peggy of the plan. "There's no rush, obviously, but just—whenever you've got a mo—maybe ping me over some dates for when you're free for our dinner thing," he said, as casually as possible, even throwing in a yawn for good measure. Peggy looked up from the Tupperware box containing the last will and testament of Charles Edwards, which she'd just discovered under the kitchen sink.

"Oh aye, will do. Next week I reckon. I'll check my diary back at the ranch."

"Cool. Sure . . . like I said, no rush," Andrew said, knowing that he'd spend the rest of the day refreshing his inbox until he was on the verge of a repetitive strain injury.

When the day of their dinner arrived the following week, Andrew found himself immediately anxious from the moment he got up. By the time he was at the office he'd managed to work himself up so much that at one point Meredith sneezed and he spontaneously apologized. He tried to tell himself to calm down, that it was ridiculous to be so anxious. *It's just dinner, for god's sake!* But it was no good. Peggy had spent the morning in an adjacent room that held the office safe, storing away the unclaimed items of value from a recent property visit in preparation for their sale, and had been on a training course away from the office in the afternoon. This, he decided, was probably why he felt so tense. Not being able to see her to exchange a friendly word all day, he couldn't convince himself that she wouldn't rather be doing anything else than spending her evening with him.

As if to confirm his gloom, he knew the restaurant was a poor choice by the look the waiter gave him on arrival, as if he were a stray dog who'd wandered in looking for a place to die.

"Your . . . friend is on their way, sir?" the waiter asked after Andrew had been sitting there for less than five minutes.

"Yes," Andrew said. "I hope—I'm sure—she'll be here soon."

The waiter gave him a seen-it-all-before smirk and poured two inches of water into his glass. Twenty minutes went by, during which Andrew refused and then reluctantly accepted some incredibly hard bread.

"Are you sure you don't want to order something now for when your friend arrives?" the waiter said.

"No," Andrew said, annoyed at the waiter and annoyed at himself for having the temerity to get out of the little box he lived in.

Then, with the muscles in his toes tensed as he prepared to rise and make as dignified an exit as possible, he saw a flash of color at the door and there was Peggy in a bright red coat, hair sopping wet from rain. She plonked herself down in the chair opposite with a half-mumbled greeting and thrust a crust of bread into her mouth.

"Christ," she said. "What's this I'm eating—a hubcap?"

"I think it's focaccia."

Peggy grunted and, with some difficulty, swallowed.

"You know when you married Diane?" she said, ripping a bit of bread in two.

Andrew's heart sank. Not this. Not this already.

"Mmm-hmm," he said.

"Did you ever think that there'd be a point where you'd be staring at her as she sat on the living room floor with a beer can balanced on her belly like a drunk, horizontal Christ the Redeemer and think to yourself: *How the hell have we ended up here?*"

Andrew shifted awkwardly in his seat.

"Not word for word, no," he said.

Peggy shook her head slowly, gazing into the middle distance. There was a lock of rain-damp hair hanging down at the side of her face. Andrew felt a strange urge to reach over and tuck it behind her ear. Was that something he'd seen in a film? The waiter appeared at the table, his smirk replaced by a slightly disappointed, almost apologetic smile now that Peggy had shown up.

"Would you like to look at the wine list, sir?"

"Yes please," Andrew said.

"Don't bother about asking me, mate," Peggy muttered.

"I apologize, madam," the waiter said, bowing theatrically before sauntering off.

"Annoys me, that," Peggy said. "For all he knows I'm an off-duty sommelier. The wanker."

On the one hand Andrew was enamored of Peggy's righteous ire. On the other, he feared the chances of piss in their linguine had just been significantly increased.

After a glass of wine and the arrival of the starters, Peggy seemed to relax a little, but there was still an undercurrent of frustration and as a result conversation was hard going. Andrew began to panic in the increasingly long stretches where they weren't talking. Being silent during meals was for married couples on holiday in brightly lit tavernas with only their mutual resentment of each other left in common. This wasn't going according to plan at all. What he really needed was something to snap them out of it. His wish was granted, but perhaps not quite in the way he would have wanted, when a man in a yellow coat straining against his enormous form barged into the restaurant. His sleeves were stretched over his hands and he had his hood drawn tight over his head, the effect of which made it look like an incredibly large child was barreling toward them. As he stomped closer he yanked his hood away from his face, showering some nearby diners with raindrops. Heads were turning. The look on each face conveyed that very particular fear when someone is behaving outside the normal boundaries in a public space, namely: *What is about to happen and am I going to be able to trample my way out first if it all kicks off?*

"I could be wrong," Andrew said, trying to sound calm, "but I think your husband's just walked in."

Peggy turned around and immediately got to her feet. Andrew folded his hands in his lap and stared at them, feeling pathetically scared in the face of the inevitable confrontation.

"So you're following me now?" Peggy said, hands on hips. "How long have you been standing out there? And where are the girls?"

"With Emily from next door," Steve said in a voice so low it sounded like he was in slow motion.

"Okay, and just to check, that isn't just another lie?"

"Course not," Steve growled. "And who the fuck's this little shite?"

Andrew somewhat optimistically hoped it wasn't him Steve was referring to.

"Never mind who he is," Peggy said. "What the hell are you doing here?"

"I'm just nipping to the loo," Andrew said with a manic brightness, as if this would make him impervious to being punched. The waiter stood aside to let him past, the smirk returned to his face.

When Andrew plucked up the courage to come back to the table, Peggy and Steve were nowhere to be seen, and Peggy's coat was gone. Some of the other diners were risking covert looks up at him as he took his seat. Others were looking out of the window, where Andrew could now see Peggy and Steve. They were standing in the street outside, hoods up, both gesticulating furiously.

Andrew hovered by the table. He should go out there. He should at least *pretend* to himself, if not the rest of the restaurant and the snarky fucking waiter, that he was going to go out there. As he drummed his fingers on the back of his chair, still deciding what he was going to do, the yellow blob was suddenly gone, as if carried off downriver by a strong current, and Peggy was heading back inside. She looked like she'd been crying—it was hard to tell because of the rain—and mascara had snaked down her cheeks in two thin lines.

"Are you o—"

"I'm really sorry, but please can we just eat?" Peggy interrupted, her voice hoarse.

"Of course," Andrew said, shoving some more shrapnel bread into his mouth and consoling himself with the fact he hadn't been punched in the face by a giant Geordie.

———

Peggy went to eat the last mouthful on her plate, changed her mind, and set her knife and fork down together with a clang.

"I'm sorry you got called a shite back then," she said.

"No need to apologize," Andrew said, thinking that it should really be him apologizing, for being such a coward. "I'm guessing we'll skip the puddings then?" he said.

The hint of a smile returned to Peggy's face. "You're joking, I hope. If there was ever a time for emergency sticky toffee, then it's now."

The waiter came over and cleared their plates.

"I don't suppose sticky toffee pudding's on the menu?" Andrew said, with his best stab at a winning smile.

"As it happens, sir, it is," the waiter said, seeming disappointed at this.

"Oh, champion," Peggy said, offering the waiter a thumbs-up.

———

They both finished their puddings at the same time, returning their spoons to the bowl with simultaneous clinks.

"Snap," Peggy said. "How much food have I got on my face, by the way?"

"None," Andrew said. "How about me?"

"No more than usual."

"Glad to hear it. Actually, you have got a little bit of . . ."

"What?"

"Mascara, I think."

Peggy snatched up her spoon and looked at her reflection. "Ah Jesus, I look like a panda, you should have said something."

"Sorry."

She dabbed at her cheeks with her napkin.

"Do you mind me asking if everything's okay?" Andrew said.

Peggy continued to dab. "I don't," she said. "But there's not much to say, so . . ." She smoothed the napkin flat on the table. "This might be a bit weird, but can I ask you to do something?"

"Of course," Andrew said.

"Okay, so close your eyes."

"Um, sure," Andrew said, thinking this was the sort of thing Sally used to make him do that would invariably end up with him being in pain.

"Can you picture a moment, right now, where you and Diane were at your happiest?" Peggy said.

Andrew felt the heat rising on his cheeks.

"Have you got something?"

After a moment, he nodded.

"Describe it to me."

"How . . . how do you mean?"

"Well, when is it? Where are you? What can you see and feel?"

"Oh, okay."

Andrew took a deep breath. The answer came to him not from something written on a spreadsheet, but from somewhere deep inside.

"We're just out of university, starting our lives together in London. We're in Brockwell Park. It's the hottest day of the summer. The grass is really dry, practically charred."

"Go on . . ."

"We're sitting back to back. We realize we need a bottle opener for our beers. And Diane pushes her back against me to try and get to her feet. And she nearly falls, and we're just giggling, and giddy in the heat. She walks up to these strangers—a couple—to borrow their lighter. She knows this trick where you can use one to open a bottle. She cracks the tops off and hands the lighter back. She's walking back to me, and I can see her but I can still see the couple, too. They're both looking at her. It's like she's left an impression on them in that moment that means they'll be thinking about her for the rest of the day. And I realize how lucky I am, and how I never want this day to end."

Andrew was startled. Both at the clarity of what he'd just pictured, and by the tears pooling fast under his eyelids. When he finally opened his eyes, Peggy was looking away. After a moment, he said, "Why did you want to know that?"

Peggy smiled sadly.

"Because when I try and do the same thing, I can't seem to see anything. It's that more than anything that's making me think I can't see a happy ending. The truth is I've given Steve an ultimatum: to clean up his act or that's it. Trouble being, I don't really know which way I want things to go. Ah well, I'm sure whatever happens will be for the best."

Andrew was feeling a peculiar mixture of emotions. Anger at the big flapping daffodil, and pain at the sight of Peggy, her posture slumped slightly, her defiance undermined by her watering eyes. But there was something else there, too. It struck him that, up until now, he'd been too eager to find an excuse to get close to Peggy, that this had been far too much about him and the fear of where his life was heading. Part of him had *wanted* a reason to be able to step in and be there for her, which meant perhaps part of him hadn't cared if she was upset. Well, if he was going to be that cynical and selfish, then he didn't deserve a friend. And now, as he desperately searched for something reassuring to say to Peggy, he realized the pain he was feeling concealed a different truth. In that moment, he didn't care about himself. All he wanted to do was make Peggy happy. The pain was there because he didn't know how.

CHAPTER 14

The following fortnight was dominated by death. The coroner seemed to be on the phone practically every hour, struggling to remember which cases she'd discussed with them. ("We talked about Terrence Decker, right? Newbury Road? Choked on a marshmallow? Oh, no, wait, that was someone else. Or possibly a dream I had.")

Such was the glut of property inspections they were having to do, at times Andrew and Peggy regretfully sacrificed respectfulness for pragmatism, sorting through the chaos and the mess or the soulless, empty rooms as quickly as possible. The houses varied from a cramped maisonette complete with a dead rat sporting a grotesque grin on its face, to a seven-bedroom house backing out onto a park, its interior overwhelmed with cobwebs, every room feeling pregnant with secrets.

Peggy had been struggling even before the frequency of the inspections increased. Whether Steve had messed up again and she'd been forced to act on her ultimatum, Andrew wasn't sure. The first time he'd seen her returning from the loos in the office with puffy red eyes he'd started to ask her if she was all right, but she very calmly interrupted and asked him a question about an upcoming job. From then on, every time he saw her looking upset or happened to hear her in the stairwell having an angry phone call, he made sure to make her a cup of tea, or e-mail something silly and distracting about Keith's latest hygiene horror. He even attempted to bake some biscuits, but the end results had resembled something a child might use for snow-man's eyes, so he had abandoned them in favor of shop-bought. Some-how, it just didn't seem enough.

During a brief respite in the break-out area one afternoon, eating what Peggy referred to as "alternative bananas" (a Twix and a KitKat Chunky, respectively), Andrew happened to mention Ella Fitzgerald.

"She that jazz one?" Peggy said through a mouthful of nougat.

"*'That jazz one'*?" Andrew said. He was about to admonish Peggy for her description, but then an idea struck him. People still liked getting mix tapes, didn't they? And what could be better than Ella to cheer someone up? If she could have the same effect on Peggy as she'd had on him over the years, it could even be a revelation, a cornerstone of comfort like it had been for him since he'd first listened to her all those years ago. And so began a series of agonizing evenings spent trying to choose songs that perfectly encapsulated Ella's essence. He wanted to capture the whole spectrum—upbeat and downbeat num-bers, polished and loose—but also just how joyously, infectiously funny she could be on her live albums. The outtakes and the between-song badinage meant as much to him as the most soaring melody.

After evening five, he began to wonder if it was actually an impos-sible task. There was never going to be *the* perfect tape. He'd just have to hope what he'd chosen would have the right sort of alchemy to make it a source of comfort to Peggy whenever she needed it. He de-cided to give himself one more night to finish it, eventually collapsing into bed way past midnight, his stomach rumbling angrily, at which point he realized he'd been so ensconced he'd forgotten to have any dinner.

When he presented the end result to Peggy on the stairs outside the office he affected an air of nonchalance to try to hide the nagging voice telling him this might have been a weird thing for him to have done. "By the way, I knocked up an Ella Fitzgerald mix tape for you. Just chose a few songs I thought you would like. No pressure, of course, to listen to it straightaway, or even over the next few days, or weeks, or whatever."

"Ah, thanks, pet," Peggy said. "I solemnly swear to listen to it within the next few days, or weeks, or whatever." She turned the CD over and read the back. It had taken seven attempts for Andrew to write the tracks out in acceptably neat handwriting. He realized Peggy was looking at him with a twinkle in her eyes. "How long did it take for you to 'knock this up,' out of interest?" she said.

Andrew blew a dismissive and unintentionally wet raspberry. "Couple of hours, I suppose."

Peggy opened her bag and dropped the CD inside.

"I've no doubt you're an excellent mix-tape maker, Andrew Smith. But you're a terrible liar." And with that she walked calmly into the office. Andrew stood there for a moment, grinning, albeit slightly confused as to why it felt like Peggy had taken his stomach, heart and several other vital organs with her as she'd left.

———

There's nothing like a PowerPoint presentation to stamp out green shoots of happiness, especially one involving sound and visual effects. Cameron was particularly pleased at getting letters to spiral onto the screen soundtracked by typewriter clacks, jauntily revealing that there had been an increase of 28 percent of elderly people describing themselves as feeling lonely and/or isolated. His pièce de résistance was an embedded YouTube clip of a midnineties sketch-show skit that bore no relevance to the presentation but was just, he explained, "a bit of fun." They sat there in rigid silence, apart from Cameron, who chuckled away with increasing desperation. Just as it seemed the damn thing was finally about to end, an e-mail notification appeared in the bottom right-hand corner of the screen:

Mark Fellowes
Re: potential cutbacks

Cameron immediately scrabbled to close the window. But it was too late. The rest of the sketch played on, the studio audience's laughter horribly at odds with the new atmosphere. Andrew couldn't work out if anyone was going to say something. Clearly also anticipating this, Cameron shut down his laptop and made a swift exit, like someone who's just given a short statement outside court escaping the paparazzi, ignoring Meredith, who'd started to ask him the obvious question of what that e-mail had been about.

"Shit the bed," Keith said.

———

Later that morning, Peggy and Andrew arrived for a property inspection at 122 Unsworth Road feeling shell-shocked.

"I really can't lose this job," Peggy said.

Andrew decided to try to stay calm rather than add fuel to the fire.

"I'm sure it'll be fine," he said.

"And you're basing that on . . . ?"

"Um . . ." The calm quickly deserted him. "Blind optimism?" He laughed nervously.

"I'm glad you're not a doctor giving life-expectancy odds to a patient," Peggy said.

They got into their protective gear, and Andrew looked at the frosted glass window of number 122 and really rather wished he and Peggy were anywhere else but here.

"Nothing like sorting through a dead bloke's stuff as a cheery distraction, eh?" Peggy said, putting the key in the lock. "Ready?"

She shunted the door open and gasped. Andrew braced himself for what lay beyond her. He must have carried out more than a hundred property inspections in his time, and all these homes, no matter what their condition, left an impression on him, some little detail standing out: a gaudy ornament, a troubling stain, a heartbreaking note. Smells, too, stayed with him. And not just the horrendous ones. There had been lavender and engine oil and pine needles too. As time passed he stopped being able to match the memory to the person or the house. But once Peggy stood to one side and he saw past her, he knew for sure that he would always remember Alan Carter and 122 Unsworth Road.

At first, it wasn't clear what exactly he was looking at. The floors, radiators, tables, shelves—every available surface—were covered with little wooden objects. Andrew dropped down to the floor and picked one up.

"It's a duck," he said, suddenly feeling a bit stupid for saying that out loud.

"I think they all are," Peggy said, crouching down next to him. If this was a dream, Andrew wasn't quite sure what his subconscious was going for here.

"Are they little toys—was he a collector or something?" he said.

"I don't . . . blimey, you know what, I reckon he's carved all of these himself, you know. There's got to be thousands of them."

There was a path through the middle of the carvings, presumably made by those first on the scene.

"Remind me who this guy is?" Peggy said.

Andrew found the document in his bag.

"Alan Carter. No obvious next of kin, according to the coroner.

God, I know it's been busy but you'd have thought she'd have mentioned this."

Peggy picked up one of the ducks from a dressing table and ran a finger across the top of its head, then down the curve of its neck.

"So the question currently running through my mind, other than 'What the fuck?,' of course, is . . . why ducks?"

"Maybe he just loved . . . ducks," Andrew said.

Peggy laughed. "*I* love ducks. My daughter Suze actually painted me a mallard for a Mother's Day present a few years ago. But I'm not so much of a fan that I'd want to go and whittle a million of them."

Before Andrew had a chance to speculate further there was a knock at the door. He went to answer it, for some reason briefly imagining a human-sized duck on the other side, there to offer its condolences in a series of solemn quacks. Instead, it was a man with beady blue eyes and Friar Tuck hair.

"Knock knock," the man said. "You from the council? They said you'd be around today. I'm Martin, from next door? It was me who called the police about Alan, the poor chap. I thought I might . . ." He trailed off as he saw the carvings.

"Didn't you know?" Peggy said. The man shook his head, looking bewildered.

"No. I mean, the thing is, I'd knock on Alan's door every now and then, say hello, but that was it. Come to think of it, he never opened the door more than to show his face. He kept himself to himself, as the saying goes." He gestured to the carvings. "Is it okay if I have a closer look?"

"By all means," Andrew said. He exchanged a glance with Peggy. He wondered if she'd been starting to think the same as him, that despite all the intricacy and craftsmanship, at some point they would likely have to work out if the ducks had any discernible value that could be used to cover Alan Carter's funeral.

When Martin the neighbor left, Andrew and Peggy reluctantly got on with the job they were there to do. An hour later they were packing up and getting ready to leave, a thorough search of the place for documents revealing only a folder with neatly filed utility bills, and a *Radio Times* that looked like it had been rolled up for the purposes of killing flies, but nothing that gave any clues to a next of kin.

Peggy stopped by the front door so suddenly that Andrew nearly walked straight into her, just about managing to keep his balance, like a javelin thrower post-throw.

"What is it?" he said.

"I just don't want to leave this one without trying absolutely everything to find out if he's got family, you know?"

Andrew checked the time. "I suppose one more sweep couldn't hurt."

Peggy beamed, as if Andrew were sanctioning one more go on a bouncy castle rather than an additional search through a dead man's belongings.

"Take a room each?" he said.

Peggy saluted. "Sir yes sir!"

Andrew thought he might have something when he found a piece of paper that had fallen behind the drawers in a kitchen cupboard, but it was just an old shopping list, yellowed with age. It looked like they were all out of options, but then Peggy had a breakthrough. Andrew found her kneeling on the floor, reaching around the side of the fridge.

"I can see a bit of paper or something trapped there," she said.

"Hang on," Andrew said. He took hold of the fridge and rocked it back and forth in little jerks to move it to one side.

Whatever it was, it was covered in a thin layer of grime.

"It's a photo," Peggy said, wiping it clean with her sleeve to reveal two people looking back at them. They wore slightly sheepish smiles, as if they'd been waiting a long time to be exposed by someone clearing the dirt away. The man was dressed in a wax jacket with a flat cap tucked under his arm. His silver hair was fighting a losing battle against the wind to stay in place. There were pronounced crow's-feet around his eyes and wavy wrinkles on his forehead like ridges on a sand dune. The woman had frizzy brown hair tinged with gray, and was wearing a mauve cardigan and matching hoop earrings, an element of fortune-teller about her. She looked to be in her fifties, the man perhaps in his sixties. The photographer had cut them off at the waist, making enough space for a sign above their heads that read: "And a few lilies blow." There were more signs behind that but the writing was out of focus.

"Is that Alan, do we think?" Andrew said.

"I guess so," Peggy said. "What about the woman?"

"They're obviously together in the photograph. His wife? Or ex-wife? Hang on, is that a name badge on her cardigan?"

"It just says 'staff,' I think," Peggy said. She pointed to the sign. "'And a few lilies blow.' I feel like I should know that."

Andrew decided that this was enough of a reason to break his usual rule and use his phone.

"It's from a poem," he said, scrolling down the screen. "Gerard Manley Hopkins:

> I have desired to go
> Where springs not fail
> To fields where flies no sharp and sided hail
> And a few lilies blow."

Peggy ran her fingertips slowly over the photo, as if hoping to glean information simply by touch.

"Oh my god," she said suddenly. "I think I know where this is.

There's this big secondhand bookshop near where my sister lives—oh, what the hell's it called?" She flicked the photo back and forth impatiently as she tried to remember, and that's when they both caught a glimpse of something written on the back, in slanting blue pen:

"B's birthday, April 4th, 1992. We met after lunch at Barter Books and strolled down to the river. Then we had sandwiches on our favorite bench and fed the ducks."

CHAPTER 15

Andrew watched the funeral director lay the simple wreath at the unmarked grave and wondered how long it would be before it wilted away to nothing. The council usually paid for the wreaths, but recently when he'd asked for funds to do so it had led to increasingly tedious and depressing exchanges of e-mails that got him nowhere. At least he was still able to pay for obituaries in the local paper, as long as the wording was kept to a minimum. In this particular case he'd only been able to achieve an acceptable length by omitting the deceased's middle name, the sparsity of the notice barely leaving room for sentiment: "Derek Albrighton, died peacefully on July 14th, aged eighty-four." He supposed one small advantage of the restricted word limit was that he couldn't act on the temptation to add, "post-cake, mid-wank."

He met Peggy in a café that overlooked some railway tracks.

"You know cranes, right?" she said, looking out of the window as Andrew sat down.

"The construction machine or the long-necked bird?" Andrew said.

"The former, obviously."

"Obviously."

"When you see one of those massive ones by a skyscraper, do you ever wonder if they had to use another crane to build *that* crane? Or did it just get up there by itself? I suppose it's all a metaphor for how the universe was created. Or something."

A commuter train rattled past.

"I'm glad I'm sitting down," Andrew said. "That's quite a lot to take in." Peggy stuck her tongue out at him.

"So how was it today—did anybody show up at the church?" she said.

"Sadly not."

"You see, this is what I'm worried about," Peggy said, taking a swig of ginger beer.

"What do you mean?" Andrew said, wondering if maybe *he* should start drinking ginger beer.

Peggy looked sheepish and reached into her bag, bringing out the photo of Alan Carter and "B."

"I just can't stop thinking about this," she said.

It had been a week since they'd visited Alan's house and Andrew had tried to convince Peggy that they'd done all they could, that she'd go mad if she kept thinking about it, but she clearly hadn't let it go. Reluctantly, he took the photo from her. "And you're sure it's . . . where was it again?"

"Barter Books. It's a secondhand bookshop in Northumberland. I Googled it just to make sure, and it's definitely the right place. My sister moved to a village nearby a few years ago and we usually pop in on the way to visiting her."

Andrew studied the now familiar sight of Alan and his grinning companion.

"I just can't bear the thought of him being buried alone if there's someone out there who loved him and should be there—or at least be given the opportunity to be there."

"But that's the point, isn't it?" Andrew said. "Unfortunately, the cold truth of it is that when we get in touch with these people there's usually a reason they're not in contact with the person who's died."

"Yeah, but that's not always the case, is it?" Peggy said, her eyes wide, imploring Andrew to understand. "It's hardly ever because there's been some great dramatic falling-out. At worst it's a stupid argument over money, and more often than not it's just out of laziness that they've fallen out of touch."

Andrew went to speak but Peggy jumped in again.

"What about that woman you called last week—the one whose brother died. She didn't have a bad word to say about him—she was just embarrassed more than anything because she'd stopped bothering to call or visit him."

Andrew immediately thought of Sally and felt his neck starting to prickle.

"I mean, what a sorry state of affairs society's in," Peggy continued, "and so utterly *British*, to be that stubborn and proud. I mean . . ." She stopped, seemingly aware from Andrew's body language that he was uncomfortable with where this was going. She quickly changed the subject and offered to buy him an "overpriced, possibly stale" cookie.

"I couldn't possibly ask you to do that," Andrew said, putting his hands up in mock earnestness.

"Oh, but I insist," Peggy said. As she went up to the counter, Andrew looked at the photograph again. Perhaps he shouldn't have been so dismissive. Maybe there was a way of pursuing this without getting too deeply invested. He looked over at Peggy, who was taking the cookie-selection process very seriously despite the obvious impatience of the waitress. As usual, Andrew had made his textbook packed lunch that morning, but he'd pretended he hadn't when Peggy suggested they go out for lunch. He looked again at the photo. Maybe there wasn't too much harm in hearing Peggy out.

"So, what do you want to do?" he said when she returned, proffering cookies.

"I want to go there," she said, tapping the photo. "To Barter Books. And find this woman—find 'B.'"

"Isn't that a bit . . . I mean, isn't it incredibly unlikely that she's still working there?"

Peggy scratched at an imaginary stain on the tablecloth. Andrew narrowed his eyes.

"Have you already contacted them?"

"Maybe," Peggy said, her mouth twitching as she tried to hide a burgeoning smile.

"And?" Andrew said, and Peggy leaned forward and began to speak with a rapidity unusual even for her: "I phoned a lass there and spoke to her about it and I explained about the photo and what I did for a living and that I was a regular visitor and I asked whether there was anyone working there whose name began with B with brown and gray frizzy hair that might now actually be a bit more gray than brown and if they used to know someone called Alan."

She paused for breath.

"Right. And . . . ?" Andrew said.

"*And*, well, she said she couldn't give out specific details about staff members, but there were some people who'd been working there for a good long while and I was very welcome to pop in the next time I was up visiting my sister." Peggy opened her arms wide as if to say, *See?*

"So you're saying you want to go to this bookshop on the off chance that the person in the photograph with Alan is still working there?" Andrew said.

Peggy nodded emphatically, as if there had been a language barrier and she had finally broken through to him.

"Okay," Andrew said, "to play devil's advocate—"

"Oh, you bloody love playing bloody devil's bloody advocate," Peggy said, flicking a crumb in his direction.

"Say it *is* her—the woman in the photo—what will you say?" Andrew flicked the crumb back to signify the ball was in her court again.

Peggy thought for a moment. "I think I'll just have to do that on the day. Improvise, you know?"

Andrew went to speak but Peggy jumped in first. "Oh, come on, where's the harm?" she said, reaching over and taking his hand, which was halfway to delivering a cookie to his face. "Look, I've got it all worked out, right. I hadn't even thought about a holiday this summer, but god knows I need one—the kids, too, and"—she released Andrew's hand and a bit of cookie fell onto the table—"Steve's been staying at a friend's, recently . . . Anyway, my plan is to go up and see my sister the week after next and drop in on Barter Books while I'm there."

Andrew tilted his head from side to side, weighing this up. "Okay, well in fairness, if you're going up to see your sister, it's not quite as . . . mad."

Peggy put the photo back in her bag.

"I'd invite you to come up too, but I assume you'll be busy with the family."

"Ermm, well . . ." Andrew floundered, trying to think on his feet. It had seemed like a genuine invitation from Peggy, not simply out of politeness. "I'll have to check," he said, "but, actually . . . Diane was planning to take the kids down to visit her mum that week. In Eastbourne."

"And you're not going too?" Peggy said.

"No, probably not," Andrew said, willing his brain into gear. "I, um, don't really get on with Diane's parents. Bit of a long story."

"Oh?" Peggy said. She wasn't going to let him finish there, clearly, but this wasn't something that had ever made it to Andrew's master spreadsheet.

"It's a bit complicated, but basically her mum never approved of us getting together in the first place, because I was always seen as a bit unsuitable. So we've never really been able to see eye to eye and it just causes tension whenever we meet."

Peggy went to say something, then stopped.

"What?" Andrew said, a little too defensively, panicking at the thought that she wasn't convinced by this story.

"Oh, nothing. It's just, I can't imagine you being deemed unsuitable," she said. "You're far too . . . nice . . . and . . . you know . . ."

Andrew really *didn't* know. He took advantage of Peggy's being flustered for once and thought about what he should do. The simplest option would be to stay at home and avoid further questions about his family life. But there was just something about the idea of getting to spend a whole week with Peggy—on what felt like an adventure, too— that was too exciting and scary a prospect to miss. If this wasn't going out of his comfort zone, then what was? He had to go for it.

"Anyway," he said, as casually as possible, "I'll have a think about Northumberland. There's a good chance I can come and it, er, wouldn't be weird or anything, for me to do that, would it."

He hadn't quite thought this last bit through, and it came out halfway between a normal question and a rhetorical one. Peggy seemed like she might be about to answer but luckily someone at a neighboring table knocked an entire pot of tea onto the floor, whereupon five members of staff appeared from nowhere and cleared up the mess with the efficiency of Formula 1 mechanics in the pit lane, and the moment passed. Peggy seemed to use the distraction to do some weighing up of her own. "If you're free then you should definitely come," she said, once the pit lane crew had done their cleanup. Andrew recognized that tone. It was the way someone spoke when they were trying to convince themselves as much as the person they were talking to that what they were suggesting was a good idea.

They left the café and walked most of the way back to the office without speaking. Andrew glanced at Peggy, saw her furrowed brow and knew that like him she was replaying the conversation from the café over in her mind. They crossed at some lights and stepped around either side of a woman with a pram. When they came back together their arms bumped and they both apologized at the same time, then laughed at their politeness, the tension of the silence broken. Peggy raised an eyebrow at him. It seemed like such a daring gesture, to Andrew. As if she was on the verge of acknowledging what they were both thinking about the trip, that it was much more important to both of them than they were letting on. Furthermore, Andrew had the sudden realization that it was, in fact, one of the most spectacularly perfect eyebrows he'd ever seen, and that his heart was starting to beat uncomfortably fast.

"So what's Barter Books like, then?" he said, trying to restore normality to the conversation.

"Oh, it's amazing," Peggy said. She was attempting to put her coat on but was having a hard time finding one of the armholes. "It's a huge old place, rows and rows of books, comfy sofas dotted around."

"Sounds lovely," Andrew said. For some reason, putting one foot in front of the other had become an impossible task. Was this really how he walked? It seemed so unnatural.

"It really is," Peggy said, finally getting her arm through the coat sleeve. "It used to be a station and they've kept the waiting room and turned it into a café. The best part is there's a model train that runs all the way round the shop above the bookshelves."

Andrew stopped dead in his tracks before hurrying to catch Peggy up.

"Say that again?"

– CHAPTER 16 –

To Andrew's dismay, the trip was nearly scuppered before they'd even booked train tickets.

Cameron, for reasons that were unclear, had taken to getting people's attention by whistling at them. At first it had been a sharp, enthusiastic toot. But recently, in parallel with his mood, the whistle had become a low, melancholy sound, like a farmer instructing his sheepdog on its last outing before it was to be put down.

It was by this method that Andrew was beckoned into Cameron's office. There were folders and documents all over the place, and he had to gather a bunch of them up and move them off a chair so he had somewhere to sit. Distressingly, Andrew realized the office had started to resemble a room he might usually find himself searching through with surgical gloves and a litter picker.

"Rightio then, Drew," Cameron said. "This holiday you've booked. In future please check with the others in the team about timings because Peggy's away at the same time and that's just not ideal.

Please just be a bit more nimble about things, okay? It's so easy to cascade this sort of thing."

"Ah right, yes," Andrew said. He and Peggy hadn't deliberately concealed the fact they were going away together, but Andrew couldn't help but enjoy how illicit that seemed to make it. He realized that Cameron was looking at him expectantly.

"I'll check next time," he said quickly.

"Good. Thanks," Cameron said.

Andrew hoped that was going to be the end of it, but the next day he was at his desk when he heard raised voices coming from Cameron's office. "It's just absolutely outrageous," Meredith was saying, with typical understatement. "I'm sorry, literally the last thing I like doing is complaining, but you can't just turn around to me and say I can't take holiday when I want to, that's against my rights. I don't see why Andrew and Peggy can just swan off at the same time and I can't. It's ludicrous. It's completely unfair."

Cameron followed her out, wringing his hands with an alarmingly tight-looking grip.

"As I have told you, Meredith," he said, his voice ominously quiet, "you *can* take a holiday. I have just asked you *not* to go away the one week Peggy and Andrew are."

"Well how was I supposed to know when they were away? I'm not Mystic Meg, am I?"

"You're supposed to plan in advance and look at the log," Cameron said.

"What?"

"THE LOG! THE FUCKING LOG!"

Cameron covered his mouth with his hands, seemingly more shocked than anyone about his outburst. It was at that point that Keith wandered into the office, humming something a semitone out of tune and brandishing a heart attack between two slices of bread.

He looked at them in turn and took a massive bite, ketchup dripping onto his chin.

"What have I missed?" he said.

Andrew got to his feet. He had to act quickly so the trip wasn't endangered. "Look, I think what Cameron was trying to say, Meredith, is that we just need to make sure this log . . . thing . . . is filled out from now on. It's a bit of miscommunication, that's all. I'm sure he didn't mean to shout. Right, Cameron?"

Cameron looked at Andrew as if only just realizing he was there. "Yes," he said. "Yes, that's right. Tough week. Clara and I . . . Not that I want to get into all that business but . . . I'm sorry."

Andrew decided to ignore the Clara comment and quickly moved to settle things. "I'm happy to take on some of your workload this week to make up for it, Meredith."

Peggy was looking at him slightly curiously, perhaps equally as surprised as he was at him taking charge like this. It felt sort of liberating—for a moment he had a taste of what it would be like to send cold food back in a restaurant, or ask people to move down on the tube.

"Well," Meredith said. "It doesn't make up for not being able to go away. I was planning on going on a yoga retreat, so that will need rescheduling. Not ideal, as you can imagine. But yes, I am hugely snowed under, as it happens. So thanks, I suppose."

"Yoga, eh?" Peggy said, licking the lid of a yogurt she'd produced seemingly out of nowhere. "Downward dogs and all that bollocks?"

Andrew widened his eyes at her.

"I mean, good for the old joints and that, I'll bet," she said.

"And flexibility," Meredith said, glancing at Keith, who smirked and took another huge bite of his sandwich.

"I know what," Cameron said suddenly, with a startling return to his usual bright self. "How about I go out and buy us a cake?"

"A . . . cake?" Andrew said.

"Yes, Andrew. A cake. A big lovely cake. Right now. That's what you hardworking lot need." And before anyone could say anything else Cameron walked out, not even stopping to pick up his coat despite the torrential rain.

Keith sucked his fingers clean.

"Fifty quid says he's in the papers tomorrow morning."

Peggy rolled her eyes. "Don't say things like that," she said.

"I *do* beg your pardon," Keith said, in his best attempt at a snooty voice. Meredith giggled. "Besides," Keith went on, "if he's out the way maybe we keep our jobs."

Nobody, it seemed, had a response to this. There was just the sound of Keith giving his fingers one final clean.

Come on, come on, come on.

Andrew was pacing back and forth—as much as you *can* pace back and forth in a train vestibule. The train was scheduled to leave King's Cross at 9:04, and he and Peggy had arranged to meet on the concourse at 8:30. In retrospect, alarm bells should have rung when she'd said "eight thirty—or thereabouts."

He'd messaged her three times so far that morning:

Just on the concourse. Let me know when you get here—sent at 8:20.

It's platform 11. Meet you there?—sent at 8:50.

Are you near . . . ?—sent at 8:58.

He couldn't write what he really wanted to, namely, *WHERE IN GOD'S NAME ARE YOU??*, but he hoped the ellipsis would get the general gist across.

He planted his foot so that it was halfway out of the train door, ready to defy every fiber of his being and jam it open. He could just get off, of course, although they *had* bought specific tickets for this time that *were* nonrefundable—not that he cared about that sort of thing, *obviously*. He swore under his breath and dashed over to the luggage racks to retrieve his bag. Ideally he would have been traveling with an elegant little suitcase, the sort of thing you saw BBC4 travel documentary makers in white linen suits wheeling through Florence. But what he actually had was a great, cumbersome, bright purple backpack that at one time in his life he'd used to carry every single possession he had to his name. While he hadn't upgraded his bag (or bought a linen suit for that matter), he had spent far too much money on an extensive clothes overhaul: four new pairs of trousers, six new shirts, some leather brogues and, most daringly, a charcoal-gray blazer. On top of this he'd also had his quarterly haircut, choosing a more upmarket place than usual, and bought a bottle of the stinging lemon aftershave the barber had splashed unbidden on his cheeks, which made him smell like a sophisticated dessert. At the time, looking at himself in the barber's mirror, in his new garb and new haircut, he was pleasantly surprised at his reflection. Would it be too much of a stretch to think he looked handsome? Perhaps even—dare he say it—Sean Bean-esque? He had been secretly quite excited to see what Peggy might make of his new look, but by the time he got to the station the unfamiliarity of it all was actually making him feel even more self-conscious than usual. It was as if everyone in the station were judging him. *Well well well*, the man in Upper Crust seemed to be thinking, eyeing his jacket scornfully. *A bold fashion choice for a middle-aged man who still clearly uses a combined shower gel and shampoo.*

Andrew felt something itching at his hip, and realized to his embarrassment that he'd left a label on his shirt. He twisted the material around and began pulling and yanking at the label, until eventually it snapped off. He shoved it into his pocket and looked at his watch.

Come on, come on, come on.

There were two minutes before the train was scheduled to depart. Resignedly, he swung his rucksack onto his back, nearly falling over in the process. He took one final look down the platform. And there, miraculously, flanked by her two girls, waving tickets at the guard and hurrying through the barriers, was Peggy. The three of them were laughing, urging each other on. Peggy too wore a ludicrously bulky rucksack, loosely secured, which was wobbling violently from side to side as she ran. Her eyes scanned down the carriages until she saw him. "There's Andrew," he heard her say. "Come on, you two slowcoaches—run to Andrew!"

They were only feet away from Andrew now, and suddenly he was overcome with a desperate desire to stop and bottle the moment. To see Peggy rushing toward him like that, for him to be needed, to be an active participant in someone else's life, to think that maybe he was more than just a lump of carbon being slowly ushered toward an unvarnished coffin; the feeling was one of pure, almost painful happiness, like a desperate embrace squeezing air from his lungs, and it was then that the realization hit him: he might not know what the future held—pain and loneliness and fear might still yet grind him into dust—but simply feeling the possibility that things could change for him was a start, like feeling the first hint of warmth from kindling rubbed together, the first wisp of smoke.

CHAPTER 17

Andrew jammed the doors open, incurring both the anger of the guard on the platform and the unbridled tutting of passengers in the vestibule. Peggy frantically ushered the kids onto the train before jumping on herself, and Andrew released the doors.

"Well that's probably the most rebellious thing I've ever done," he said. "I imagine this is the same feeling you get after a skydive."

"What a hell-raiser you are," Peggy said, struggling to catch her breath. When she looked at him she seemed to do a double take. "Wow, you look . . ."

"What?" Andrew said, running a hand through his hair self-consciously.

"Nothing, just . . ." Peggy picked a stray bit of cotton from his blazer. "Different, that's all."

They held eye contact for a moment. Then the train began to pull away.

"We should find our seats," Peggy said.

"Yep. Good plan," Andrew said, and then, suddenly feeling rather devil-may-care: "Lead on Mac . . . lovely . . . duff."

To Andrew's great relief, Peggy had turned to her daughters, who were waiting patiently behind her, and didn't seem to have heard this. He decided to leave devil-may-careness for another day. Perhaps when he was dead.

"Kids, say hello to Andrew," Peggy said.

Andrew had been worried about meeting Peggy's girls, and had turned to the subforum for advice, waiting for a spirited but good-natured debate about the best way to replace valve gear pins from driving wheels to finish before bringing the conversation around to his nerves at meeting Peggy's children.

This might sound rather odd, **BamBam wrote,** but the best advice I can give is NOT to talk to them like they're children. None of that patronizing, slow-talking nonsense. They'll spot such bullsh*t a mile off. Just ask lots of questions and essentially treat them like you would an adult.

So with a general air of suspicion and mistrust, Andrew thought. Though he replied: Thanks, mate! and worried for two hours about the implications of his now being the sort of person who used the word "mate."

As it turned out, Peggy's eldest, Maisie, happily ignored them all for the duration of the journey—only lifting her head away from the book she was reading to ask where they were, or what a particular word meant. Her younger sister, Suze, on the other hand, conversed entirely through the medium of "would you rather" scenarios, which made things infinitely easier than Andrew was expecting. She had a twinkle in her eye that made it seem like she was constantly on the cusp of laughing, so Andrew was finding it hard to treat the questions with the gravitas they clearly warranted.

"Would you rather be a horse that can time-travel or a talking turd?" was the latest conundrum.

"Would it be okay for me to ask follow-up questions?" Andrew said. "That's what Peggy—your mum, I mean—and I normally do."

Suze yawned as she deliberated. "Yeahhh, okay," she said, apparently satisfied that this was aboveboard.

"Okay," Andrew said, suddenly aware that both Peggy and Suze were looking at him intently, and trying not to feel embarrassed. "Can the horse speak?"

"No," Suze said, "it's a horse."

"That is true," Andrew conceded. "But the *turd* can talk, though."

"So?"

Andrew didn't really have a response to that.

"The problem you've got here," Peggy said, "is that you're trying to apply logic to the question. Logic is not your friend here."

Suze nodded sagely. Next to her, Maisie closed her eyes and took a deep breath, frustrated at the constant distractions. Andrew made sure to lower his voice.

"Okay, I'm going to go with the horse."

"Obviously," Suze said, apparently baffled as to why it had taken Andrew so long to get there. She tore open a bag of lemon sherbets and, after briefly contemplating, offered the bag to Andrew.

As the train snaked into Newcastle, the Tyne Bridge sparkling in the sun, Peggy took out the photograph of Alan and "B."

"What do you reckon, kiddos. Think we're gonna find this lass?"

Maisie and Suze shrugged in unison.

"That seems about right," Andrew said.

"Oi," Peggy said, kicking him gently in the shin, "whose side are you on?"

———

Peggy's sister, Imogen, was, by her own admission, "a cuddler," and Andrew had no option but to submit to her bosomy bear hug. She drove them to her house in a car with an alarming amount of gaffer tape holding it together, with Andrew sitting in the back next to the girls feeling a bit like an awkward older brother.

Imogen had obviously been busy that morning as the kitchen was teeming with cakes, biscuits and puddings, many of which Andrew lacked the critical vocabulary to describe.

"I see you're catering for village fetes now," Peggy said.

"Oh give over, you all need fattening up," Imogen said. Andrew was glad that while cuddles were compulsory, pokes to the belly were apparently restricted to family.

Later that evening, with the kids in bed, Imogen, Peggy and Andrew settled down in the living room and half-watched a romcom, Imogen thankfully interrupting a dire scene involving bodily fluids to ask about Alan and the ducks.

"You've never seen anything like it, honest to god," Peggy said.

"Well, it's very sweet what you're doing," Imogen said, stifling a yawn. "I mean, you're both mental, obviously . . ."

Peggy started to make their case again. She was sitting with her legs tucked back to one side, her sweater slipped off her shoulder. Andrew felt an ache somewhere in the region of his stomach. It was then he glanced over and saw that Imogen was watching him. More specifically, she was watching *him* watching Peggy. He looked away and focused on the TV, glad the room was dim enough to hide his reddening cheeks. He got the impression that Imogen wasn't someone easily fooled, and just as he'd had that thought she cut across Peggy's questioning of the protagonist's Irish accent.

"So what does your wife make of your chances of finding this person, Andrew?" she said.

Well, what *would* she make of them?

"She hasn't said much about it, to be honest," he said.

"Interesting," Imogen said.

Andrew hoped that was the end of it, but then Imogen spoke up again.

"Surely she must have been curious, though?"

"*Imogen* . . . ," Peggy said.

"What?" Imogen said.

"I don't tend to talk too much about my work at home, to be honest," Andrew said, which *was* technically true, he supposed.

"How long have you two been together?" Imogen said.

Andrew kept his eyes on the screen.

"Oh, a long old time," he said.

"And how did you get together?"

Andrew scratched at the back of his head. He really wasn't in the mood for this.

"We met at university," he said, as casually as possible. "We were friends for a while—mainly bonding over our shared hatred of all the idiots on our course, or the ones who'd taken to wearing berets, at least." He took a sip of wine. He wasn't sure why, but he felt compelled to keep going. "She had this way of looking at me over the top of her glasses. Used to make me feel a bit faint. And I'd never met anyone I found it so easy to talk to. Anyway, we were at this party and she took me by the hand and led me away from all the noise and people and, well, that was that." Andrew looked at his hand. It was the strangest thing. He could practically feel the sensation of that firm grip, confidently pulling him out of the room.

"Ah, sweet," Imogen said. "And she wasn't particularly intrigued about you coming all this way . . . with Peggy," she added pointedly.

"Imogen!" Peggy snapped. "Don't be so bloody rude. You've just met the man."

"No, no, it's fine," Andrew said, keen that this didn't end up in an argument. Thankfully, a neat solution presented itself. "In actual fact, I better give Diane a ring now, if you'll excuse me." His left leg had gone numb from his sitting position, so he had to limp away to the guest bedroom as fast as he could, like an injured soldier retreating from no-man's-land. The room was freezing, the window having been left open on the latch. He wondered if he should actually fake the phone call in case anyone could hear him. Just come out with some generic stuff about how the journey had been, what he'd had for dinner—the sort of thing he imagined most people would say in real life.

In real life. He was going to get fucking committed for this. He slumped onto the bed. Out of nowhere, the tune came into his head—*Blue moon, you saw me standing alone*—and then came the feedback and static like a wave smashing against rock. He tried to shake it away, getting so desperate for it to end he found himself facedown on the bed, pounding the duvet with his fists, shouting into the pillow.

Eventually, the chaos subsided. He lay still in the resulting silence, fists clenched, short of breath, praying that his shouts hadn't traveled. He looked at his reflection, pale and tired, in the dressing table mirror, and suddenly he felt desperate to be back in the front room with a glass of wine in his hand and the rubbish telly on in the background and—even if half of it was suspicious about him—the company.

He wasn't sure what made him do it, but he found himself pausing outside the living room door, which was open just wide enough for him to hear Imogen and Peggy speaking in hushed tones.

"You really think his missus is fine with this?"

"Why wouldn't she be? She's away herself, remember. With her parents. They don't get on with Andrew, apparently."

"That's not what I meant, and you know it."

"What then?" Peggy hissed.

"Come off it, you really think he isn't interested in you?"

"I'm not answering that."

"Okay, well, are you interested in *him* then?"

". . . I'm not answering that either."

"I don't think you have to."

"Please can we just change the—"

"I know things are shite with Steve but this isn't the answer."

HOW NOT TO DIE ALONE

"You've no idea what things are like with Steve."

"Of course I do, I'm your sister. He's obviously up to his old tricks again. And the sooner you get out of that the better. It's just like Dad—constantly begging for forgiveness and saying it won't happen again. I can't believe you're being so naive."

"Don't. Just don't, okay?"

There was a pause, then Peggy spoke again.

"Look. It's so lovely being here. You know how much the girls adore you, how . . ."—her voice broke ever so slightly— ". . . how I do, too. I just want to relax for a few days, get myself together again. If things go the way I think they are—with Steve, with work—I need to be in a good frame of mind to deal with it all."

Another pause.

"Ah, pet, I'm sorry," Imogen said. "I just worry about you."

"I know, I know," Peggy said, her voice muffled by what Andrew guessed was another bear hug from Imogen.

"Peg?"

"Yeah?"

"Pass us the cookies."

"*You* pass *us* the cookies, they're equidistant."

"Are they bollocks," Imogen said, and Peggy let out a slightly tearful giggle.

Andrew retreated a few steps, both in an attempt to calm his thumping heart and to make his entrance seem more genuine.

"Hello hello," he said. Peggy was sitting on the sofa where he had been before so she could look at her phone, which was charging nearby, meaning he had to choose whether to sit next to her or Imogen. Peggy smiled at him as he hovered, the light from the TV showing the dampness in her eyes.

"Everything . . . okay?" he said.

"Oh, aye," Imogen said, patting the space next to her. "Sit yer arse down here."

Andrew was glad to have his mind made up for him, even if it meant a missed opportunity to be closer to Peggy.

"Let's finish these buggers off then," Imogen said, divvying up the remaining cookies.

"You get through okay?" Peggy said.

"Huh? Oh, yes. Thanks."

"Good-o," Imogen said. "The signal can be pretty patchy that side of the house."

"My luck must have been in," Andrew said.

It was then that his phone—which had been on the mantelpiece where he'd put it when he'd first arrived that afternoon—began to ring.

CHAPTER 18

*S*o, *yeah, I've got two phones. One's a work one that I got ages ago. I'm not sure if Cameron even knows about it so, you know, best keep shtum!"*

Andrew kept replaying his garbled explanation over and over in his mind. Neither Peggy nor Imogen had seemed to know what he was blathering on about, which just meant he carried on and on, digging an increasingly large hole. Thankfully, they'd continued to just look at him blankly, like two bored customs officials ignoring a foreign traveler's desperate attempts to explain their plight, and the climax of the romcom provided enough of a distraction for the conversation to move on.

Andrew had assumed that they would be going to Barter Books the next morning, but Peggy and Imogen had other plans. What followed over the next couple of days were boat trips to the Farne Islands, where Andrew was unceremoniously shat on by a puffin (much to Suze's delight), and blustery coastal walks punctuated by tea and cake pit stops (much to Imogen's delight), followed by delicious dinners back at Imogen's and two occasions where Peggy fell asleep on Andrew's shoulder (much to Andrew's delight).

Alone in the guest room, he thought of the conversation he'd eavesdropped on.

"Okay, well, are you interested in him *then?"*

". . . I'm not answering that either."

"Interested in him." Could that have meant anything other than romantic interest? Maybe it was from a purely anthropological point of view—that Peggy was planning to make scientific field notes: *A squat specimen, frequently observed making a twat of himself.* Either way, Peggy had refused to answer the question, and Andrew had watched enough episodes of *Newsnight* to know this meant she was avoiding telling the truth. He only wished Imogen had gone full hostile BBC interviewer on her.

———

Finally, the following morning they headed to Barter Books. Andrew got the sense that Peggy had been delaying the visit not because she'd somehow lost interest, but because she was scared that it was going to end in failure.

The kids had stayed behind with Imogen, who had promised to make them a cake so chocolatey it would send Bruce Bogtrotter into a diabetic coma. Peggy had taken Imogen's Astra, Imogen explaining all the car's various problems and how to cope with them, many of which involved punching things and swearing.

"Bastard," Peggy grumbled, yanking the gear stick violently back and forth and making a joke about her first boyfriend's eyes watering that caused Andrew to wind down the window for a moment.

They passed a sign saying they were fifteen miles from Alnwick.

"I'm feeling a bit nervous," Andrew said. "How about you?"

"Dunno. Yeah. Sort of," Peggy said, but her attention was on the rearview mirror as they merged onto a busy road.

The more miles they chewed up, the more fraught Andrew felt, because the closer they got to the bookshop, the closer they were to their adventure's ending. Most likely they'd just be returning home, deflated with defeat, and Alan would be buried with just them and a disinterested vicar for company. Then it would be back to the daily grind.

They passed another sign for Alnwick. Five miles, now. Someone had somewhat unimaginatively graffitied the word "shit" onto the sign in angry red. Andrew was reminded of something he'd seen coming back from a rare school trip to the Ashmolean Museum in Oxford. He remembered the evening sky being scorched pink, his eyes following the telegraph wires silhouetted against it as if they were a blank musical score, when he noticed the letters painted white and bold on a fence in the distance: "Why Do I Do This Every Day?" The memory had stayed with him despite his not understanding its commuter-baiting message at the time. It was as if his subconscious was saying, *This won't mean much to you at the moment because you're too young and your major concern is whether Justin Stanmore is going to Chinese-burn you again, but just give it thirty years or so and its significance will really hit home.*

He sat forward.

Maybe he'd just tell Peggy everything. Now. Here. In an overheating Vauxhall Astra on a dual carriageway.

He shifted in his seat, half exhilarated, half terrified at the possibility. Everything could be out in the open. Not just about his growing feelings for her, but about the big lie, too. Peggy would hate him, maybe never even talk to him again, but it would end just . . . *this*. This relentless misery—of still clinging on to something that barely provided him solace anymore. The realization came to him like a radio signal finding its way through static: a lie can only exist in opposition to the truth, and the truth was the only thing that could free him of his pain.

"Why are you wriggling around so much?" Peggy said. "You're like my old dog dragging its arse along the floor."

"Sorry," Andrew said. "It's just . . ."

"What?"

". . . Nothing."

————

Andrew lost Peggy almost as soon as they walked into the bookshop, his focus drawn immediately to what was happening five feet above his head. A beautiful, dark green engine (an Accucraft Victorian NA Class, if he wasn't very much mistaken) was sliding effortlessly around the tracks positioned above the book stacks. The aisles beyond were bridged by signs bearing lines of poetry. The nearest read:

Yon rising Moon that looks for us again / How oft hereafter will she wax and wane.

The train flashed past again, a soft breeze rippling in its wake.

"I'm in heaven," Andrew whispered to himself. If anything was going to slow his pulse back to normal after what had nearly just happened in the car, it was this. He was aware of someone standing next to him. He glanced to his side and saw a tall man in a gray cardigan, his hands held behind his back, looking up at the train. He and Andrew exchanged nods.

"Like what you see?" the man said. Andrew had only ever heard this phrase used by bolshy brothel madams in period dramas, but despite its seeming so out of context, at the same time he really *did* like what he was seeing.

"It's mesmerizing," he said. The man nodded, eyes briefly closing, as if to say: *You're home now, old friend.*

Andrew took a deep breath, feeling properly calmed now, and turned slowly on the spot so he could take in the rest of the place. He certainly wasn't the sort of person who would use the word "vibe," but if he *were*, he'd have said Barter Books' vibe was one he was very much "down with," to borrow one of Sally's old phrases. It was so serene, so quiet. People browsed the shelves with a sense of reverence, their voices lowered. When someone took a book off a shelf they did so with the delicacy of an archaeologist bringing ancient pottery out of the soil. Andrew had read that the shop's claim to fame was that it was where the original "Keep Calm and Carry On" poster had been unearthed. And while it had spawned thousands of annoying variations (Meredith had a mug in the office with the slogan "Keep Calm and Do Yoga" written on it, possibly the most prosaic sentence ever committed to ceramic), here it felt like the perfect emblem.

But they weren't here for the atmosphere. Andrew found Peggy sitting low in a chair that looked almost obscenely comfy, her hands linked behind her head, a contented smile on her face.

"Argh," she moaned as Andrew approached. "I suppose we better get on with this, then?"

"I think we had better," Andrew said.

Peggy looked at him determinedly and held out her hands. At first Andrew stared at them uncomprehendingly, then snapped into action and pulled Peggy to her feet. They stood side by side, shoulders touching, facing the polite queue by the tills.

"Right," Andrew said, rubbing his hands together to suggest industry. "So are we just going to go up there and ask them whether a 'B' works here?"

"Unless you've got a better idea?" Peggy said.

Andrew shook his head. "Do you want to do the talking?"

"Nope," Peggy said. "You?"

"Not particularly, if I'm honest with you."

Peggy pursed her lips. "Rock Paper Scissors?"

Andrew turned so he was facing her. "Why not."

"One, two, three."

Paper. Paper.

"One, two, three."

Rock. Rock.

They went again. Andrew thought about going scissors, but at the last minute he changed it to rock. This time, Peggy went paper. She closed her hand over his.

"Paper covers rock," she said quietly.

They were standing close now, hands still touching. It felt for a second like the hubbub had died away, that all eyes were on them, that even the books on the shelves were holding their breath. Then Peggy suddenly dropped her hand. "Oh my god," she whispered. "Look."

Andrew forced himself to turn around so that they were side by side once more. And there at the tills, cup of tea in hand, glasses around her neck on a chain, was a woman with green eyes and frizzy gray hair. Peggy dragged Andrew by the arm over to the waiting room café.

"That's definitely her, right?" she said.

Andrew shrugged, not wanting to get Peggy's hopes up. "It could be," he said.

Peggy manhandled him once more, this time out of the way of an elderly couple who were slowly carrying trays laden with scones and mugs of tea over to a table. Once settled, the man set about spreading cream onto his scone with a trembling hand. His wife looked at him askance.

"What?" the man said.

"Cream before jam? Ya daft apeth."

"That's the way it's supposed to be."

"Is it heck. We have this argument every time. It's the other way round."

"Nonsense."

"It isn't nonsense!"

"It bloody is."

Peggy rolled her eyes and gently prodded Andrew forward. "Come on," she said. "We've buggered about far too much already."

As they made their way toward the counter, Andrew felt his heart starting to thump faster and faster. It was only when they reached the woman and she looked up from her crossword that Andrew realized Peggy had taken his hand. The woman put down her pen and asked in the soft yet slightly raspy voice of a smoker how she could help.

"This is going to sound like a slightly strange question," Peggy said.

"Don't worry, love. I've been asked some very strange questions in here, believe me. Belgian chap a few months ago asked me whether we sold books about bestiality. So fire away."

Peggy and Andrew laughed slightly robotically.

"So," Peggy said. "We just wanted to ask, well, whether your name begins with 'B.'"

The woman smiled quizzically.

"Is that a trick question?" she said.

Andrew felt Peggy tighten her grip on his hand.

"No," she said.

"In that case, yes it does," the woman said. "I'm Beryl. Have I sold someone a dodgy book or something?"

"No, nothing like that," Peggy said, glancing at Andrew.

This was his cue to take the photograph from his pocket and hand it over. The woman took it from him and there was a flash of recognition in her eyes.

"Blimey," she said, looking at them in turn. "I think this calls for another cup of tea."

– CHAPTER 19 –

Beryl responded to the news of Alan's death with a short, sad exhalation, like a week-old birthday balloon finally admitting defeat.

Andrew had only ever given news to relatives on the phone, never face-to-face. Seeing Beryl's reaction in person was a very uncomfortable experience. She asked him the questions he'd been expecting—how had Alan died, who had found him, where and when was the funeral going to be—but he got the sense she was holding back about something. And then, of course, there was the other thing . . .

"Ducks?"

"Thousands of them," Andrew said, pouring tea into their cups.

Peggy showed Beryl Alan's note about feeding the ducks on the back of the photograph. "We assumed it was something to do with this."

Beryl smiled, but her eyes started to water too, and she reached into her sleeve and retrieved a hanky to dab them dry.

"I remember that day. It was miserable weather. As we were walking to our usual bench we saw an ice-cream van parked on the side of the road. The bloke inside looked so depressed we went and bought a 99 each just to cheer the poor bugger up. We ate it before we'd had our sandwiches—it felt so decadent!"

She lifted her mug to her lips with both hands and her glasses momentarily steamed up.

"Do you remember having the picture taken?" Peggy asked.

"Oh yes," Beryl said, wiping her glasses with her hanky. "We wanted a snap of us in the shop because that's where we first met. It took Alan about ten visits to pluck up the courage to talk to me, you know. I've never seen someone spending so long pretending to look at books on Yorkshire farm machinery of the eighteenth century. At first I thought he might just really love farming, or Yorkshire—or both—but then I realized he was only standing there because it was the best way to keep sneaking glances at me. Once I saw him holding a book about seed drills upside down. That was the day he finally came over and said hello."

"And you became an item straightaway?" Peggy said.

"Oh no, not for a long time," Beryl said. "The timing was rubbish. I'd just divorced my husband and it hadn't been the easiest of rides. Looking back now I don't know why I made such a fuss about waiting. It just seemed like I should pause for the dust to settle a bit. Alan said he understood that I needed time, but that didn't stop him coming in and pretending to still care about bloody farming for the next six weeks, sneaking over to say hello whenever there was a gap between customers."

"Six weeks?!" Peggy said.

"Every day," Beryl said. "Even when I had five days off for tonsillitis he still came in, despite my boss telling him I was going to be off for the rest of the week. Eventually, we had our first date. Tea and iced buns in this very café."

They were interrupted by one of the staff, who was noisily clearing away crockery from the adjacent table. She and Beryl exchanged slightly frosty smiles. "She's the worst, that one," Beryl said when the woman was out of earshot, without providing further explanation.

"But you and Alan were together properly after that?" Peggy probed.

"Yes, we were inseparable actually," Beryl said. "Alan is—oh, I suppose I should say *was*—a carpenter. His workshop was in his house just down the road, near the little cemetery. I moved in just after Christmas. I was fifty-two. He was sixty but you'd never have known it. He could have passed for a much younger man. He had these great big strong legs like tree trunks."

Andrew and Peggy looked at each other. In the end, Beryl realized what the unspoken question was.

"I suppose you're wondering why we aren't still together."

"Please don't feel obliged to tell us," Andrew said.

"No, no—it's fine."

Beryl composed herself, polishing her glasses again.

"It was all down to my relationship with my ex-husband. We'd got married when we were twenty-one. Kids, still, really. And I think we both knew as soon as we came home on our wedding night and gave each other a chaste little peck on the cheek that we didn't properly love each other. We stuck it out for years but eventually I couldn't stand it anymore and I decided to end it. And I made a decision then and there"—she rapped her knuckles on the table for emphasis—"that if I were to ever find someone else to share my life with it would have to be for love and nothing else. I wasn't going to settle for the sake of it being the done thing, or just for companionship. And at the first sign of feeling like we were going through the motions, that we'd fallen out of love, that would be it. Bish, bash, bosh. I'd be out."

"And that's what happened with Alan?" Peggy said.

Beryl took another sip of tea and replaced the mug carefully on its saucer.

"We were very much in love to start," she said. She eyed Andrew mischievously. "You might want to cover your ears for this part, but we practically spent the first few years in bed. That's the thing with someone who works with their hands. Very skilled, you see? Anyway, aside from *that* side of things, for a long time we were very happy. Even though his family had buggered off a long time before, and mine had never approved of the divorce, it didn't matter. It just felt like me and him against the world, you know? But then, after a while, Alan started to change. It was subtle at first. He'd say he was too tired to work, or he'd go for days at a time without shaving or getting out of his pajamas. Occasionally I'd find him—" She broke off and cleared her throat.

Peggy leaned across the table and put her hand on Beryl's. "It's okay," she said, "you don't have to . . ." But Beryl shook her head and patted Peggy's hand to show she was okay to continue.

"Occasionally, I'd find him sitting cross-legged on the living room floor, back against the sofa, just looking out into the garden through the French windows. Not reading. Not listening to the radio. Just sitting there."

Andrew thought of his mother in the dark of her bedroom. Inert. Hidden away. Unable to face the world.

"He was a proud old sod," Beryl said. "Never would have admitted to me that he was struggling with whatever it was. And I could never find the right words, or the right moment, to ask him about it all. Then his back went. Whether it was psychosomatic or what I don't know, but he had to sleep in another room because otherwise he'd disturb me getting up—or so he said. Then one evening we were having tea, watching some rubbish on the telly, and out of nowhere he turned to me and said: 'You remember what you told me right after we met, about what you'd do if you stopped loving the person you were with?'

"'Yes,' I said.

"'Do you still believe that?' he said.

"'Yes, I do,' I said. And I *did*. I should have said something reassuring, of course, but I just assumed he knew I still loved him as much as I always had. I asked him whether he was okay but he just kissed me on the top of my head and went off to do the washing up. I was worried but I thought he was just having one of his difficult days. The next morning I went off to work as usual, but when I got home he wasn't there. And there was a note. I can still remember holding that piece of paper, my hands shaking like mad. He'd written that he knew I didn't love him anymore. That he didn't want to put me through any pain. He'd just gone. Never left an address, never left a phone number. Nothing. I tried to find him, of course. But as you know there were no relatives to get in touch with, and he didn't have any friends I knew of. I did actually look into getting a whatchamacallit, a private investigator, but the thought always dogged me that maybe he'd just lied, that he'd run off with some other lass. Looking at this though"—she picked up the photograph—"and hearing about this duck business . . . Well, you tell me—" At this, a sob escaped her, and she clasped both hands to her chest. "Maybe I should have tried harder after all."

————

After they'd made sure Beryl was okay, with promises to be in touch soon, Andrew and Peggy emerged from the shop like two people leaving a cinema: blinking into the sunlight, thoughts consumed by the story they'd just been told.

They stood in the car park and checked their phones. Andrew was really just scrolling up and down his short list of existing texts—offers from pizza companies he'd never ordered from, PPI scams, work nonsense. He couldn't shake the desperate sadness of Beryl's story.

Peggy was gazing into the middle distance. An eyelash had fallen to her cheek, looking like the smallest of fractures on a piece of porcelain. Somewhere nearby, a car horn sounded with one sharp blast and Andrew reached out and took Peggy's hand. She looked at him with surprise.

"Let's go for a walk," Andrew said.

They left the car park and made their way toward the town center, hand in hand. Andrew hadn't planned to go this way, but it just felt right, as if they were being drawn along by an invisible force. They walked along the high street, weaving past parents with pushchairs and a group of tourists who'd slowed to a stop in the street as if their batteries had run down, then on further to Alnwick Castle, with its red and yellow Northumberland flags strained taut by the breeze. Without exchanging a word they made their way around the castle to the surrounding field, newly cut grass collecting on their shoes. Down, further, past kids throwing a dog-eared tennis ball around and pensioners resting on picnic tables watching the moody clouds closing in on the sun. Down, further still, along a path carved out by footfall, until finally they reached the river and found a solitary bench half-covered in moss at the water's edge. They sat and listened to the gurgling water and watched the reeds struggling against its flow. Peggy was sitting upright, her hands in her lap, one leg crossed over the other. They were both very still, at odds with the rushing river, like the model figures Andrew arranged on his living room floor. But even in that stillness, there was movement. Peggy's foot was stirring almost imperceptibly every second or so, like a metronome. It was, Andrew realized, not because of tension or nervousness, but purely because of the pulse of her heart. And suddenly he was gripped by possibility once again: that as long as there was that movement in someone, then there was the capacity to love. And now his heart was beating faster and faster, as if the power of the river were pushing blood through his veins, urging him to act. He felt Peggy stir.

"So," she said, the faintest of tremors in her voice. "Quick question. With scones, do you go with jam or cream first?"

Andrew considered the question.

"I'm not sure it really matters," he said. "Not in the grand scheme of things." Then he leaned across, took Peggy's face in his hands, and kissed her.

Somewhere, he could have sworn he heard a duck quack.

CHAPTER 20

It was fair to say, if you were to really drill down and examine the data, and then draw conclusions *from* said data, that Andrew was, to a certain extent, drunk. He was dancing around Imogen's living room, with a giddy and giggling Suze, singing along raucously to Ella's "Happy Talk." They were, by now, the firmest of friends.

He still couldn't quite believe what had happened earlier that day. The moment he'd taken Peggy's hand and set off without knowing where he was going, it had felt like an out-of-body experience. The memory was somehow sharp and blurry all at once. They'd sat for a long time on the bench, their foreheads touching gently, their eyes closed, until Peggy broke the silence. "Well now. I'm not entirely sure I saw this coming."

As they made their way back to the car Andrew felt like he'd been drugged. He spent the entire journey home trying to stop grinning. He watched the fields flash by, getting the occasional glimpse of the sea, sunlight shimmering on its surface. A sunny August day in England. Perfection.

"That was an eventful day, then," Peggy said when they were back at Imogen's, as if they'd just been for a ramble and come across an unusual bird's nest on the ground.

"Oh, I dunno. Pretty run-of-the-mill stuff for me all told," Andrew said. He leaned across to kiss her but she laughed and gently nudged him away. "Give over, what if someone sees? And before you say anything, earlier it would just've been a pensioner on a bench, not . . ." *Imogen or the kids*, was the unspoken thought. The spell might not have been completely broken, but it was certainly damaged. Andrew was about to get out of the car but Peggy made an exaggerated show of looking around before leaning over and giving him a peck on the cheek, before quickly fixing her makeup in the mirror. It was all Andrew could do not to skip up the drive, Morecambe and Wise–style.

Dancing around the living room to Ella would have to do instead. Maisie, who up until now had been summarily ignoring them in favor of her novel, waited until the song was over before asking who the singer was. Andrew put his hands together as if in solemn prayer. "That, my friend, was Ella Fitzgerald. The greatest singer there's ever been."

Maisie gave the subtlest nod of approval. "I like her," she said, with the tone of someone weighing in calmly to settle a fierce debate, before going back to her book.

Andrew was about to find a new tune (he was in the mood for "Too Darn Hot," next) and, more importantly, get another lager from Imogen's booze fridge in the garage, when Peggy appeared at the living room door and asked the girls to come and help her lay the table.

Andrew retrieved a fresh beer and flopped down onto the sofa, allowing himself a moment to take everything in. He let the music wash over him, listened to the animated voices coming down the hallway, and breathed in the delicious cooking smells drifting in from the kitchen. All of it was intoxicating. He decided this should be part of some governmental scheme: that everyone should be legally entitled to have at least one evening a year where they could sink down into soft cushions, their stomachs rumbling in anticipation of ravioli and red wine, listening to chatter from another room, and feel for the briefest flicker of time that they mattered to someone. It was only now he could truly see how deluded he'd been to think the fantasy he'd created could be anything more than the weakest facsimile of the real thing.

After he'd listened to "Too Darn Hot," Andrew headed to the kitchen and asked whether there was anything he could do.

"You could give the girls a hand," Peggy said. Andrew saluted back, but Peggy had turned away and missed it. She and Imogen were having to chop, peel and stir in close proximity, but, as if carefully choreographed, they managed to avoid getting in each other's way. Andrew, on the other hand, now fully buzzed by the beer, quickly became an increasingly frustrating presence as he tried to help. There was something about being in another person's kitchen that meant everything he was looking for seemed to be in a totally illogical place. So when he confidently opened the cutlery drawer all that was inside was a warranty for a sandwich toaster, and the cupboard that should have housed glasses contained just a novelty eggcup in the shape of a hollow-backed pig, and some birthday cake candles. "Andrew, Andrew," Imogen said with an air of frustration as he tried to pull open a false drawer next to her, "glasses top left, knives and forks here, water jug over there, salt and pepper here." She pointed out each item like a football manager on the touchline indicating who the defenders should be marking.

Table now laid, Andrew sat down at it with a fresh beer and some Pringles Suze had brought him (two in her own mouth poking out to make it look like she had a duck's beak) and drank in the atmosphere. The kitchen, like the rest of the house, was well kept but with lots of character—a bunch of flowers in a quirky vase on the windowsill, a print on the wall with a picture of a woman cooking and sipping from a glass with the caption "I love cooking with wine—sometimes I even put it in the food." The windows had steamed up to reveal handprints and a wonkily drawn heart.

"I never know whether you're supposed to eat the top bits of peppers," Peggy said to no one in particular. "Don't want to make people ill but don't want to be wasteful either. I end up walking to the bin, nibbling on it till I get there, then chucking what's left away."

Jesus Christ, Andrew thought, unable to stifle a hiccup. *I think I'm in love.*

———

As the old drinking adage goes: beer before wine, then you'll be fine; *six* beers before *half a bottle* of wine, then you'll be dizzy and believe the story you want to tell to be much more important than anyone else's.

"Yeah, so, yeah," Andrew slurred, ". . . yeah."

"You were in the kitchen?" Imogen prompted.

"Yes, Imogen, we were! But then we thought we'd check the bedroom because that's where they usually leave their money if they have any—cash, you know, rolled up in socks or in a Tesco's bag shoved under the mattress. So anyway, anyway, we went in there—didn't we, Peggy?"

"Mmm-hmm."

"And the impression we'd had up till then was that the man had been fairly quiet, fairly normal . . ."

"Andrew, I'm not sure this is okay . . . the kids . . . ?"

"Ohhh it'll be fine!"

Peggy took his hand under the table and squeezed it firmly. It would only be much later that he'd realize this wasn't an affectionate gesture but an attempt to get him to stop talking.

"So, the bedroom's bare apart from a telly, and I accidentally turn it on and lo and behold—"

"Andrew, let's talk about something else, eh?"

"—he'd been watching a dirty film called *Quim Up North*!"

Peggy had spoken over him, so the impact of the punch line was deadened.

"Come on, girls, shall we play cards or something?" Imogen said. "Maisie, you can help teach Suze."

While Maisie went to get the cards, Andrew—as is the preserve of the drunken—suddenly decided it was imperative he be as helpful as possible while doing so ostentatiously enough to be praised for it.

"I'll do the washing up," he announced determinedly, as if volunteering to go back into a burning building to rescue some children. After a while Peggy came up to him at the sink as he struggled to pull on washing-up gloves.

"Oi, you, you lightweight," she said in a low voice. She was smiling, but there was a firmness to her voice that went some way to sobering Andrew up.

"Sorry," he said. "Got a bit carried away. It's just . . . you know. I'm feeling quite . . . happy."

Peggy went to say something but stopped herself. She squeezed his shoulder instead. "Why don't you go and relax in the living room for a bit? You're the guest, you shouldn't be doing the washing up."

Andrew would have protested, but Peggy was standing closer to him now, her hand on his arm with her thumb gently caressing it, and he very much wanted to do exactly as she asked.

The girls and Imogen had briefly abandoned cards to see how fast they could play pat-a-cake, pat-a-cake, baker's man, their hands a blur, collapsing into giggles as they finally lost coordination. Andrew heard the tail end of their conversation as he left.

"That pasta we just ate now," Maisie said.

"Yes, pet," Imogen said.

"Was it *al dente?*"

"I think it was Jamie Oliver, love," Imogen said, cackling at her own joke. *At least I'm not the only one who's pissed, then*, Andrew thought. He slumped onto the sofa, feeling exhausted all of a sudden. All of this euphoria was very tiring, but it didn't stop him from wanting the day to go on forever. He just needed to rest his eyes for a minute.

———

In the dream, he was in an unfamiliar house, dressed for a property search in his regular protective suit, except it was beginning to feel suffocatingly tight against his body. He couldn't remember what he was supposed to be searching for; he had a feeling it was to do with some documents. "Peggy, what are we looking for again?" he shouted. But her reply was muffled, and though he looked in every room he couldn't seem to find her. And then he was lost—and more and more rooms kept appearing, so that every time he crossed a threshold he was in a space he didn't recognize, and he was calling Peggy's name and asking for help and his protective suit was starting to constrict him to the point where he thought he might pass out. And there was music—jarringly out of tune, so deep it was vibrating through his body. The song was Ella's, but her voice sounded like it was playing at half speed. *Bluuuue moooooon, you saw me standing aloooonnnne.* Andrew tried to shout for someone to turn it off, to play anything—anything—but that, but no sound came out of his mouth. And then suddenly he was in his own flat and Peggy was in the corner, her back to him, but as he approached and screamed her name, the music getting louder all the time, he saw it wasn't Peggy at all, but someone with brown, wavy hair, a pair of orange-rimmed glasses in her hand at her side, and then the glasses had slipped through her fingers and were falling in slow motion toward the floor—

"Andrew, are you okay?"

Andrew opened his eyes. He was on the sofa and Peggy was leaning over him, her hand cupping one side of his face.

Is this real?

"Sorry—I didn't know whether to wake you, but you looked like you were having a nightmare," Peggy said.

Andrew's eyelids flickered and closed.

"You don't have to say sorry," he mumbled. ". . . Never . . . ever have to say sorry. You're the one who's saved me."

CHAPTER 21

Trust me, it'll help."

Andrew took the can of Irn-Bru from Peggy with a trembling hand and took a tentative sip, tasting what seemed like fizzy metal.

"Thanks," he croaked.

"Nothing like a four-and-a-half-hour trip on a train that smells of wee to cure a hangover," Peggy said.

Suze nudged Maisie and gestured for her to take her earphones out. "Mum said 'wee,'" she said. Maisie rolled her eyes and went back to her book.

Andrew was never drinking again, that much he knew. His head was throbbing, and every time the train took a bend he felt a horrible pang of nausea. But far worse were the incomplete flashbacks from the previous night. What had he said? What had he done? He remembered Peggy and Imogen looking annoyed. Was that the point when he'd started a sentence three times with increasing volume and urgency ("I was . . . So, anyway, I was . . . *I WAS*") because people didn't seem to be concentrating? He'd at least managed to get to bed rather than sleeping on the sofa, but—*shit*—he remembered now that Peggy had practically had to drag him there. Luckily, she hadn't lingered there long enough for him to embarrass himself further. Ideally now they'd be re-creating the spirit of excitement and adventure of the journey up there, but Andrew was having to focus all his attention on not puking himself entirely inside out. To make matters worse, there was a small child sitting directly behind him whose favorite pastime appeared to be kicking Andrew's chair while asking his father a series of increasingly complex questions:

"Dad, Dad?"

"Yes?"

"Why is the sky blue?"

"Well . . . it's because of the atmosphere."

"What's a atmosphere?"

"It's the bit of air and gas that sort of stops us from getting burned by the sun."

"So what's the sun made of?"

"I . . . Um . . . why don't we find you your bear, Charlie? Where's Billy the Bear gone, eh?"

I hope Billy the Bear is a nickname for a strong sedative, Andrew thought. He tried to will himself into unconsciousness, but it was useless. He noticed Peggy was looking at him, arms folded, her expression unreadable. He scrunched his eyes shut, Peggy's face slowly fading away into nothing. He fell into a horribly uncomfortable pattern of falling asleep but almost immediately jolting awake. Eventually he managed to doze, but when he woke, expecting to be south of Birmingham at least, it turned out they were stationary, having broken down before they'd even gotten to York.

"We apologize for the delay," the driver said. "We appear to be experiencing some sort of technical delay." Apparently unaware that he hadn't turned off the loudspeaker, the driver then treated them all to a peek behind the magician's curtain: "John? Yeah, we're fucked. Have to chuck everyone off at York if we can even get a shunt there."

After said shunt finally materialized, Andrew and Peggy hauled their bags off the train along with a few hundred other passengers traveling back that Saturday whose phasers were all set to "grumble," only to be elevated to "strongly worded letter" when they were told it would be forty minutes before a replacement train could get there.

The brief sleep had revived Andrew enough that he could now, with horrible clarity, consciously consider how much he'd ruined things. He was just deciding how to carefully broach the possibility that maybe he and Peggy could possibly *have a little chat, about, you know, everything*, when Peggy returned from the café with crisps and apples for the girls and coffees for her and Andrew and said, "Right, we need to have a word."

She bent down and kissed the top of Suze's head.

"Won't be a minute, pet. We're just going to stretch our legs, but we'll not go far."

She and Andrew walked a little way along the platform.

"So," Peggy said.

"Look," Andrew said quickly, cursing himself for butting in but desperate to get his apology in as soon as he could. "I'm so sorry for last night—like you said I'm clearly a lightweight. And I know, especially, that to do that when that's what Steve's been doing is so stupid of me, and I just promise to you now—on my life—that it won't happen again."

Peggy swapped her coffee from one hand to the other.

"Firstly," she said, "getting tipsy on a few beers and being a bit of a tit doesn't make you Steve. It makes you a bit of a tit. Steve's got an actual problem." She blew on her coffee. "I haven't told you this, but it turns out he's been sacked for drinking at work. He had a bottle of vodka in a drawer, the moron."

"Jesus, that's awful," Andrew said.

"He's getting help, so he claims."

Andrew chewed his lip. "Do you believe him?"

"I don't really know. In fact, to be truthful, the only thing I can be sure about, with all that's happening at the moment, is that everything's a huge mess and there's no way someone's not going to get hurt." The jaunty musical jingle that precedes an announcement sounded and everyone on the platform pricked up their ears, but it was just warning them of a train that was not stopping there.

"I know that things are complicated," Andrew said, because that seemed like something people said in these sorts of conversations.

"They are," Peggy said. "And you can see that maybe my head's been a bit all over the place recently. That maybe I haven't been thinking straight, and that I've been a bit, well . . . reckless."

Andrew swallowed, hard.

"You mean with you and me?"

Peggy scrunched her hair tight at the back of her head, then let it go.

"Listen, I'm not saying I regret what happened yesterday, not for one second, and I honestly mean that."

There was a "but" coming. Andrew could sense it hurtling toward him quicker than the approaching train.

"But . . . the thing is . . ." As Peggy grasped for what to say next there came the familiar two-tone blast from the onrushing train, warning people to stand back. "I just think," Peggy said, stepping closer to Andrew, her mouth close to his ear to make herself heard over the noise of the train that was now tearing toward them, "that I don't want you to get carried away, and that this should just be something lovely that happened. A one-off. Because meeting you and becoming friends has been such a wonderful, unexpected thing . . . but friends is all we can be."

The train thundered past and disappeared into the tunnel. Andrew wished, very much, that he were on it.

"Does that make sense?" Peggy said, taking a step back.

"Yeah, sure," Andrew said, waving his hand in what he hoped was a casually dismissive way. Peggy took him by the hand.

"Andrew, please don't be upset."

"I'm not upset. Honestly. Not in the slightest."

He could tell from the way Peggy was looking at him that this pretense was pointless. His shoulders slumped.

"It's just . . . I really feel like we've got something, here. Can't we at least give it a chance?"

"But it's not as easy as that, is it?" Peggy said. Andrew had never felt so pathetically desperate. But he had to keep going, had to keep trying.

"No, you're right. But it's not impossible. We could get divorced, couldn't we? That's an option. It'll be hard—obviously—with the kids and everything, but we would work it out. Find a way to be a family."

Peggy put a hand up to her mouth, fingers splayed across her lips. "How can you be so naive?" she said. "In what universe does that happen so smoothly, so quickly, with all the logistics sorted and none of the fucking pain of it all? We're not teenagers, Andrew. There are consequences."

"I'm getting ahead of myself, I know. But yesterday has to count for something, right?"

"Of course it does, but . . ." Peggy bit her lip and took a moment to compose herself. "I have to think of the girls, and that means making sure I am in the best possible state of mind so that I'm there for them whatever."

Andrew went to speak but Peggy cut across him.

"*And*, at the moment, given what I've been going through with Steve, what I really need—even if this is hard to hear—is an understanding friend with a good heart, who's there to support me. Someone honest, that I can trust."

They had been promised a replacement train, but in reality this just meant they were forced to cram onto the next service, which was already full. It was an every-man-for-himself affair, but Andrew managed to get into position by a door to let Peggy and the girls onto the train first, before some opportunists snuck on before he could. In the end, with no hope of reaching the others, he was forced to perch uncomfortably on his stupid purple rucksack in the vestibule. The toilet door opposite was malfunctioning, perpetually sliding open and shut and letting out a cocktail of piss and chemical smells. Next to him, two teenagers with an iPad were watching a film where old ladies played by grotesquely made-up men farted and fell into cakes, all of which the teenagers observed without a flicker of emotion.

When they finally reached King's Cross and traipsed off the train, Andrew realized he'd lost his ticket. He didn't even bother to fight his case, instead shelling out more money on the new fare so they'd let him through. At the other side of the barrier, Suze wore the telltale creased face of a grumpy child after a long journey, but to Andrew's surprise, when she saw him she ran over and reached her arms up to hug him good-bye. Maisie opted for a formal but still affectionate handshake. As the girls bickered about who deserved the remaining strawberry bonbon, Peggy approached Andrew warily, as if he might try to carry on their earlier conversation. Sensing this, Andrew managed a reassuring smile and Peggy relaxed and leaned in to hug him. Andrew went to let go but Peggy took him by the hands. "We shouldn't forget, in all of this, that we actually found Beryl!" she said. "That was the reason for the trip after all."

"Absolutely," Andrew said. It was too painful, this intimacy. He decided to pretend his phone was vibrating, apologizing and backing away with one finger pressed to his free ear as if to block out the noise of the station. He made for a pillar, still holding the phone up to his ear and mouthing silently to nobody, as he watched Peggy and the girls walk away until they were lost in the crowd.

———————

Later, he stood outside his shabby building, which had seemingly aged ten years in the last week, and considered finding a pub or somewhere else where he could sit and pretend for another few hours at least that he wasn't back home. He thought back to how uncharacteristically rushed he'd been when he'd left the house, feeling jarred by the change in routine but dizzy with excitement at spending so much time with Peggy. He'd barely had time to turn off his PC before—weighed down by his backpack—he'd hurled himself down the stairs and out of the building.

Eventually he resigned himself to going indoors, into the shared hallway with its familiar scent of his neighbor's perfume, the scuff marks on the wall, and the flickering light.

He was about to unlock his front door when he became aware of a noise apparently coming from the other side. God, surely it wasn't a burglar? Gritting his teeth, he swung his bag up in front of him to make an improvised shield, unlocked the door, and threw it open.

Standing there in the semidarkness, his heart pounding, he realized that the sound was coming from the record player in the far corner. In his haste to leave he must not have turned it off properly, so the needle was skipping, and the same note was stuttering away on a loop, over and over and over again.

– CHAPTER 22 –

His name was Warren, he was fifty-seven years old, and it had taken eleven months and twenty-three days for anyone to realize he was dead. The last record of his being alive was when he'd been to the bank to deposit a check, whereafter he'd returned home, died, and rotted away apologetically on a sofa under a throw patterned with hummingbirds.

The only other flat in the building was unoccupied, which explained the fact that the smell, which was currently causing Andrew to gag even before he'd set foot in the flat itself, hadn't been the thing to alert someone to Warren's death. In fact, the only reason it hadn't been longer before his body had been discovered was that direct debits for his rent and energy bills had bounced back at the same time. An unfortunate debt collector—who'd apparently been scrambled to the property with the urgency of a counterterrorist operative—had peered through the building's letterbox only to be met by a volley of flies.

Peggy had messaged him on Sunday evening, the day after they'd returned from Northumberland, to say she'd developed "a stinking cold" and wouldn't be coming into work the next day. In truth, Andrew was quite relieved she wasn't with him. He wasn't sure how he'd be able to act normally around her after all that had happened. And so it was that he found himself at his first solo property inspection in weeks, a heavily aftershave-soaked mask pressed to his face, bracing himself to enter. Though he'd tried to prepare himself as best he could, he was still unable to stop himself from dry-heaving. He dropped his bag to the floor and batted away the flies excited from the disturbance. He worked as quickly as he could, separating trash bags of indiscriminate rotting food and soiled clothes as he looked for any sign of a next of kin. He searched for nearly two hours without finding anything. With all the usual places covered, he even forced himself to look inside the oven, which was caked in congealed fat, and the fridge, which was empty save for a single summer fruits Petits Filous yogurt. When he finally left, not having found a single trace of evidence that Warren had family, or any concealed cash, he headed to his flat rather than the office. As soon as he was inside he tore off his clothes and showered, turning the water as hot as he could bear and scrubbing feverishly at his skin, using a whole bottle of shower gel. All the while he struggled to think of anything other than Warren. What must his last few weeks before he'd died have been like, living in all that filth? He'd always thought he preferred the chaos to the sterile, but on a purely sensory level it was hard to reconcile how someone could have lived like that. Surely he must have been of unsound mind not to know how bad it was. It made Andrew think of the frog boiling to death, unaware that the water's getting hotter.

Later, he headed back to the office smelling like the Body Shop had vomited on him, and arrived to find Cameron sitting on Meredith's yoga ball, his eyes closed in contemplation, a mug of what looked like swamp water steaming away next to him.

"Hello, Cameron," Andrew said.

Cameron kept his eyes closed and showed Andrew the flat of his hand, like a sleepwalking traffic cop halting imaginary cars. There wasn't enough space for Andrew to squeeze around the exercise ball to his desk, so he had to wait while Cameron finished whatever the hell it was he was doing. Eventually, he let out such a long, powerful breath that Andrew thought at first the ball had developed a puncture.

"Good afternoon, Andrew," Cameron said, rising with as much dignity as is possible when clambering off an oversized plastic testicle. "And how was the property inspection?"

"Truthfully, it was probably the worst one I've ever had to do," Andrew said.

"I see. And how does that make you feel?"

Andrew wondered if this was a trick question.

"Well . . . bad."

"I *am* sorry to hear that," Cameron said, rolling his shirtsleeves up to the elbow before changing his mind and rolling them back down again. "No Peggy today then, poor thing."

"No," Andrew said, slumping down into his chair.

"Meredith and Keith are off on their hols," Cameron said, running his finger along the top of Andrew's screen.

"Uh-huh."

"So that means it's just us two here . . . holding the old fort."

"Yep," Andrew said, unsure where this was going, wondering if he should suggest that Cameron's next move toward enlightenment should be an enforced period of silence. It was horribly clear, though, that Cameron had some sort of an agenda. Andrew watched him go to walk away before making a big show of changing his mind, snapping his fingers as he turned back.

"Actually, do you mind if we have a quick chat? I can make you some herbal tea if you want?"

The break-out area had evolved since Andrew had been away. There were blue and purple throws over the sofas and a coffee table book about transcendental meditation artfully placed on a beanbag where the coffee table used to be. Andrew was just glad that there weren't any obvious hooks to hang wind chimes from.

"Are you looking forward to Thursday night?" Cameron asked.

Andrew looked blankly back at him.

"It's Meredith's turn to host us for dinner," Cameron said, clearly disappointed that Andrew had forgotten.

"Oh, yes, of course. Should be . . . fun."

"You think? Look, I know it was a bit of a funny old evening when Clara and I hosted . . ."

Andrew wasn't sure whether he was supposed to agree with this or not, so he kept his mouth shut.

"But I'm sure it'll be a more chilled-out evening this time around," Cameron said.

They sipped their tea and Andrew chanced a look at his watch.

"I'm glad it's just us two, actually," Cameron said. "It gives me a chance to touch base with you about something."

"Right," Andrew said, resisting the temptation to scream, *IF YOU MEAN "TALK" JUST SAY "TALK,"* at him.

"You'll remember my presentation a little while back, where a certain notification appeared on the screen."

Cutbacks. With all that had been going on, Andrew had barely had time to think about that.

"The truth is," Cameron continued, "I just don't know yet whether it's going to be *us* that'll need to have fewer people wearing more hats, or another department."

Andrew fidgeted in his seat. "Why are you telling me this, Cameron?"

Cameron flashed him a particularly desperate grin, his teeth on full display.

"Because, Andrew, it's been playing on my mind to the point of distraction, and I just felt I had to say something to someone here and because . . . we're mates, right?"

"Sure," Andrew said, guiltily avoiding Cameron's eye. If Cameron was telling him this, did it mean he would be safe? His optimism quickly vanished when he realized that meant that Peggy could be the one to go.

"Thanks, mate," Cameron said. "Feels loads better getting that off my chest."

"Good," Andrew said, wondering if perhaps he should try to make the case for Peggy now.

"So how's the old fam-fam, then?" Cameron said.

The question caught Andrew off guard. Troublingly, it took a moment for him to realize Cameron meant Diane and the children. He made to reply but his mind was blank, no false anecdotes or news coming to mind as usual. *Come on, think! Just make something up like you normally do.*

"Um . . . ," he said, then, panicking that Cameron would take his hesitation to mean something might be wrong, quickly followed up with, "They're fine. Just all good, really. Listen . . ." He got to his feet. ". . . I've actually got loads to do, so I better get back to it. I'm sorry."

"Oh, well if you're—"

"Sorry," Andrew said again, nearly tripping over an errant throw on the floor as he hurried away, feeling suddenly short of breath, just making it to the toilets in time to cough up bile into the sink.

———

That evening, he chatted with BamBam, TinkerAl, and BroadGauge-Jim, and tried not to think about what had happened with Cameron. It had been terrifying to go blank like that. Maybe he was just rustier than usual because his focus had been on Peggy. The closer he'd gotten to her, the more distant Diane had become. He'd neglected his "family," the people he relied on for support, and the guilt he felt was deep and real. The strength of the feeling was horribly troubling. *This. Isn't. Normal*, he told himself, digging his fingernails into his thigh.

He felt bad for interrupting the current subforum conversation (Which type of rubberized horsehair is best for creating bush scenery?), but there was nowhere else for him to turn.

Chaps, not to bring the mood down, but remember when I told you about that person who I was starting to get along with really well? It turns out there was something more than just friendship there, but now I've blown it.

BroadGaugeJim: Sorry to hear that, T. What happened?

Tracker: It's a bit complicated. There's someone else in her life. But that's not even the main problem. Basically, I've been holding something back from her, and I know that if I come clean she'll probably never talk to me again.

BamBam67: Yikes, that does sound rather serious.

TinkerAl: Tricky one, mate. What I would say is maybe you should just be honest with her? Maybe you're right—she might never talk to you again, but if there's even the smallest chance she'll be okay with it, then isn't that worth fighting for? This time in a week you could be together! Bit of a cliché I know, but isn't it better to have loved and lost, and all that???

The discordant "Blue Moon" arrived in an instant, and the screeching feedback and stabbing at Andrew's temples was so severe that he had to slide to the floor and clap his hands to his head, drawing his knees up to his chest, waiting for the pain to subside.

———

He slept fitfully that night. He'd developed an earache and a raw, scratchy throat, and his body was starting to ache all over. As he lay awake in the early morning, listening to the rain hammering at the window, he thought of Peggy, and wondered whether he'd caught this cold off her, or just a stranger.

– CHAPTER 23 –

Peggy was still off sick the following day. Andrew had texted her asking if she was feeling better, but there was no reply.

The cold he'd caught had evolved into something that sapped him of energy but left him too uncomfortable to sleep. Instead, he sat shivering or sweating under a duvet watching mindless action films, the moral of each story appearing to be if you drive a car fast enough a lady will take her top off.

He was halfway to work the following morning, feeling like he was trudging through thick mud, when he suddenly remembered it was the day of Alan Carter's funeral. He forced himself to turn back and flag down a taxi.

The vicar—a squat man with piggy eyes—greeted him at the church's entrance.

"Relative?"

"No, council," Andrew said, glad that he *wasn't* a relative given the brusqueness of how the vicar had spoken to him.

"Ah yes, of course," the vicar said. "Well, there's one lady inside.

But it doesn't look like anyone else is coming so we better crack on." He raised a fist to his mouth to cover a burp, his cheeks bulging like a frog's neck.

Beryl was sitting in the front row of the empty church. Andrew tucked his shirt in and flattened his hair down as he walked up the aisle. "Hello, dear," Beryl said when he arrived at her side. "Gosh, are you okay? You look ever so peaky." She put the back of her hand to his forehead.

"I'm fine," Andrew said. "A bit tired, that's all. How are you?"

"Not so bad, pet," Beryl said. "Have to say, it's been a long time since I've been in a church." She lowered her voice to a whisper. "I'm not exactly a believer in the beardy bloke upstairs. Neither was Alan, truth be told. I'm sure he'd have found all this palaver funny, really. Is Peggy coming, do you know?"

"I don't think so, I'm afraid," Andrew said, looking back toward the door just in case. "She's really poorly, unfortunately. But she sends her love."

"Oh well, not to worry," Beryl said. "More for the rest of us."

Andrew couldn't think what Beryl meant until he looked down to see she was holding an open Tupperware box full of fairy cakes. After a moment's hesitation, he took one.

The vicar appeared and stifled another belch, and Andrew feared the worst about the sermon, but thankfully the vicar's delivery was heartfelt enough. The only blip in the service came when a man wearing a baseball cap and waterproof trousers—a gardener, Andrew presumed—shunted the church door open and whispered, "Oh bollocks," just loudly enough for them to hear before slipping back out.

Beryl remained composed throughout. Perhaps because Andrew had more of a personal investment than usual, he listened intently to the vicar's words and, to his intense embarrassment, found himself on the verge of tears. He felt a wave of shame hit him—he hadn't ever met this man; it wasn't his place to cry. And yet that guilt only made things worse and eventually he was unable to stop a single tear from spilling down onto each of his cheeks. Luckily, he managed to wipe them away before Beryl saw. He'd have to blame his cold if she said anything about his puffy eyes.

As the vicar asked them to join him in reciting the Lord's Prayer, the realization suddenly came to Andrew that he hadn't been crying for Alan, or even for Beryl, but for the future version of himself, his death unmourned at a service in a drafty church with only the walls to receive the vicar's perfunctory words.

———————

They said polite if stiff good-byes to the vicar ("I don't trust men with handshakes that firm—you have to think they're overcompensating for something," Beryl said) and were walking arm in arm along the churchyard path when Andrew asked Beryl whether she needed accompanying back to the station. "Don't worry, love. I'm actually visiting a couple of old friends. 'Old' being the operative word; I think they've got about seven teeth between them these days, Sheila and Georgie."

They'd reached the end of the path. The wind was rushing through the branches of the imposing yew tree that stood just inside the churchyard walls. They were only in mid-September, but the sublime August day in Northumberland seemed a long time ago.

"You got time for a cuppa before I go?" Beryl said.

Andrew scratched at the back of his head. "Sadly not."

"Time waits for no man, eh? Hang on, though." Beryl scrabbled in her handbag and found a pen and paper. "I'm around for another few days. Give me your number. I've got my special old-lady mobile phone the size of a brick with me, so maybe we could meet up later in the week or something."

"That would be lovely," Andrew said.

Another gust of wind came, stronger this time. Beryl readjusted her hat and took Andrew by the hand.

"You're a good man, Andrew, coming here today. I know my Alan would've appreciated that. Take care now."

She walked away, looking brittle against the wind, but after a few steps she stopped and came back.

"Here," she said, digging the box of cakes out of her bag. "Share these with Peggy, won't you?"

– CHAPTER 24 –

Andrew stooped to double-check, but there were no two ways about it: he was looking at a dead mouse.

He'd been searching for a bucket because water was leaking from an unidentifiable hole in the ceiling above the back stairs. Cameron had called the maintenance team but they'd fobbed him off. His response had been to repeat some sort of mantra over and over under his breath, his eyes tightly shut.

"Back in a sec," Andrew had said, edging slowly away.

As he opened the cupboard underneath the kitchen sink he was hit by the familiar stench of death, and sure enough, lying there on its back among bleach bottles and a hi-vis jacket was a mouse. This wasn't exactly under Andrew's remit, but he couldn't just leave it there, so he put on a single washing-up glove and picked it up by its tail. He caught his distorted reflection in the shiny side of the coffee machine and saw the mouse swinging back and forth, as if he were performing some sort of macabre hypnotism. Since he didn't want to disturb whatever mindfulness ritual Cameron was going through, his only option was to go back through the office and out of the front entrance to find somewhere to dispose of the corpse. So it was with a horrible inevitability that he had managed to get all the way to the main doors without passing a soul, only to be met by Peggy coming the other way. She was distracted by collapsing her umbrella, and making a split-second judgment, Andrew opened his coat pocket and stuffed the mouse inside it. Her umbrella now folded away, Peggy spotted Andrew and made her way over.

"Hello," she said, "how's tricks?"

Aside from the dead mouse in my pocket?

"Yes, okay. Nothing new, really. You're feeling better then?"

He had meant it as a genuine question but in his flustered state it came out almost sarcastically. Thankfully, Peggy didn't seem to take it that way.

"Yep, much better," she said. "What's the craic today then?"

"Oh, just the usual."

Mouse in my pocket, mouse in my pocket, mouse in my pocket.

"Keith and Meredith?"

"Not in yet."

"Thank god for small mercies. And we've not been fired, yet?"

"Not that I know of."

"Well, that's something."

For the first time since Andrew had known Peggy, there was an awkward pause.

"Well, I better crack on," Peggy said. "Coming?"

"Sure," Andrew said. "I've just got to . . . I'll see you in there."

He disposed of the mouse in some weeds in a corner of the car park. He had only just gotten back inside when he looked out of the window to see Keith arriving on his scooter next to the burial ground. Such was his size relative to the machine it reminded Andrew of a clown on one of those ankle-height tricycles. Barely half a minute later Meredith drove up in her custard-yellow hatchback, and Andrew watched her and Keith take a sly look around before locking lips, Keith wrapping his arms around Meredith as the kiss became more passionate, so it looked as if she'd fallen into quicksand.

———————

Andrew was trying to write an obituary for Warren but kept distracting himself by stealing glances at Peggy, who despite her earlier assurances that she was feeling better still looked pale and worn out. Though that might have been something to do with having to listen to Meredith banging on about some sort of "retreat" where she'd just been on holiday. He was considering going over to rescue Peggy, but things felt so different now. He couldn't bear the idea of her smiling warily as he approached, worried that he might try to bring up what had happened in Northumberland. Instead, he trudged to the kitchen and went to make tea. Someone had finished the milk and put the empty carton back in the fridge. Andrew wished that whoever it was (and let's face it, it was Keith) would tread on an upturned plug in bare feet sometime soon. From the kitchen doorway he could see into Cameron's office. Cameron was sitting at his computer, arms aloft, viciously squeezing a stress ball in each hand. He saw Andrew and his grimace turned into a slightly pained smile, the same expression a baby pulls in the process of filling its nappy. *At least today can't get any worse*, Andrew thought, and as if Cameron had read his mind he chose that moment to wheel himself over on his chair.

"Remember, guys, it's dinner party mark two tonight."

CHAPTER 25

Andrew peered out from behind a tree across the street from Meredith's house, picking at the price label on the cheapest bottle of wine he'd been able to find in the corner shop. (He was no expert, but he was pretty sure that Latvia wasn't famed for its rosé.)

He braced himself to enter the fray. Cameron had been suspiciously quiet since the cutbacks conversation, and even though they were supposedly "mates," Andrew wasn't going to assume for a minute that he was safe. He would have to be on his best behavior tonight. Cameron was continuing to give a disproportionately large shit about these stupid dinner parties, so if pretending to be the sort of person who enjoyed talking about school catchment areas over an underbaked flan stood him in good stead, then so be it.

He was about to cross the road when a car pulled up outside and he shrank back as he saw Peggy climb out of the passenger side, waving good-bye to Maisie and Suze in the backseats. The window lowered and Andrew heard Steve's gruff voice. Peggy turned and leaned in through the window to retrieve the handbag Steve was proffering, and there was just enough light in the car for Andrew to see them kiss. He waited after Peggy had gone inside and watched as Steve cracked his knuckles before taking what was unmistakably a hip flask from the glove compartment and taking a deep swig before driving off, tires shuddering against the tarmac.

———

Meredith opened the door and bestowed a kiss on each of Andrew's cheeks, a greeting he received while motionless, as if he were a statue she was kissing for luck. The music that was playing from concealed speakers throughout the house was, Meredith cheerfully informed him, by someone called Michael Bublé.

"It's jazz!" she added, taking the wine from him.

"Is it?" Andrew said, looking around for something hard and pointy to bash his face into.

The others were all there. Keith, to Andrew's surprise, was dressed in a gray suit with a purple tie, the knot of which was largely obscured by the folds of his neck. He looked troublingly happy. Cameron—who was already sitting at the dining room table with a large glass of red wine—was wearing a white shirt with three buttons undone, graying chest hair poking through, and had a bracelet of wooden beads around his wrist.

Andrew bumped into Peggy coming back from the loo and they performed an interminably awkward shuffle as each tried to let the other past.

"You know what, I'm just going to stand still and close my eyes until you've found a way past," Peggy said.

"Good plan," Andrew said. As he passed her he caught what smelled like a new scent—something subtle and fresh. For some reason this floored him even more than seeing the kiss. He felt his stomach plunge.

"I thought we'd start with a bit of a game, just to loosen us up," Meredith said once they were all assembled in the dining room.

Oh joy, Andrew thought.

"Let's go around the group, saying a word each, until we've improvised a story. It can be about anything. First person to go blank or crack up loses. Andrew, why don't you start."

Oh god.

Andrew: "We."

Peggy: "All."

Cameron: "Went."

Meredith: "To."

Keith: "Meredith's."

Andrew: "House."

Peggy: "And."

Cameron: "We."

Meredith: "All."

Keith: "Really."

Andrew: "Hated."

Andrew looked over to Peggy. Why was she staring at him like that? Did that mean she'd lost? And then he realized what he'd said.

Thankfully, Peggy came to his rescue, saying "having," and the rest of the story went on until Cameron inexplicably started guffawing and the game was quickly brought to a close. The dinner itself passed uneventfully. Meredith delivered several courses, all of them seemingly varieties on the theme of hedge cuttings, which left Andrew starving. He'd worked his way through most of his bottle of Latvian wine, which was surprisingly nice (so he was a racist as well as cheap), drumming his fingers on the table as he listened to the others talking about a Scandinavian crime box set he'd yet to watch.

Meredith prefaced her thoughts by saying, "This isn't a spoiler," before revealing the death of a lead character, two plot twists, and the dialogue from the final scene of the show in its entirety. He'd cross that one off his list, then.

Cameron had been his usual animated self, edging toward the giddy end of the spectrum. Andrew hadn't thought his behavior particularly unusual, but when Cameron stood up to go to the loo he wobbled on his feet, grabbing on to a cabinet for support, before weaving unsteadily out of the room.

"He got here an hour early," Meredith whispered gleefully. "Got stuck into the malbec like you wouldn't believe. I think there's trouble in paradise with Clara."

"And where's your feller tonight?" Peggy asked, just as Keith went to brush a crumb from Meredith's sleeve. He withdrew his hand sharply but Meredith grabbed it, like a lion being fed a hunk of meat in a zoo, and slapped it down on the table, locking her fingers with his.

"Well, in fact," she said, "I was—*we* were—going to wait until after the homemade profiteroles, but we've actually got something to tell you."

"You're shagging?" Peggy said, stifling a yawn.

"Well, there's no need to be so crude about it," Meredith said, a fixed smile on her face. "But, yes, Keith and I are officially partners. As in lovers," she added, in case anyone thought they were about to float a company on the stock market.

The dining room door swung open and banged against the wall as Cameron staggered over to his chair. "What have I missed, then?" he said.

"Them two are 'lovers,' apparently," Peggy said. Andrew went to top up her glass but she put her hand over the top and shook her head.

"Well, that's, I mean, good . . . Good for you," Cameron said. "Now, that's what I call team bonding!" He laughed raucously at his own joke.

"Keith, would you mind helping me in the kitchen for a moment?" Meredith said.

"Yeah, sure," Keith said, the familiar leer back on his face.

"I'm just going to get some air," Peggy said. She looked at Andrew and raised her eyebrows.

"I think I will, too," Andrew said.

"There's a surprise," Keith said quietly.

"What's that?" Peggy said.

"Nothing, nothing," Keith said, hands raised defensively.

The four of them stood and Cameron looked up at them, confused, like a little boy lost in a crowd.

Outside, Peggy produced a cigarette and offered one to Andrew, who accepted despite having no intention of smoking it. He lowered his arm, letting the cigarette burn, and watched Peggy inhale deeply.

"Cheek of that knobber Keith," Peggy said, tilting her head up as she exhaled smoke. Andrew again caught a hint of her new perfume and felt like he might overbalance. He wasn't sure why it was affecting him like this. He hummed tunelessly, the silence too much to bear.

"What?" Peggy said, seemingly taking this to mean he wasn't in agreement with her about Keith.

"Nothing," Andrew said. "He's a knobber, like you said."

Peggy exhaled again. "You haven't . . . said anything to him, have you?"

"No, of course not," Andrew said, cringing.

"Okay. Good."

This was miserable. To hear the concern in Peggy's voice at the thought of their secret coming out, knowing that her primary concern was jeopardizing her reconciliation with Steve, was torture. Should he tell her he'd seen Steve drinking as he'd driven off? Regardless of what had happened between them, surely she had a right to know if Steve was lying to her, especially if he was endangering the girls. Peggy was eyeing him suspiciously.

"Just so we're clear, you're not going to do anything silly, are you? No mad gestures inspired by those two idiots in there? Because believe me, that won't work."

This time, it was anger Andrew felt. He hadn't asked to come and stand in the cold and be humiliated like this.

"Oh, don't worry," he said, "I wouldn't dream of ruining things for you."

Peggy took a final drag on her cigarette and threw it to the ground, crushing it with her boot heel, fixing Andrew with a steely expression.

"Just so you know," she said, her tone so harsh it made Andrew take a step back, "this hasn't been an easy week for me. It's been pretty grueling, in fact, largely because I've spent the entire time doing what that moron Cameron would no doubt describe as a root-and-branch review of my marriage. But thankfully, for all the pain involved, it's resulted in Steve cleaning himself up and deciding to be a husband and a father again. And that's how things have to be for me. There's no other option. It's not my place to say, but if you're not happy with Diane then maybe you need to have an honest conversation with her too."

Andrew was going to let her walk back inside, but these last words had stung him too much and he couldn't stop himself.

"I saw Steve drop you off earlier," he blurted out. "With the girls in the car."

"And?" Peggy said, her hand on the door handle.

"When you'd gone inside he took out a hip flask."

Peggy bowed her head.

"I'm sorry," Andrew said. "I just thought you should know."

"Oh, Andrew," Peggy said. "Did all that stuff we talked about before—about being friends, about being there for each other . . . did it not mean anything to you?"

"What? Of course it did."

She shook her head sadly.

"Yet you're fine with lying to me?"

"No, I . . ."

But Peggy didn't stay to hear him out, closing the door firmly behind her.

Andrew stood listening to the faint strains of music and voices coming from inside. He looked at Peggy's cigarette smoldering on the floor and realized he was still holding his own. He took aim and dropped his onto hers, then mashed them together with his heel.

————

For the rest of the evening he retreated into himself, picturing his Ella records and all the model train components he owned neatly laid out on the floor, debating what he could live with selling should he be the one to get sacked. There was *Souvenir Album*, maybe. It was probably the record he listened to the least. The DB Schenker Class 67 had seen better days, too, he supposed. It looked magnificent still but barely made it around the track without slowing to a melancholy stop at least a couple of times, no matter how much he serviced it.

Peggy sat glumly while Cameron, Keith and Meredith entered the stage of drunkenness where one-upmanship masquerades as badinage. There were boasts of drinking sessions, crowbarred anecdotes about meeting celebrities and, most alienating of all, talk of sexual exploits.

"Come on then, come on then," Keith said, raising his voice above the others'. He had seemed unusually awkward earlier, before Meredith had made their affair public, but now he was relaxing into his old self, shirt untucked, tie loosened, like Mr. Toad on dress-down Friday. "Who here's done it in public?" he said.

So far Andrew had gotten away with staying quiet and eating his food, occasionally smiling or nodding to give the impression he was engaged with the conversation. But now their plates were cleared and he had nowhere to hide. Keith caught his eye and Andrew knew instantly that he wasn't going to miss the opportunity to embarrass him.

"Come on, Andy-pandy. You and your missus have been together how long?"

Andrew took a sip of water. "A long time."

"So come on, have you . . . ?"

"Have we what?"

"Got down and dirty somewhere public!"

"Ah. Um. No. Not to my knowledge."

Meredith sniggered into her wineglass. Cameron laughed too, but his glassy eyes suggested he was too drunk to understand what was going on.

"Not to your knowledge?!" Keith said. "You do know how sex works, Andrew? It's not like you can do it behind your own back."

"Well . . . depends how flexible you are," Meredith said. As she cackled at her own joke, Andrew excused himself to go to the toilet.

"Don't think we've forgotten about you," Keith called after him.

Andrew was in no hurry to return to the dining room–turned-school-playground, but there was something disconcerting about Meredith's bathroom—namely the picture of her and, presumably, her now-former partner. It was a professional shot—all fluffy white shag pile and unnatural body language. Andrew looked at the man smiling gamely at the camera and wondered where he was at that moment. Maybe he was out drowning his sorrows with friends, that same fixed smile on his face, telling everyone that no, seriously, honestly, this was the best thing that'd ever happened to him.

Back in the dining room, there was no sign of things having calmed down, although Cameron did appear to have passed out. Keith was standing next to him holding a marker pen, apparently preparing to draw something on his face. Meredith was at his side, bouncing on her feet and wheeling her arms excitedly like a toddler who's just learned to stand unaided. Just as Andrew approached the table he saw Peggy clearly lose patience and stomp over to Keith, making to whip the pen out of his hand.

"Oi!" Keith said, ripping his hand away. "Come on, it's just a bit of fun."

"Could you be any more immature?" Peggy said. She went to make another grab for the pen but this time Meredith stepped in front of her, eyes fiery with defending Keith. "I don't know what your problem is, Mrs. Uptight," she hissed.

"Oh, I don't know," Peggy said. "How about the fact he's clearly in a bad way about his wife, as you so kindly brought up earlier. Just because you two are apparently so happy doesn't mean you get to humiliate him."

Meredith tilted her head to one side and stuck her bottom lip out. "Oh, hon, you sound ever so stressed. You know what you need? A good yoga sesh. I know this great place—Synergy—where I was last week? Get all that frustration out of you, yeah?"

Synergy, why does that sound familiar? Andrew thought, edging around the table to stand next to Peggy. He'd planned to try to calm things down, but Peggy had other ideas.

"You know what?" she said. "Every time I've had to be in the same room as you these last few months, the only thing that's given me any sort of pleasure is trying to work out what exactly it is you both look like."

"Peggy," Andrew said, but she raised a hand. A hand that wasn't to be trifled with.

"And, I'm very pleased to say, I've finally reached my conclusion, because it's now very clear to me that you, Keith, look like a health warning on a pack of cigarettes."

Meredith made a strange gurgling sound.

"And as for you, *hon*, you look like the result of a dog being asked to draw a horse."

As much as Andrew was enjoying the looks on Keith's and Meredith's faces he knew this silence was his last chance to stop things from getting out of hand.

"*Look*," he said, startling himself with how loudly he'd spoken. "Remember the cutbacks thing we saw in Cameron's presentation? You really think this sort of behavior is going to go down well if he's got to make that decision? I know he can be an idiot, but he's still the most important person in this room."

It was at that moment that Cameron began to snore.

"Ha, yeah, he looks really important right now," Keith scoffed. "You're just scared, as fucking usual. I, for one, am sick of trying to pretend he's anything other than a streak of chamomile-tea piss. Let him fire me, see if I fucking care."

He took the lid off the pen with his teeth and spat it onto the floor, doubling down on his bravado. For the first time, Meredith looked uneasy, Andrew's words about the cutbacks clearly getting through to her at least. Andrew and Peggy exchanged a look. He wanted to tell her that they should just get out of there, let these two idiots seal their own fate. But before he could say anything Peggy darted toward Keith and grabbed the pen.

"You bitch," Keith snarled, grasping at thin air as Peggy dodged him.

"Oi!" Andrew yelled, rushing over, banging his hip on the table in the process. Peggy feinted one way, then doubled back and climbed up onto a chair, where she held the pen aloft, Keith and Meredith straining to reach it. If a stranger had walked into the room they might have been under the impression that they'd just chanced upon a strangely angry Morris dance. Just as Andrew reached the melee Peggy pushed Keith away with her foot so that he stumbled backward. Andrew could see the fury in Keith's eyes, and as he lurched back toward Peggy, Andrew instinctively reached out and pushed him in the side as hard as he could. Unbalanced, Keith stumbled away and slammed backward into the wall with a horrible double thwack of back followed by head against the doorframe.

At that moment, several things happened at once.

Cameron woke with a start.

Keith reached for the back of his head, looked at the blood on his fingertips, and promptly collapsed to the ground with a thud. Meredith shrieked.

And then, as Andrew's brain finally clicked—*Cynergy*, not Synergy—he felt his phone vibrating and pulled it out of his pocket. It was Carl.

– CHAPTER 26 –

Andrew wasn't sure how long he'd been in the bath (or why he'd decided to run one in the first place), but it had been scaldingly hot when he'd lowered himself gingerly in, and now it was barely lukewarm. He'd put Ella on in the living room, but the bathroom door had swung shut so he could only just hear the music. He'd considered getting out and opening the door, but there was something different about experiencing the music like this, where he had to train his ears so intently that he heard every key change, every subtle shift in vocal inflection, as if for the first time. He felt overwhelmed at Ella's capacity to surprise and thrill him after all this time, but now the record had come to an end and every time he shifted position he felt the coldness of the water seeping into his flesh.

He couldn't really remember leaving Meredith's earlier that evening. He'd stumbled out, his phone still ringing, vaguely aware that Meredith was screaming, "He's killed him! He's killed him!" as Peggy tried to calmly explain the situation on the phone to the emergency services. The next thing he could recall was the scuff marks and the strip light and his neighbor's perfume. Maybe he was in shock.

He finally worked up the courage to get out of the bath and sat shivering on his bed with a towel wrapped around him, looking at his phone on the floor in the corner where he'd dropped it. He'd turned it off after the third time Carl called, but he knew he couldn't ignore him for much longer. Carl and Meredith. Meredith and Carl. There was no way Carl's calling him now was just a coincidence. And then there was Keith. Maybe he should call Peggy first, see what had happened. He couldn't really have hurt him that badly, surely?

He went to the living room and sat with his phone, switching between the two numbers, unable to make a decision. Eventually, he pressed "call." Digging his fingernails into his arm, he waited for Carl to answer, the silence horribly absolute. He was suddenly desperate to puncture the stillness, and he rushed over to his record player and clumsily dropped the needle, Ella's voice filling the room. It was the closest to backup he was ever going to get. He walked around the train tracks in a figure eight, the phone still ringing out.

"Hello, Andrew."

"Hello."

There was a pause.

"Well?" Andrew said.

"Well what?"

"I'm returning your call, Carl. What do you want?"

Andrew heard Carl swallow. A disgusting protein shake no doubt.

"I met one of your colleagues last week," Carl said. "Meredith."

Andrew's head swam violently, and he crumpled slowly to his knees.

"She came to a yoga class of mine. Business has been slow, so it was only her and a few others. We've not been able to afford proper advertising, of course."

"Right," Andrew said, clinging on to the slimmest hope that Carl wasn't going where he thought he was with this.

"We got to chatting after the class," Carl said. "It was a bit awkward, really. She suddenly started going on about some miserable affair she's having. I don't know why she thought I'd be interested. I was desperate to get rid of her and then suddenly, out of the blue, she mentioned where she worked. And, lo and behold, it was with you. Small world, isn't it?"

Andrew considered hanging up. He could take the SIM from his phone and flush it away and never have to speak to Carl again.

"Andrew, are you still there?"

"Yes," Andrew said, through gritted teeth.

"Good," Carl said. "I thought someone might be distracting you. Diane, perhaps. Or maybe the kids."

Andrew balled his free hand into a fist and bit down on it hard until he could taste blood.

"It's funny how our memories distort," Carl said. Andrew could tell he was trying to keep his voice level. "Because I could have sworn that you lived on your own in a bedsit just off the Old Kent Road, that you hadn't been in a relationship since . . . well . . . But according to this Meredith person you're a happily married father of two living in a fancy town house." Carl's voice was vibrating with repressed anger. "And there are only two explanations there. Either Meredith has got things spectacularly wrong, or it means you've been lying to her and god knows who else about having a wife and children, and Christ I hope it's the first one, because if it's the second then I think that might be the most pathetic, awful thing I've ever heard. And I can only imagine what your boss would think of that, were he to find out. You're working with vulnerable people a lot of the time, and for the council too. I can't imagine such a revelation would go down particularly well, do you?"

Andrew brought his hand away from his mouth and saw the cartoonish bite mark on his skin. A memory swam into his mind of Sally throwing a half-finished apple over a hedge and protesting to their mother when she told her off.

"What do you want?" he said quietly. At first there was no reply. Just the sound of their breathing. Then Carl spoke.

"You ruined *everything*. Sally could have gotten better, I know she could, if only you'd made things right. But now she's gone. And guess what? I spoke to her lawyer today, and she tells me that the money—Sally's life savings, just to remind you, Andrew—will be paid to you any day now. Christ, if only she'd known the sort of person you really are. Do you honestly think she'd have done the same thing?"

"I don't . . . That's not . . ."

"Shut up and listen," Carl said. "Given the fact I now know just how much of a liar you are, let me make it very clear what's going to happen if you decide to go back on your promise to give me what's mine. I'm going to text you my bank details, right now. And if you don't transfer the money to me *the moment* you get it, then all it takes is one phone call to Meredith, and everything's over for you. Everything. Got that? Good."

With that, he hung up.

Andrew took the phone away from his ear and gradually his brain tuned back in to Ella's voice: *It wouldn't be make-believe, if you believed in me.* He immediately logged in to his online banking on his phone. When the screen showed his account, it took him a moment to realize what he was looking at: the money was already there. His phone vibrated—Carl's bank details. Andrew started a new transfer, entering Carl's details, his heart racing. One more click, and the money would be gone, and this would be over. But, despite every instinct, something stopped him. For all of Carl's words about what Sally would make of his lies, would she really take a better view of what Carl was doing right now? This money was the last thing that connected him and Sally. It had been his sister's last gift to him. The last emblem of their bond.

Before he could stop himself, he'd hit "cancel," dropping the phone onto the carpet and putting his head into his hands, taking long, calming breaths.

He'd been sitting on the floor, thoughts flitting between weary defeat and desperate panic, when his phone rang again. He was half expecting it to be Carl—that somehow he'd worked out Andrew had the money already—but it was Peggy.

"Hello?" he said. The background noise was chaotic, people shouting over each other, clamoring to have their voice heard.

"Hello?" he said again.

"Is that Andrew?"

"Yes, who's this?"

"It's Maisie. Hang on. Mum? *Mum?* I've got him."

Andrew heard a collective "Whoa!" and the sound of blaring horns, then everything went muffled with the sound of fingers scrabbling at the phone.

"Andrew?"

"Peggy? Are you okay? Did Keith—"

"You were right about Steve. Got back and he was shouting at the girls, drunk out of his skull and on god knows what else. I can't do it anymore, I just can't. Grabbed as much stuff as I could and shoved the girls into the car. Steve was too busy smashing the place up to stop me leaving but he jumped on his motorbike and came after me."

"Shit, are you all right?"

Another horn blared.

"Yes, well no, not really. I'm so sorry, Andrew, I should have believed you earlier."

"It doesn't matter, I don't care—I just want to know you're safe."

"Yeah, we are. I think I've lost him. But the thing is, look, I know it's late and everything but I've tried everyone else and . . . I wouldn't normally ask but . . . could we come to yours, just for an hour or something, till I figure out what to do?"

"Yes, of course," Andrew said.

"You're a lifesaver. We won't be a hassle, I promise. Okay, what's your address? Maisie, grab that pen, darling, I need you to write Andrew's address down for me."

Andrew felt his stomach somersault as he realized what he'd just agreed to.

"Andrew?"

"Yes, I'm here, I'm here."

"Thank god. What's your address?"

What could he do? He had no choice but to tell her. And almost as soon as the words were out of his mouth the line went dead.

"It's fine," he said out loud, the words swallowed by the yawning indifference of his flat, the four walls that comprised living room, kitchen and bedroom seeming to have encroached.

Okay, let's look at this logically, he thought. Maybe this could be a second house? A little place he had all to himself for a bit of . . . what was that dreadful phrase Meredith had said the other day? "Me time," that was it. He turned slowly on the spot and took the place in, trying to imagine it was the first time he'd seen it. It was no good. It felt too lived-in to be anywhere other than his home.

I'm going to tell her everything.

The thought caught him off guard. Moments later came the sound of a car pulling up outside. He looked around. Maybe he should try to clear up—though there was hardly any mess. As usual, there were one plate, one knife and fork, one glass, and a single saucepan on the draining board. Nothing else was out of place. God, what was the use?

He took one last look around, then grabbed his keys and headed for the door. Down the stairs. Past the scuff marks. Through the faint cloud of perfume. The lower he got, the colder the air became, and he felt his confidence starting to drain with it.

No, you've got to do it, he urged himself. *Do it. Don't turn back now.*

He was in the corridor, just one set of doors separating him from Peggy and the girls, their shapes blurred through the frosted glass.

Do it. No going back.

His hand was on the door handle. His legs were shaking so much he thought they might give way. *Things just have to get worse before they can get better. Do it, you fucking coward—do it.*

Peggy threw her arms around him and he felt her tears on his cheeks. He hugged her back so tightly he could feel her loosen her own grip in surprise.

"Hey now, hey," she whispered, and the softness of it brought tears swimming into his own eyes. He could see Suze trying to carry three different bags out of the car at once, struggling to keep her balance. Maisie was at her side, her face pale, her arms folded tightly around herself. Peggy put her hands on Andrew's chest. "Shall we go inside?" she said. Andrew watched her eyes searching his, concern now dawning.

"Andrew . . . ?"

– CHAPTER 27 –

Andrew was sitting on a dead man's bed wondering if he'd broken his foot. It had ballooned up grotesquely since last night, fluid expanding underneath spongy flesh, and it was now throbbing and hot, as if infection were setting in. He hadn't been able to fit a shoe on it that morning—the best he could do was a knackered old flip-flop he'd found at the bottom of a cupboard. The pain was excruciating, but nowhere near as bad as what he felt when he closed his eyes and pictured again the disappointment dawning on Peggy's face.

It had all happened in such a blur—his garbled apology to her and the girls (no, sorry, they couldn't come in after all, he was so so sorry, he'd explain when he could, it just wasn't possible tonight)—then the confusion on Peggy's face, and the hurt, and finally the disappointment. He'd fled inside, unable to watch Peggy shepherding her confused daughters back into the car, jamming his fingers in his ears so he couldn't hear them questioning why they were leaving already. He was back in the corridor, past the scuff marks and through the cloud of perfume, and up the stairs, and inside, and then he was listening helplessly as the car drove off, and when he could no longer hear its engine he looked down and saw the train set laid out with all its precision and care and expense and then he was kicking and stamping at it, bits of track and scenery slamming against the walls, until all that was left was carnage blanketed by silence. He hadn't felt a thing at first, but then the adrenaline wore off and the pain hit him in a dull, sickening wave. He crawled to the kitchen and found some frozen peas, then searched the cupboard next to him, optimistically hoping to find a first aid kit. Instead, there were two bottles of cooking wine covered in a thick film of dust. He drank half a bottle in one go, until his throat stung and the wine spilled over his mouth and down his neck. He shifted so he was sitting against the fridge, and that's where he eventually fell into a fitful sleep, waking just after three and crawling to his bed. He lay there, tears leaking down his cheeks, and thought of Peggy driving through the night, her face intermittently illuminated by streetlights, pale and afraid.

He'd turned off his phone and thrown it in a drawer in the kitchen. He couldn't bear to hear from anyone about anything. He still had no idea what had happened to Keith. Maybe he'd already been fired for hurting him like that.

When the morning came, he couldn't think what to do other than carrying out the property inspection he'd been scheduled to do. He sat on the tube among the rush-hour commuters, the pain in his foot now so severe it strangely emboldened him to stare at everyone in turn, feeling miserable at just how much he wanted someone to ask if he was okay.

The address for the property inspection had rung a bell, but it was only when he'd limped onto the estate that he recognized it as the place he and Peggy had come on her first day. (Eric, was that the man's name?) As he prepared himself to enter the property of the late Trevor Anderson, he looked across the rain-slick concrete slabs, a hopscotch game still faintly outlined, and saw a man carrying two off-license bags' worth of shopping struggling to open the door to the flat where Eric had lived. Andrew wondered if the man knew about what had happened there. How many thousands of other people, in fact, might at that very moment be about to open the door to a house where the last occupant had died and rotted without anybody noticing.

————

According to the coroner, Trevor Anderson had died having slipped and banged his head on the bathroom floor, adding that conditions in the house were "pretty poor" in the bored tone of someone reviewing a disappointing quiche from a gastropub. Andrew had put on his protective clothes, forcing himself to ignore a fresh wave of pain in his foot, and observed his usual ritual of reminding himself why he was there and how he should behave, before going inside.

It had been clear Trevor had found it hard to cope in his last days. Rubbish was piled up in the corner of the living room—the collection of stains on one particular spot of the wall suggesting various things had been thrown at it before sliding down to join the pile. There was a fiercely strong smell of urine because of the bottles and cans of all sizes filled to the brim, which were spread out in a halo around a small wooden stool just feet from a television on the floor. The only other things that could count as possessions were a pile of clothes and a bicycle wheel resting up against a beige radiator shot with scorch marks. Andrew had searched through the rubbish but knew in his heart of hearts that he'd find nothing. He'd gotten to his feet and peeled off his gloves. In the side of the room that functioned as the kitchen, the oven door hung open in a silent scream. The freezer buzzed for a moment, then clicked off again.

He'd hobbled into the bedroom, once separated from the living room by a door, but now just by a thin sheet secured by parcel tape. Next to the bed was a mirror, flecked with shaving foam, leaning up against the wall, along with a bedside table improvised from four shoeboxes.

The pain had suddenly been too much and Andrew had been forced to hop over and sit on the bed. There was a book on top of the shoeboxes, an autobiography of a golfer he'd never heard of, the cheesy smile and baggy suit placing it firmly in the 1980s. He opened the book at random and read a paragraph about a particularly arduous bunker experience at the Phoenix Open. A few pages on, a light-hearted anecdote about a charity match and too much free cava. As he flicked forward again something came loose and fell into his lap. It was a train ticket, twelve years old: a return from Euston to Tamworth. On the back there was an advert for the Samaritans. "We don't just hear you, we listen." Below, in a small patch of white space, something had been drawn in green pen.

Andrew spent a long time studying Trevor's drawing. He knew it was his, because it consisted of three simple oblongs, each with a name and dates inside them:

Willy Humphrey Anderson: 1938–1980

Portia Maria Anderson: 1936–1989

Trevor Humphrey Anderson: 1964–????

The only other words: *Glascote Cemetery—Tamworth.*

Andrew had so many questions. Had the drawing been intended for someone specific to see, or purely for the first person who found it? How many years after this man had drawn where he wanted to be buried had he sat waiting for death?

Andrew wanted to think that Trevor Anderson had lived a life of glorious hedonism. That this little piece of admin was a rare moment of practical planning in among the chaotic fun. Looking around at the grimy flat, Andrew realized this was a desperately optimistic assessment. The reality would be that in the last few years Trevor would have opened his eyes each morning, checked for sure that he wasn't dead, and gotten up. Until one day he didn't.

It was the waiting, that was the worst part—when the days were exclusively about eating enough food and drinking enough water to keep yourself alive. Maintenance. That was all it was. Andrew suddenly thought of Keith's dull eyes the moment before he crashed to the ground. Christ, what had he *done*? At some point he'd have to face the consequences. And then there was Carl. How was he to deal with that? He could simply fold and transfer the money. But would that really be the end of it? Carl seemed so angry and bitter . . . What was to stop him from flipping at any moment and picking up the phone to Meredith? The waiting. It would be torture. He could never truly think about being happy with that hanging over him. And then there was Peggy. He thought of that afternoon in Northumberland. At the time he'd felt so full of possibility, convinced that everything was going to change. How wrong he had been. There was no way he could expect Peggy to understand his lies, not after he'd refused to help her when she'd needed him most.

There was, of course, one very simple way to fix everything. It was a thought that had occurred to him a long time ago, now. Not in some moment of crisis, but simply registering itself as a possibility, as he went about his business. He had been waiting in line somewhere. A supermarket checkout perhaps, or maybe the bank. As soon as he'd acknowledged the thought, it was with him permanently. It had been like a stone hitting a windscreen, leaving a tiny crack in the glass. A permanent reminder that, at any time, the whole sheet of glass could smash. And now, he realized, it made complete and utter sense. Not only did he have a way out, but, for once in his life, he would be in complete and total control.

He looked at himself in the mirror, his face partially obscured by a streak of dirt. He set the ticket down carefully on top of the book and got slowly to his feet, standing still for a moment, listening to the gentle hum of the estate—canned laughter from a television next door, gospel music coming from the flat below. He could feel his shoulders slacken. Decades of tension were beginning to lift. Everything was going to be fine. The opening bars of Ella's "Isn't This a Lovely Day?" came into his head. There was a renewed flash of pain in his foot. But this time he barely registered it. It didn't really matter. Not now. Nothing did.

In the kitchen, the freezer buzzed into life for a few moments, shuddered, then clicked off.

———

He made one final pass of Trevor's flat and e-mailed a report to the office. Hopefully he'd given enough information for someone to make the funeral arrangements.

He took the bus home, standing with one leg raised like a flamingo, feeling liberated at how little of a shit he gave about the way people were looking at him. As soon as he was home he went straight to the bathroom and ran a bath. As he waited for it to fill he limped to the kitchen and, almost as if trying to hoodwink himself, reached into a drawer without looking until his hand touched what he was after. He ran his fingers against the scarred plastic handle of the knife, feeling oddly comforted by its familiarity. He ran it under the tap, supposing it should be clean, though it didn't really matter. He started toward the kitchen but stopped and turned back. This wasn't going to change anything, he told himself, but it felt like he should check, just in case. He opened the drawer and pulled out his phone. It seemed to take an age to turn on. When it vibrated, Andrew nearly dropped it in surprise. But then he saw that the message was from Carl. *Is the money with you yet? You better not be having second thoughts.* He shook his head, slowly. Of course Peggy hadn't messaged him. He was already dead to her. He threw his phone onto the countertop, where it skidded along.

He flicked through his Ella records and decided what he was going to play. Normally, it would be on instinct. But for this, he felt the need to find the album that encapsulated everything he loved about her. In the end he decided on *Ella in Berlin*—the reissued import version. He lowered the needle and listened to the volume fade up on the crowd, their excited applause sounding like rain on a windowpane. He undressed where he stood, halfheartedly folding his clothes and leaving them on the arm of a chair. He thought perhaps he should write a note, but only because that's what people did. What was the point if you didn't have anyone to say anything to? It would just be another piece of paper waiting for the litter picker's pincers.

By the time he'd lowered himself into the bath, gasping with pain as the hot water stung his foot, applause was ringing out again at the end of "That Old Black Magic," and the gentle double bass and piano of "Our Love Is Here to Stay" filled the air.

He'd intended to drink the rest of the wine but had forgotten to bring the bottle from the kitchen. It was better this way, he decided. To be completely lucid. In control.

The rumbling thud of the bass drum and the rushed coda from the piano signaled the end of the song, and Ella thanked the crowd. Andrew always thought she sounded so genuine when she did that; it was never forced, never false.

He was beginning to feel woozy. He hadn't eaten for hours and steam was fogging the room and his senses. He tapped his fingers on his thighs under the water and felt the ripples go back and forth. He closed his eyes and imagined he was floating down a languid river somewhere on the other side of the world.

More applause, and now they were on to "Mack the Knife." This was where Ella forgot the words. Maybe this time it would be different, Andrew thought, feeling along the side of the bath until he found the plastic handle, gripping it tightly. But no, there was the hesitation, then the breathless, audacious reference to wrecking her own song, and now the cheeky improvisation where her voice morphed into Louie Armstrong's rasp, the roar of the crowd. They were with her, cheering her on.

He lowered his hand into the water. Tightened his grip. There was barely time to pause for breath before the urgent drums of "How High the Moon" and Ella launching into her scat-singing. The music chased after her words, but she was always too quick, always too quick. He twisted his arm and clenched his fist. He felt the sharpness of the metal, his skin straining against it, about to give way. But then there was another noise, cutting through the music, vying for his attention. It was his phone ringing, he realized, opening his eyes, his fingers unclenching from around the knife's handle.

– CHAPTER 28 –

I t was Peggy.

"You're in the shit for not being here. Cameron's properly fuming, and he's taking it out on the rest of us. Where the hell are you?"

She sounded angry. Glad, perhaps, to have an excuse to call and vent at him without explicitly mentioning the other night.

He'd managed to crawl to the bedroom, where he was now sitting on the floor, naked, exhausted. It felt like he'd just woken from an intense dream. He had a sudden vision of blooms of scarlet muddying the clear bathwater and had to grip his knees to stop the sensation that he was falling. Was he still here? Was this still real?

"I'm at home," he said, his voice thick and unfamiliar.

"You've thrown a sickie?"

"No," he said. "It's not that."

"Right. Well, what's going on then?"

"Um, well, I think I sort of nearly tried to kill myself."

There was a pause.

"Say that again?"

They met at the pub, once Andrew had refused Peggy's several demands to take him to the hospital. The post-work Friday evening drinkers would be descending soon, but for now the place was empty, save for a man sitting at the bar making conversation with the polite yet clearly bored bartender.

Andrew found a table and slowly lowered himself onto a chair, folding his arms around his chest. He felt incredibly fragile all of a sudden, like his bones were made of rotten wood. A few moments later Peggy shoulder-barged the door open, hurrying over to him and smothering him with a hug that he accepted but couldn't reciprocate because he'd begun to shiver uncontrollably.

"Wait here, I know what'll sort you out," Peggy said.

She returned from the bar with what looked like a glass of milk. "They didn't have honey so this'll have to do. Not a proper hot toddy but ah well. My mam used to give them to me and Imogen when we had colds. At the time I thought it was a proper cure but looking back she clearly just wanted to knock us out so she could get some peace."

"Thank you," Andrew said, taking a warming sip and feeling the not unpleasant sting of the whisky. Peggy watched him drink. She looked anxious, fidgeting with her hands, twiddling her earrings—delicate blue studs that looked like teardrops. Andrew sat inert opposite her. He felt so detached.

"So," Peggy said. "You, um, said on the phone about the whole, you know . . ."

"Killing myself?" Andrew said.

"That. Yes. Are you—I mean it's a stupid question I suppose but—are you okay?"

Andrew thought about it. "Yes," he said. "Well, I suppose I feel a bit sort of . . . like I might *actually* be dead."

Peggy looked down at Andrew's drink. "Okay, I really do think we need to get you to a hospital," she said, reaching over and taking his hand.

"No," he said firmly, Peggy's touch bringing him out of his daze. "There's really no need. I didn't hurt myself. I'm feeling better now. This is helping." He took a sip of whisky and coughed, clasping his hands together until his knuckles were white in an attempt to stop them from trembling.

"Okay," Peggy said, looking skeptical. "Well, let's see how you feel after this."

Just then the door of the pub opened and four extremely loud sets of suits and ties containing men came in and arranged themselves at the bar. The old regular finished his pint, tucked his newspaper under his arm and left.

Peggy waited until Andrew had nearly finished his whisky before seeming to remember she had a beer to drink and taking two hearty gulps. She sat forward and spoke softly. "So what happened?"

Andrew shivered in response and Peggy reached over and cupped her hands around his. "It's okay, you don't have to tell me details, I'm just trying to understand why you'd . . . want to do something like that. Where were Diane and the kids in all of this?"

Andrew's synapses instantly fired as he searched for an explanation. But nothing came to him. Not this time. He smiled sadly as the realization hit him. This time, *this time*, he was going to tell the truth. He took a deep breath, trying to settle himself, to stamp down on the part of him desperately trying to stop him from going through with this.

"What? What's happened?" Peggy said, looking even more worried. "Are they okay?"

Andrew started to speak, hesitantly, having to pause every few seconds: "Have . . . have you ever told a lie so big that you felt there was no way out of it . . . that you . . . that you had to just carry on pretending?"

Peggy looked at him evenly. "I once told my mother-in-law that I'd crisscrossed the bottoms of sprouts when I hadn't. That made for a tense Christmas Day . . . but that's not quite what you mean, is it?"

Andrew shook his head slowly, and this time the words came out before he could stop them.

"Diane, Steph and David don't exist," he said. "It came from a misunderstanding, but then I kept the lie going, and the longer I did the harder it was to tell the truth."

Peggy looked like she was thinking and feeling a hundred different things at once.

"I don't think I really understand," she said.

Andrew chewed his lip. He had the strangest sensation that he was about to start laughing.

"I just wanted to feel normal," he said. "It started off so small but then"—he let out a strangely high-pitched bark of a laugh—"it's sort of got a bit out of hand."

Peggy looked startled. She'd fiddled with one of her earrings so much that it came free in her hand and bounced onto the table like a little blue tear that had frozen as it fell.

Andrew stared at it, and then the tune came into his head. This time, though, he willed it on. *Blue moon, you saw me standing alone.* He started to hum the tune out loud. He could sense that Peggy was beginning to panic. *Ask me. Please*, he begged silently.

"So, just so I'm clear," Peggy said. "Diane just . . . doesn't exist? You invented her."

Andrew grasped his glass and tipped the remaining liquid into his mouth.

"Well, not entirely," he said.

Peggy rubbed her eyes with her palms, then reached into her bag for her phone.

"What are you—who are you calling?" Andrew said, starting to get to his feet, yelping at the pain, having forgotten about his bruised foot.

Peggy waved her hand at him, getting him to sit back down.

"Hi, Lucy," she said into her phone. "I'm just calling to check you're all right to look after the girls for another couple of hours. Thanks, pet."

Andrew readied himself to speak but Peggy held up a hand. "I'm going to need an oil change before we go any further," she said, downing the rest of her drink, snatching their empty glasses and marching to the bar. Andrew clasped his hands together tightly. They were still so cold he could barely feel them. When Peggy returned with their drinks she had a new resolve about her, a steely look in her eyes that said she was prepared to hear the worst and not appear shocked by it. It was, he realized, exactly the sort of look Diane used to give him.

– CHAPTER 29 –

Andrew had gone to Bristol Polytechnic the summer after his mother's death. With Sally in Manchester with her new boyfriend, it had been less about a yearning for higher education and more about finding some people to talk to. Without any real research he settled on some digs in a part of the city called Easton. The house was just off a stretch of grass with the optimistically bucolic name of Fox Park, which in reality was a tiny patch of green separating the residential street from the M32 highway. As Andrew arrived outside the house, hauling his possessions in a bulky purple rucksack, he saw a man in the park dressed entirely in trash bags kicking a pigeon. A woman appeared from a bush and dragged the man away from the bird, but to Andrew's horror this was only so she could continue the assault herself. He was still recovering from having witnessed this harrowing tag-team display as he was ushered into his lodgings by the landlady. Mrs. Briggs had a fierce blue rinse and a cough like distant thunder, and Andrew quickly realized she had a good heart underneath her stern exterior. She seemed to be constantly cooking, often by candlelight whenever the electricity meter ran out (which it regularly did). She also had an unnerving habit of slipping in criticism halfway through an unrelated sentence: "Don't worry about that feller and the pigeon, my love, he's bit of a funny one, that lad—gosh, you need a haircut, m'duck—I think he's one sandwich short of a picnic, truth be told." It was the conversational equivalent of burying bad news.

Andrew soon grew fond of Mrs. Briggs, which was just as well, because he hated everybody on his course. He was savvy enough to work out that philosophy was going to attract a certain type, but it was as if they'd all been grown in a lab somewhere purely to annoy him. The boys all had wispy beards, smoked shitty little roll-ups and spent most of their time trying to impress girls by quoting the most obscure passages they knew from Descartes and Kierkegaard. The girls were denim-clad and seemed to spend all the lectures stony-faced, anger broiling away underneath the surface. Andrew only worked out later that this was largely due to the male tutors, who engaged in lively debate with the boys but spoke to the girls the way you might to a rather intelligent pony.

After a few weeks he made a couple of friends, a pudding-faced, largely benign Welshman called Gavin who drank neat gin and claimed to have once seen a flying saucer going over Llandovery rugby ground, and Gavin's girlfriend, Diane, a third-year who wore bright orange-rimmed glasses and didn't suffer fools gladly. Andrew quickly realized that Gavin was obviously the biggest fool of all, constantly testing Diane's patience in increasingly creative ways. They had been together since before uni ("Childhood sweethearts, you see," Gavin told him for the seventh time one evening, after his sixth gin), and Gavin had followed her to Bristol to do the same course. (Later, Diane would confide that this had been less Gavin's not bearing for them to be apart and more that the simplest of tasks were too hard for him. "I came home once to find him trying to cook chicken nuggets in the toaster.")

For reasons that were unclear to Andrew, Diane was the only

person he'd ever met in his brief adult life whom he found it completely unproblematic to talk to. He didn't stutter or stumble over his words when he was with her, and they shared a very specific sense of humor—dark, but never cruel. In the few instances where they were alone—waiting for Gavin to meet them at the pub, or in snatched moments when he was in the toilet or at the bar—Andrew began to open up to her about his mum and Sally. Diane had a natural gift for helping him to find the positives in what he was going through without trivializing anything, so when he spoke about his mum he found himself recalling the rare occasions when she seemed unburdened and happy, which usually occurred when she was gardening in the sunshine with Ella Fitzgerald playing in the background. When he spoke of Sally, he remembered a phase around the time they were watching Hammer horrors with Spike when she started to come back from the pub with presents she'd "acquired" (clearly from a dodgy regular who'd got them off the back of a lorry), including a Subbuteo set, a little wooden instrument apparently known as a "Jew's harp," and, most magnificently of all, an R176 Flying Scotsman with an apple-green engine and a teak carriage. He loved that engine, but it was Diane who made him realize that it was more than just an appreciation of the thing itself, that it was really emblematic of that brief period of time when Sally had been at her most affectionate.

Occasionally, through a haze of smoke in a rowdy pub, he would catch Diane looking at him. Unembarrassed at being caught in the act, she would hold his gaze for a second before rejoining the conversation. He lived for those moments. They started to be the only thing keeping him going. He was failing in his coursework to the point where he'd stopped bothering with it completely. He was resigned to dropping out at Christmas. He'd get a job somewhere and save some money. He told himself he'd go traveling, but in truth he'd found it hard enough moving to Bristol.

One night, he, Diane and Gavin were invited to an impromptu

party in a fellow philosophy student's halls of residence room, the caveat to the invite being they had to bring a crate of beer each. A large gang of them crammed into a bedroom and cracked open cans. Nobody wanted to talk about uni work, but Gavin found a copy of *On Liberty* and began drunkenly reading out passages as everyone tried to ignore him. As Gavin searched for a new book (perhaps Kierkegaard was what this party needed!), Andrew reached for what he was 50 percent sure was *his* Holsten Pils, but someone took his free hand from behind and pulled him outside. It was Diane. She led him through the corridor, down the three flights of stairs and out into the street, where snow was falling in thick clumps.

"Hello," she said, putting her arms around his neck and kissing him before he could reply. By the time he opened his eyes again there was a carpet of snow.

"You know I'm going back to London later this week," he said.

Diane raised her eyebrows.

"No! I didn't mean that . . . I just . . . I just thought I should tell you." Diane politely advised him to shut up and kissed him again.

They snuck back to Mrs. Briggs's that night. Andrew woke the next morning and thought Diane had left without saying good-bye, but her glasses were still on the bedside table, pointing toward the bed as if watching him. He heard the toilet flushing in the shared bathroom and then the sounds of two different sets of footsteps meeting on the landing. A short standoff. Awkward introductions. Diane climbed back into bed and punished Andrew for not coming to her rescue by clamping her ice-cold feet to his legs.

"Don't you ever warm up?" he said.

"Maybe," she whispered, pulling the duvet over their heads. "You'll just have to help me, won't you?"

Afterward, they lay on their sides with their legs still entwined. Andrew traced his finger on the little white scar above Diane's eyebrow.

"How did you get this?" he asked.

"A boy called James Bond threw a crabapple at me," she said.

————

Five days later, they stood on the train platform as the sun warmed them through a gap in the fence. They'd been on their first official date the previous night, to see *Pulp Fiction* at the cinema, though neither of them would be able to remember a great deal about the plot.

"I wish I'd worked harder," Andrew said. "I can't believe I've messed this up so badly."

Diane took his face in her hands. "Listen, you're still grieving for goodness' sake. The very fact you managed to get out of the house is something you should be proud of."

They stood huddled together until the train came. Andrew bombarded Diane with questions. He wanted to know everything about her, to have as much as possible to cling on to after he'd gone.

"I promise to come and visit you whenever I can afford the ticket, okay?" Andrew said. "And I'll call. And write."

"What about a carrier pigeon?"

"Oi!"

"Sorry, it's just you *are* talking a little bit like you're being shipped off to a war somewhere, not Tooting."

"And remind me again why I can't just stay here?"

Diane sighed. "Because a) I think you should spend some time with your sister, especially at Christmas, and b) because I think you need to move home for a bit and decide what you want to do next independently of me. I have to concentrate on my degree, for one thing, and when that's finished I'll probably end up moving to London anyway."

Andrew pulled a face.

"Probably."

After a moment of silence he realized how unattractive his sulking must have been to Diane, but as she hugged him good-bye she gripped him so fiercely that he felt the warmth of her all the way back to London.

———————

He moved into the spare room of a house currently occupied by two Dubliners who'd just discovered speed, and whom he managed to largely avoid apart from when they'd summon him to help settle entirely incomprehensible debates. (He tended to side with the one who looked most likely to set fire to something if he wasn't declared the winner.) He survived entirely on Rice Krispies and the thought of the next time he'd get to speak to Diane. They had an arranged time every week when he'd go down to the pay phone at the end of the road and call her, Diane demanding they start every conversation with him telling her about the newest "busty" or "exotic" woman being advertised in the phone box. He kept an empty Nescafé jar on his bedroom windowsill where he saved up money for train fares to Bristol. He'd found work behind the till in a video rental store exclusively patronized by shifty-eyed drunk men buying porn, something he'd only told Diane after much carousing in the pub.

By this point he'd all but given up on the idea of coming back to try to finish his degree. Summer was creeping toward them and it made him anxious just thinking about the idea of being back in classes again.

"So you're just going to sit about in London working in a porno shop?" Diane asked him. "What happened to you making decisions, or is this really the height of your ambition? You need to find out what you want to do for yourself. If you're not going to finish your degree you need to work out how you're going to have a career."

"But—"

She waved away his protests. "I'm serious. I won't hear another word about it." She put her hands on the sides of his face and squeezed, turning his mouth into a comedy fish. "You need to believe in yourself a bit more and just bloody get out there. What's your dream job, your dream career?"

She released the fish and waited for him to answer.

What *was* his dream job? More importantly, what could he say that she wouldn't laugh at?

"Working in the community somehow, or something, I suppose."

Diane narrowed her eyes, searching his face for signs of facetiousness.

"Well then, good," she said. "So that's the first positive step. You know the area you want to work in. You just need some experience. That means an office job, first up. So as soon as you're back in London you're going to find one. Agreed?"

"Yeah," Andrew mumbled.

"Don't sulk!" Diane said, and when he didn't respond she moved down the bed and blew a fierce raspberry on his belly.

"What about you then?" Andrew laughed, pulling her up so that she was lying on top of him. "What's *your* dream job?"

Diane rested her head on his chest. "Well, as much as I spent my entire adolescence saying I'd do the complete opposite of my parents, hence the philosophy degree blah blah blah, I'm thinking about a law conversion."

"Oh yeah? Brokering deals for drug-dealing informants, that sort of thing?"

"The fact that's your first thought makes me think you've been watching lots of terrible straight-to-video films from your shop."

"It was either that or the porn."

"And you've not watched any of that."

"Absolutely not."

"So if you want to have some 'alone time' you just picture . . ."

"You. Exclusively you. Wearing nothing but a smock made out of pages from Virginia Woolf novels."

"I thought as much."

She rolled off him so they were lying side by side.

"So, you're going to be a lawyer then," Andrew said.

"Either that or an astronaut," she yawned.

Andrew laughed. "You can't have a Welsh astronaut. That's ridiculous!"

"Um, why not?" Diane said.

Andrew prepared his best Valleys accent. "Well there now, rrrright. That's a small step for man, that is, and a great big giant one for mankind, see."

Diane huffed and went to climb out of bed, but Andrew dived and grabbed her arm that she'd left deliberately dangling there. He loved it when she did that. Teasing him. Knowing that she would only get as far as a step away before he pulled her toward him.

Back in London, he spent his time behind the video shop counter circling jobs in the paper. He'd just sold a horrific-looking video to a gaunt-faced man who explained, "Wanking helps me with the comedowns," when the phone rang. Five minutes later he replaced the receiver and considered the possibility that the woman who'd just asked him to come in for an interview might have been hired by Gavin as some sort of cruel act of revenge.

"Firstly, you're insane," Diane said when he spoke to her from the phone box later that evening (Bella, gorgeous busty blonde). "Secondly, I'm pretty sure I'm entitled to say I told you so. So we can do that now or wait till after you've actually got the job. It's up to you . . ."

The interview was for an admin assistant at the local council. He borrowed one of the Irish boys' suits, which had once belonged to his father. Checking his pockets as he sat in the waiting room, he found a ticket stub from a 1964 production of a play called *Philadelphia, Here I Come!*, which had been performed at the Gaiety Theatre, Dublin. Had Sally gone to Philadelphia when she was in the States? He couldn't remember, and he'd long since thrown away the postcards. He decided that the optimism of the title was a good omen.

The following morning, Diane's opening line as she picked up the phone to him was "I told you so."

"What would you have done if you'd said that and I hadn't got it?" Andrew laughed.

"Um, pretended it was one of my other boyfriends?"

"Oi!"

A pause.

"Wait, you are joking, right?"

A sigh.

"Yes, Andrew, I'm joking. Hamish Brown accidentally touched my boob while trying to fix an overhead projector last week, that's about as close as I've come to cheating on you . . ."

Despite himself, Andrew spent possibly 70 percent (okay, 80; 90, tops) of the time worrying about Diane's being enticed away by someone. He always pictured a floppy-haired rower called Rufus, for some reason. All broad shoulders and old money.

"Luckily for you, fictional Rufus is no match for a real-life skinny philosophy dropout who works in a porno shop and lives with two speed freaks."

Andrew was so nervous on his first morning at the council that he was forced to make a decision on whether it was less strange to spend the entire time on the toilet or to be sitting at his desk wincing with stomach cramps every five seconds. Thankfully, he managed to get through the day, and then a week, and then a month, without shitting himself or accidentally setting anything on fire. ("We really need to work on your benchmarks," Diane told him.)

Then the most glorious of days arrived: June 11, 1995. Diane's course was over, and she was coming to London. Andrew said good-bye to the two Irish boys, who were surprisingly emotional (though that could have been because they'd been up for three days straight) and piled all his stuff into the taxi waiting to take him to the flat he'd found for him and Diane, who'd managed to get everything into a couple of suitcases and taken the train from Bristol.

"Mum wanted to drive me," she said, "but I was a bit worried you might've rented us a crack den or something and I didn't want her having a panic attack."

"Ah. Hmm. Funny you should say that . . ."

"Oh god . . ."

Andrew couldn't be sure the tiny flat he'd found off the Old Kent Road *hadn't* ever been used as a crack den—it was a rough-and-ready sort of building with scuff marks on the corridor walls and a dewy smell about the place—but as he lay in bed that night, Diane sleeping next to him, her knees curled up to her chest, he couldn't stop smiling. This already felt like home.

Their moving coincided with a summer that brought with it a fiercely cloying heat. July was particularly punishing. Andrew bought a fan and he and Diane sat in their underwear in the front room when it got too hot to go out. They both became mildly obsessed with Wimbledon that month, Steffi Graf being a particular hero to Diane.

"This is just too bloody hot, isn't it?" Diane yawned, lying down on her front as Graf signed autographs before leaving center court.

"Might this help?" Andrew said before fishing two ice cubes out of his glass and carefully dropping them onto Diane's back, innocently apologizing as she half shrieked, half laughed.

The heat was unrelenting into August. People eyed each other nervously on the tube, looking out for potential fainters. Roads cracked and split. Garden watering bans were out in force. On the hottest day of the year, Andrew met Diane after work and they sprawled on the parched grass in Brockwell Park as all around them people kicked off shoes and rolled up sleeves. They'd brought bottles of lager but had forgotten to bring an opener. "Not to worry," Diane said, confidently approaching a nearby smoker and borrowing his lighter to somehow crack open the beers.

"Where did you learn that trick, then?" Andrew asked as they re-settled themselves on the grass.

"My granddad. He could use his teeth too in an emergency."

"He sounds . . . fun."

"Good old Granddad David. He used to say to me"—she affected a deep, booming voice—" 'If there's one lesson I've learned, Di, it's never go cheap on your booze. Life's too short.' My granny would just roll her eyes. God, I loved him, he was such a hero. You know what, if I ever have a son I really want to call him David."

"Oh yeah?" Andrew said. "What about if you have a girl?"

"Hmmm." Diane inspected her elbow, creased with a crisscross patch from the grass. "Oh, I know: Stephanie."

"Another relative?"

"No! Steffi Graf, obviously."

"Obviously."

Diane blew the froth from her beer at him.

Later, at home, she straddled him on the sofa as lightning seared the sky.

The rain came while the city slept, a deluge of greasy water pound-ing the streets. Andrew stood by the window as dawn broke, sipping a cup of coffee. He couldn't tell if he was still a bit drunk, or whether there was a hangover lying in wait. One of those nasty ones that creeps up on you, the sort where you're eating bacon while it's en route to the plate from the frying pan. He heard Diane stir. She sat up in bed and let her hair fall over her face.

Andrew laughed and went back to looking out of the window. "Have you got a hurty-head?" he said.

"I've got a hurty-everything," Diane croaked. He heard her shuffle over and felt her arms go around his waist, her cheek resting at the top of his back. "Shall we have a fry-up?" she said.

"Sure," Andrew said. "We'll just have to grab a few things from the shop."

"Whadoweneed?" Diane yawned, Andrew feeling it resonating through him.

"Oh, just bacon. And eggs. And sausages. And bread. Beans, possibly. Milk definitely, if you want tea."

He felt her grip slacken slightly and she groaned in defeat.

"Whose turn is it to *do a thing*?" he asked innocently.

She buried her face into his back. "You're only saying that because you know it's mine."

"What? Never!" Andrew said. "I mean, thinking back: I changed the channel, you put the kettle on, I put the bins out, you bought the paper, I did the washing up . . . Oh, you're quite right, it *is* your turn to do a thing."

She poked her nose into his back several times.

"Oi," he said, eventually giving in and turning to take her in his arms.

"Do you promise everything will be better after bacon and beans?" she said.

"I do. I absolutely do."

"And you love me?"

"Even more than bacon and beans."

He felt her slide her hand into his boxers and squeeze him.

"Good," she said, kissing him on the lips with an exaggerated "mwah" and abruptly walking off to slip on some flip-flops and throw a thin sweater over her pajamas.

"Well that's not fair," Andrew said.

"Hey, it's my turn to do a thing, I'm just going by the rules . . . ," Diane said with a shrug, trying to keep a straight face. She reached for her glasses, grabbed her purse and left, humming a tune. It took Andrew a second to realize it was Ella's "Blue Moon." *Finally*, he thought. *She's a convert.* He stood there grinning stupidly, feeling so hopelessly in love it was like he was a punch-drunk boxer desperately trying to stay upright.

He allowed himself two listens of "Blue Moon" before heading to have a shower—guiltily hoping that by the time he came out he'd be able to smell bacon sizzling. But there was no sign of Diane when he emerged. And there still wasn't ten minutes later. Perhaps she'd bumped into a friend—a fellow Bristol Poly alumnus; small world and all that. But something about this just didn't feel right. He quickly dressed and left the house.

He could see the gathering of people from the other end of the street where the shop was. "That's the thing," he overheard someone in the gaggle muttering just as he reached them. "All that hot weather and then suddenly a big old storm . . . bound to cause damage."

There were police officers standing in a semicircle, blocking anyone from going further. One of their radios crackled into life, a confusion of feedback and static that made an officer on one end of the ring wince and hold his radio out at arm's length. Then a voice cut through the interference: ". . . confirm it's one deceased. Falling masonry. No one's been able to ascertain who owns the building, over?"

Andrew felt the dread seeping into him as he moved through the last line of the crowd and toward the edge of the police ring. He was trembling as he walked, as if an electric current were flowing through him. He could see some blue plastic sheets ahead on the ground rippling in the breeze, a pile of smashed slate to one side. And there, next to it, perfectly intact, looking just the same as on the bedside table in Mrs. Briggs's house, was a pair of orange-framed glasses.

A policeman had his hands on his chest, telling him to get back. His breath smelled of coffee. There was a birthmark on his cheek. He was angry, but then he suddenly stopped shouting. He knew. He understood. He tried to ask Andrew questions but Andrew had crumpled to his knees, unable to support himself. There were hands on his shoulders. Concerned voices. Radio static. Then someone was trying to pull him to his feet.

The noise of the pub flitted back in and the policeman's hands became Peggy's, and it was like he was coming up from underwater, breaking the surface, and Peggy was telling him it was okay, squeezing him tightly, muffling his sobs. And even though he couldn't stop crying—it felt like maybe he'd never actually stop—he slowly became aware of a tingling in his fingers, warmth finally returning.

CHAPTER 30

He barely had the energy to get back to his flat. Peggy walked him there, half supporting his weight, and insisted that she come in with him. He protested halfheartedly, but now that Peggy knew the truth there wasn't much point.

"It's either that or the hospital," Peggy said, which settled the matter.

The model train set still lay wrecked, untouched since he'd smashed it up. "Hence the limp," he mumbled.

He lay down on the sofa and Peggy covered him in a blanket and then her coat. She made him tea and sat cross-legged on the floor, occasionally squeezing his hand, calming him down each time he jolted into consciousness.

When he woke, she was sitting in an armchair reading the *Ella Loves Cole* sleeve notes and drinking coffee from a mug he'd not used in a decade. There was a crick in his neck—he must have slept in a funny position—and his foot was still throbbing, but he felt more like himself.

He could vaguely remember a dream he'd had about Meredith's dinner party, and a question suddenly struck him. "What happened to Keith?" he asked.

Peggy looked up at him. "Morning to you too," she said. "Keith, you'll be glad to hear, is fine."

"But I heard you calling an ambulance," Andrew said.

"Aye. By the time it had arrived he was awake and trying to persuade the paramedics not to take him. To be honest, they seemed more worried about Cameron—silly sod sat there passed out with pen all over his face. I think they thought we'd kidnapped him into a mad cult, or something."

"Is Keith back at work?"

"Yep."

"Is he, you know, angry at me?"

"Well, he's not exactly delighted. But Meredith is treating him like a war hero, constantly fussing over him, so I think he's secretly quite enjoying it. She's the one you want to—" Peggy stopped herself.

"What?" Andrew said.

"She kept talking about getting Keith to press charges."

"Oh god," Andrew groaned.

"Don't worry, it's fine," Peggy said. "There is a chance I may have had a little word with her about it, and that she's not mentioned it since."

Andrew couldn't be sure, but it seemed like Peggy was trying to suppress a smile.

"You sound like a Mafia boss," he said. "But I'm very grateful, whatever you said." He looked across at the oven clock and scrabbled to sit upright. "Jesus," he said. "Have I really been asleep for twelve hours? What are you still doing here? You should be at home."

"It's all right," Peggy said. "I've FaceTimed the girls. They're staying in Croydon with one of Imogen's friends. They got to stay up and watch something horrifically inappropriate on the telly last night so they couldn't care less that I'm not there."

She turned the sleeve over. "I've got a confession to make. I haven't listened to the mix tape you made me."

"I'll let you off," Andrew said. "Like I said"—he winced as he rubbed at his swollen foot—"it barely took any time to put together."

Peggy placed the record carefully back on top of the pile.

"Your mam was a big fan, you said?"

"I don't really know. I've just got really vivid memories of her putting these records on and singing along as she did stuff in the kitchen, or playing them out of the window as she gardened. She always seemed, I don't know, like a completely different person when she let herself go like that."

Peggy drew her knees up to her chest. "I'd like to say I have similar memories of my mam when I was younger, but if she was dancing around the kitchen it was usually because she was trying to wallop one of us, or there was something on fire. Or both. Right, you look like you need some toast."

"It's fine, I'll do it," Andrew said, starting to get to his feet, but Peggy told him to sit still. Andrew just hoped to god she didn't judge him too much about the three cans of baked beans and possibly stale loaf of bread that made up the contents of the cupboard. Before he could make preemptive apologies his phone vibrated. He read the message and felt faint again. He waited until Peggy brought over a plate of generously buttered toast and a mug of tea.

"There's something else I need to tell you," he said.

Peggy took a big bite of toast. "Okay," she said. "I'll be honest with you, Andrew, after last night I'm not sure there's much you can say that'll shock me. But go for it . . ."

By the time he'd finished telling her about Carl and the blackmail

Peggy had lost interest in her toast, which she'd thrown onto her plate in disgust. She was pacing back and forth, hands on hips.

"He can't do that to you. There was a reason Sally gave you that money, and the fact he's threatening you is outrageous. You're going to call him right now and tell him to get fucked."

"No," Andrew said. "I can't."

"Why the hell not?"

"Because . . ."

"What?"

"It's not that easy. I can't . . . I just can't."

"But it's just an empty threat now, because it's not as if . . ." Peggy stopped pacing and looked at him. "Because you *are* going to tell the others at work the truth about everything, right?"

Andrew didn't say anything.

"Well," Peggy said, matter-of-factly, "you're going to have to. In two weeks' time you're supposed to be hosting the next dinner party so you haven't really got a choice."

"What?!" Andrew said. "But what about what happened at Meredith's—that was a disaster. Surely Cameron doesn't want that happening again."

"Oh, on the contrary, he's got it in his head that it's the perfect way for you and Keith to make up. He was so hammered that night he didn't really understand what had happened, other than that you and Keith had 'fallen out.' I managed to wipe his face clean and pour him into a taxi. He kept mumbling something to me about 'redundancies,' but god knows what's happening there."

Andrew folded his arms.

"I'm not telling them," he said, in a voice barely louder than a whisper. "I can't."

"Why not?"

"What do you mean, why not? Because I'll get fired! I can't afford for that to happen, Peggy. I've got no transferable skills, for one thing."

They were silent for a moment. Andrew really wished there were music playing. Peggy moved over to the window and stood with her back to him.

"I actually think you do have transferable skills," she said, "that you could do something else. And I think you know you do, too."

"What's that supposed to mean?" Andrew said.

Peggy turned around and went to speak, but then stopped, seemingly changing her mind.

"Can I ask you something?" she said eventually.

Andrew nodded.

"How much has this place changed since you moved in?"

"How do you mean?"

Peggy looked around. "When did you last buy new things? Have you, in fact, changed anything since the day Diane . . ."

Andrew suddenly felt horribly self-conscious.

"I don't know," he said. "Not a lot. A bit, though. The computer's new."

"Right. And how long have you been doing your current job?"

"What is this, an interview?" Andrew said. "Do you want another cup of tea by the way?"

Peggy came to sit next to him and took his hand in hers. "Andrew," she said softly. "I'm not even going to pretend to know how much shit you've had to go through, but I do know from experience what it's like to live in denial, to not confront things. Look at me and Steve. I knew in my heart of hearts that he wasn't going to change but it took me sinking to absolute rock bottom to do something about it. Didn't you have that same realization last night? Don't you feel now that it's time to try and move on?"

Andrew felt a tightness in his throat. His eyes began to sting. Part of him wanted Peggy to keep on at him like this, part of him just wanted to be alone.

"People won't be as kind as you," he said quietly. "And you couldn't exactly blame them. I just need more time—to think about how I'm going to do it, you know?"

Peggy lifted Andrew's hand and used hers to press it against his chest. He could feel his heart pounding against his rib cage.

"You've got to make a choice," Peggy said. "Either you can try and keep up with the whole pretense—pay that money to Carl even though it's yours, keep on lying to everyone—or you can tell the truth and start accepting the consequences. I know it's hard, I really do, but . . . okay, that day in Northumberland. When we had our 'moment,' shall we say."

Andrew really, *really* wished he didn't blush so easily.

"Yeah," he mumbled, rubbing his eyes.

"Look at me. Please."

"I can't."

"Okay, then just close your eyes. Think back and picture that moment. You don't have to tell me, but just think about how that made you feel. How lovely and *different* and . . . intense it was. I don't know. I'm only going on how it felt for me."

Andrew opened his eyes.

"Later," Peggy said, "when you were falling asleep on the sofa. You kept saying, 'You've saved me.' You thought I was your way out of all this. But, and you've got to trust me on this, only you can change things. It *has* to come from you."

Andrew's eye was drawn to the railway debris. It was as if the crash had just happened.

Peggy looked at her watch. "Look, I should probably think about going now. I need to make sure the girls have been given something else to eat other than Curly Wurlys." She stood up—letting Andrew's hand go—and retrieved her coat and bag. "Just think about what I've said, okay? And if you start feeling . . . you know . . . then call me straightaway. Promise?"

Andrew nodded. He really didn't want her to leave. He wasn't going to be able to do this without her, whatever she might think. "I'm going to do it," he blurted out. "I'll tell the truth, to everyone—but it just *can't* be now, when Cameron's talking redundancies. I just need to find a way of getting through the stupid bloody dinner party with my reputation intact, and then when things have settled down I'll fix everything, I promise. So all I'm asking for is a bit of help, short term, for how I'm going to . . ." His words petered out as he saw the disappointment in Peggy's eyes. She moved toward the door and he limped after her.

"What are you . . . please don't—"

"I've said my piece, Andrew. I'm not going to change my mind. Besides, I've got my own mess I need to sort out."

Andrew just about managed to stop himself from begging her to stay.

"Sure," he said. "Of course. I understand. And sorry, I didn't mean to drag you away. And I'm sorry for lying to you. I wanted to tell you the truth, I really did."

"I believe you," Peggy said, giving him a peck on the cheek. "And I believe in you, too."

Andrew stood there for a long time after Peggy had gone. He looked down at the wine stain on the carpet. It was in the same spot where he'd stood, rigid in his own despair, the phone ringing and ringing as Sally tried to get him to speak to her, the day after Diane's death. He felt impossibly guilty for how he'd behaved then—how cowardly and weak he'd been to hide himself away, too broken to face the funeral, refusing to let Sally comfort him—and even more so now thinking about how he'd indulged in the fantasy of how his life might have gone if Diane had never walked out of the house that morning. He couldn't believe how kind and understanding Peggy had been after she'd learned the truth. He'd expected her to run a mile. Unless of course she was just lulling him into a false sense of security before she dashed to the nearest mental hospital to report him as a deluded, dangerous fantasist . . . Surely, *surely*, nobody else would be as understanding as her, if he were to simply come out and tell them? He pictured Cameron's beady eyes widening, Keith and Meredith turning from stunned to scathing in the blink of an eye.

He heard his mobile vibrate again. Another message from Carl, no doubt. The autopilot in him wanted to put on some Ella, but he stopped by the record player, his hand above the needle. Without music or the gentle whooshing of a train he was more aware of what he could hear. He opened the window. Sparrows were singing; a bee—a queen surely, judging from its size—buzzed past.

Despite the fact he was feeling jittery from caffeine, he made himself another cup of tea, enjoying the comforting warmth of it as he drank, his thoughts percolating. He understood why Peggy was frustrated that he wasn't simply going to come clean with everyone now that he'd revealed the truth to her, but what she perhaps hadn't fully grasped was how potent the fantasy was, how tied to it he felt. It wasn't something he could just walk away from.

He stood and surveyed the train wreck. It was hard to tell what damage was repairable and what was ruined for good. The locomotive he'd had set up at the time—an O4 Robinson class—was probably a write-off, as were the carriages. Thank Christ it hadn't been any of his really prized locomotives. Most of the scenery—the lighter stuff—was definitely irreparable. Trees and animals were flattened and bent. Figures lay prone on the ground. All of them, he realized, except three farmhands who were still upright in what used to be an orchard, a look of defiance about them.

Peggy had told him he alone had to choose what to do, and maybe she was right. But what if that meant he chose only to tell people the truth when he actually felt ready? That was still him taking control, wasn't it? He ignored the dissenting voice at the back of his head by focusing on what he told himself was the more immediate concern: namely, the approaching dinner party. It was absolutely vital that he keep Cameron happy. What he really needed was some help. Peggy was out of the question. So that left . . . well, "Nobody," he said out loud. But as he looked again at the stoic farmhands, he remembered that, actually, that wasn't strictly true.

CHAPTER 31

Saturday afternoons weren't the busiest times on the subforum, but Andrew could still picture BamBam67, TinkerAl and BroadGaugeJim checking in before the evening was out—a quick glance as they waited for dinner to simmer, just in case someone had posted to confirm that the new Wainwright H Class 0-4-4T really *did* justify the insane hype.

It worked in his favor that recent events had meant his activity on the forum had been limited in the previous week, as the last two messages mentioning him, from TinkerAl and BroadGaugeJim, were written with genuine concern:

Tracker, you've gone a bit quiet. All good?

Was just thinking that! Don't say old T-bone's gone cold turkey??

The fact that they were obviously concerned for his welfare made him feel a little more comfortable about asking for help like this. He composed a message in a blank document, tweaking and rewording from start to finish several times.

He was still finding it hard to get completely warm, so he'd rooted around in a cupboard and found some blankets, which he'd washed and tumble-dried before wrapping around his shoulders, so that it looked like his head was poking out through the top of a wigwam. He had also—in a moment of madness, suddenly consumed by derring-do—made some soup from scratch.

He copied and pasted his message into a new post on the forum, gave it one final check, and then, before he could back out, he hit "send."

———

Andrew took a sip of lager and made a note to remind himself that his instincts—much like burgers bought from rest-stop vans and people who started sentences with "I'll be honest with you"—were not to be trusted. He'd chosen the pub near King's Cross because it was called the Railway Tavern, and that felt like a good omen. He had visions of Barter Books—the same ambience, but substituting tea, scones and books for thick pints of bitter and interesting crisps. Instead, the pub felt like the sort of place you only ever heard mentioned in the same breath as "fled the scene" and "unprovoked attack." Andrew had long since lost track of which clubs were battling it out at the top of Division One, or whatever it was called now, but the twenty or so other men in the pub were, to put it mildly, invested. Insults were leveled at the screen with furious relish. More confusingly, a man with ginger sideburns kept clapping whenever a decision went his team's way or there was a substitution, as if his applause could actually travel through the screen and reach the player coming on. Another man in a leather jacket worn over his team's colors periodically threw his arms up in the air and turned to try to make conversation with a group of fans who steadfastly ignored him. A young woman was standing further up along the bar, pulling nervously at her hair, which was purple and looked like it had the consistency of cotton candy. Never had Andrew seen so many people in the same place, supporting the same team, wearing the same shirt, looking so alone.

Under other circumstances, he would have left and found somewhere else, but that wasn't an option. He'd concluded his message on the forum by naming the pub and the time. For all he knew there might've been three instant replies, apologetic or otherwise, rejecting the plan, but he hadn't been able to face looking to see if anyone had responded. The closest he'd gotten was scrolling down with one hand over his face, peeping through a gap between his fingers, as if he were looking at an eclipse.

He fiddled nervously with a coaster, eventually giving in to the urge to tear it into strips, leaving a pile of cardboard on the table like a hamster's nest. He was suddenly very aware of how desperate he felt. He cringed at his cheery sign-off on the forum (Besides, it would be fun for us to actually meet up in person, no??), which now seemed glaringly ripe for dismissal and ridicule. It went against pretty much everything they stood for. The forum was a place where you could pretend to be someone else and, more importantly, do so naked while eating cheese if you wanted. How was real life supposed to compete with that?

He took a careful look around (remembering how Peggy had admonished him for his obviousness in the pub on her first day), hoping to see someone he thought might be one of the forum lot. He was doing his best not to make eye contact with the man in the leather jacket, who, when Andrew was ordering a pint from the grizzled barman, had turned to him showing his bloodshot eyes and grunted, "All right?" Andrew had pretended not to hear before scuttling away, also pretending not to hear the man muttering, "Wanker," after him.

He straightened his coat lapel so that the little model train badge he'd affixed to it was visible. He'd hoped it was a subtle touch that would make him recognizable to the others without drawing undue attention. So it was all he could do not to burst out laughing when he looked up to see the man who'd just entered the pub was wearing a T-shirt bearing the slogan: "Model Trains Are the Answer. WHO CARES WHAT THE QUESTION IS?!"

Andrew half stood, half waved to the man, who—to his overwhelming relief—grinned back broadly.

"Tracker?"

"Yes! My name's Andrew, you know, in real life."

"Nice to meet you, Andrew. I'm BroadGauge—Jim."

"Great!"

Andrew reached out and shook Jim's hand, possibly a bit too enthusiastically judging by Jim's expression, but Andrew felt too excited to be embarrassed. Somebody had come!

"Cracking badge, by the way," Jim said.

"Thanks," Andrew said. He was going to return the compliment about Jim's T-shirt when evidently a goal was scored and the pub erupted into howls of disapproval. Jim briefly appraised the commotion, then turned back, his eyebrows raised.

"Sorry, it's a rubbish choice of venue," Andrew said quickly.

Jim shrugged. "Nah, it's fine. What are you drinking then?"

"Oh thanks, lager please," Andrew said, waiting till Jim was heading to the bar before downing the last third of his pint.

As Jim returned with their drinks he was followed over by the young woman with purple hair, who'd just come out of the ladies'. Before either Jim or Andrew could say anything she'd sat down at the table and offered them a nervous hello.

"Um, sorry," Jim said, "but we're actually waiting for someone." Andrew gave the woman an apologetic smile.

"Yeah, that'd be me," the woman said.

Andrew and Jim looked at each other.

"Hang on," Andrew said, "You're . . ."

"TinkerAl," the woman said.

"But . . . but you're a woman!" Jim said.

"Well spotted," the woman laughed. Then, when neither Andrew nor Jim could work out how to respond, she rolled her eyes and said, "The 'Al' part comes from Alexandra. But people call me Alex."

"Well," Jim said. "That's, you know . . . good for you!"

"Thanks," Alex said, smothering a smile before launching into a passionate monologue about her latest acquisition. "I honestly reckon it outclasses the Caerphilly Castle 4-6-0," she said.

"No way!" Jim said, eyes nearly popping out of his head.

The three of them continued to talk trains, occasionally having to raise their voices over the men shouting at some perceived injustice on the big screen. Despite the occasional angry glare from leather jacket man, Andrew was beginning to relax. Though if BamBam wasn't going to turn up, then that posed a big problem. He needed him the most.

It was during a melee of celebrations as the home team pinched an equalizer that a man sauntered through the door and pulled up a chair at their table with the nonchalance of someone who was meeting people he'd seen every day for twenty years. He was wearing a dark blue denim shirt tucked into some beige slacks and smelled of expensive aftershave. He introduced himself as BamBam, then Rupert—which the others tried and failed not to seem surprised by. Jim watched Rupert shake Alex's hand and couldn't help himself. "She's a woman!" he said.

"It's true," Alex said. "I've got a certificate and everything. Right, who wants crisps?"

The four of them drank and ate from bags of potato chips that were democratically opened out on the table. As they talked about new purchases and various upcoming conventions—already promising to meet up at an exhibition day at Alexandra Palace—Andrew was starting to wish he didn't have to upset the balance by bringing his plan into the mix. But after he returned from the toilet, the others clearly using the opportunity to discuss his message, Jim cleared his throat and said, "So, Andrew, you, um, invited us here for a . . . thing?"

Andrew had carefully rehearsed what he was going to say, but he could still feel the blood thumping in his ears. He'd decided to get everything out as quickly as possible, revealing only as much as he had to. He spoke rapidly without pausing to draw breath, so much so that he was actually light-headed by the time he'd finished.

"That's it," he concluded, taking a big gulp of beer.

There was a horribly long pause. Andrew grabbed another beer mat and started to tear and twist it.

Then Rupert cleared his throat.

"Just to be clear," he said, "you need my house to host a dinner party in?"

"And for all of us to help you cook for said dinner party?" Alex said.

"And just generally be on hand to help out . . . and stuff," Jim added.

"Because," Alex said, "redundancies are on the cards and you need to keep your boss on your side."

Andrew realized how mad it all sounded, laid bare like that. "I honestly can't explain to you how insane my boss is. I thought he was just making us do these dinner parties because he wanted to be friends with us all, but it seems like it's more to do with him trying to decide who he likes the most and who he can bring himself to let go. And I . . . well, I really can't afford to be that person right now."

The others exchanged glances, and Andrew sensed they might want to confer.

"I'll get a round in," he said. Despite worrying about what Jim, Rupert and Alex were deciding to do, he couldn't help but grin to himself as he made his way to the bar. *I'll get a round in*—so casual! As if it were the most natural thing in the world!

"I need to change the barrel for the pale ale," the barman said.

"That's fine, take your time," Andrew said, realizing too late that this might have sounded sarcastic. The barman stared at him for a moment before heading to the cellar.

"You wanna be careful," leather jacket man said. "I've seen him kick seven shades out of a bloke for less. He's fine one minute, mental the next."

But Andrew wasn't listening. There was a mirror just above the row of spirits, and in the reflection he could see the others deliberating at the table. He was suddenly very aware of the ebb and flow of noise from the fans around him, as if the groans and expletives and shouts of encouragement were the soundtrack to the conversation he was watching.

"Why you ignoring me, mate?" leather jacket man piped up.

Andrew acted oblivious and counted out his money for the round.

"Helllooooooo," the man said, reaching over and waving a hand in front of Andrew's face.

Andrew pretended to be surprised. "Sorry, I'm not really with it today," he said, wishing he didn't sound quite so much like a flustered substitute teacher.

"No excuse to totally ignore me like that," the man said, poking him in the shoulder. "Basic fucking human politeness, that."

Now Andrew was desperate for the barman to return. He looked at the mirror. The others still seemed to be in deep discussion.

"So what you reckon?" the man said, indicating the screen.

"Oh, I don't really know," Andrew said.

"Have a guess, mate. Bit of fun." The man poked him in the shoulder again, harder this time.

Andrew backed away as subtly as he could. "A draw?" he said.

"Pah. Bollocks. You West Ham in disguise? Oi, everyone, this one's West Ham!"

"I'm not, I'm nobody," Andrew said, his voice going falsetto.

Luckily, no one paid them any attention, and to Andrew's relief the barman finally reappeared and finished pouring drinks.

When he arrived back at the table it was to what felt like an awkward silence, and he realized he'd forgotten one vital point. "I forgot to say, I'm not asking you to do this for free. We can work out, you know, a payment, whether that's cash or you taking your pick of my kit. I managed to damage my O4 Robinson recently, but there are my other locomotives, and scenery, so just let me kn—"

"Don't be silly," Alex interrupted. "Of course you don't need to pay us. We're just trying to work out logistics."

"Oh. Good," Andrew said. "I mean, great, that you're on board and everything."

"Yep, definitely," Alex said. "We're friends, after all," she added, in a voice that made it sound like she was settling the issue. She widened her eyes at Rupert.

"Oh, yes, indeed," he said, "and you're welcome to have your soiree at mine. My partner's actually away with work next week, so the timing's decent. Though I'm a lousy cook, I'm afraid."

Jim linked his fingers together and extended his arms, cracking his knuckles. "You can leave the cooking to Jimbo," he said.

"So. There we go. Sorted," Alex said.

They talked a little more about the whens and wheres, but after a while conversation turned back to trains. For the second time that afternoon, Andrew had to concentrate on hiding the goofy grin that kept trying to wriggle onto his mouth.

———

The football was finished—it *was* a draw in the end—and most of the fans had already filed out, shaking their heads and grumbling. Leather jacket man had other ideas, however, and Andrew groaned inwardly as he watched him meander over and pull up a chair at the table next to them.

"Model trains, eh," he said, eyeing Jim's shirt before resting his feet on the back of Andrew's chair. "Fuck me, do people still actually bother with that crap?"

Alex raised her eyebrows at Andrew. "Do you know him?" she mouthed. Andrew shook his head.

"Sorry, mate," Alex said, "we're a bit busy. Mind giving us some space?"

The man made a big show of looking Alex up and down. "Well, well, well, if I was ten years younger . . ."

"I'd still utterly ignore you," Alex said. "Now go away, there's a good boy."

The man's leer turned into a scowl. He kicked the back of Andrew's chair. "You wanna tell that bitch to shut her mouth."

"All right, that's enough," Andrew said, getting to his feet. "I'd like you to leave us alone now." His voice was shaking.

"Yeah, and what happens if I don't?" the man said, standing and drawing himself up to his full height. This was the cue for Rupert, Jim and Alex to stand up, too.

"Jesus, look at this lot," the man said. "A wimpy prick, a slag, a tubby ticket inspector and a shit Sherlock Holmes."

"Well that's not very nice, now, is it?" Rupert said, sounding remarkably calm. Andrew would have questioned whether such a sarcastic tone was the right approach, but then he noticed what Rupert had already. Namely, that unbeknownst to leather jacket man, the barman was walking toward him, rolling his head around his shoulders as if he were about to run the hundred meters. He waited for the man to take one more step toward Andrew before he advanced swiftly, grabbed him by his collar, hauled him toward the exit and shoved him through the door, aiming a kick at his backside for good measure. As he made his way back to the bar he even rubbed imaginary dirt off his hands, something Andrew had only ever seen in cartoons.

Andrew, Jim, Alex and Rupert all just stood there for a moment, nobody seeming to know what to say. It was Jim who broke the silence. "Tubby ticket inspector? I'll take that, I reckon."

CHAPTER 32

Peggy was worried about Andrew's coming straight back into work. *You should take some time off, get your head together*, she texted him. *Remember how grim this job can be. You're not an ice cream taster.* But Andrew was struggling with being at home. It was just him and his own thoughts, and he hated his own thoughts; they were largely bastards. Since Peggy had come to his flat he was also beginning to realize quite how ridiculous the state of the place was. He spent the evening after the subforum meet-up cleaning everywhere until he was sweaty and exhausted.

As he left the building the following morning he caught a tantalizing glimpse of perfume woman's door closing behind her. He was so surprised to actually see evidence that she existed he very nearly called out.

———

The evening of the dinner party coincided with Andrew and Peggy's first property inspection for two weeks (Malcolm Fletcher, sixty-three, massive heart attack on a lumpy futon), and for once it only took them a few minutes before they had a breakthrough.

"Got something," Peggy called from the bedroom. Andrew found her sitting cross-legged on the floor of a walk-in wardrobe, surrounded by pairs of pristinely polished shoes, nearly identical suit jackets hanging above her, like she was a child playing hide and seek. She proffered Andrew a posh-looking address book. He flicked through but there was nothing written on any of the pages from A to Z.

"Last page," Peggy said, reaching up for Andrew to pull her to her feet. Andrew flicked to the "Notes" section at the back of the address book.

"Ah," he said. *Mum & Dad* and *Kitty* were written at the top of the page in small, spidery handwriting, with corresponding phone numbers next to them. He took out his mobile and called *Mum & Dad*, but it was a young-sounding woman who answered who'd never heard of anyone called Malcolm and had no record of the previous occupants. Andrew had more luck with Kitty.

"Oh goodness, that's . . . he's my brother . . . poor Malcolm. God. What a horrible shock. I'm afraid we'd rather fallen out of touch." Andrew mouthed along with the last six words for Peggy's benefit.

———

"So how are things?" Andrew said as they left the flat, deciding to keep the question vague enough that Peggy could respond however she wanted.

"Well, Steve came to collect the last of his stuff yesterday, which was a relief. He told me he hadn't had a drink in ten days, although he did smell like a distillery, so unless he got very unfortunate and someone spilled an awful lot of vodka on him, I think he was probably lying."

"I'm sorry," Andrew said.

"Don't be. I should have done this a long time ago. Sometimes you just need that extra little push. A reason to help you make the decision."

Andrew could sense Peggy had turned her head to look at him, but he couldn't quite bring himself to meet her eye. He knew what she was getting at—and he didn't want to concede that she was right.

Just then, he received a text from Jim with the menu for that evening (the food sounding reassuringly posh—what, indeed, was kohlrabi?) and asking him to pick up some booze. He shook the doubts from his mind. He had to focus on everything going perfectly tonight, no matter what Peggy thought.

"I just need to make a quick detour," he said, taking them into Sainsbury's and heading for the alcohol aisle.

"That person you spoke to today—Kitty, was it?" Peggy said.

"Mmm-hmm," Andrew said, distracted by reading the label on a pinot noir.

"She must've been the hundredth person you've heard saying 'we'd rather fallen out of touch,' right?"

"Probably," Andrew said, reaching for a bottle of champagne and passing it to Peggy. "Is this classy?"

"Erm, nope, not really. How about this?" She handed him a bottle with some silver netting around the neck. "What I mean is," she said, "it's all very well doing what we do, but it all feels a bit 'after the fact,' you know? I mean, wouldn't it be nice if everyone did more to at least give people the option of finding company, to be able to connect with someone in a similar position, rather than this sort of inevitable isolation?"

"Yeah, good plan, good plan," Andrew said. *Nibbles. Do we need nibbles? Or are nibbles passé these days?* He hadn't felt that anxious up until then, but he was really starting to feel the nerves bubbling now.

"I was wondering," Peggy continued, "if there was, like, a charity that did that, or—I know this sounds a bit mad—whether we could actually look at setting one up ourselves. Or if not that, then finding a way to make sure at least *someone* other than one of us turns up to the funerals when we can't find a next of kin."

"Sounds great," Andrew said. *Why does paprika have such a monopoly on spice-flavored crisps, anyway? Fuck, what if someone is allergic to paprika, or any of the food Jim is cooking? Okay, just calm down. Deep breaths. Deep. Fucking. Breaths.*

Peggy sighed. "And I'd also like to ride an elephant into the sea, naked, while singing the words to 'Bohemian Rhapsody.'"

"Mmm-hmm, good plan. Hang on, what?"

Peggy laughed. "Never mind." She took the bottle out of his hands and replaced it with another. "So, tonight . . . ," she said.

Andrew winked. "Got that all figured out," he said.

Peggy stopped dead, waited for him to turn around and face her. "Andrew, did you just wink at me?"

———

As soon as he got back to the office from the supermarket, he walked straight over to Keith's desk.

Keith was eating a donut and chortling at something on his screen. But when he saw Andrew he dropped the donut and scowled.

"Hello, Keith," Andrew said. "Listen, I just wanted to apologize for what happened the other week. Things got really out of hand, but I am so, so sorry for pushing you like that. I really didn't mean to hurt you. I hope you can forgive me."

He handed over the champagne Peggy had picked out and offered Keith a handshake. Initially, Keith seemed taken aback by this charm offensive, but it didn't take him long to regain his composure. "Cost-cutter own brand, is it?" he said, ignoring Andrew's hand and turning the bottle over to read the label, as Meredith hurried over to stand protectively at his side.

"Well, this doesn't exactly make up for what happened," Meredith said.

Andrew held his hands up. "I know. I agree. It's just a little gesture. I really hope that we can all get together tonight at mine, have a lovely time, and put it all behind us. What do you think? Sound like a plan?"

Okay, okay, keep a lid on it, don't sound so desperate.

"Well," Keith said, clearing his throat. "I suppose that I was maybe being a bit out of order myself. And, well, I guess you weren't trying to deliberately knock me out."

"No," Andrew said.

"Obviously given another day I'd have probably sparked you out for hitting me, if you'd not got that lucky shot in."

"Definitely," Meredith said, looking at Keith admiringly.

"But, for the sake of, you know, moving on, I'm happy to say bygones be bygones, and all that shit."

This time Keith shook his hand.

Just then, Cameron walked past, doubling back to see what was happening. He had dark rings under his eyes and looked horribly gaunt.

"Everything okay, chaps?" he said, slightly warily.

"Yes, absolutely," Andrew said. "We were just saying how much we're looking forward to dinner tonight."

Cameron searched Andrew's face for signs of sarcasm. Apparently satisfied of its absence, he smiled, put his palms together and said, "Namaste," before backing away into the corridor and heading to his office with a new spring in his step.

"What a weirdo," Keith said.

Meredith, realizing that Keith's label was poking out of his shirt collar, reached over and tucked it in. Keith, Andrew noticed, looked a little embarrassed at this.

"So, Andrew," Meredith said, "do we finally get to meet Diane tonight?"

"No, afraid not," Andrew said. "She and the kids have tickets for a show. Crossed wires on the dates." Even though he'd rehearsed this line several times, it still took all his concentration to make the words sound genuine. As he sat down at his desk, a fresh pile of paperwork in his in-tray, a new lot of death to be tackled, he couldn't help but picture Peggy's reproachful look as he begged her to help him. *Only you can change things. It* has *to come from you.*

– CHAPTER 33 –

Andrew walked out of the office laden down with booze, looking both ways before he crossed the road, and promptly dropped the bag of wine on the pavement, where it landed with a crunch. "Unlucky, mate," called a white-van man inevitably driving past at that moment. Andrew gritted his teeth and made his way to another Sainsbury's. What was it about going into a supermarket already carrying a bag of shopping that made it feel like you were returning to the scene of a botched murder?

He just about remembered which bottles of wine he'd previously bought and added another bottle for good luck. The woman behind the till—Glenda, according to her name badge—scanned the bottles through and hummed approvingly. "Big night tonight, m'love?"

"Something like that," Andrew said.

Innocent though they'd been, Glenda's words opened the floodgates to Andrew's nerves. He could feel his heart starting to race as he hurried along, sweat beginning to pool under his armpits. He felt like everyone he passed was giving him a meaningful look, as if there were something at stake for them too, and every half-overheard snippet of conversation seemed to be charged with meaning. His anxiety wasn't helped by the fact that Rupert's directions to his house seemed needlessly complicated. (He'd told them all to ignore Google Maps—"It thinks I live in a shop called Quirky's Fried Chicken. I've sent several e-mails"—and go by his own instructions.) When Andrew did eventually find the place, sweat was pouring off him and he was out of breath. He jabbed at the doorbell and heard a slightly pathetic and oddly discordant response, as if it were on the verge of breaking.

The door was answered by a cloud of smoke, followed by Jim.

"Come in, come in," Jim coughed.

"Is everything okay?" Andrew said.

"Yes, yes, just a minor accident involving a paper towel and a naked flame. I'm cracking on with the starters nicely though."

Andrew was just about to ask whether there was a smoke alarm in the kitchen when it went off and he stood helpless, weighed down with the shopping, as Jim frantically flapped a tea towel in the air.

"Stick the wine on the island for now," Jim said, indicating the pristine granite worktop complete with wine rack and artfully arranged Sunday supplements. "I need to work out what I'm pairing with what."

"It's not an island," came Rupert's voice from the doorway. "According to our estate agent, anyway. It being connected to the wall on one side, it's actually a peninsula." Rupert was wearing similarly smart attire to when they'd met in the pub, but with the addition of a purple dressing grown tied loosely at the waist. He noticed Andrew looking at it.

"It gets quite cold in my office but I can't bring myself to turn the heating up. Don't worry, I'm just an IT consultant, not Hugh Hefner or anything."

Jim pulled some ingredients from a bag and, having lined them up on the counter, began to scrutinize each item closely, as if he were judging a village fete competition.

"All good?" Andrew said.

"Yes. Absolutely," Jim said, tapping a finger against his chin, his eyes narrowed. "Absolutely."

Andrew looked at Rupert, who raised an eyebrow at him.

Andrew was about to ask Jim if he was sure he knew what he was doing when the doorbell rang, the sound even more weary and out of tune than when he'd rung it himself. Rupert put his hands in his dressing gown pockets.

"Well it's your house tonight, you better answer it."

As Andrew left the room he heard Jim asking if Rupert owned "a cleaver, or something," and felt his heart rate increase another notch.

Andrew opened the door to find Alex. Her hair was dyed a shocking white-blond, although it wasn't altogether rid of the purple, which was clinging on in the odd streak.

"So I've got loads of decorations and stuff," she said, thrusting one of the two bags she was holding into Andrew's hands. "Gonna really set the mood and make it all *massively, extremely* fun! Look—party poppers!"

She skipped past Andrew down the corridor.

"Um, Alex, when you say 'massively, extremely fun'—obviously I want it to be *fun* but I don't want anything too extreme or . . . or massive."

"Sure, gotcha, don't worry about it," Alex said. Andrew followed her into the dining room in time to see her enthusiastically scattering glitter onto the dining table.

"Shit," she said suddenly, slapping a hand to her forehead.

"What's wrong?" Andrew said.

"Just realized I've left a whole bag of stuff at the shop. I'll have to go back." When she took her hand away there was glitter in her hair.

Back in the kitchen, Jim was indiscriminately hacking at a butternut squash with a cleaver as if he were hastily dismembering a corpse.

"Everything all right?" Andrew said, hovering nervously.

"Yes, yes," Jim said. "Ah, that's what I was going to say: Rupert, do you have anything that we could use as a trolley to transfer the food to the dining room on?"

"A trolley? Can't I just carry it?" Andrew said.

"Yes, but I thought it might look quite fancy if you were to prepare the last bits and pieces of the main next to the table, gueridonstyle, you see?"

"*Gueridon?*" Rupert said. "Didn't he play left-back for Leeds?"

The doorbell warbled again. Andrew was wondering about what else in the way of party decorations Alex might have returned with, but when he opened the door it was with horror that he found Cameron standing on the step.

"Hellooo!" Cameron said, stretching the word out as if he were calling into a tunnel to hear the echo. The smile disappeared from his face. "Oh, crumbs, I'm not mega-early, am I?"

Andrew just about managed to regain his composure. "No, no, of course not, come in, come in."

"Something smells good," Cameron said after he'd stepped inside. "What's a-cookin'?"

"It's a surprise," Andrew said.

"How intriguing," Cameron said with a knowing grin. "I've brought some vino rouge, but I'll probably stick to the Adam's ale this evening after my—how shall I put it—overindulgence last time."

"Right, sure," Andrew said, taking the bottle and guiding Cameron into the dining room.

"Clara and I had sort of clear-the-air talks when I got home that night, truth be told—unpacked everything and really drilled down. It always helps to talk things through, doesn't it?"

"Absolutely," Andrew said, realizing with some concern that Cameron looked even paler than earlier.

"Well, I like the glitter," Cameron said. "Very jazzy."

"Thanks," Andrew said. "Take a seat and I'll be back with your water in a sec. Don't move!" he added, making a gun with thumb and forefinger. Cameron raised his hands meekly in surrender.

Andrew sprinted into the kitchen and closed the door. "Okay, we have a very big fucking problem," he said. "One of the guests—my boss, in fact—has arrived and is just sitting there in the dining room. So you need to keep as quiet as possible—and don't let anybody through this door who's not me."

Rupert was swiveling back and forth on a tall chair, looking completely unfazed. "Can't we pretend to be staff or something?" he said.

"No," Andrew said. "Too weird. They'll ask too many questions. Right, what am I doing? Ah yes, water."

Andrew turned to the cupboards, looking for a glass.

"Hmm, slight issue," he heard Rupert say.

"What? And where do you keep your glasses?"

"Top-left cupboard. And the issue is there's a woman just outside, staring at us."

Andrew nearly dropped the glass as he spun around to look at the window. Thankfully, it was Peggy. And as she caught his eye and smiled, one eyebrow slightly arched in amusement, it was then that Andrew was overwhelmed by now happy and relieved he was to see her—that this was how he felt whenever she came into the same room as him.

He walked over and slid the French windows open.

"Hello," Peggy said.

"Hello."

Peggy widened her eyes slightly.

"Shall I come in?"

"Oh, right, yes," Andrew said, quickly stepping aside. "Everyone, this is Peggy."

"Hello . . . everyone," Peggy said. "I think your doorbell's kaput."

Andrew started to garble an explanation but Peggy put up her hand to stop him. "It's fine, it's fine, you don't have to explain. I'll go through, shall I?"

"Good idea," Andrew said. "Cameron's already here, actually."

"Spectacular news," Peggy said. "Down here, is it?"

"Yep. Second—no, third—door on your right."

Andrew watched her leave, then turned back to the countertop, leaning on it for support and taking some steadying breaths.

"She seems nice," Jim said.

"She is," Andrew said. "So nice in fact that I *think* there's actually a very good chance I'm in love with her. Anyway, how's the butternut whatever coming along?"

When Jim didn't answer, Andrew looked around to see that Peggy had reappeared without him realizing it. There was a moment when nobody did anything. Then Peggy stepped forward and reached past Andrew, avoiding his eye. "Glasses in here, are they? Lovely. Just getting Cameron's water."

She filled the glass from the tap and left, whistling softly.

"Oh great," Andrew said. He was about to follow this up with some less family-friendly words when there was a knock at the front door.

"I'll get it," Andrew said, heading off down the hall. He opened the door to find a panicked-looking Alex bookended by a confused-looking Meredith and Keith.

"Just picked up those things you asked for," Alex said robotically.

"Ah. Right. Yes," Andrew said. "Thank you very much."

"No problem . . . neighbor."

Andrew took the bag and ushered Meredith and Keith into the hallway, gesturing to Alex that she should go around to the French windows.

"Good luck!" she mouthed, giving him a double thumbs-up.

"Can I use the loo?" Meredith said.

"Yes, of course," Andrew said.

"Where is it?"

"Um, good question!"

Meredith and Keith didn't join in with Andrew's forced laughter. "It's just through there," he said, pointing vaguely down the hallway, then scratching at the back of his head. Meredith went through a door and Andrew breathed a sigh of relief when he heard the bathroom fan come on. He showed Keith into the dining room and asked him to take Alex's bag in with him.

"Should be some fun bits and pieces in there. Party stuff, you know?"

He patted Keith on the back, wondering when it was he'd become a back-patter, and dashed away to the kitchen.

Jim had his hands over his face and was muttering through his fingers.

"What's happened?" Andrew said.

Jim took his hands away. "I'm so sorry, mate. I don't know what's happened, but I think in technical cooking terms, I've bollocksed it."

Andrew grabbed a spoon and took a tentative slurp.

"Well?" Jim asked.

It was hard to adequately explain what Andrew's taste buds had just experienced. There was too much information to process.

"Well, it certainly has a tang to it," Andrew said, not wanting to hurt Jim's feelings. His tongue was probing at his back teeth seemingly of its own accord. *Wine*, he thought. That was the answer. If they were drunk enough they wouldn't care about the food.

He uncorked two bottles of merlot and headed to the dining room. As he came around the corner he was just thinking how ominously quiet it was—that it was the sort of silence that hung in the air following an argument—when he was met by a series of loud bangs.

Startled, he felt both bottles slip from his hands. There was a moment where they all looked at the red wine spilling out onto the light blue carpet, and the falling streamers from the party poppers nestling in the resulting puddle, before everyone burst into life, offering different advice.

"Blot it, you need to blot it. Definitely blot it," Peggy said.

"But only with up-and-down movements, not side to side—that just makes it worse, I saw it on QVC," Meredith said.

"Salt, isn't it?" Keith said. "Or vinegar? White wine?"

"I think that's a myth," Andrew said, just in time to see Cameron leap forward with half a bottle of white wine, which he deposited onto the carpet.

"He's going to kill me," Andrew breathed.

"Who is?" Meredith said.

"No one. Everyone, please just . . . wait here." Andrew dashed back down the corridor and into the kitchen. He explained the situation to Rupert, who listened to his rambling, took him by the shoulders and said, "Don't worry. We'll sort it later. You need to give those people some food. And I rather think I've found a solution." He pointed to the counter, where five frosted Tupperware boxes sat. They were all labeled with "Cannelloni."

Andrew turned to Jim, about to apologize.

"It's fine, do it," Jim said. "They might've found my dish a bit on the . . . challenging side anyway."

A period of relative serenity followed as they cooked the cannelloni in batches in the microwave and cleaned up the mess. Andrew even felt relaxed enough that when Rupert wryly observed the absurdity of what they were doing, and Alex joked that she couldn't believe Andrew had talked them into it, he nearly dissolved into hysterics, having to shush the others good-naturedly. He periodically returned to the dining room to hand out breadsticks and olives, while Alex took on the role of continuity adviser on a film set, making sure he carried an oven glove over his shoulder and wiped a damp cloth on his forehead to give the impression of slaving away at a hot stove.

When the food was finally ready to dish up, Andrew felt the most composed he had that evening. The cannelloni wasn't exactly awe-inspiring, and neither was the conversation, but it really didn't matter. Civility was exactly what was needed, and thus far everyone was on the same page. Keith, who had been quieter than usual, and less inclined to sarcastic asides, related a story, falteringly, about a voicemail he'd received the previous week. A woman had seen in the local paper the story of a pauper's funeral and had only then realized it was her brother, whom she'd not spoken to in years. "She told me they'd fallen out because of a table. They thought it was an antique passed down through ten generations. They'd fought over it when their parents died and eventually she came out on top. It was only after she'd seen that he'd died that she decided to get the thing valued, and it turns out it was a fake. A cheap knockoff. Barely worth a fiver." Keith suddenly seemed uncomfortable in the reflective silence. "Anyway," he said. "Just makes you think, I suppose. About what's important."

"Hear hear," Cameron said. They were quiet after this, creating the inevitable awkwardness after someone's said something profound, nobody wanting to be judged for bursting the bubble by following up with something trivial in comparison.

It was Peggy who broke first. "What's for pudding then, Andrew?"

"You'll have to wait and see," Andrew said, hoping that the others weren't beginning to get annoyed with all this vagueness when it came to the food.

He headed back to the kitchen and took in the scene from the doorway. Jim, Rupert and Alex were all huddled around the counter, where they were carefully adding strawberries and crushed pine nuts to bowls of something that looked genuinely delicious. Andrew stayed still for a moment, not wanting to announce his presence just yet. The three of them were hushed in their concentration, all working as a team, and Andrew felt the faint soreness of tears beginning to form behind his eyes. How kind these people were. How lucky he was to have them on his side. He cleared his throat and the others looked back, concern on their faces, smiles appearing when they saw it was him.

"Ta-dah!" Alex whispered, making up for having to lower her voice with some extravagant jazz hands.

Andrew brought the plates into the dining room and received some admiring oohs and aahs.

"Blimey, Andrew," Cameron said through a mouthful of ice cream. "I didn't realize you were such a whiz in the kitchen. This one of Diane's recipes?"

"Ha, no," Andrew said. "She's . . ." He searched for the words. Something light. Something funny. Something normal. As he racked his brain, the memory came to him, crisp and clear, of Diane taking his hand and leading him away from the party, down the stairs, out into the snowy night. He shivered involuntarily.

"She's not here," he said eventually. He looked at Peggy. She was digging around with her spoon in her bowl, despite the fact it was empty, her expression betraying nothing.

Cameron was drumming his fingers on the table. He seemed to be waiting for them all to hurry up and finish, and Andrew noticed him check his watch surreptitiously. Peggy finally stopped pretending to eat and Cameron got to his feet.

"I actually have a few words I need to say to you all," he said, ignoring the others' exchanging nervous looks. "It's been a challenging few months. And I think that sometimes the personal has got in the way of the professional—to some extent at least—for all of us at one point or another. On my part, I apologize for anything that I've done that's not sat well with you. I know this, for example—these evenings—haven't been to everyone's taste, but I hope you understand it was simply an attempt to help bring us all together. Because, as you may have gathered by now, it was my feeling that top brass were much less likely to try and break up a strong, cohesive team in the event of cuts. That, I suspect, was naive on my part. And you'll have to forgive me for that, and for not being as explicit with you as I should have been, but I was just trying to do what I thought was best. However, it turns out that the statistics—and it feels strange to say this, I promise you— are on our side. The number of public health funerals rose even more sharply this year than any of us were expecting. And I'm incredibly proud of how you have dealt with that as a team. In truth, to be completely blunt, I have no idea what's going to happen next. A decision has been delayed on whether cuts are needed until at least the end of the year. Here's hoping that isn't the case. All I can promise is that, if it comes down to it, I will fight your cause to the absolute best of my abilities." He looked at them all in turn. "Well, thank you. That's it."

They sat in silence as they digested the news. Clearly, Andrew thought, things were still up in the air, but it seemed they'd been given a few months' respite at least. After a while the atmosphere returned to something approaching how it had been before, though they were understandably more subdued. Before too long it was time for everyone to leave. Andrew fetched their coats. *You're nearly there*, he told himself. As he watched the others readying to go, he was expecting to feel a great wave of relief at having survived the evening, especially now that it seemed his job was safe, at least in the short term. But instead, with each good-bye he said, he felt not relief but fear, and it seemed to spread up through his body like he was edging slowly into freezing water. He pictured Carl composing his next message— demanding to know where his money was, or maybe telling Andrew that he was about to bring his world crashing down instead. And then there was Diane. Ever since he'd told Peggy everything, the memories that he'd repressed for so many years had been begging for attention, and tonight they were coming to him thick and fast. It was as if a trapdoor had opened above his head and Polaroids were cascading down on him: A lingering look across a smoky room. Kissing as the snow fell. The fierce hug on the platform, the embers of that embrace warming him until he was home. The parched grass of Brockwell Park. The paleness of her skin illuminated by lightning. Orange frames next to cracked slate.

Peggy leaned in to hug him good-bye.

"Well done," she whispered.

"Thank you," he said back automatically. As she let him go, it felt like all the breath had been taken from him, leaving him light-headed. Before he knew what he was doing, he'd reached out and taken Peggy's hand. He was aware of the others looking at him, but in that moment he just didn't care. In that moment, he realized that all he wanted was for Peggy to know how wonderful he thought she was. And even though the thought of saying those words was terrifying, the very fact he was considering doing it had to mean something. It had to mean he was ready to let go.

That was when Cameron opened the front door and a rush of cold air came down the hallway, eagerly searching out warmth to attack.

"Wait!" Andrew said. "Sorry, everyone, but would you mind just waiting for a minute?"

After a moment, the others filed reluctantly back into the dining room like schoolchildren who'd been kept back after class.

"Um, Andrew . . . ?" Peggy said.

"I'll be right back," he said. He could feel his heart starting to thump again as he skittered into the kitchen. Jim, Alex and Rupert all looked at the door, frozen in fear that they'd been discovered. When Andrew asked them to follow him they exchanged confused looks, but Andrew forced a reassuring smile.

"It's fine," he said. "This won't take long." He ushered them down the corridor and into the dining room, where he introduced the two equally perplexed groups.

"What's going on, Andrew?" Cameron asked, once they'd arranged themselves in a semicircle.

"Okay," Andrew said. "I've just got a few things I need to tell you all."

CHAPTER 34

A ndrew listened to the phone ringing out and gulped down half a glass of tepid pinot grigio.

"Andrew, what a pleasant surprise."

"Hello, Carl."

"Funny you should call—I've just checked my bank account and I still don't seem to have my money."

"It's only just come into my account," Andrew said, trying to keep his voice even.

"Well," Carl said, "you've got my bank details, so as long as you transfer it straightaway then we won't have a problem."

"The thing is though," Andrew said, "I don't think I am going to transfer it."

"What?" Carl snapped.

"I said I don't think I am going to transfer it."

"You are," Carl said. "You *absolutely* are, because remember what happens if you don't. All I need to do is pick up the phone and you're fucked."

"This is what I mean," Andrew said. "I appreciate that I may not exactly deserve this money—that perhaps my behavior did cause some of Sally's unhappiness, and maybe more than that. But the thing is, we still loved each other, and I know that what I've been lying about might've been hard for her to deal with, but I think it would have been easier for her to understand that than the fact you're blackmailing me."

"Oh *please*. You really don't get this, do you? I am *owed* that money. I wouldn't be having to do this in the first place if you'd just done what was right. So you listen to me. It's very simple, okay? If that money isn't in my account within twenty-four hours, then your life as you know it is over."

The line went dead.

Andrew let out a deep breath and felt his shoulders slacken. He leaned forward in his chair and looked at his phone, which was on the dining room table. There were seven others placed in a circle around it, all of which showed that they were still recording. There was silence in the room. Andrew looked down, his cheeks burning. There was a flash of movement, and for a second Andrew thought he was about to be attacked, but then he realized it was Peggy, a split second before she threw her arms around him.

CHAPTER 35

Andrew waited until the taxi had wound its way out of the cul-de-sac, stopping to let a fox diligently trot across a zebra crossing, before he spoke.

"Am I going to get fired, then, do you think?"

Peggy handed him the bottle of wine she'd smuggled into the taxi and he took a surreptitious sip. "Honestly? I've no idea," she said.

The work lot had left in another cab. Jim and Alex had decided to stay a little longer at Rupert's, not being able to resist the opportunity to see his attic and its dedicated Rocky Mountains–themed train setup.

"I couldn't quite tell how everyone reacted at first, when I told them everything."

Andrew had only given the short version of events to the others, and describing his deception that way made it sound all the more stark. He'd braced himself for scathing interruptions from Keith and Meredith, but neither of them said anything. Nobody did, in fact, until he got to the part about Carl, at which point Alex launched into a furious rant about how they weren't going to let him get away with it. She demanded that Andrew call Carl right there and then, explaining to him impatiently exactly how he'd need to play the conversation to get Carl to reveal unambiguously what he was doing. She cajoled the others into giving her their phones, lining them up on the table and setting them to record. Afterward, they listened back on each one and decided that Meredith's recording was the clearest.

"Great, so you just need to send that to Andrew now," Alex told her.

"Oh right, yes. How do I . . ."

Alex rolled her eyes and took the phone out of Meredith's hand. "Andrew, what's your number? Right, there. Done."

Afterward, Rupert had suggested bringing out some "decent" brandy to toast the plan's working so well, but the suggestion was met with only a halfhearted response. Cameron, in particular, seemed eager to leave.

"Well. That was obviously . . . what a funny old evening," he said to Andrew. "I'm away for a few days, did I mention that? Training courses and whatnot. But we should talk properly when I'm back. About all this."

"That could just mean he wants to talk to you and make sure you're okay," Peggy said as the cabbie casually veered across two lanes of traffic without signaling.

A thousand thoughts were clamoring for attention in Andrew's mind, and he didn't even notice that Peggy had slid across the seats until he felt her head on his shoulder.

"How are you feeling?" she said.

Andrew puffed out his cheeks.

"Like someone's just removed a splinter I've had in my foot for a hundred years."

Peggy rearranged her head on his shoulder.

"Good."

The cabbie's radio crackled into life—the control room telling him he could go home after this job.

"God, it's no good, I'm falling asleep," Peggy said. "Wake me up when we're at Croydon, eh?"

"I think you're the first person in history ever to have said that," Andrew said. Peggy elbowed him halfheartedly.

"So, earlier, when you came into the kitchen," Andrew said, feeling unusually uninhibited given all that had just gone on. "I couldn't tell if you'd heard what I'd just said. About, well, me maybe being in love with you."

For a moment he thought Peggy was choosing how to respond, but then he heard the soft sounds of her breathing. She was asleep. He rested his head gently against hers. It felt entirely natural, in a way that made his heart soar and ache at the same time.

He'd be lucky if he got a minute's sleep that night, his brain was so wired. He had already sent the recording to Carl, but there had been no response. He wondered if there ever would be.

He found himself thinking of Sally—the moment where she'd handed him that beautiful green model train engine, winking at him and ruffling his hair. Maybe, if they had their time again, they'd have been able to fix things. But he shook the thought from his head. He was tired of fantasizing. He'd done enough of that for one lifetime. He drank the last dregs from the wine and raised the bottle in a silent toast to his sister.

CHAPTER 36

Two mornings later Andrew woke with a start. He'd been dreaming about what had happened at Rupert's house and for a horrible few seconds he couldn't be quite sure what was real and what his subconscious had decided to twist. But when he checked his phone the message Carl had sent him the morning after the phone call was still there: "Fuck you, Andrew. Enjoy your guilt money."

Andrew knew at some point he'd have to think about that guilt, and how he was going to deal with it—and what he was actually going to do with the money—but for now he was just hopelessly glad that everything with Carl was over.

He went to put the kettle on, feeling the unusual sensation of stiffness in his legs. The previous evening he'd been for what he'd ambitiously billed as a "run," which in actual fact had been closer to a "stagger" around the block. It had been agony at the time, but there was a moment when he'd gotten back—post-shower, post–meal-made-with-something-green-in-it—where he felt a rush of endorphins (previously a thing he'd imagined were mythical, like unicorns or something) so strong that he finally understood why people put them-selves through this. There was life in the old dog yet, it seemed.

He fried some bacon and looked directly into the tile-camera. "So you may have noticed I have accidentally burned this rasher, but given I'm about to put a Lake Windermere's worth of brown sauce on it, it doesn't really matter."

He stretched his arms up behind his head and yawned. The whole weekend lay in front of him, and unusually, he had plans that didn't involve Ella Fitzgerald and browsing the forum.

———————

It was going to be a long journey, but he was well prepared. He had a book and his iPod and had dusted off his old camera so he could take some snaps if the mood took him. When it came to his packed lunch he had gone entirely rogue, making sandwiches with white bread and experimenting with new fillings, one of which, in a move so daring he was barely able to contain himself, was crisps.

To his dismay, he got onto his train at Paddington with time to spare, only to find his reservation meant he was slap-bang in the mid-dle of a bachelor party, who were already getting stuck into the beers. It was three hours to Swansea, and that allowed for a lot more drink-ing time and wee quaffing, or whatever it was people did on these things. They had personalized T-shirts commemorating "Damo's Stag" and already seemed quite tipsy. But, against all the odds, they actually turned out to be pleasant company, offering snacks to every-one else in the carriage, helping people put their suitcases on the over-head shelves with faux competitiveness, before breaking out crosswords and quizzes to pass the time. Andrew found himself so caught up in the general air of bonhomie that he ended up scoffing his packed lunch before midday, like a naughty schoolboy on a trip. The onward journey from Swansea was a more somber affair, although a lady with purple hair knitting a purple bobble hat offered him a purple boiled sweet from a tin, like something out of an advert from a bygone era.

The station was so small it barely had a platform—one of those stops where you practically walk straight out onto the street as soon as you alight. Checking the route on his phone, Andrew took a turning onto a narrow lane where the houses on opposite sides seemed to lean toward each other, and for the first time he began to truly feel the nerves that had been bubbling away under the surface ever since he'd left London.

The church was unassuming, its spire small enough to be concealed from view by two modest yews. The place had a wildness about it—the gate at its entrance covered with moss, the grass in the graveyard was overgrown—but the early autumn air felt still.

He'd prepared himself for a lengthy search. A process of elimination. He half remembered holding the phone to his ear and a voice telling him this was where the funeral was to be held, then the confusion and hurt following his mute response. The only detail he could remember was that the church was near the rugby ground where Gavin had claimed to have seen the flying saucer.

In the end, he'd barely walked past half a dozen headstones when he saw the name he was looking for.

Diane Maude Bevan.

He thrust his hands into his pockets, rocking on the balls of his feet, building up the courage to approach. Eventually he did, slowly, as if moving to the edge of a cliff. He hadn't brought anything with him—flowers, or anything like that. That just didn't feel right, somehow. He was in touching distance now. He dropped down to his knees and gently ran his hand across Diane's name, tracing each letter's contour. "Well," he said. "I'd forgotten how much you hated your middle name. It took me a whole Sunday to get it out of you, remember?"

He took a deep breath, hearing the tremor as he let it out. He leaned forward until his forehead was resting gently against the headstone.

"I know this doesn't count for much now, but I am so sorry for never coming to see you. And for being so scared. You probably worked this out much sooner than I did, but you know I never really was able to accept that you were gone. After Dad, and Mum . . . and then Sally leaving . . . I couldn't let you go too. And then somehow I got the chance to build this place, this world, where you were still here, and I couldn't resist. It wasn't supposed to be for long, but it got out of control so quickly. Before I knew it I was even inventing the *arguments* we'd have. Sometimes it was just silly stuff—you despairing about me and my silly model trains, mostly—but other times it was more serious: disagreements about how we were bringing up the kids, worrying that we'd not lived our lives to the full and hadn't seen enough of the world. That's the tip of the iceberg, really; I thought about everything. Because it wasn't just one life with you I imagined, it was a million different ones, with every possible fork in the road. Of course every now and then I'd feel you pulling away from me, and I knew that was your way of telling me to let go, but that just made me cling on more. And, the thing is, it was only after the game was finally up that I was actually able to pull my stupid, self-absorbed head out of my arse and think about what you would have actually said if you knew for one single second what I was doing. I'm just sorry I didn't think of that sooner. I just hope you can forgive me, even though I don't deserve it."

Andrew was aware that someone else had appeared to tend to a grave a few feet away. He lowered his voice to a whisper.

"I wrote you a letter, once, very soon after we got together, but I was too scared to give it to you because I thought you might run a mile. It started life as a poem, too, so you were really let off the hook. It was full of hopelessly romantic sentiment that you would have quite rightly laughed your head off at, but I think one bit remains true. I wrote that I knew the moment we first held each other that something in me had changed forever. Up to that point I'd never realized that life, just sometimes, can be wonderfully, beautifully simple. I only wish I'd remembered that after you'd gone."

He had to stop to wipe his eyes with his coat sleeve, smoothing his hand along the stone again. He stayed there, quiet now, feeling a pure and strangely joyful pain wash over him, knowing that as much as it hurt, it was something he had to accept, a winter before the spring, letting its ice freeze and fracture his heart before it could heal.

———

The next train to Swansea was pulling into the station as Andrew got there, but he felt reluctant to leave so soon. He decided to stop in a pub nearby instead. As he approached the door old habits kicked in and he hesitated just outside. But he thought of Diane watching on, no doubt mouthing swear words in his direction, and he pressed on. And though the regulars looked at him somewhat curiously, and the barman poured him a pint and threw a packet of salt and vinegar on the bar without much enthusiasm, their reaction to him was benign rather than unwelcoming.

He sat in the corner with his beer and his book, and felt, for the first time in a very long while, content.

CHAPTER 37

Andrew turned the pair of tights inside out and shook out a bundle of notes onto the bed.

"Bingo," Peggy said. "Enough to cover the funeral, do you reckon?"

"Should be," Andrew said, leafing through the money.

"Well, that's something. Poor old . . ."

"Josephine."

"Josephine. God, I'm the worst. It's such a lovely name, too. Sounds like the sort of woman who'd always bring loads of food to a harvest festival."

"Maybe she did. Did she talk about church in the diary?"

"Only when she was slagging off *Songs of Praise*."

Josephine Murray had penned scores of diary entries, as she'd noted, "in an old Smith's notebook, using a chopping board resting on my lap as a makeshift desk, much like I imagine Samuel Pepys did."

The diary's subject matter was largely mundane—short, spiky critiques of television programs or comments on the neighbors. Often, she combined the two: "Watched a forty-five-minute advert for

Findus Crispy Pancakes interrupted sporadically by a documentary about aqueducts. Could barely hear it over the noise of Next Door Left rowing. I really wish they'd keep a lid on it."

Occasionally though, she'd write something more reflective:

"Got in a bit of a tiz this evening. Put some food out for the birds and felt a bit dizzy. Thought about calling the quack but didn't want to bother anyone. Silly, I know, but I just feel so embarrassed about taking up someone's time when I know I'm probably fine. Next Door Right were out having a barbecue. Smelled delicious. Had the strongest urge—for the first time in goodness knows how long—to take a bottle of wine round there, something dry and crisp, and get a bit tiddly. Had a look in the fridge but there wasn't anything there. In the end I decided that dizziness and tiddlyness wouldn't have been a good mix anyway. That wasn't the tiz, by the way, that came as I was trying to drop off to sleep when I suddenly remembered it was my birthday. And that's why I'm writing this now in the hope it helps me to remember next year, if I haven't kicked the bucket by then of course."

Peggy put the diary in her bag. "I'll have a look through this back at the office."

"Right you are," Andrew said. He looked at his watch. "Sandwich?"

"Sandwich," Peggy confirmed.

They stopped off at a café near the office. "How about here?" Andrew said. "I must have walked past this place a thousand times and I've never been in."

It was warm enough to sit outside. They munched their sandwiches as a group of schoolchildren in hi-vis bibs were led along by a young teacher who was just about managing to keep track of them all while taking the time to tell Daisy that Lucas might not appreciate being pinched like that.

"Give it ten years," Peggy said. "I'll bet Lucas will be dying to get pinched like that."

"Was that your flirting technique back in the day?"

"Something like that. Bit of pinching, few vodka shots, can't go wrong."

"Classic."

A man marched by them in an electric-blue suit, shouting incomprehensible business jargon down the phone, like a peacock who'd managed to learn English by reading Richard Branson's autobiography. He strode out into the road, barely flinching as a bike courier flashed inches past and called him a knobhead.

Andrew felt something vibrating against his leg.

"I think your phone's ringing," he said, passing Peggy's bag over to her.

She pulled out her phone, looked at the screen for a second, then dropped the phone back in the bag, where it continued to vibrate.

"I'm going to guess that was Steve again," Andrew said.

"Mmm-hmm. At least he's down to two calls a day now. I'm hoping he'll get the message soon enough."

"How are the girls doing with it all?"

"Oh, you know, about as well as you'd expect. We've got a long old road ahead of us. But it's still absolutely for the best. By the way, Suze asked about you the other day."

"Really? What did she say?" Andrew said.

"She asked me whether we'd be seeing 'that fun Andrew man' again."

"Ah, I wonder which Andrew she was thinking of there, then," Andrew said, mock-disappointed, but unable to entirely conceal how proud he really was, judging from the smile on Peggy's face.

Peggy reached into her bag again and brought out Josephine's diary, flicking through the pages.

"She seems like such a lively old lass, this one."

"She does," Andrew said. "Any mention of a family?"

"Not that I can see. There's lots more about the neighbors, though never by name, so I'm not sure how friendly they all were. I suppose if one lot of them was always rowing then maybe she didn't feel like talking to them. The others, though, the barbecuing lot—I might go back later and have a chat with them if I can't find anything here. Part of me's just intrigued as to whether she *did* ever decide to go round there for a drink or anything."

Andrew shielded his face from the sun so he could look Peggy in the eye.

"I know, I know," she said, holding her hands up defensively. "I'm not getting too invested, honestly. It's just . . . this is yet another person who spent their final days completely alone, right, despite the fact she was clearly a nice, normal person. And I bet if we do find a next of kin it'll be another classic case of 'Oh, dear, that's a shame, we hadn't spoken in a while, we sort of lost contact, blah blah blah.' It just seems like such a scandal that this happens. I mean, are we all really content to say to these people, 'Sorry, tough luck, we aren't even going to bother trying to help you poor lonely bastards,' without at least offering them the chance to have some company or something?"

Andrew thought about what he might have done if somewhere down the line someone had offered him companionship. All he could really picture, unhelpfully, was a Jehovah's witness standing at his door. But that figured, because, truth be told, he'd have rejected help outright. He said as much to Peggy.

"But it doesn't have to be like that," she said. "I wanted to talk to you about this, actually. I mean, I haven't exactly got it all mapped out, but . . ."

She began to rout around in her bag, producing empty water bottles, an old apple core, a half-empty bag of sweets and fistfuls of receipts. Andrew watched, mesmerized, as she swore and continued to pull things out like an angry magician. Eventually she found what she'd been looking for.

"So it's just a rough outline," she said, smoothing out a piece of paper. "Really rough, actually, but it's a summary of what a campaign to help people could look like. The gist of it is that people can apply to have the option of a phone call or a visit from volunteers. And the thing is it doesn't matter if you're a little old lady or a thirty-something high flyer. It just gives you the option of having someone you can connect with."

Andrew studied the paper. He was aware that Peggy was watching him anxiously.

"What?" she said. "Is it mental?"

"No. It absolutely isn't. I love it. I just wish you'd told me about it sooner."

Peggy narrowed her eyes.

"What?" Andrew said.

"Oh, nothing," Peggy said. "I was just thinking about a moment in Sainsbury's about a week ago when I nearly punched you in your stupid face."

". . . Right," Andrew said, deciding not to probe that one any further.

"There's something else I want to show you too," Peggy said, reaching into her Tardis bag again and pulling out her phone. "Obviously it's a bit too late to help poor old Josephine find company, bless her, but what do you reckon about this?" She passed her phone over to Andrew, who wiped his fingers on a paper napkin before he took it. It was a post Peggy had drafted in Facebook.

"You know what?" Andrew said, once he'd finished reading it.

"What?"

"You're actually brilliant."

Andrew wouldn't have thought Peggy capable of blushing, but her cheeks were definitely tinged pink.

"So shall I post it?" she said.

"Abso-bloody-lutely," Andrew said. He handed her phone back

and watched her upload the post just as his own phone started to ring.

"Yes, no, I understand, thanks, but like I said that's out of my price range, I'm afraid. Okay, thank you, bye."

"'Out of my price range, I'm afraid,'" Peggy said. "Are you buying a yacht or something?"

"That's next on the list, obviously. For now, I'm trying to move house."

"Wow. Really?"

"I think it's for the best. Time to move on."

"So now you're experiencing the joy of speaking to all those lovely lettings agents."

"Yep. I've never had so many people lie to me in such a short space of time."

"You have much to learn, my friend."

Andrew rubbed his eyes and yawned. "All I want is to live in a converted train station on top of a mountain with sea views and Wi-Fi and easy access to central London, is that so much to ask?"

"Have another cookie," Peggy said, patting him on the top of the head.

———

They were nearly back at the office—despite coming close to making an executive decision to dedicate the afternoon to Scrabble in the pub.

Andrew had been building up the courage, again, to ask whether Peggy had overheard him in Rupert's kitchen, and this felt like the most opportune moment he'd had in the last few days.

"So, the other night . . ."

But he didn't get a chance to finish, because Peggy suddenly grabbed his arm. "Look," she muttered.

Cameron had arrived at the office ahead of them and was skipping nimbly up the stairs. He stopped to search for his building pass, only finding it once Andrew and Peggy had caught up with him.

"Hi, Cameron," Peggy said. "We weren't expecting you back till next week."

Cameron busied himself with his phone as he spoke. "Had to come back early," he said. "Last day of the course got canceled. Salmonella, it would seem. I'm the only one who managed to escape it. Well, hopefully," he added.

The three of them walked down the corridor in silence. When they got to their office Cameron held the door open so Peggy could go through, then turned to Andrew and said, "Could we have a quick word in my office when you have a moment?"

"Sure," Andrew said. "Can I ask wha—"

"See you in a minute then," Cameron said, walking away before Andrew could say anything else. He didn't know exactly what was coming, but he could make a reasonable guess that he wasn't going to be awarded a knighthood.

A few weeks ago he would have been panic-stricken. But not anymore. He was ready for this. He dumped his stuff by his desk and made his way straight to Cameron's office.

"Andrew," Peggy hissed from across the room, her eyes wide with concern.

He smiled at her.

"Don't worry," he said. "Everything's going to be fine."

– CHAPTER 38 –

Another day, another funeral.

Today was the day Josephine Murray said good-bye to the world, and Andrew was the only one returning her farewell. He shifted his position on the creaky pew and exchanged smiles with the vicar. When Andrew had greeted him earlier that morning it had taken him a moment to realize he was actually the floppy-haired youngster whom he'd watched conduct his very first funeral service. Though that had only been earlier that year, he already looked to have aged considerably. It wasn't just that his hair was neater, in a more conservative side parting, it was also in the way that he carried himself—it was more assured. Andrew felt oddly paternal, seeing how much he seemed to have matured. They had spoken briefly on the phone beforehand and Andrew, after discussing it with Peggy, had decided to relate parts of Josephine's diary so that the vicar was able to add a bit more color to the service, and make it more personal.

Andrew swiveled to look to the back of the church. Where, then, was Peggy?

The vicar approached. "I'll give it another minute or so, but then I'll really need to start, I'm afraid," he said.

"Of course, I understand," Andrew said.

"How many were you expecting?"

That was the problem. Andrew didn't have a clue. It all depended on how Peggy had gotten on.

"Don't worry too much," he said. "I don't want to cause a holdup."

But just then the church door swung open, and there was Peggy. She looked flustered at first, but then relief flooded her face when she saw that the service hadn't started yet. She held the door for someone behind her—there was at least one other person, then—and made her way up the aisle. Andrew watched as first one, then two, then three people came in after her. There was a short gap, and then, to Andrew's amazement, a steady stream of people filed in until he lost count at over thirty.

Peggy arrived next to him. "So sorry we're late," she whispered. "We had a decent response on the Facebook page but then we managed to round up a few people from Bob's Café across the road last minute." She nodded at a man wearing a blue and white checked apron. "Including Bob!"

The vicar waited until everyone was seated before making his way to his lectern. After the initial formalities he decided—spontaneously, it looked to Andrew—to leave his lectern, and his notes with it, so that he could be nearer to the congregation.

"As it happens, I have a little something in common with Josephine," he said. "My grandmother was her namesake—she was always Granny Jo to me—and they both kept diaries. Now, my granny's, which we were only allowed to read once she'd passed away, was of course of great intrigue to us. It was only when we were finally able to read it that we realized she'd written most of the entries after a couple of strong gin and tonics, and so they were pretty hard to read in places." There was a warm ripple of laughter from the congregation and Andrew felt Peggy take his hand.

"From what I gather from the good people who've looked after Josephine's affairs, her own diary shows her to be witty, bright and full of life. And while she was someone not shy of a strong opinion, especially when it came to television schedulers or weathermen, her warmth and strength of character are what leap off the pages."

Peggy squeezed Andrew's hand and he squeezed back.

"Josephine may not have had family or friends around her when she died," the vicar continued. "And today might well have felt like a lonely occasion. So what a wonderful thing it is to look out over so many of you who have given up your time to be here today. None of us can be sure at the start of our lives just how they will end, or what our journey there will be like, but if we were to know for sure that our final moments would be in the company of good souls such as yourselves, we would surely be comforted. So thank you. May I invite you now to stand and join me in a moment of contemplation."

———

The service over, the vicar waited by the church door and took a moment to thank everyone individually for coming. Andrew even overheard him telling Bob that of course he'd love to pop over later "for a cuppa," but saying he'd probably pass on the muffins. "But they're massive!" Bob remonstrated. "You won't get a bigger one for miles around, honestly."

"I think he's made about twenty new customers today," Peggy said. "Good on him, the cheeky bugger."

They strolled toward a bench and Andrew brushed away some fallen leaves so they could sit down.

"So, are you actually going to tell me how it went with Cameron?" Peggy said.

Andrew leaned back and looked up at the sky, watching a distant plane leaving the faintest of vapor trails. It felt good, stretching his neck like this. He should do it more.

"Andrew?"

What was there to say?

The conversation had been meandering and inconclusive. Cameron had been at pains to say how much he was on Andrew's side, how if it was up to him he'd let the revelations from the dinner party go. But then he'd started to pepper what he was saying with phrases like "duty bound" and "following protocol."

"You understand I have to say something?" he'd concluded. "Because, whatever the reasons for doing what you . . . did, it's all still rather troubling."

"I know," Andrew had said. "Believe me, I know."

"I mean, bloody hell, Andrew, if you were in my position, what would you do?"

Andrew had gotten to his feet. "Cameron, listen, I think you should do what your instincts tell you, and if that means reporting me to someone up the chain, or if it gives you a neat solution to the cutbacks issue were it to come up again, then I understand. I won't hold it against you."

"But—"

"Honestly. To have everything out in the open, to have been able to move on, that's more important to me than keeping this job. If it helps you out with a tricky decision, then I'm genuinely fine with that."

God, what a relief it had been to be able to speak as freely as this.

To open himself up to new possibilities. He'd thought of Peggy's campaign. The more they'd discussed it, the more energized he'd felt.

"Besides," he'd said to Cameron. "It's about time I finally figured out what I'm going to do with my life."

———————

Peggy brought him back to the present as she took his hand. "It's okay, we don't have to talk about it now."

Andrew shook his head. "No, we can. So, it looks like I'm going to be let go."

"Oh my god," Peggy said, clapping her hands to her mouth, eyes wide.

"*But*," Andrew said, "Cameron has promised to try and find me a position in another department."

"And you'll go for it, you think?"

"Yes," Andrew said.

"Right, well that's . . . good," Peggy said, a tinge of disappointment in her voice.

"Though only temporarily," Andrew said.

"Really?" Peggy said quickly, eyes searching Andrew's. He nodded.

"I've been doing a bit of research. About charity funding. You need a fair wedge up front to start one, around five thousand pounds. But I have the money Sally left me. I've not had any better ideas about how to spend it, and I know she'd be really happy with me using it for something like this."

Peggy was looking at him with such a strong mixture of confusion and excitement that Andrew had to stop himself from laughing.

"I'm talking about your campaign idea, just in case you weren't quite there," he said. "And I was thinking, maybe you could, you know, help me. See if we can make a proper go of it."

"This is . . . Andrew . . . I don't quite . . ."

"I'm not saying it's definitely possible," Andrew said. "We might fall at the first hurdle. But we can give it our best shot."

Peggy was nodding at him very firmly. "We can, we absolutely can," she said. "Let's talk about it more over dinner tonight—if the offer's still on, that is?"

"It very much is," Andrew said. He'd found a new flat that morning—a chance spot on one of the four bewildering apps he'd downloaded—and even though it meant he'd have to move the following week he'd made the decision to do it on the spot. Part of him did feel a little sad about moving, but at least with Peggy's coming around that evening he'd be able to see the old place off in style.

"Quick question," he said. "You do like beans on toast, right?"

"My favorite, obviously," Peggy said, looking at him with slightly narrowed eyes, not sure if he was joking or not. "But right now, I don't know about you, but I could murder a massive muffin."

"Why not," Andrew said. They held each other's gaze for a moment.

He saw again her and the girls rushing down the platform toward him at King's Cross, and his heart flickered once more with a sense of possibility.

He had given up on how he was going to broach the subject of whether Peggy *had* overheard him talking about his feelings for her in Rupert's kitchen. He was just stupidly happy that she was there now, at his side, knowing everything there was to know about him. That, he realized, was more than enough.

ACKNOWLEDGMENTS

To my wonderful agent, Laura Williams. Words can't express how grateful I am for everything you've done for me.

To Clare Hey at Orion and Tara Singh Carlson at Putnam. I am so lucky to be working with two such brilliant editors and publishers. Thanks for everything.

Thank you to everyone at Orion, especially Virginia Woolstencroft, Katie Moss, Harriet Bourton, Sarah Benton, Oliva Barber, Katie Espiner, Lynsey Sutherland, Anna Bowen, Tom Noble and Fran Pathak. And to all at Putnam, especially Helen Richard, Alexis Welby, Katie McKee and Sandra Chiu.

To the awesome Alexandra Cliff—I shall remember *that* phone call for a very long time. Also, to the brilliant Marilia Savvides, Rebecca Wearmouth, Laura Otal, Jonathan Sissons and everyone else at PFD.

To Kate Rizzo and all at Greene & Heaton.

Special thanks to Ben Willis for reading this at an early stage and giving me invaluable advice in a Camberwell Wetherspoons, and for being there for me from the beginning. So too has been Holly Harris (official). Thank you for everything, especially stopping me from going insane in Wahaca when I found out I was getting published. I am very lucky to call two such excellent people my friends.

To my good pals Emily "Half Pint" Griffin and Lucy Dauman. You're the absolute best.

Thank you to Sarah Emsley and Jonathan Taylor—I couldn't wish for two more kind, wise and good-natured people as mentors and as friends.

To the rest of the gang at Headline for being wonderful to work with, and whose celebratory messages to me the moment the news came out gave me so much joy. Special thanks to Imogen Taylor, Sherise Hobbs, Auriol Bishop and Frances Doyle.

To the following, for their encouragement, support and advice: Elizabeth Masters, Beau Merchant, Emily Kitchin, Sophie Wilson, Ella Bowman, Frankie Gray, Chrissy Heleine, Maddy Price, Richard Glynn, Charlotte Mendelson, JJ Moore, Gill Hornby, Robert Harris.

To Katy and Libby—wonderful, supportive sisters. Love you guys.

Finally, to my mum, Alison, and dad, Jeremy, to whom this book is dedicated—this is all down to you.